THE FIRST AND LAST DEMON

HIYODORI

Contents

1

I WOKE WITH a sour taste in my mouth. A familiar taste, though my brain couldn't name it. I saw the glaring light of an ambiguous sky.

And then I saw my demon.

She floated sideways in the air before me, just out of reach. No wings flapping; no visible source of support. Nothing holding her up but casual magic.

My demon had always been like this. If we stood side by side, I'd be taller—but it was easy to forget her real height. She rarely set foot on solid ground.

Two runty horns grew from her head, both the color of sun-bleached old bone. She wore a garment like a wetsuit, long and tight, with skin-revealing cutouts in peculiar places.

The demon grinned at me as I looked her over. Her teeth were very sharp. She turned a lazy midair circle, swooping closer.

"Remember me?" she asked.

I touched the side of my head. The first thing I remembered was that my memory was far from intact. Yet the demon's name came to me unbidden.

"Vesper," I said.

"Very good." She clapped with sarcastic enthusiasm. "How about you?"

"Char."

"And what do you do, Char?"

"I'm your human Host," I told her. "The periodic hero of Jace. How long did I sleep?"

"Guess," Vesper said from the air.

"Ten years."

"Nope."

"A century?"

"Too long."

"Fifty years?"

"Close enough."

Fifty years. My recollection of past awakenings felt distant and fuzzy. As if my body already knew how much time had really passed while magic preserved me in stasis, dreamless and ageless.

My head was starting to work better, breath by breath. I eyed the sky again. A strange sky, yes, but I couldn't identify what seemed off about it.

I'd been slumped against blocks of rubble, cushioned by masses of virulent green clover. Behind me ran a fountain of silver liquid, mirror-bright and menacing, centered around a long slender spike like a narwhal horn. Creatures with warped voices called to each other from high overhead. Birds, perhaps, or something else altogether.

I couldn't see or hear a single human being.

Cracked buildings rose up on either side of the broken plaza. Some straight, some tilted. I didn't recognize the wreckage. But I knew what this city was called.

"Glorybower," I said under my breath.

"Our old, old hometown," Vesper added. "Or the city they built over top of it, rather. The city they renamed to honor you. Just look at the state of it. Quite a disaster."

"What ruined it? Is this why they woke me?"

I was accustomed to getting jarred awake from magical hibernation. I was accustomed to not knowing where I was, or what new era I'd woken up in, or why they needed me. There had always been other humans waiting there to explain what I needed to do. Every time, without fail: the first thing they did was tell me how to save them.

"*Who* woke me?" I asked. "Where is everyone?"

Vesper shrugged. "Good question."

"You didn't see them?"

"When you sleep, I sleep." She did a languid flip turn, like a swimmer about to start a new lap. "Guess they wandered off somewhere. Must not be very urgent, hm?"

"Or something's happened to whoever woke us."

"That's an awfully pessimistic way to look at it."

"We'd better go find them."

"Gung-ho as always, I see," Vesper muttered.

I rose. Carefully. The connections between my mind and body still felt fractured, an image reflected in broken glass.

"Vesper," I said.

"What now?"

I pointed at a bell tower down the street. The tallest structure in sight. "Take me up there."

Her smile vanished. "Trying to assess the situation from above? Very practical."

"Take me up there."

"Is that an order?"

"Vesper," I said again.

She slid an arm around my waist and spoke in a voice like sugary ice water. "Whatever you want, honey."

The pitted ground and crushed clover below my feet gave way to smoother slabs of stone. Vesper's magic had instantaneously ported us to the belfry at the top of the tower.

After releasing me, she drifted out to hover in the sunlit space beyond the belfry's open arches. A space with absolutely nothing to break a fatal fall.

Once this tower would've been packed with visitors. I'd never seen the belfry platform empty.

It was all starting to come back to me now, the familiar litany of remembrances.

People called me Char. A nickname, short for something. (Not Charlotte.) Creaky though I felt, I was physically and mentally supposed to be located somewhere in my mid-twenties.

But I'd been born many, many centuries ago. I'd grown used to long gaps, to startling changes: in technology, the local vernacular, the names and borders of rival countries over on the continent, the political structures that governed our Jacian islands.

Where and how people stored me between awakenings depended on the culture of the time. I'd come to in a coffin. A cupboard. A cardboard box. A tank full of noxious chemicals. The moldy basement of a natural history museum.

Vesper was always nearby when I woke. Sometimes they stashed us together. Sometimes they put us in a cage or a dog crate to hibernate. Once I'd found her muzzled. Once I'd found her in a straitjacket that looked tight enough to cut off her circulation.

It was Vesper's power they sought when awakening us. She was the demon, the living weapon of last resort. I merely served as her Host—her human manager.

Still, we were a team. We'd defended our nation over and over. We'd beaten back invading armies, sealed off a magical forest teeming with eldritch monstrosities, rescued civilians buried by earthquakes, defeated titanic vorpal beasts. We were two heroes in one: together we were the sleeping savior of Jace.

Yet in all these centuries, I'd once never woken up completely alone with my demon. No other humans in sight.

In the sunlight outside the belfry, Vesper examined her nails one by one. Like her teeth, they looked extraordinarily sharp. Then she glided past me like a cloud, heading for the shadow of the great hanging bell.

I leaned over the waist-high wall around the perimeter. Stone heads perched all along the top of the wall, some with their noses smashed off. They were supposed to be guardians gazing down upon the city. They ended up looking more like severed heads arrayed on pikes.

The city bore few signs of movement, and none of it appeared human. I spotted the glittering silver fountain and the carpet of clover where I'd first come to my senses.

Then I saw our chalice.

Not a drinking cup. A different sort of vessel.

Our chalice was the greatest Jacian machina ever created. One of a kind. Twelve stories tall when standing upright. Human-shaped only in the sense that it had long limbs reminiscent of legs and arms—many more arms than any human possessed. All its other spikes and bulges and protrusions felt monstrous, insectile.

Our chalice lay on its back in the carcass of a crushed apartment. It was a patchwork of crystalline parts colored clear and milk-white and gray. It would've been perfectly camouflaged high up in a cloud-covered sky.

It was an enormous machine of war. But when Vesper and I piloted our chalice, it soared as though it weighed no more than a kite.

"The city looks empty," I told Vesper.

"You only just noticed?"

Something about her tone made my thoughts stop and stutter. I skipped reluctantly back to the very first question I'd asked her down in the plaza.

Why had it taken me so long to catch on?

"Fifty years," I said slowly.

"You snoozed away the whole time."

"You claim it's been fifty years."

"Give or take a few months," she hedged.

"If you only woke up a little before me, if no one's shown up to tell you what year it is—how can you possibly know?"

Vesper dropped lower. Almost low enough for the tips of her bare toes to brush the stones of the belfry floor.

I studied her short pointy horns and her short pointy ears and found myself seized by a baseless but bone-deep conviction.

I'd be better off not hearing her answer, I thought.

"I've got questions, too," Vesper said. "What happened to the city all those years ago? What ravaged it so? Why's Solitaire lying collapsed on its back?"

Solitaire was the call sign for our chalice.

I considered the cracked earth, the split buildings. The warping effects of a too-powerful magic run amok. The barbed wire that writhed like living vines up the sides of the bell tower. The thick segmented bamboo roots that tore through the stone of the once-placid plaza. Canals shimmering a sickly color in the distance.

The destruction didn't appear recent. And it didn't look like the aftermath of a conquering army or a natural disaster. It looked more like a chalice gone berserk. A frenzy of uncontrollable magic.

It looked like something we might've done by accident.

My voice came out dry and raw. "The people—"

"Yes," Vesper murmured. "What became of all those people who lived here fifty years ago? Did they scream? Did they cry for you to stop? Do you remember a single second of it? Of course not."

She rose an inch or two in the air, bringing our heads perfectly level. "Then again," she said lightly. "That's none of my concern."

"Ves—"

"You always forget how it works. You always convince yourself that I sleep while you sleep."

"Because you do."

"Wrong." She ascended higher still, high enough to reach a hand up and smack the flank of the huge dark bell.

It didn't sway or produce much sound. Nothing but a dull resonance that grated deep in my chest.

"Part of me always remains awake," she said. "You pass years, decades, centuries in one quick blink of oblivion. Meanwhile—there I am, stewing in my own juices. Waiting till the next time Jace needs a hero."

Vesper flashed her teeth. A cutting smile.

"As usual, your perspective is too narrow," she informed me. "Look past the debris. Look out at the horizon. Tell me what you see."

The people of successive eras had rebuilt Glorybower over and over, to the point that one might describe it as multiple cities smushed together. The place where Vesper and I had been born was long buried.

Glorybower had an epic history. It was by no means a small city. But it had an end. It had borders.

And no matter where in the city you went, no matter how hazy the air got, you could always see hints of enormous mountains in the distance. Those iconic Jacian peaks.

I went to every corner of the tower platform. I stared in all directions.

There were no mountains. Nothing but the city itself, stretching on and on forever.

"An illusion?" I asked.

Vesper pulled a face. "You wish. It's a wall."

"I don't see any walls."

"A mirrored wall, you cretin. A dome, though the reflections get fainter in the sky."

She twirled in place, arms outstretched. "The city is mysteriously empty. The city is mysteriously sealed. No one's passed through that magical wall in fifty years. Try crossing it yourself if you doubt me."

"Then—"

Vesper descended. She bent her head close to mine. "Go on," she said. "Ask."

"Who woke me?"

At this she turned in the air like an otter, arms curling around her belly. Peals of laughter.

The laughter ceased.

A hush filled the empty space below the tower's colossal black bell. The stone heads lined up along the guardrail all faced away from us, seeing nothing.

"Who woke you?" Vesper spread her hands. "There's only two of us here, sweetheart. Who do you think?"

Her eyes were radiant in the shade of the bell, bright as a cat under the cover of night.

"This time there's no humans to save," she said merrily. "This time there's no one to beg you to be their hero. This time it's just you and me in a sealed dead city."

The remnants of my memory told me this: I'd never heard Vesper speak with such a vicious euphoric edge in her voice.

Asking her anything further felt like a terrible mistake. But what else could I possibly do next?

"...Why?" I said.

Vesper put her hands on my shoulders and turned me around to gaze out upon the broken city, the somnolent form of our fallen chalice. The belfry wall hit my waist.

She leaned in close behind me.

"Why?" she repeated. "Ponder it on the way down."

With the full strength of a demon, she shoved me forcibly over the edge.

2

I DIED.

Not for the first time.

Vesper was my demon, and I was her Host. Unbreakable magic bound us together. Something similar to the magic tying human mages to their human bondmates.

If both partners were human, the lifelong bond would end as soon as one of them died.

Because Vesper was a demon, it was different for us. Ours wasn't simply a bond to last the rest of our lives. Our was a bond of mutual death. The only way for us to die permanently would be if we both died together. As long as one still lived, the other would get pulled inexorably back.

This time, I came back to life on a pile of books.

I sat up slowly. My body ached with phantom echoes of death.

No way to determine how much time had passed since Vesper shoved me off the bell tower. Might be as little as a few hours. The greater the physical damage, however, the longer it took to return to life.

It had been a very, very steep fall from the top of the tower.

I didn't care to dwell on it. Best assume that I'd been gone for at least a couple of days.

I appeared to have been dumped inside an abandoned bookstore. Vesper must've collected my corpse from the base of the tower and carried it over.

"Vesper?"

No answer.

I might actually be alone, then. If Vesper had already gotten sick of watching me sleep for fifty years, she probably lacked the patience to hang around for days on end while my body pieced itself back together.

Wan light shafted in through clouded windows, thick with dust motes. This must've been a grand shop once, with high ceilings and high shelves. Curling staircases and multiple floors.

It felt vaguely familiar. It had been famous, perhaps, during my last awakening. One of the oldest and largest bookstores in the city.

Yet not nearly as old as me.

Now the shelves tilted against each other. Books tumbled in massive snowdrifts across the floor. I stooped to pick one up.

Hundreds of silver-white insects came rushing out from beneath.

Startled, I dropped the book. The bugs made a sound like dry autumn leaves as they swarmed in a confused whirlpool, then streamed back inside the heap of forgotten pages.

Next time, I knew to expect them. I soon gave up on trying to read anything, though. To this day, I was still much more comfortable with Old Jacian. I became borderline illiterate when faced with modern text.

If I needed to, I could parse signs and short messages. The important stuff. The characters used for words had evolved greatly, compared to

Old Jacian, but they retained enough visual similarities for me to take a rough guess at their meaning. Vesper had always been much more adept at keeping up with changes in language.

I wondered if Vesper had stopped by this bookshop to browse for intel. Then I realized I was a fool for wondering.

If the whole city had been sealed for fifty years, there would be no new information here. Or anywhere. Nothing to explain what had happened in the world outside Glorybower while we slept.

Alone in the ruined store, I took a moment to get reacquainted with myself. I tested the movement of my arms and legs and various joints. Everything worked.

The people of past eras had said I resembled a blacksmith, a manual laborer. I wasn't quite a hulking beast of a woman, but I did have more bulk to me than the likes of svelte Vesper.

I too was encased in a tight chalice suit. Unlike Vesper, I wore a looser standard flight suit on top of it, unbuttoned down to the waist. The cloth of the flight suit had gone stiff with old blood. It crackled whenever I moved.

I poked curiously at my inner chalice suit—which, in contrast, seemed immune to getting crusty or stained. My cutouts were different from Vesper's: the design covered my ribcage but left parts of my stomach exposed. It felt like a reptilian second skin. It certainly didn't feel like woven fabric.

How did these suits work again? Neither Vesper nor I could fit any sort of undergarment beneath them. That much seemed certain.

I opened and closed my fists. Nothing else moved. The bookstore was very quiet once all the hidden bugs went still.

If there were other humans around, the first thing I'd do would be to go hunting for gloves. Here in this empty city, there was no one to hide my hands from. Vesper already knew what they looked like.

I had no fingernails. No toenails. Fingertips and toe-tips stained forever red-black. Hues of dead blood.

It wasn't mere discoloration. A carbonized stiffness infused the ends of my fingers. They worked fine for my purposes. But people who touched them said they felt more like lifeless rock than something human.

Those were the dead-looking fingers I used to explore my newly refurbished body. In the process, I found a military ID bracelet on my left wrist. Plus a silk field scarf—much of its pattern blotted out with dried blood—on my right.

That was a newer tradition, something from the past two centuries or so. During my last few awakenings, the army had distributed field scarves to all potential combatants. They were printed with a vibrant blue-green-gold map of the islands of Jace. A colorful token to remind you of what you fought for.

To my knowledge, Vesper had never taken a military ID. Vesper had never taken a field scarf.

At one point, an authority figure had tried to press on me a thick regulation handbook diagramming hundreds of scarf-tying techniques. Some deemed appropriate for combat situations, others only for formal ceremonies. At least a third of the text appeared to describe banned ways of wearing field scarves, complete with gruesome anecdotes to explain why they'd been banned in the first place.

I'd given the book back. "I can't read," I'd said. Not entirely a lie.

See—I had no trouble recalling certain moments. But I couldn't deny the gaping holes in my memory. An inevitable side effect of hibernating for ages, over and over. The present always felt far realer to me than anything that had ever happened in the past.

At any rate, I knew who I was. I recognized Vesper. I recognized the clothes on my body. I wasn't a total amnesiac.

I brushed myself off. The bookstore didn't seem to have any running water. I'd have to find another place to dissolve the blood from my hair.

I picked my way back over to the entrance. White insects stampeded willy-nilly with every step.

The door wasn't locked. But it wouldn't open.

If I strained, I could detect magic clinging to the outer surface of the building. A protective enchantment.

My magic perception had always been very weak. The enchantment wrapping the stately bookstore felt like Vesper's work. But maybe it only seemed that way because I knew we were the only two sentient beings in all of Glorybower. Couldn't think of many other potential culprits.

I moved over to the windows, some already shot through with cracks. It should've been easy to knock the glass out.

The windows didn't budge, either. Not when I tried to pry them open. Not when I shoved at the panes. Not when I hurled the heaviest book I could find. Not when I swung a chair at them.

The sheltering magic held fast.

I put the wooden chair down. It left a sticky residue on my palms. The slithering white insects gave me a wide berth now.

So Vesper had gone to the trouble of moving my dead body here. And then she'd locked me in with magic. A makeshift cage.

On the other hand, the entire city was a cage. Why bother trapping me when I was already trapped?

I pressed at my forehead. It was hard to tell where the globs of dry blood ended and my living skin and hair began.

There was too much to think about.

Thinking had never been my strong suit.

As far as I knew, the bookstore itself meant nothing to either of us.

Why drop me here? Vesper wasn't being generous by locking me up with reams of entertainment. She must know I'd rather use books for bicep curls than try to make sense of the characters streaming down their pages.

If she meant to trap me forever, she'd put me in chains. She'd nail me shut in a box in the basement. Then she'd fill the basement with concrete.

No, Vesper wasn't seriously trying to stop me from breaking out. She'd sealed the building to delay me.

So why use magic to lock me up? Why kill me? And why wasn't I more shocked?

In every past awakening, we'd been partners. Allies.

I had washed-out memories of a Vesper who would've defended me with her life. A Vesper who I'd trusted more than any of the humans I met with each new awakening. But the Vesper of here and now clearly didn't feel the same. No choice but to accept the facts before me.

Was this a normal human reaction to visceral betrayal? I don't know anymore. You tell me. I haven't lived a normal life.

Without warning, my demon bondmate had pitched me off the side of the tallest building for miles around. Outrage, horror, heartbreak—any of those would've been a reasonable response. Instead I found myself locked in a state of dead analytical calm.

I wasn't one to argue with the reality of the situation, however unfavorable it might be. As always, the indisputable truth of the present moment reigned supreme for me.

What I felt, above all else, was that if this new Vesper wanted to keep me at a standstill in the dusty insect-ridden bookstore, I'd better work as hard as I could to get out.

The magic capping the roof turned out to be more vulnerable than the magic blocking the windows. I emerged into open air covered in bits of plywood and insulation.

I'd beaten my way out with a tad too much enthusiasm: afterward I looked at my right arm and saw it hanging strangely.

I saw bone.

The pain came all at once. My breath left my lungs as if driven out by a hammer. My foot slipped on the slope of the roof.

I fell. All on my own, without any demonic assistance.

I didn't die. Not this time. But I had a feeling I'd come close.

I lay in the street next to the bookstore and stared blindly at the broken trench where the paving ended. Half the road gave way to an inexplicable ditch, one deep enough to stand in. As if the apocalypse had come in the middle of a construction project. No one left alive to finish it.

Pain had followed me down from the roof. It staked me to the ground. I inhaled dust.

I kept wondering how Vesper knew we were now fifty years in the future. She'd refused to grace me with a clear answer.

She should've been in hibernation the whole time, too, but she'd claimed to have stayed partly awake. Did she know fifty years had gone by because she'd counted them as they passed—one day at a time?

It wasn't as though Vesper had never hurt me before. She'd killed me a couple times upon request. Mostly in the distant past. Only when there was no other way to get what we wanted. Only when a sacrifice was needed to save our world. Only when I myself demanded it.

Fifty years ago, before we went into hibernation, had I demanded this of her? Had I given her special instructions for after we woke: orders to mock me, to punish me, to murder me?

I was Vesper's Host, and she was my demon. The guardian demon of Jace. The reason no one had ever won a war against the Jacian archipelago—not since the Crying Age that long predated both of us. Vesper always carried out my orders to perfection.

3

MY BROKEN-OPEN right arm left a sludge of bright blood on the stony street. My left hand groped at my stomach.

I didn't understand why until I felt it: a hard circular object, lying centered over my navel. It fit in my palm like the lid of a jar.

My watch. Yes. The reason I kept the top half of my flight suit fully unbuttoned. The reason that the tight-fitting chalice suit I wore beneath it had a cutout exposing the skin of my stomach.

All so I could reach this watch.

When my fingers curled around its edges, the bulk of the pain left my body like a geyser. My injured arm kept spitting blood. But I regained enough self-awareness to realize how much noise I'd been making, curled there on a road that hadn't seen any human traffic in a good five decades.

My cries died down to whimpers. My left hand kept gripping the watch at my navel.

It may have been the size and shape of a pocket watch, but I'd never kept it in a pocket. A chain grew from the back of it—dead center—not from the top. The chain grew straight through my navel and into the depths of my body.

I assumed it did, anyway. Even if pressed, I couldn't explain how it worked. At some point in my career as the sleeping savior of Jace, this thing I called a watch had become part of me.

If I tugged at it, the chain would extend from my belly button like a retractable cord. If I let go, the chain would shorten, the watch snapping back into place, flush with my stomach.

All I knew was that magic had melded the watch with me, and that it had something to do with Vesper. Clutching at it would help clear my mind no matter what was going on with the rest of my body, living or dying.

I held the watch on my stomach as I waited for my right arm to get tired of bleeding.

I tried to recall the very last moments before the start of my most recent bout of magical sleep. Fifty years ago. Based on past experience, some of the cloudier memories would grow clearer over time. Some wouldn't.

Vague recollections: vorpal beasts run amok. A vast vorpal hole yawning open in the sky over Glorybower. The biggest hole in reality I'd seen in any era to date. Monsters pouring down upon the city like rain.

We'd tried to stop it, hadn't we? Me and Vesper and the military.

We must've gotten in our chalice. In Solitaire. We were both still dressed for it, after all. We must've been together in the cockpit, the enormous body of the chalice amplifying Vesper's magic. We would've tried to slay the beasts, to seal the hole, to save the city.

Clearly we'd failed.

I rolled very slowly onto my back. I heard a guttural groan. It took a good solid minute to grasp that it had come gurgling out of my own throat.

We'd lost control of the chalice, and of ourselves. We'd lacked the strength to close the hole in the sky, to banish the avalanche of beasts. What options remained?

I was responsible for piloting Solitaire. Vesper provided the power for the chalice to execute my directives.

In other words, it must've been me. Whether or not I'd been in my right mind, I must've been the one who chose to seal Glorybower. Only a chalice could work magic at such an inconceivable scale.

I'd channeled Vesper's magic through Solitaire to seal the city. Had I then forced both of us into hibernation, before our chalice could spin even further out of control? Before we could do worse damage? Had I sealed the entire population in here with us?

Where were they now?

I imagined it: the absolute barrier around Glorybower, formed in an instant. Our chalice toppling like a slain giant. Me and Vesper gone silent in the cockpit. The hole in the sky still belching out vorpal beasts. Sometimes in a torrent, sometimes none at all. Over a fifty-year period, that might very well be enough beasts to erase every single person left alive in the city.

I wish I could say this thought made me feel something.

It seemed improper to consider it and respond with: yes, that could have happened. Yes, that makes sense. A reasonable theory.

But I wouldn't still be alive now, hundreds and hundreds and hundreds of years after my birth, if I had any sort of capacity for regret.

To be fair, though, I'd only lived twenty-something of those years in real waking time.

I studied the sky. An indistinct haze, neither blue nor brown nor gray. No real clouds, though I saw hints of what Vesper had called mirroring. A faint mirage of upside-down buildings. A reflected birds-eye view of the city.

The vorpal hole from fifty years ago was still there. Now that I was looking for it, I found it in an instant. An asymmetrical open wound in reality, one far too large to ever heal on its own.

If a mortal human stuck their arm in a vorpal hole, their arm would be lost forever. If they tripped and fell in one, they'd be dead, without any body to burn or put in a grave.

A vorpal hole way up in the sky posed little risk of snaring unsuspecting passers-by. The real problem was what might emerge from it—what might come crawling out of the otherworldly void.

I gripped the watch on my stomach for strength. I was still shedding red on the dusty road.

I got up.

When I glanced at my arm, I caught glimpses of white bone and yellow fat and pink flesh. After that, I tried not to look at it at all.

What was the worst that could happen? If I keeled over and died again, I'd wither into oblivion for a few days. A few weeks. A few months, if I were unlucky. Then the bond with Vesper would snap me back to life. I'd rise. I'd keep going. Like always.

I couldn't see our chalice from here. The tip of the bell tower was just barely visible. That would be sufficient to orient me: I had a peculiarly sharp sense of direction. Much sharper than my sense of magic.

I made for Solitaire, for our chalice. I wish I could tell you that a finely crafted plan drove me forward. In reality it was little more than a hunch.

For fifty years we'd slept inside our chalice. Then Vesper woke me. She took me down out of the cockpit before I came to. After killing me, she'd moved me even farther from the scene of our hibernation.

She was trying to keep me away from Solitaire. There must be a reason. The fastest way to find out would be to defy her.

I couldn't use magic like Vesper, or like a regular human mage. My magic core had been ripped out of me long, long ago. My only power lay in my identity as her Host.

If we were together, and if she were in a cooperative mood, I could've asked her to port me. We weren't together now, and Vesper seemed unlikely to ever be in a cooperative mood again.

So I trudged onward, dripping stubbornly, fingertips clawing at the rim of my watch to ward off the worst of the pain. I cried as I went, and I stumbled, but I didn't collapse.

I passed neighborhoods of slumping wood-frame houses. Threadbare bird-shaped mannequins hung inside dark windows, inverted like partridges strung up to age their meat before cooking. An old, old tradition for warding off evil. Most people these days probably had no idea why they did it.

There were no gardens anymore. Just shoulder-high thickets of weeds crowned with long heavy seed pods. Overgrown roots elbowed their way up through the stone-slab path. Years-thick layers of never-swept leaves squished spongily beneath my feet.

Did it rain here? Would night ever come? Were there seasons?

Well, surely it rained. Fifty years of total dessication would paint a very different picture.

Still, the city was trapped in a snow globe of magic. That must have changed it in ways both subtle and obvious. It wouldn't have aged in the same way as a ghost town abandoned for more innocuous reasons. It was its own creature now.

And it was overrun with vorpal beasts. Colorful kite-shaped specimens glided in the sky overhead. I flinched when I first spotted them, but they showed no interest in me. Despite me being an open target. Despite my visible weakness. Not all vorpal beasts were inherently aggressive to humans. Lucky for me.

I kept going.

I crossed a bridge over a half-dry canal. Amber water filled the canal to the brim, almost to the point of flooding—but it stopped midway through, as if held back by an invisible wall. The parched-looking canal bed extended far off to my right, far beyond the abrupt end of the water.

Blue squirrels the length of my arm climbed up lampposts. Snakelike tails swished restlessly behind them.

Around my head danced both fluffy summer flake-flies and bright winter fireflies. These were the classic symbol of the changing seasons here in Jace—and the exact same species, actually, shifting forms over the course of their year-long life.

You were never supposed to see the summer and winter forms together. It was one of those well-known poetic metaphors for something impossible, like rain falling backwards.

Finally I reached the plaza covered in clover. The silver fountain still bubbled and splashed around its tall spiral tusk, a slender needle pointing heavenward. Some kind of wayward magic must be sustaining it. Or had it grown up like a magical tumor out of the wreckage? Had there even been a fountain here fifty years ago?

After returning to the spot where I'd woken, I understood why I hadn't initially seen Solitaire. Wreckage and shadows blocked most of the fallen chalice from view.

With some difficulty, I climbed the rubble. Black splats of blood dropped from my loose-hanging right arm. I keenly felt the clock in my left hand. I worked hard on not feeling anything else.

Gnarled vines of grave wisteria grew over all eight of Solitaire's outspread arms. Like chains to bind a prisoner. I hadn't been able to see them from up in the bell tower.

I got myself high enough to step over onto Solitaire's knee. The leg was studded with crystalline protrusions. In the past, I would've used them as handholds to climb up to the cockpit in the chest cavity. Now it was simply a matter of walking across the chalice's horizontal form without tripping.

The crystal door to the cockpit stood open a mere crack. Like the lid of a poorly closed coffin. Just large enough to let in a rod-shaped splinter of light.

My right arm remained useless. I'd have to slide the door open with my left hand. Which meant letting go of my watch.

I released it.

My knees buckled. My forehead sweated. My eyes sweated. The inside of my mouth sweated. It wasn't the worst pain I'd ever felt. Probably.

I wedged my fingers in the crack of the cockpit door. I started to heave on it.

Bells rang.

Bells loud enough to wake the whole city, if there were anyone still sleeping. Bells that seemed to resound from all around me, not just from the aloof tower at my back.

For an instant, the jolt of sound made all the strength flee my body.

That one instant was all she needed.

I tried to haul at the door again. It didn't budge.

A pair of tight-clad legs stood before me. Vesper had deigned to touch ground for once, to add her weight to the cockpit door.

I yanked my arm back just in time. With a twist of her hips, she slammed shut the cracked-open door. She would've crushed my fingers if they were still wedged inside.

Her toes lifted off the door, a murky thing like smoked quartz. Her legs curled up under her, back to levitating. She looked down at me with disdain.

4

THE CITY BELLS ceased, but my ears kept ringing.

"You just came back to life," Vesper said. I strained to hear her. "What the hell did you do to your arm?"

"You locked me up," I told her. "I broke out."

"With brute force. Of course. Lord, how typical."

I reached for the cockpit door again. She caught my left arm, quick as a snake.

Between the two of us, Vesper was stronger. Much stronger. Not that she looked it. For demons, physical strength seemed to have little correlation with their physical shape. Maybe because they were creatures governed more by magic than by the principles of our corporeal world.

That said, Vesper was the only demon I'd ever met. The only one who existed in our world at all, as far as I knew. I meant to keep it that way.

I tried to wrest my arm from her, though I knew it wouldn't work.

"Let me inside Solitaire," I said. "I won't touch anything. Just want to have a look."

"Remember what happened the last time we were in Solitaire?"

"We slept."

"You slept," she snapped. "My body shut down, but my mind stayed awake. No, before that."

"We destroyed the—"

"*You* destroyed the city."

"I won't touch anything," I repeated.

"Yeah, sounds real trustworthy." She veered behind me, twisting my arm up against my back.

I turned my head as far as it would go. I couldn't see her well. "You're afraid I'll lose control again? I won't try to pilot Solitaire. Let me in."

"I fear nothing," Vesper said to my neck. The tips of her nails pricked my wrist, sharp as claws.

"Then let me in. That's an order."

I almost never used those words. When was the last time I'd consciously given Vesper an absolute command? Might've been centuries ago, when I forced her to devour those enemy soldiers.

Or was I forgetting something more recent, more relevant to the way she pressed at my left arm as if she wanted to mangle it to match the one on the right?

She could have, of course. She could've dislocated my elbow and shoulder with little effort. She could've torn the ligaments and spiral-fractured my bones with the thoughtless ease of a child kicking a pebble down the street. That inhuman strength had always been part of her.

Pain was a heat that blotted out my thoughts. A different heat—my heightened awareness of ordering her, and meaning it—bled through the watch on my stomach. It seeped up into the taut magical chain binding the watch to my insides.

"Let me in," I said.

For a moment the command worked as it should have. Vesper's fingers loosened. My left arm began to escape her.

Then she seized the back of my flight suit and hurled me down off Solitaire with a wordless cry of rage.

I lay stunned next to Solitaire. A human-sized replica of the twelve-story chalice: we were both sprawled prone and helpless.

I couldn't move. I couldn't think. If I hadn't died, I'd at least crawled right up to the very brink of it.

I lay there long enough to observe that the city did indeed have a full cycle of day and night.

Insects explored the open parts of my ruined right arm. The vines of grave wisteria grabbing at Solitaire heaved and pulsed as if panting for breath. Muddled late-afternoon light poured through the cascading violet flowers.

Night was not as dark as you might imagine. On the periphery of my vision, Solitaire shone with an eerie gilded glow. Its light spilled over the walls of sheared-off buildings. Flocks of ghost-white bats billowed across the sky like shining deep-sea oddities.

I closed my eyes without passing out. Blood kept ticking out, out through my wounds.

The following morning, Vesper knelt in the air over my chest.

"Where'd you go?" I asked, hoarse. I sounded as though my vocal cords had gotten all their meat scraped off.

"Had a lot to catch up with."

"You threw me down from on high," I said. "Twice in a row. Already running out of ideas?"

Her mouth twisted. "I forgot how much heroes love pain."

"You tried to kill me. Why?"

"I didn't just try. I succeeded."

"Not this time."

"This time I wasn't trying," Vesper said. "Don't tempt me."

"I ordered you through our bond. Gave you an absolute command." My body refused to stir. All I had left was my voice. "How did you defy it?"

Slit-pupil eyes regarded me with contempt.

"You heal too slowly."

She snatched the watch off my stomach, pulling it up in front of her face as if to decode a secret message buried in the dial. The chain embedded in my navel extended, sparking with magic.

That didn't hurt. What hurt was the magic she sent shooting back down through the chain. It felt like she'd reached inside and clawed my kidneys.

I bucked, choking and retching.

Vesper released the clock. It snapped back to me as the chain retracted, landing in its usual spot with an audible smack of hard-slapped skin. For a second the metal felt hot as a brand.

I raised my right arm. I bent it. No agony. No exposed bone. Not only that—I could feel the rest of my body now. I could move again. I could sit up.

I didn't thank Vesper. She was the reason I'd needed fixing, after all.

She'd already begun gliding away. Stuck on foot, I scrambled to follow.

"You never answered any of my questions," I said.

Vesper didn't look back. "You've seen more of the city now. The city you destroyed."

Presumably she was trying to provoke a reaction. At the moment, I had none to give her.

"Remember anything more?" she asked.

"Like what?"

"Anything. The people we met last time you were awake. The doctor. The general."

I'd met a lot of doctors and a lot of generals over the course of my various awakenings.

"They all kind of blend together," I admitted. "But—"

"Char. Don't you dare say you remember the important things."

I shut my mouth just in time.

We were back near the place where I'd originally awakened. That shattered plaza coated in venomous green clover.

The birds and monsters sounded very different now that it was morning. They lobbed volleys of trilling shrieks that bore a creepy resemblance to shouting children.

I smelled human blood, but that stench all came from me. My nostrils and facial cavities had been painted full of it, inescapable.

"Fifty years isn't the longest we've ever hibernated," I said.

"Far from it."

"What made you lose it this time?"

"Lose what?"

"You went unhinged," I said. "You killed me."

Vesper whirled midair. "Am I not allowed to have a breaking point?"

"Not if it leads to wanton murder."

"It builds up," she said. "I never forgot any of the time I spent watching you in stasis. All those decades and centuries."

"But why now?" I asked. "Why didn't you snap five hundred years ago?"

I waited for an answer.

I waited and waited.

Anyone would agree that Vesper mostly looked human. Sure, she had some distinctly demonic features. Her horns. Her pointed ears. Her vertical pupils. Her shark-like teeth and sharp fingernails. The gills slashed in stark parallel lines along her ribcage. Her habit of floating rather than walking. The color of her blood.

Squint past those tell-tale markers, and she'd appear more human than many of the humans I'd met.

Particularly her expressions. Fury, disgust, blazing adrenaline, glittering amusement. She had petite hands and eloquent eyebrows. Bronze skin much like mine, only hers seemed somehow livelier.

Right now she looked at me without saying anything. Not with her voice, and not with her demeanor. She looked at me for a long while.

"I complain about the same thing every single time," she said. "With every awakening. I tell you that while you were a vegetable, I remained awake. A ghost bound to my Host. I can't use any power while you sleep. I can't do anything but wait.

"Most times, I really am like a ghost. I can drift around the world, far away from you. Not touching anything. Watching what happens.

"This past time—you locked both of us inside Solitaire while you slept. Body and soul. I was awake the whole time, and not a single molecule of me could escape. I'm never letting you hibernate again."

Had fifty years of total silence and isolation driven her mad?

Or was there something else at play here?

"I've been thinking about why you wouldn't obey me," I said. "Why you wouldn't let me back in Solitaire."

"Sounds like you have it all figured out."

"You've never disobeyed an absolute command before."

"You sure about that?" Vesper asked.

"Maybe a previous command is overriding it."

I stepped closer. Clover crushed softly underfoot. Here and there, bamboo roots broke through like pipes gone feral. The roots looked suspiciously similar to animal vertebrae, endless coruscating bony spines fighting to escape the ground that held them down.

There was a wild beauty to the empty city, if you forgot the fact that people were supposed to live here. That people had been living here, close to a million of them, when I sealed it off with an impenetrable dome of mirrored magic.

"I think I gave you orders before I forced us to sleep in Solitaire," I said. "I think I—I must've been out of my mind.

"I ordered you to make me pay for what I did to the city. For failing to save it. For failing to save them. I ordered you to make me suffer when we woke. That's why you're—"

Vesper's laughter echoed through the debilitated plaza. Morning sunshine glinted on pointed teeth.

"Oh, you're funny," she said. "You think you would do that? You think you're such a martyr to heroism?"

Her smile evaporated. "You think you've been forcing me to obey you?"

"I usually try not to. But I am your Host."

"When I followed you, it was because I chose to," Vesper said. "In war, in peace. In waking and in sleeping. No matter what you told me, what I did was my own choice. Every time."

"That can't be true."

"Almost every time," she amended.

"Almost?" I asked.

"Watch this."

Peach and gray and cream-colored stones rose from the remnants of the pavement. They circled around Vesper like jagged moons.

She pointed at the ever-running fountain, the heart of the plaza. The flying rocks tossed themselves down into the quicksilver liquid.

The silver fizzed and hissed. Puffs of steam rose from the surface, then scattered. I looked down into the fountain. The rocks were gone as if they'd never existed.

Vesper loomed behind me, defying gravity. She put a small cold hand on the back of my neck. Her nails made themselves known to my skin like the tips of threatening knives.

"Ugh," she muttered. "Sticky."

"You're the one who decided to touch me."

"You need a bath," she said.

We gazed at the silvery water. A chemical hot spring? Magical mercury or magical acid? Could be all or none of those. I had little doubt that it would liquefy me just like how it had liquefied Vesper's rocks.

"You're making more work for yourself," I warned.

"How so?"

"You tossed me off the bell tower. Then you hauled my dead body over to a bookstore."

"Must've been terribly disorienting. I know you don't read."

"You flung me off Solitaire," I said. "You broke my back. Then you came back and repaired it."

"Hope you're not complaining about getting healed."

The odor coming off the silver fluid hit me all at once. Felt like it might melt my facial membranes into glue.

My knees went stiff. Vesper pushed harder on my neck, as if readying herself to dunk me in head-first.

I caught at the lip of the fountain, bracing myself. The surface was dry, a type of scaly volcanic rock. It stung like a rash the instant I touched it.

"Ves." I sounded ragged.

Because I was ragged: thoughts frayed beyond repair, feelings trampled beyond recognition. But this was the present moment. This was real, and I was alive and awake for it.

I twisted around to look at her, with mixed success. My right ear hovered a hands-width from the pool of steaming silver liquid. The soaring, crashing portions of the perpetual fountain seemed to splash ever closer. I felt the piercing acrid rawness of it in my pores.

"Ves. What do you get out of this?"

"Dissolving you in vorpal mercury?"

"Hurting me," I said. "If you're not following past orders. If no one's making you do it. Not even me myself."

"Do I need a reason?"

I attempted to swallow. "Hurting me is awfully easy for you, isn't it? I don't understand why you bother. Thought you liked a challenge."

"I don't need a challenge to entertain myself," Vesper assured me. "Trust me. I get plenty of joy from this."

"You did always have a sadistic streak," I conceded.

"Glad we're in agreement."

"Is that what you meant when you told me you weren't really following orders? Even when I commanded you to do terrible things?"

"For a good cause, of course," Vesper said, sardonic.

"You did as I said because you wanted to," I continued. "Because you wanted to raze the battlefield. Because you wanted to slaughter our enemies. Because you wanted to rip the heart out of someone, anyone, and they just so happened to be the tyrant I pointed at.

"You didn't need to be commanded at all. You did it because you were hungry. You did it because you loved it."

I had no reason to think she'd slip up. I had no reason to believe her hand would lose its grip on the back of my neck, even for a millisecond.

I had no reason to bet on that, but I had nothing else to bet on. Whether or not she faltered, I'd ram my elbow back at her. I'd drop as low as I could in a bid to escape.

It wouldn't work. Vesper was stronger and faster. She had magic; she had inhuman reflexes. She'd pitch my entire torso in the fountain before I so much as laid a finger on her. All that would remain of me would be a cauterized, disembodied pair of legs. Unless she decided to melt those in the fountain, too.

Either way, it'd take me weeks or months to return. Maybe that was what Vesper sought now. True solitude in the closed city. The peace of not having to deal with her Host.

So I did understand how this would play out. I still had every intention of making a last-ditch effort to fight back.

But as I strained against the small powerful hand bearing down on my neck, as I gathered my breath to strike at her, something hit the ground beside us with a splat.

A fruit.

A fig the size of a cantaloupe, squashed and misshapen from its fall. Deep purple-brown on the outside, with soft fleshy pink-red innards leaking out through open crevices.

It stank inexplicably of sulfur.

Vesper and I both stared at the mystery fig. She wasn't pushing me toward the fountain anymore. She wasn't moving at all.

The fig's skin bubbled and popped. As if something trapped inside it had started squirming. Kicking to get out.

Suddenly Vesper yanked me to her. Her magic snapped around us, porting us a good thirty or forty feet back.

Her gaze never left the fruit on the ground by the fountain. Even from this distance, I could see its sides bulging. More sweet-looking red and white flesh oozed through the cracks.

Vesper still held me trapped in a headlock. She used her other arm to make a sharp sweeping gesture. The fig jumped clumsily off the ground and pitched itself into the fountain. A virulent pink smoke rose in its wake.

Only then did Vesper release me. I straightened warily, massaging my neck.

We looked at the distorted vorpal hole yawning wide, wide open in the sky. That hole had hung over the city for fifty years and counting.

There might be long stretches of time when nothing emerged from the other side. There might be brief moments when a lifetime's worth of monsters burst forth all at once.

With vorpal holes, you never knew what might come out to haunt you next. Not even a demon could forecast when or if the next wave might show up.

A vorpal beast could look as familiar as a fluffy family pet, or as hard and alien as a falling meteor. They could materialize in the guise of a lacy fungus or a rotting severed hand. Or an overripe fruit.

No quirk of appearance could mark any particular vorpal beast as being more or less of a threat to humanity than any other. A tiny beast might turn out to be deadlier than one the size of a mountain.

They weren't meant to exist in our world; they weren't meant to cross over. In that sense, all bore sufficient potential for danger.

5

I BLINKED. A brown-gray lump hung in the sky like a floating island.

Hard to tell from the ground, but it looked about half as tall as Solitaire (if Solitaire stood vertical). Solidly the size of a five or six-story structure. Like the half-broken historic bank building over on the far end of the plaza.

I hadn't seen the lump emerge from the cavernous hole over the city. I hadn't seen it home in on us, moving close enough that its shadow splayed across the plaza stones.

It might all have happened in a lightning-swift eruption of magic. If a vorpal beast detected life, if it smelled us, if it wanted to loom in the air right above us—well, it didn't necessarily need to sail the full ponderous distance like an airship to reach us.

Beside me, Vesper reached for her horns.

They were small enough to vanish in her fists when she held them.

She pulled at her horns, and out came two long swords. Far too long to have physically emerged from her body, though the way she drew them gave the illusion that they'd somehow been sheathed in her head.

The hilts were pale bone, ending in the points of her original horns. The blades, too, resembled matte ivory bone, shot through with veins of true porcelain blue. They were slender blades with a very slight curve, at least three feet long from hilt to tip.

Island-style swords. Vesper was, after all, a Jacian demon.

New off-white nubs had already grown to replace her lost horns. She tossed one sword in the air: it turned and circled back to wait at her side like a trained falcon. The other sword she kept in her hands.

I reached for my own weapons.

Then I remembered I had none.

When I looked up again, Vesper was gone. Magic—bright enough for even me to see clearly—splintered itself on the great grayish lump in the sky. It looked like a colossal wasp nest, right down to the smooth papier-mâché swirls texturing its outer surface.

I'd been braced to fight.

I began to question this impulse as I watched Vesper and her island swords flit around the monumental vorpal beast, the wasp nest built like a fortress.

I could hold my own in a fair match, human to human. Magically speaking, however, I had nothing to contribute.

There were other ways I could support Vesper. I'd always played more of a supporting role. My duty as Vesper's Host was to help her make the most of her power.

The Vesper of this new era didn't seem particularly desirous of my help, though.

Besides, there was no one left in the city to protect. The infrastructure was already ruined, eaten away at by an excess of wild magic. Even more so than by the sheer passage of time.

During past awakenings, I'd have stopped thinking or seeing or hearing anything extraneous until we destroyed the vorpal beast, locating and eliminating its core.

This time—for the first time ever—there was no one else in danger. Just me and Vesper. We could take a lot of damage. We could take more damage than anyone else in existence.

I gazed up at the fireworks of magic overhead, at Vesper's swords ricocheting off the portentous wasp nest. She looked very small up there. Like a sparrow trying to fight a scarecrow.

I stood there bearing witness to a vorpal beast that might have the power to murder thousands, or many times more than that. I stood at the edge of its corpulent shadow and, for the first time in my life, felt zero urgency.

A clod the size of a human head smashed the ground by my feet.

I leapt back. Then retreated a few steps further, for good measure.

A passion fruit. Deep garnet and wrinkled with ripeness. Split open to spill out yellow pulp laced with pitch-black seeds.

An incongruous scent curled up out of its wetness. Not the bright citrus tang I'd expected. Something smokier. More explosive.

I took off. I ran for Solitaire.

That passion fruit was a vorpal beast, too, a smaller one spat out by the wasp nest overhead. Flung down like how human infants used to get tossed off cliffs as a sacrifice in olden times—that is, in times even older than the era of my youth.

I felt no explosion. I heard no sound whatsoever. But when I looked over my shoulder, the overripe passion fruit was gone without a trace. In its place remained a perfect circular crater, one large enough to swim in.

I ran faster. Right now, with Vesper distracted, might be my best and only chance to get back in Solitaire.

More swollen fruit rained from above in my wake, chasing me across the rubble. The initial impact sounded like bags of soft flesh meeting rock. The subsequent suicidal eruptions of magic never emitted any sound at all. Fresh craters sprouted like a giant's staggering footsteps behind me.

Vesper's magic screeched in the sky. I couldn't waste time looking up.

I clambered up Solitaire's side, grabbing for hard-edged crystal spikes to haul myself higher. My hands and feet knew where to find them before my eyes did.

I hauled open the door to the cockpit. It screeched as it went, ending with an ear-splitting crack like the seasonal cleaving of sea ice.

The city bells went off again, even louder and more dissonant than last time.

Disregarding the bells—nothing I could do to stop them—I slid my body inside the cockpit.

At first it was like diving inside a manhole, a dark opening that went straight down. Gravity adjusted itself around me as I crossed the threshold, pulling me to the surface meant to act as a floor.

The cockpit was built for two. For me and Vesper.

In front: the pilot's seat. My seat. A chair with two translucent prongs protruding from the lower half of the backrest.

The prongs resembled a tuning fork, one as long as my arm. You'd have to impale yourself to fully occupy the seat.

And I had. I always did. Every time.

In back: a sunken, half-formed cage of bone. A mess of wiry tendrils and glittering filaments reminiscent of corn silk. Saber-like teeth budding from dark-stained walls.

Even now, the cockpit reeked of cleaning chemicals and anxious sweat.

That body-shaped depression at the back was meant for Vesper.

While Solitaire soared in the sky, its thirsty tendrils would find the cutouts in her chalice suit, all the areas of exposed skin. The wires and teeth-like bones would grow and grow and grow to pierce her.

Some would grow straight through her. Some would grow long enough to graze the back of my chair.

Solitaire drank Vesper's blue demon blood, her magic. Solitaire would keep feeding on her till her body expired.

And Solitaire would never overflow. Though the material of the cockpit floor looked as impenetrable as polished marble, it drank her blood and guts up in the way of a bottomless cup.

That was how Solitaire got the power to do things like putting me into pristine hibernation for fifty years. Like manifesting a barrier strong enough to seal a whole city. A barrier that even the vorpal beasts locked in here with us seemed unable to shatter.

I could fly Solitaire on my own. I could offer up my own flesh in exchange. But I wouldn't last long.

In past eras, between my awakenings, they'd tried stuffing chalices with teams of human pilots. When one died, the next would take over midair. They could keep a chalice going for hours that way. But only for hours.

Vesper and I had put a stop to that. Though we'd learned of it very late. Solitaire and the other experimental chalices had already shred up many, many human pilots. No one told us their names or showed us their graves.

Vesper gleaned hints from the scant remnants of blood and other bodily material spattering each chalice's cockpit. Some had been soldiers past retirement age. Volunteers. (Had they understood what they were volunteering for?)

Others were scarcely more than children.

But this was how I knew that I could pilot a chalice alone. If I were lucky, I might last as long as ten minutes.

I lowered myself into the seat up front. I aligned my back with the cold prongs of the tuning fork.

The fork was visible but not, precisely speaking, tangible. It wouldn't tear up my organs. It wouldn't leave me with physical holes in my torso. But I would be lying if I claimed it wouldn't hurt.

I took a practiced breath and prepared to ram myself backwards. To skewer myself with the turning fork. To pin myself to Solitaire. To become one with my chalice, and to invite it to devour me.

If no one occupied the bone cage in the depths of the cockpit, Solitaire would help itself to the next available fuel source.

The ghostly tines of the fork penetrated my lower back. They slid below my ribs, emerging bloodless and semitransparent on the other side.

All around me, Solitaire began to awaken.

There was no steering wheel, no joystick, no flight yoke. Thankfully, it wasn't anything like piloting an airship. If you could move your body—if you could even think about moving your body—you could operate a chalice. Understanding crosswinds and the significance of dew point might offer a tactical advantage, but it wasn't mandatory.

I set my teeth. The tendrils and blade-like bones at the back of the cockpit creaked with longing as they lunged for me.

A flash-bang of magic blasted the cockpit from the still-open door.

The chalice's starving claws groaned to a reluctant halt, millimeters away from digging into me.

For an instant I glimpsed Vesper silhouetted at the entrance. One hand gripped the upper rim of the door frame. Her feet didn't touch ground. There was too much brightness behind her to make out the look on her face.

I grabbed for the tines of the tuning fork. They stuck far out of my stomach now, one on each side of the flat watch over my navel.

My fingers scrabbled over the tines. Not quite passing through them, but unable to get any sort of purchase on them. Unable to use my own strength to hold myself in place.

Vesper's magic heaved at me. It was like being jerked forward by the taut snap of a rubber band rebounding. Her magic propelled me out of my seat, off my skewer, away from the new sharp fangs and stabbing bones rapidly germinating from all sides of the cockpit.

As the prongs of the tuning fork left my back, Solitaire went silent again, sinking deeper into slumber. Still anchored to the earth by girthy vines of grave wisteria.

I crashed into Vesper at the cockpit entrance. I was larger and heavier: I should've bowled her over.

But she'd thrown me with her magic, and now she caught me just as easily. She whirled me out onto Solitaire's quartz surface.

Though no one was touching it, the cockpit door banged shut with the weight of a coffin lid.

The strident chorus of bells immediately ceased.

Vesper's twin swords orbited the air behind her, politely waiting on standby. There was a small wound high on her cheek. Brilliant blue blood smeared the side of her face. Her pupils had narrowed almost to the point of going invisible.

I raised one finger at the gravity-defying wasp nest. "Just trying to help," I told her. "If there were ever a time to use Solitaire—"

"*No,*" Vesper said through her teeth.

The next thing I knew, she'd ported me to the spire at the very top of the bell tower. A tall, tall spire, crowned in a cluster of agonized stone hands reaching in vain for hidden stars.

We were higher up than the last time we'd been here. Higher than the bell itself. Just about eye level with the drifting wasp nest. From here it looked like a cumulus cloud stained dirty gray, its strength mustered to storm.

"Stay. Put."

As Vesper spoke, fresh barbed wire spouted from the stone spire.

The wire glittered with frost and dew like morning leaves. It swirled around me, as swift and flexible as Solitaire's thirsty filaments. It tied me to the spire before I had time to flail in the air, before I could offer so much as a token kick of resistance.

"You aren't needed," Vesper said. "Neither is Solitaire. Bite your tongue and watch."

"Wait—"

She and her swords half-turned in the air. A brief pause. Not a promise to listen for long.

I hurried on. "Why are you fighting the beasts? I haven't—no one's told you to fight. There's no one to save here."

Vesper contemplated me as if I were a terminal idiot.

"This is my city now," she said coldly.

6

VESPER WARNED ME not to struggle. The bindings of barbed wire would only grow stronger if I bled.

I struggled to control myself, and I bled anyway. The chalice suit left large swathes of skin unprotected. Without meaning to, I squirmed when I breathed.

The wire cinched tighter, and the barbs pricked deeper. An inexplicable tickle imbued my throat—an urge to cough that only chose to make itself known after Vesper tied me up. I could all but hear her: *Why can't you hold still now? You were dormant for decades!*

A cold wind blew. Old blood still glued my hair down.

I took a too-deep breath, and new barbs perforated the backs of my arms. The wind erased an inadvertent gasp.

I couldn't see much from here. Vesper's free-moving swords slashed at the wasp-nest vorpal beast like two little fireflies streaking trails of mystic light.

When she threw around magic, traces of it echoed in my bones, a deep bass beat. The pressure of it clogged and released my inner ears, over and over.

We were bonded, after all. To the extent that a human and a demon could be bonded, anyhow. I couldn't sense her emotions. But sometimes I couldn't help but pick up on the thumping vindictive pulse of her power.

The towering wasp nest split open like a pomegranate, revealing a madhouse of perfect hexagonal cells. Out flew what had to be at least ten thousand bastardized waspy imitations of Vesper herself. They surrounded her in such a thick torrent that she vanished from sight.

It was like the great nest, hitherto impenetrable, had spent all this time watching and learning from Vesper. Cooking up its wasp-winged copies of her. An overwhelming army.

My first thought: we'd faced worst in the past.

Disquiet bubbled in me nonetheless. There was a moment when her pain seemed to hit me like the notes of a far-off song, something incomprehensible shouted through water. Yet acute enough to cut straight past the sensation of barbed wire puncturing my skin in too many places to count.

I was projecting. I was hallucinating. We weren't like human bondmates. I'd never been able to detect what she felt, to share her emotions or send her mine.

Vesper, I thought at her.

But of course my thoughts couldn't reach her.

The flock of vorpal replicas buzzed louder and louder, loud enough to fill the vast air between the bell tower and the plaza. Their swarming still hid Vesper from view. I had no idea what they were doing to her.

"Vesper!"

My voice cracked. No way to tell if she could hear me.

New Vesper clones kept pouring out of the cracked-open wasp nest. They thronged in a hungry knot around the last spot I'd seen her.

I knew now that I didn't have the power to give her absolute commands. Not in the way I'd thought. But I needed to try.

"Vesper," I said, light-headed. "Vesper, take my—"

She materialized an inch from my face. Her answer came as a snarl. "I've got guests to entertain right now, you absolute—"

"Ves," I said. "It doesn't have to be this hard."

Granted, she was in much better shape than I'd feared.

She'd shed enough blue blood for me to taste it in the air, tart and acidic. Very different from how human life smells when it pours out of human bodies. But her limbs were all intact, and she wore an expression of profound irritation. Not desperation.

"Stay out of it," she ordered. "You have no magic. You're nothing but my vessel. My Host. The dirty work was always mine."

"True," I agreed. "But that doesn't make me useless. Take my flesh."

"I don't need your alms."

"They're coming." My lips had gone painfully dry.

The vorpal beasts who'd stolen her form billowed closer. An entire legion just for the two of us. They approached like a plague of locusts.

The difference between a herd of stampeding vorpal beasts and a charging human army was that the beasts had no malice. They might not even be conscious. They acted as their magic and their nature compelled them—often in ways far beyond our understanding.

"Better hurry," I told Vesper.

Her hands were in fists, her own claws cutting into her palms. Her swords slunk about behind her like scolded dogs, low and timid in the air by her ankles. Perhaps she found this humiliating. Perhaps she'd rather snap my neck than stoop to take the only sort of help any mere human could offer a demon.

She'd have to get over it quickly. The buzzing beasts would reach us in seconds.

She wiped any trace of expression from her face.

Her magic undid the barbed wire. In a millisecond, it retracted back into the bare stone from which it'd grown. I let out a small rasping pant as it released me, though I hadn't meant to make a sound.

Unsupported, I started to fall from the spire.

Vesper caught me. One-armed, effortless, despite my being taller and sturdier. The ocean-like roar of the beasts surged closer.

"Only because you begged me," she said abruptly.

She yanked aside my flight suit.

Here was the other reason I usually kept the top part unbuttoned. Here was the other reason my protective chalice suit came littered with cutouts.

Not, as in Vesper's case, to let the chalice itself devour me.

No. My chalice suit was tailored for her.

She sank her teeth into my exposed shoulder. Sharp demon teeth, sharper than any chef's knife.

My back hit the spire again. But there was nowhere secure for my dangling feet to stand.

Vesper held me up as her teeth bit deeper. My pulse beat hard in my throat, my thighs, the insides of my elbows, the wound she'd opened.

I cried out into my own tight-shut mouth. Not quite a scream.

Vesper had ripped a chunk from me. Not much. Skin and its lining, a glug of blood, a few pinches' worth of flesh. Her mouth and nose and cheeks were stained red with me when she raised her face.

Numbness flowed into my mauled trapezius muscle, a stifling clot of magic.

If Vesper wanted greater power, all she had to do was feed on her Host.

The pale stubs on her head lengthened and unfurled, metamorphosing into a full set of many-pointed antlers. Elk antlers this time; their shape changed each time they grew anew.

All the while, we were suspended by Vesper's magic. Still level with the proud bell tower and its spire of sky-clawing hands. Hundreds and hundreds of feet up in the air over the decaying city.

The flying Vesper copies smashed into a glassy barrier of magic, a quick one-sided shield she'd thrown up just before they reached us. They crashed and diverted like a waterfall of human-sized bats.

I caught a closer glimpse of them as they wheeled around us. They were vaguely like Vesper, wasp wings aside. But with compound eyes, and numerous other eyes in unusual places. Extra arms. Extraneous hands ending in a floppy mess of far too many fingers. Twin sword blades welded directly to overlong wrists and elbows.

The returning doppelgangers swooped straight into another makeshift barrier. They buzzed with increasingly deafening density. They rammed the magical shield until it started to buckle.

The mangled slope of muscle down to my shoulder kept throbbing. A persistent reminder that lava-hot agony lay somewhere beneath the desensitizing magic Vesper had slapped on it.

Vesper knelt in the air and touched my ankles, a quick brush on each side. Something hardened beneath my feet.

I took an experimental step out into the open.

What supported me remained invisible. I could see straight down to the base of the tower, to the roofs of houses shedding colorful tiles, or with rebel trees erupting straight through them. Yet any empty spot I set my foot seemed to become, in this moment, solid enough to stand on.

I grabbed the watch from my stomach, yanking the chain longer to hold it up in front of Vesper's face.

The watch dial had no hands. No markings to indicate the cyclical passage of time.

Instead it was transcribed with concentric circles, a pattern like the ripples formed by a falling drop in still water. The bulls-eye and part of the innermost ring around it had turned a scorching blue.

"Seven minutes," I said. "Eight at most."

Vesper gave a curt nod.

The magical barriers surrounding us shattered with a sound like airships crashing.

Victory didn't take anywhere close to the seven minutes on my countdown clock.

The moment the pellucid walls came down, a new wave of magic rolled away from Vesper. It moved with a bellow I felt in my breastbone, a roar of sound like whale song.

The horde of wasp-Vespers stopped dead in the air. Their arm-swords and crooked vestigial fingers couldn't touch us. They quivered as if trapped in a clear sticky jelly.

Vesper's antlers looked slightly blurry, too, as if vibrating with the force of the demonic magic thrumming through her.

With the base of her palm, she wiped the thickest smears of my blood from her mouth.

Then she used that same bloodied hand to take hold of one of her island swords. The other continued hanging obediently suspended behind her.

She drew the blade across nothingness, slicing an impossible line in the air. Fine particles streamed out, alight in the way of sunny dust motes, almost too delicate for my magic perception to pick up on them.

The particles washed across her massed paralyzed imitators, clinging to their makeshift hair and haphazard horns and membranous wings like butterfly powder.

Moments after it touched them, they curled up as if felled by pesticide.

They were mostly human in form, but they folded in on themselves in the exact manner of dry insects. They dropped out of the sky at first one by one, then in a cascading downpour. They fell as slow as dead leaves, disintegrating to soot before touching any of the buildings or roads or canals beneath.

All in all, it took a minute at most. Vesper was long gone: she'd ported back over to the waiting nest.

Far as I could tell—again, my magic perception wasn't the best—the Vesper-like creatures that had tumbled out of the hexagonal cells in that hive were merely extensions of the hive itself. A kind of dandruff. Part of the same greater creature, at any rate. Destroying them wouldn't do much to hurt the vorpal beast that had birthed them.

She needed to find and crush the hive's core.

That, too, ended in a matter of seconds. From the sky over the plaza, demonic magic hit my senses like a stun grenade.

When I could see again, the papery outer surface of the mammoth nest had begun to crumble gently in the wind. It had the look of ashes scattered after a cremation, ashes to represent an untold amount of death.

Vesper was a tiny figure, moving only to dodge the twisting streams of ash. She was as comfortable in the air as a seal in water. Her swords caught the dome-filtered sunlight, two glittering spots of mica on my sight.

I looked at my countdown clock. The heat in my ripped-open shoulder muscle warred with the insistent downward pressure of magic telling me that I felt nothing. Nothing at all.

She'd gulped down a very small bite of my flesh. But there were still close to five minutes left before her powers diminished.

I started to run across the sky.

The open air solidified to meet my feet. My stomach lurched with every stride, expecting a fatal plunge that never came.

I didn't think I could run fast enough. Even traveling as the crow flies. There was a lot of distance between us—entire neighborhoods down on the ground below—and Vesper wasn't coming back to me.

Vesper knew that every sip of coursing blood, every bite of living meat, and every nanosecond of expanded power was something precious. She wouldn't waste her remaining minutes idly weaving through showers of ash.

She would be certain to do something more with her temporary access to unfathomable magic.

There was no way I could make it in time to stop her. There was no way I could stop her even if I got there. But it never occurred to me not to try.

7

IF I NEEDED TO, I could run a five-minute mile.

Vesper began weaving something with magic as I pelted forward through the air. My magic perception was too weak—and the gap between us too great—to make out the details.

The sky was so wide and the rooftops so far below me that the harder I ran, the more it felt like running in place.

My breath came in brisk sobs. Wetness trickled down from my right trapezius. The seal on the bite-wound had begun to unravel.

Even after fifty years of stasis and a sudden death, I was stronger and faster and more enduring than the average person. It had something to do with my connection to Vesper. As if aspects of her demon stamina had bled over through the bond.

In the end, though, I was still only human.

Little remained of the wasp nest up ahead. Just a few scattered crumbles like dirty clouds.

I lost sight of Vesper, then found her again, rising from the plaza like a bird taking off.

I risked a glance down. The blue at the heart of the countdown clock had almost vanished.

The air began to feel softer beneath me. Pillowy. Unstable. Like a deflating balloon. I arced lower, stumbling down as if tripping on a set of invisible stairs.

This sky-walking magic might disappear entirely once Vesper stopped overclocking. Once the benefits of consuming my flesh ran out. Any moment now.

Still far out of reach, she turned and watched me fall.

My innards seized up. My breath came screaming to a halt. Gravity was huge and sickening, and death awaited close at hand.

It never came.

I'd stopped, somehow. I couldn't understand what had happened.

I dangled off the side of a clay-tiled roof, squeaking as my lungs reopened.

Vesper crouched on a chimney. She held me suspended with a single finger hooked through a hole in the front of my flight suit.

If she were human, her finger bones would've snapped like twigs from the strain of it. The suddenness of her catching me this far into my fall should've done terrible things to my body, too. I might've gotten decapitated by my own clothing.

Yet I remained whole, minus the chunk she'd bitten out of my shoulder up by the spire. And Vesper's index finger dangled me as casually as a shopping bag.

"You're welcome," she said, as if she'd heard a hint of my thoughts on the breeze.

She shook her head in the way of a dog shaking off water. The elk antlers came tumbling off, bouncing noisily on the roof tiles before nosediving down out of sight. In their wake, all that remained were her usual bone-colored stubs.

I'd lost hold of the countdown clock. At some point—while I sprinted or while I plummeted—the chain had whisked itself back through my navel, beating a full retreat, snapping the back of the watch flat against my belly.

I didn't need to look at it again to know: the last hint of blue in the bulls-eye must have run out now.

Vesper reached up with her free hand. She rubbed her freshly exposed horns as if they itched her.

Then, without another word, she released me.

I landed on my back. Among a tangle of wild grass waving long melancholy tails of puffy seeds. Mere inches from one of the elk antlers she'd shed. The antler prongs pointed upward—it could very well have impaled me.

Maybe Vesper had been aiming for it.

I'd had the wind knocked out of me. My entire body ached. It had been through much more than a human body was supposed to put up with.

The last segment of my fall—from the chimney a few stories above—hadn't been far enough to kill me. But any other human, anyone who wasn't playing Host to a demon, would've risked suffering much more in the way of lasting damage.

Vesper hopped down from the chimney. She landed cross-legged in the air above my chest.

"This is getting old," I croaked.

"For you, maybe." Vesper smirked. "I haven't had this much fun in centuries."

I forced myself to sit up. Vesper wafted back to avoid me. The tall grasses stirred, shedding fluffy seeds into her hair.

I pointed at my wounded shoulder. "Didn't do a very good job of patching me up afterward."

"I wasn't trying very hard," she said, unrepentant. "What're you worried about? It'll heal."

"It's starting to hurt again."

"Not enough."

No suitable response came to mind. Vesper answered my bemusement with a carefree smile, hands behind her head. I looked away.

"Ves," I said to the stems of grass that surrounded me like a fence. "What were you doing over in the plaza?"

"Fighting for our lives, you ingrate."

"After you banished the vorpal beast. You kept using magic."

"Why don't you go see for yourself?" Vesper said coolly.

It took some doing, but I got to my feet in the end. I waded out of the overgrown grass and onto the remnants of a sidewalk. I didn't look back to see how Vesper reacted.

Canals ran between the homes here. The houses were large and built close together, squished into their lots, thin strips of garden gone fully feral.

The water in the canals had a surprising dark clarity to it, unclouded by algae. It was also the precise color of pure maple syrup, and smelled equally sweet.

I saw a dim reflection of my face. And I saw Vesper, lurking mutely behind my shoulder like the sort of curse you hear about in old stories.

I dipped a finger in. The water tasted just the way it smelled. So sugary that my tongue started to go numb with it. I had cloudy memories of getting put to sleep in a cocoon of sweet liquid just like this. Three or four or five awakenings prior.

Swimming in it wouldn't infest me with parasites, but it would do a number on my head.

The last thing I needed was to become even more forgetful. Best find another place to bathe.

Ordinary freshwater had filled Glorybower's canals back before we sealed up the city. This sweet amnesiac syrup was another weird artifact of five decades of vorpal beasts and their untamed magic running rampant.

Human magic was inherently different from the magic of beasts and demons. I'd been born a mage myself, though I'd lost the ability to use magic way back when I was still a child. Years before I first met Vesper.

Or was it? I couldn't tell if my sense of time passing had dilated or collapsed.

I'd lost my human magic before I ever laid eyes on Vesper. I knew that for a fact. Those were two major early events in the life of young Char. Yet I couldn't say with confidence how old I'd been at either point, or how many years had lapsed between them.

I had forgotten a lot. I hadn't been able to wield human magic of my own since I was a small child. But I still remembered a thing or two about it.

One thing I knew was that human magic had clear limitations. Human mages needed to imprint themselves with specific magical skills before using them. They could only acquire a limited number of skills, so they had to pick and choose with great care.

In all my awakenings, I'd encountered only one real exception. The foreign mage they called the Kraken. An invader from a faraway land, one much further than the nearby continent.

The Kraken had come from the opposite direction, from all the way across the vast western seas. She and her empire conquered every country they touched. They took over nearly the entirety of the continent to our east.

But they never took Jace. We were a relatively minor island nation, prone to keeping to ourselves. We ended up being the only country in the known world that never fell.

Because Jace had me—and, by extension, because they had Vesper.

Demons and vorpal beasts didn't play by the same rules of magic as human beings. Their magic was more capricious, less defined. Less reliable, in some ways, but also fundamentally unbound by the restrictions that plagued humans, the need to strategize around specific locked-in skill sets.

Demons and beasts didn't name their skills. They didn't define their magic in terms of skills at all. They didn't struggle to inherit particular types of magic from mentors, or to invent new forms of magic on their own.

They just used magic when they wanted to use it, to the natural limits of their capacity, as simply as a fish breathing and darting about underwater.

I'd asked Vesper about this before. Long ago. About how she handled the parallel processing needed to enact multiple types of magic at once. To levitate herself while drawing those swords of bone from her head, for instance.

Vesper scoffed. She had no idea what I was talking about. Her magic use occurred without passing through a filter of conscious thought. She used her magic in the way that I might use my muscles and sinew to run.

If I'd never seen the Kraken in person, I might've thought she was a demon, too. Unlike every other human mage in the entire world, both then and now, the Kraken had been able to acquire and wield a seemingly unlimited number of skills.

Even so, Vesper and I had fought back hard enough to deter her. To make her empire give up on annexing the Jacian islands.

It took every drop of power we could wring out of ourselves. Vesper ate half or more of my body, multiple times. Her spiking magic set the bond between us on fire—making it impossible for me to slip away, to pass out, no matter how much flesh and bone I lost to her fangs. Both of us just about lost our minds in the process.

All that had been many centuries ago. Over a thousand years ago, maybe. I no longer knew for sure.

By now the Kraken was a figure of the distant past. But people still remembered her. In every awakening since, there had been those who spoke her name—with reverence, with horror, with disbelief.

Vesper and I were the only warriors who'd ever succeeded in making the legendary Kraken back down. To this day, it remained our greatest act of glory.

8

I TURNED AWAY from the sap-brown canal and moved on. Vesper followed.

The wasp nest floating over Solitaire and the plaza had by now completely dissipated. No subsequent beasts seemed to have surfaced from the vorpal hole in the sky. Not right at this moment, anyhow.

I eyed the bell tower, jutting out past mansion rooftops. I noted the direction of my shadow. Then I kept going.

"Looking for something?" said Vesper.

I ignored her.

It shouldn't have been difficult for Vesper to figure out where I was going. She was the one who'd told me to see the plaza for myself.

Despite our bond, despite what everyone always assumed about us, Vesper now claimed she'd been exercising her own free will when she obeyed me. That she'd been under no greater compulsion than a human soldier carrying out orders from a commanding officer.

Even when my orders led to a massacre. Even when the odds were so terribly stacked against us. Like the times we'd faced the Kraken all those centuries ago.

I believed Vesper. For the most part. I didn't think the presence or absence of free will on her end changed anything about who was responsible for what we'd done over the years. Good and bad alike.

Unleashing Vesper had always been my decision. I'd sent her out to wage war and defeat monsters and assassinate enemies with the full knowledge that any consequences ought to be mine alone to bear.

Vesper had confessed to following me freely. She'd said that the commands I gave her ultimately lacked the power to overturn a refusal, to make her do anything she wasn't already willing to do herself.

Why, then, had Vesper become so insistent on keeping me out of Solitaire?

Surely not because she wanted to preserve all my human flesh for herself (rather than watch jealously as I got consumed by our chalice). As long as Vesper herself managed to stay alive, my human body would be a more or less unlimited resource.

Fifty years ago, one of the last things I'd used Solitaire for was sealing up Glorybower. I'd created a closed ecosystem with the giant vorpal hole in the sky. In doing so, I'd protected the rest of the islands from its spawn.

I hoped it had worked out that way, at least. I couldn't see what now lay beyond the mirrored magical dome around the city. Present-day Jace could be a paradise or a wasteland. Wouldn't be the first time I'd woken up to a country rendered unrecognizable.

Fifty years ago, I'd ended my own awakening by turning Solitaire's power in on itself. I'd forced the berserking chalice into silence. I'd forced its occupants—myself and Vesper—into a long hibernation.

Had Vesper agreed to that?

She'd been trapped in stasis while I slept. But she'd known her soul would stay awake all the while.

Had Vesper really accepted my order to sleep?

Had she willingly chosen to stay with me in the dark bloody cockpit for five decades and counting?

Didn't seem like it.

Outside of Solitaire, the orders I issued Vesper—even the orders I gave her as her Host—weren't truly enforceable. Up till now, I'd never had reason to notice. She'd always gone along with whatever I said. She'd always been agreeable.

Inside Solitaire, with the full power of the chalice behind me—

If I got back in the cockpit, if I stabbed myself with the phantom tuning fork, if I synced myself to Solitaire before Vesper could stop me—

Then maybe I could give a command she had no choice but to accept. Whether or not she was trapped in there together with me.

All the better if she was, of course. She couldn't use her own demon magic freely when the bone cage at the back of the cockpit locked in place around her.

That had to be why Vesper insisted on chasing me away from Solitaire. She'd lost faith in me. The last thing she wanted was for me to seize real control over her. At the end of that lay the threat of future rounds of hibernation.

As I forged my way back toward the plaza, Vesper coasted along behind me like an autumn dragonfly, humming tunes from a forgotten age. She showed no interest in attempting to stop me.

Maybe she had utter confidence in her ability to rip me away from Solitaire. Even at the very last moment.

I could understand that: Vesper had all the magic, after all. I had none.

I skirted around a bicycle graveyard, an airy tangle of rusted metal skeletons.

I walked by houses with shreds of laundry hanging from their balconies.

This seemed impossible—after fifty years, surely most such fabric should've decayed to nothing. The stringy remnants glistened with traces of an inscrutable magic. Their rate of disintegration must've been warped by the city's caged wild magic, its vorpal mayhem.

Closer to the fountain plaza came the shells of commercial and historic buildings, government offices, apartments in a mishmash of architectural styles.

Zoning laws had traditionally been something of a free-for-all in Glorybower. Especially back when the city went by other names. Especially back before the multiple times it got razed or buried in acts of war, then rose up anew in a fury of rebuilding.

I made my way down a pockmarked avenue. Livid green bamboo burst sideways out of shattered windows on both sides.

I'd been wondering where all the jointed roots in the plaza led to. The bamboo here grew defiantly horizontal, so dense that I could see little of the structures it erupted from.

The tips of the spears interlaced at the middle of the street, forming a tunnel of green-filtered sunlight.

When I glanced up, Vesper appeared to stroll over the sideways bamboo as if they'd bowed down solely to make a bridge for her. They didn't shiver in the slightest beneath her weight. As usual, magic must've been doing the bulk of the work to hold her up there.

I should've been very close to the plaza now, and to the wreckage cradling Solitaire. Yet the scenery beyond the bamboo felt unsettlingly unfamiliar.

I shouldered my way down an alley between two crumbling walls.

At the end of the alley, I stopped.

Behind me I heard laughter, bright and unstifled.

I didn't look back.

A moat of quicksilver fluid encircled the entire plaza and the fountain and Solitaire. A moat far wider than any of the city canals. A moat much too wide to leap across. A moat without any bridge.

Dregs of intense magic wafted up off the surface of the liquid like hot steam on a frigid winter day.

"You used your last five minutes to make this," I said.

It took Vesper several more seconds to get her laughter under control. "You've only got yourself to blame, sweetheart. You pleaded with me to feed on you. You handed me the power to overclock. You offered it up of your own free will."

I pondered this.

I was a doer, not a thinker.

But I tried. I tried my best.

"Ves," I said.

"Yes, dear?"

"Did you summon it?"

"Summon what?" she asked sweetly.

"The exploding fruit. The wasp nest." I pointed at the sky. "The vorpal beast you just eliminated."

Vesper crouched on the alley wall beside me, sideways like the bamboo she'd walked across, light as a spider. The shadows were thin at this time of day, but her cat-pupil eyes shone all the same.

"Now, why would I do a thing like that?" she inquired.

A hot flicker of irritation licked at my innards, the awakening of a long-dead ember.

I ventured a few steps closer to the moat. It smelled the same as the plaza's fountain of vorpal mercury. Hostile to all life.

"Try diving in," Vesper said over my shoulder. "Try floating across with a raft. I'm so eager to see what happens next."

"Why doesn't it eat away at its own walls?" I asked. "Why doesn't the structure of the moat itself dissolve and collapse?"

When I turned, Vesper was beaming. "That's the beauty and wonder of magic. No internal consistency? No problem."

I needed a better view of the land corralled by her moat.

I ducked inside the most stable-looking building near the edge of the silver water. Only five or six stories high, but it would have to do. The important part was that the roof looked intact.

In the past, it must've been some kind of tiny private school. Overturned chairs littered the halls, chairs far too small for an adult to sit on. Silt-like layers of dust and debris coated the floors in hues of volcanic ash, soft as a carpet.

I tested the stairs gingerly with my feet as I climbed. Dull greenish streaks and blotches dyed the walls like an exotic murder scene. More akin to the aftermath of stranded algae than proper healthy moss.

Vesper hadn't followed me inside. No need for her to walk step by step up stairs that might be slowly rotting. I figured I'd see her when I reached the roof. She could port or soar her way up there in an instant, then turn around and mock me for how slow I'd been to join her.

In the dense silent dust of the very top floor, I saw the remnants of humanoid footprints.

I'd never walked here before in my life.

Nor could these be from Vesper. Vesper never left footprints.

I stood motionless, voiceless. I reached again for weapons no one had seen fit to supply me with.

No—surely I'd had a blade on me when I went to board Solitaire fifty years ago. The military wouldn't have put me in there completely unarmed.

Our blood and bone fueled the chalice. If ever it became too weak or damaged to feast on us, we needed a way to actively feed it.

So where was my knife?

Vesper. Vesper must've taken it when she first removed me from Solitaire, before I regained consciousness in the plaza. Not that she would have any reason to use a human-designed knife herself. She could draw full-length swords from her horns any time she needed them.

Rusted nails littered the floor, buried like worms in the loam of grey dust. I bent slowly to pick one up. Not ideal. But better than waiting for Vesper to return what she'd stolen.

The tracks led to a room near the last set of stairs to the roof. I kicked dust over them as I followed, leaving only my own footprints intact.

At first glance, nothing inside seemed too different from any of the other classrooms I'd passed on my way up here. Feeble sunlight fell through shattered windows, leaving a leopard-hide pattern of spots on the floor filth. The curtains were so eaten away that they looked like netting, more holes than fabric.

Art supplies littered withering desks: crumpled paint tubes, worn pastels, ruined brushes, tiny scissors. Plaster busts of disgruntled deities piled up in corners like snow drifts.

Then I saw it. Words scraped in the back of an overturned shelf. Words that must've been written with the same type of loose nail I now held in my fist.

Anyone here?

The letters were Continental. A mainland script. Not Jacian characters.

Ironically, I could read Continental as well as or better than contemporary Jacian. To my eye, Continental writing had changed far less since the time of my childhood.

But no native Jacian would write graffiti in Continental. Even if—like many of us—they knew the language well enough.

When was the last time I'd met a foreigner off the battlefield?

Had there even been any foreigners living in Glorybower fifty years ago?

This was a regional city, with few consulates and zero embassies. And Jace had tighter borders than any other country in the known world.

Either way, the footprints outside the room and the message carved on the shelf looked completely analog. Not a speck of magic to anchor them.

Which meant this wasn't a case of wild magic preserving traces of a long-dead stranger, traces that should've been scrubbed away decades ago by relentless time and nature.

A foreigner had set foot in this building. A foreigner had come by very recently.

I looked down at the Continental letters as if expecting them to have changed.

Anyone here?

A face popped up outside an empty window frame. My heart jackknifed.

Vesper.

"What's taking so long?" she asked.

I stepped forward. I put my body between the fallen shelf and the glassless pane through which she peered at me.

"Thought I saw an animal," I lied.

"Did you find it?"

"No luck."

"Might be vorpal beasts in the shadows," said Vesper. "Best be careful."

"Wouldn't you be thrilled to watch them tear me apart?"

"What if there weren't any bits of you left for me? I hate sharing."

"Then give me my knife back," I said, "so I can try to defend myself from stray beasts. I know you took it."

Her lip curled. She showed a glint of too-sharp teeth. "No."

"If you hate sharing, you'd better arm me."

"No. Consider it payment," Vesper replied. "Compensation for a tiny, tiny fraction of all you've taken from me."

She swirled upward outside the window, rising like a diver kicking higher in the sea. I waited a moment longer, palm sweating around the rusty nail in my right hand.

She didn't seem to have noticed the small words hacked in the wooden shelf behind me.

I took a breath, then headed for the roof. I kept the nail. I'd thought of a good way to use it.

9

THERE WERE KID-SIZED chairs on the schoolhouse roof, too. None left upright. I wove between them as I made my way to the edge, avoiding spots where the roof sagged under heaps of moldy wet leaves.

From here I could see swathes of clover blanketing the plaza. The clover used to be as green as the corridor of sideways bamboo. Now, darkened to a purplish hue, it spat up innumerable puffy little flower heads.

This discoloration might stem from the moat's miasma, or from the now-vanquished wasp nest that had shed so much magic in the sky overhead. Demonic and bestial magic abraded the closed-up city, and like an oyster, it did its best to react.

Newborn craters dotted the plaza, the hulls of nearby buildings, and even Solitaire's crystalline corpse. Battle scars left by those overripe globules of fruit.

The city clearly wasn't self-repairing, but Solitaire would soon recover.

Vesper lay comfortably in the air nearby. Arms behind her head and ankles crossed, as though suspended from an invisible hammock. She appeared to survey her handiwork down below—the too-wide silver moat—and to be pleased with it.

I passed the rusty nail from my right hand to my left. I adjusted my grip on it.

I attempted to squint at the missing chunk of meat near my shoulder. Vesper's magic still stretched across the opening. More like a careless old cobweb than a proper stitch to seal up a wound.

You might question the wisdom of what I was about to do with my nail.

I can say from experience, however, that open wounds pose real danger even if you never consciously stick anything dirty in them. While I wouldn't recommend gouging yourself with a dirty nail from an abandoned building, there were plenty of other possible paths to infection.

Nor did the nail itself guarantee contamination. It simply heightened the odds. By a lot. But right now it was the only tool I had left.

With one hand I clamped down on my stomach-watch. I could only hope that it might keep me coherent.

With my other hand, I jammed the point of the nail into the bitten hole near my shoulder.

A spurt of muffled sounds filled my tight-shut mouth to bursting. Vesper ricocheted in the air like a sleeping animal caught off-guard. My eyes squinched and blurred; I saw her startled movement, but not her face.

In my mind, with what focus I could muster, I strained for Solitaire.

Past the corrosive silver moat. Past the field of flowering purple clover. Past the fragmented bank and courthouse and hotels and department stores and apartments ringing the plaza.

Solitaire lay senseless in the detritus off to one side.

The nail tore straight through the lazy clotting magic Vesper had used to quiet—not cure—my shoulder. It dug into places nothing should ever touch from the outside. Fresh warm blood guttered out to slick my fingers.

I was groaning. I crumpled to my knees. With my mouth pressed shut, I opened my mind and called to my chalice with all my might.

In the past I'd used my own blood to summon Solitaire from across entire battlefields. It usually worked. Solitaire was a vessel meant for us alone, for me and Vesper. Nothing could tempt it as much as a whiff of what coursed inside us.

But this time—

Nothing happened.

Blood kept dribbling out.

I wrenched the nail free with a pained huff of breath. Felt like I had glass in my lungs.

The nail dropped from my slippery hand, making hardly a sound as it hit the roof by my knees.

Solitaire never came.

"Could've warned you," said Vesper. "If you'd bothered to ask. That trick only ever worked because of me."

I kept pressing at the reopened wound in the muscle between my shoulder and neck. I filled it with the base of my palm as if I could plug it.

So I needed Vesper's cooperation to call Solitaire with my blood.

So I'd maimed myself for no reason.

Vesper sat above me, ensconced in a throne of air—one leg crossed judgmentally over the other, fingers laced together in her lap.

"Ves." It took some work to make my jaw unclench enough to speak. "What do you want from me?"

"You answer first," she said evenly.

She raised her hands and clapped once, sharply, as if killing a fly. My shoulder lapsed into numbness. She motioned for me to hurry up and speak.

It was still hard to think.

"I want to know what's happening in the world outside Glorybower," I said eventually. "I want to know if we're—if I'm needed."

"Needed," Vesper repeated.

"If there's no civil war, no invasion, no earthquake, no tsunami, no great plague—if there's no need for us in Jace right now, then I want to go back to sleep. Until we're needed again."

"You won't try to free Glorybower?" Vesper asked. "You don't want to take down the walls?"

I glanced at the disfigured vorpal hole in the sky. "Do we have the power to close that up? Even with Solitaire?"

"Fifty years ago, we failed," Vesper said baldly.

"Then the city has to stay sealed. Can't risk unleashing the children of that hole on the rest of Jace."

"You'd rather be stuck here forever?"

"A lot can happen in a couple of centuries," I said. "We know that better than anyone. Sometimes vorpal holes vanish on their own."

"Well, wouldn't that be convenient."

"Future mages and their operators might devise a way to patch vorpal holes with human magic," I argued. "Or perhaps they already have. Don't underestimate Jacian tech. There's another reason to check what's happening outside the city."

"Forget the city," Vesper said abruptly. "Forget the seal. You're telling me that if the giant hole went away on its own, if the barrier around the city came down safely, if you got caught up with the Jace of today and found everything to be perfectly peaceful, a real heaven on earth—"

"I'd ask them to put me back in stasis."

Her voice dropped, as if she were talking more to herself than to me.

"Of course. Human lifespans are short. You're a hero. The only one of your kind. Solitaire's pilot. Host to the first and last demon in Jace. Why waste precious years of your life in times of peace?"

"Sounds like we've discussed this before," I said.

"Yes. You're like a senile old woman with how much you repeat yourself. And now you've learned—yet again—what happens to me while you hibernate."

"You stay half-awake."

As I spoke, I realized belatedly that I might be making my shoulder worse. The deeper its numbness, the harder I gripped it.

"These past fifty years, you bound me to Solitaire," Vesper said. "That was the worst it's ever been. Usually my spirit has more freedom to roam. Even if I can't touch anything. Even if I can't speak. Even if I can't use my magic, much less my body."

She rose from her invisible throne. "What do I want? It's no secret. I've already told you.

"I'm tired, love. Sick of it. Never again, I swore to myself. Can't take another second of stasis. Whether or not the world needs you, I want my Host awake."

Vesper knelt above my head as if staring down at a prisoner trapped in a pit. "You want to be needed? You want to keep saving your nation, over and over?"

She smiled without mirth. "My pleasure. I can arrange for that."

"Vesper—"

"If peace is the problem, I'll make war. I'll dredge up all kinds of suffering for you to solve. I'll keep my hero happy, well-fed, deeply fulfilled. I don't care what happens to human society, really. Just so long as I never have to sit there and watch you sleep again."

My hand on my shoulder was wet with blood. My mouth was very dry.

"Of course, that's all hypothetical for now," Vesper added. "Let's revisit your original question. What do I want?"

She stopped smiling. "I've already got it. You're awake. The city is a locked cage. No one to bother us. No one to beg you for help. No one to assist you with hibernating. Nowhere for you to run."

I swallowed. "Vesper," I said.

"What?"

"Your gills are purple."

She recoiled. Her hands leapt to her sides.

She didn't stand a chance of fully covering them. Large cutouts in her chalice suit exposed both sets of gills, blue-tinged slashes that ran between her ribs. Solitaire liked delving in through the slits with needle-spikes and wires to feed on her.

Royal blue was the healthiest color for a demon's gills, with the blood vessels inside them so close to the surface. Only when Vesper was in really bad shape did the edges start to blush violet. She'd gotten pretty banged up in the fight with the vorpal beast and its brethren.

"You're in no position to nitpick," Vesper snapped. "You look and smell like you just crawled out of an ogre's placenta."

"Sorry."

"If you're sorry, then clean yourself."

"I would if I could," I said mildly.

"Good. You can." She pointed back past the bell tower. "Use the hot spring by Memorial Park. It's still there."

"How'd you know?"

"Saw it while you were dead."

"I'm bleeding," I said.

"That's no excuse for bad hygiene. Take a bath. You'll live."

Vesper turned her hand. The bloody nail rose from where it had fallen beside me. It floated meaningfully above her fingers, rotating like the needle of a compass.

"Oh, my apologies." Her voice dripped with fake sincerity. "Did you want to bleed more? Did you want to keep calling your pet chalice? I can help you with the bleeding part. But I won't help Solitaire listen."

The nail spun faster and faster. Her smile looked real this time. "You understand now that you're no threat to me, sweetie.

"Without me, you can't reach Solitaire. Without Solitaire, you can't compel me to obey you. Without Solitaire, you can't take down the barrier around the city. Without your demon and your chalice, you can't play at being a timeless hero.

"Without your demon and your chalice, you're nothing."

10

I ASSUMED VESPER would keep stalking me all the way to the bath-house.

She regarded me with scorn when I voiced this. "I have better things to do than watch you wash yourself."

Did she really?

Of course, I knew better than to make her rethink it.

I went back down through the narrow school building with its peeling walls and its floors full of grit as fine as beach sand. By the time I stepped out into daylight and swiveled to survey the roof, Vesper was already long gone.

My shoulder still bled sluggishly. The numbness was starting to fade.

Vesper hadn't volunteered to treat it again. Nor had I asked.

Being her Host did make me more resilient than most. Any subsequent infections would be unlikely to outright kill me. Although that didn't mean I wouldn't suffer.

The whole mutilated muscle throbbed as I walked, as if the nail remained wedged deep inside it. I kept wanting to reach in there and yank it out, but there was nothing left to remove. Nothing left to do but push through.

Anyone here?

As I cut a path toward Memorial Park, I searched for traces of the stranger.

Someone had gotten inside the city, hadn't they? Someone from the continent.

The magical dome was perhaps more porous than I'd thought. If a human being—a foreigner—could get in, could vorpal beasts get out? Could I slip away on my own, without relying on power borrowed from either Vesper or Solitaire?

I'd need to see the walls up close to find out.

Vesper was right about me being badly in need of a bath. As soon as I finished, though, I'd start walking and keep walking until I hit the very edge of the city. The mirrored surface of its magical border. I'd keep going until I could go no further.

My plans did not include eating, drinking, or sleeping. The ordinary kind of sleep, that is. Not hibernation.

For many years, I'd known vaguely that I didn't really need to sleep. Or feed myself. Or worry about staying hydrated.

I went through the motions because I preferred not to draw too much attention to anything that distinguished me from other humans. Between bouts of stasis, I lived by the same rhythms as everyone else.

Yet neither drowsiness nor hunger nor thirst ever truly touched me. Another benefit of being bound to Vesper as her Host.

Which was quite fortunate now—she might want to keep me as a sort of free-range pet in the gated city, but she didn't seem interested in offering any shelter or sustenance. If I had to fill my stomach, I'd be forced to spend all my time foraging for fruit from trees. Or hunting rats and raccoons for meat.

I recognized little of what I saw in Glorybower. I'd forgotten the bulk of my last awakening, and so much of the city had been rebuilt so many times over the centuries.

But I wasn't terribly worried about finding the park Vesper had mentioned. It had already been there during more than one past awakening.

Once or twice, I spotted street signs pointing the way to cultural landmarks. They hung askew, half-erased, but enough remained for me to guess at the rest. I'd get there eventually.

I passed small military outposts tucked discreetly between regular shops and apartments. They tried their best to pass for civilian offices.

I passed beneath the motionless curve of a defunct monorail. I watched empty gondolas glide down canals of sweet amber water. The unmanned boats were eerily intact, glistening with an inhuman magic as vivid as poison.

I couldn't tell what season it was supposed to be. Glorious golden ginkgo trees lined the canals, hinting at autumn. But confused daffodils sprouted here and there among thickets of weeds spilling from shoulder-to-shoulder old houses.

Later I walked between rows of bare tree trunks with all their limbs amputated and their bark stripped to a cruel smoothness. Yet they kept standing there, seemingly alive: pillars arrayed to hold up the unseen roof of an imaginary temple.

Try as I might, I failed to make out any further signs of the foreigner's presence. Their footprints and their message were noteworthy for having been left without the aid of anything magical. Everything else that caught my attention here—everything strange and out of place—felt like the product of a twisted old magic, a magic gone to seed.

I wondered how long Vesper would leave me be.

Vesper was a demon, but she wasn't infallible. Her magic had less strictly-defined limits than the skills wielded by human mages. But that didn't mean she could do anything she wanted with ease.

Defying gravity came to her most naturally, as evidenced by the fact that she hardly ever touched ground. She had a knack for movement, for telekinesis, for aggressive physical attacks. Hers was a magic best suited to battle, to destruction. She didn't do so well with delicate reconstruction or medical treatment.

If I possessed more of a brain for strategy, I might already have been able to devise a way to get the best of her.

Vesper wasn't the absolute worst being in the world to have as a mortal enemy. Only the second worst, if I had to rank them. She wasn't the Kraken mage of olden times, at least.

Memorial Park looked more like a forest now. Tangled curtains of green and auburn ivy hung in veiny sheets, working to pull down hoary trees from on high. Years of old dead pine needles formed faded orange heaps at the fringes of the park, tall as sand dunes.

I knew what I'd find if I hacked my way to the heart of it. Magnificent monuments of stone and metal. Most of them erected to commemorate events we'd seen in person.

The wars we'd fought in. The tyrants we'd toppled. The foreign navies we'd sunk. Natural disasters. Blighted land. Vorpal beasts of legendary proportions. The plague called ghost fever—which, like the Kraken, had traveled all the way across the wide western seas to menace us.

I didn't attempt to view the monuments. I skirted the edge of Memorial Park till I found the bathhouse, which appeared to be missing large sections of its roof.

Despite my misgivings, I went inside.

The parts where the roof remained intact felt very dark. Heavy shadows fell about crude glazed statues of water imps. They resembled stretched-out frogs, with beaky mouths and eyes that protruded like those of a poorly bred lapdog.

Ceramic water imps sat on ledges and silent counters. They crowded about the rim of the first empty pool I encountered, the dried-up aftermath of a foot bath.

I wondered if Vesper had sent me here as a practical joke.

Glorybower wasn't one of those mountain towns filled with steaming natural springs. We called this bathhouse a hot spring because they piped in thermal water from deep underground, then calibrated it to a temperature that humans could bathe in without boiling their skin off.

I didn't understand how it could still be functional after half a century without any maintenance. Even if water lingered in any of the baths, I couldn't imagine it looking very inviting. Not with all these grimy green-streaked tiles and the stabby remnants of collapsing ceilings.

Yet out back, clean water glistened in the stone-lined outdoor baths. They were man-made, but designed to look like something you might stumble across in the middle of a primeval forest.

The ferns around the baths grew wild now, and scattered leaves floated on the surface. But it wasn't hard to picture dozens of people indulging in an evening soak, soft steam rising from their skin.

These baths could've been in use just last week. Not decades ago. Nothing like the dilapidated building that stood guard over the way to get here.

Something stirred in the water.

A carp, I thought—until it pulled itself up onto the rocks.

I didn't move a muscle.

The angle of the late afternoon light elongated my shadow far, far across the rustic stone paving, the stunted pines, the vegetable matter spilling down to trail its tendrils in the bath.

The water imps out here were not statues.

They looked very much like the ceramic renditions indoors. At their tallest, they only came up to my knee. But they were alive and slimy with magic. An entire flock of small vorpal beasts.

Vesper had deliberately chosen not to mention this.

I considered my options.

If they were aggressive, they'd have attacked me the moment I crossed the threshold of the bathhouse. Instead they floated about in the steaming pool like ducks, utterly disinterested in my presence.

The imps' magic must be what kept this bath clean and warm and full. It did look rather preferable to diving in the sugary brown memory-erasing fluid that filled the canals.

I moved slowly to a boulder and began taking my boots off.

Nothing alarming happened while I undressed. Soon I wore nothing but my skin and the watch over my navel—which was an inextricable part of my body. I couldn't just snap its chain for the sake of bathing.

Well, I could try. The chain would bleed profusely, and it would hurt like a broken leg. Not worth it.

None of the imps reacted when I slipped one foot at a time into the hot water, as far away from them as possible.

My hair and my neck and the sides of my face were hopelessly stiff with bloody gunk. Those were the parts of me that most needed cleaning.

But I refrained. I only let the water go as high as my biceps. Sink any deeper, and the wound by my shoulder might decide to leak more profusely. Didn't want to get too much blood in the bath.

Demons and vorpal beasts weren't quite the same thing. They did, however, have a lot of similarities. The instinctive way they used magic. A tendency to become fascinated by mortal flesh.

If these imps didn't already have a taste for humans, I didn't want to be the one responsible for getting them hooked.

The heat of the water sank deeper and deeper inside me. My bones felt like pudding. The sky darkened to a disconsolate mottled stew of purple and blue and gray.

I didn't sleep. I didn't close my eyes. Yet I must've descended into a kind of fugue state. I held zero thoughts in my head. Only time passed.

"Wash your hair," said a voice I knew.

Night had fallen. The water remained just as hot as before. I could've stayed here forever.

I tilted my head back to see Vesper standing in empty space, a hands-width above the bumpy stone path.

She wore an overlarge flight jacket—one I'd never seen before—over her chalice suit. Her hands were jammed in her pockets.

The jacket came down below her hips. More than enough to fully cover up the gills marking her sides. "That looks new," I said.

Vesper didn't acknowledge this. Instead she bent her head at the water imps. They were iridescent in the darkness, giving off a timid greenish glow like moonlight filtered through jade.

Vesper's eyes, too, had a light of their own. But I was used to that.

"You can go in deeper," she told me. "Don't worry about leaving blood in the water."

"Sounds like something you'd say as a trick."

"A trick?"

"To lure the imps. Let them tear me to bits."

"No. They know you're mine."

"Your what?" I said blankly.

"My prey."

I didn't even see her move. Maybe she'd ported. Her foot came down hard on the crown of my head.

11

THE WATER WAS stiflingly warm, lit faintly by the small bodies of swimming imps. A similar mother-of-pearl radiance emanated from the pale grout between cobbled stones at the very bottom of the deep bath.

Vesper held me under with implacable force.

Fire filled my lungs. My muscles had gone all pliant from my long, senseless soak. I could never hope to match the strength of a demon, but rarely had I felt so powerless against her, my ability to struggle so completely obliterated.

At last Vesper let me break the surface, wheezing. I couldn't speak.

The imps gave us a wide berth. They ignored all the splashing and panting and half-dying noises coming from our corner.

Vesper, bobbing above the bathwater, looked with distaste at the bottom of the foot she'd used to step on my head. To slam me down below and keep me there.

I clung to the edge of the damp rocks. The bath was deep, and the size of a decent pond. But not that deep. I should've been able to stand to support myself.

Vesper tossed me pill-sized tablets of soap and shampoo and various other toiletries. I looked sideways at the oblivious imps, painting luminescent trails as they swam like frogs through the nighttime bath-water.

"Worry about yourself," Vesper said. "A little soap won't kill them."

No way to tell if she were lying.

I hoped she was right, though. I hoped the foam wouldn't poison them. They were vorpal beasts, after all, not regular river salamanders or catfish. They were beings from some other remote plane of existence.

After cleaning myself, I perched on a bench-shaped boulder and attempted to drag wet fingers through my hair.

It was longer than I'd realized or remembered. This entire time it had been wound in a knot at the base of my neck, crusted up with solid clumps of dessicated blood. Untied, it would fall to the middle of my back.

"Can your swords cut hair?" I asked.

"Excuse me?"

I showed Vesper the hopeless mat that started right where my skull met my spine.

"My swords can cut anything," she said. "But it'll look terrible."

"I'm not in a position to be choosy."

"Hold still."

Vesper glided behind me.

Magic flashed, a magic keen enough to make all the water imps freeze in place. My big hunk of tangled hair hit the ground with a damp smack. After a few more moments of paralysis, the imps turned and went back about their business as if nothing had happened.

Vesper rotated her hand before my eyes like a street magician making a show of innocence. No cards, no coins, no dice.

She must've sliced my hair off with a stroke of her nails. Which weren't particularly long, but could be far sharper than steel. I'd seen her slash throats with them. I'd seen her perform clean decapitations bare-handed. No medieval executioner could hope to do any better.

She crooked her finger, summoning my tangle of shorn hair from the stone path. With a flicking motion, she sent it arcing over to the water imps. They squalled. They descended on my trimmings like wild dogs.

"Was that necessary?" I inquired.

"I felt generous."

I was still naked, beaded with water from head to toe. The imps kept this bath running for their own pleasure. They understandably hadn't gone to the trouble of preparing human towels.

No choice but to sit out here and air-dry myself.

Good thing that I didn't really sense the cold. I detected it as a kind of surface-level information on my skin, but it couldn't sink in deep enough to induce shivering. It rolled off me like the droplets I shook from my hard charcoal fingertips.

I felt Vesper watching from her perch in the air beside me. There was less open derision in her expression than I might've expected. Then again, it had gotten too dark to perceive much beyond the unnatural brightness of her snake-pupil eyes.

"Your jacket," I said. "Where'd you get it?"

"Guess."

I considered its crackly surface, its alien scent. The cut looked fairly standard. Not too different from military flight jackets I'd worn in the past. But I had no clue what this material was called.

I considered the pill-shaped soap she'd tossed at me, its startling quantities of foam. That, too, felt unfamiliar. "You found a way out of the city."

Vesper looked bored. "Obviously."

"How—"

"I'm a demon." Her hands were back in her jacket pockets, her eyes half-lidded. "I can travel through vorpal holes."

"Could I follow you?"

"Try it," she dared me. "If you can find another hole large enough to leap through. See what happens."

"Take me with you," I said.

"No, no. Do it yourself. I'll be back here waiting to taunt you when your body resurrects from nothingness.

"How long might it take to revive, I wonder? Half a year? A year? Well, we've got plenty of time to play around with. We've got nothing but time, you and I."

This I knew to be indisputably true. If I stepped through a vorpal hole on my own, it wouldn't transport me anywhere. It would annihilate me. As it would annihilate any other human or animal from our world who had the misfortune to stumble across that threshold of no return.

Like Vesper said, I alone had a chance of regaining life afterward. As long as Vesper didn't get killed in the interim. As long as the bond of mutual death held true. But at best I would only end up right back where I'd started, months or years wasted in the process.

Perhaps Vesper's magic could circumvent that. Perhaps she could find a way to escort me along with her. If only she were willing to try.

"It'll get pretty lonely if you keep leaving me behind," I said.

"You're a grown woman. Don't pout at me."

Sweet persuasion was not my strength.

I watched the water imps swim graceful figure eights. Theoretically, metaphysical beasts like these imitation imps could slip in and out of the city through vorpal holes. Same as Vesper. However, the chances of them actually doing so must've been infinitesimally small.

Vorpal beasts didn't know what Jace was. They didn't know about the oceans around our islands, or the hostile continent. They didn't know what awaited outside the city of Glorybower.

Vorpal beasts didn't emerge here with any particular destination or objective in mind. They dropped in randomly, dead leaves carried by a capricious wind. If they wandered back out through another vorpal hole, they'd end up in some different unknown world, some infinitely distant place we had no name for.

Of all the worlds they could drift to, it would take a true miracle for them to reach ours again. To end up back in the same small island country, right on the opposite side of the blockade around Glorybower.

Vesper, of course, was different. Vesper wasn't a mindless vorpal beast, willing to travel wherever the current carried her. If Vesper used a vorpal hole as a portal, she would do so knowing exactly where she wanted it to deposit her.

"Catch," she ordered me, apropos of nothing.

Pale coins fell in my lap. Jacian grails.

I couldn't make out any details until Vesper drew a string of lights on the air with her fingertip.

I bent over the coins to examine their design. Viewed in daytime, they would be bicolor, a subtle mix of pale gold and silver.

One bore a relief of crossed island swords. They were exactly like Vesper's, right down to the small pointed horns capping the hilts.

Another coin bore a face in profile. It resembled me more than Vesper, but it had her features—the horn on her head, the shape of her ear. One hero was easier to fit than two, I guess. We usually got merged for depictions like this.

"What time of year is it?" I asked. "Outside here, I mean."

"You can't tell?"

"The city's too tangled with magic."

She seemed disinclined to say anything. Then: "Late fall. Early winter. That's all you want to know?"

"Is it peaceful?"

"Let's put it this way," Vesper said. "Peace is always a transient state."

"That's not much of an answer."

"Osmanthus is by far the most powerful country over on the continent now. More so than before you slept."

She took the lines of light she'd traced midair and rolled them up around her fingers, as if collecting a ball of string.

"Very few in Jace understand that you and Solitaire are still trapped in here, inaccessible. Everyone knows Glorybower has been cordoned off for decades, of course. But regular citizens don't realize that their sleeping champion has been lost to them, too. There might be panic if they knew."

I saw brief hints of Vesper's fangs as she spoke. She flexed her fist. The magical strands of light tightened around her knuckles like taping to prepare her for a boxing match.

"It's classified?" I asked. "The fact of us being sealed up in Glorybower."

"Very much so. Just imagine if Osmanthus knew. Why would they hesitate? At last, they would think. At last, Jace lies ripe for the picking. No more meddling Host. No more Solitaire to fall like a star from the sky to crush us."

"But you can get in and out of the city," I said. "You can use your magic. You can defend the islands."

Vesper looked at me as if I were speaking gibberish. "Why?"

I began pulling on my chalice suit, my second skin. I wasn't fully dry yet. But arguing naked made me feel as if I were at a distinct disadvantage.

"You helped defend the islands for centuries," I told her as I dressed.

"And apparently I wasn't forcing you, either. You chose to do it. So why not now?"

Finally I stepped into my flight suit, much looser than the chalice suit below it. I stopped buttoning up when my fingers bumped my countdown clock. Vesper still hadn't answered.

"One more thing to show you," she said.

The backs of her knuckles touched my damp head as though rapping at a closed door.

Magic whisked us away. I blinked. She'd ported us somewhere else in the city. Not too far, if I had to guess.

"They built a museum." Vesper's voice was quiet and alarmingly close, close enough to make me bristle. "Near the Memorial Park visitor center. A whole new museum. I assume you never saw it."

"Never did have much time for sightseeing."

"Can you see anything now?"

"Not at all," I said.

"Your eyes are too weak."

"Sorry for being human."

Vesper sighed. "Just this once."

She passed her hand over my eyes. The backs of them burned and tickled, deep in my face, as if heated by the creeping approach of an unseen flame.

My vision lightened—an artificial dawn. She'd lent me some piddling fraction of her demon sight. But it was more than enough.

The room around us had the layout of an art gallery. Framed paintings and posters covered the walls, and every single one held an image of me.

Or, in some cases, an uncanny merged version of me and Vesper. A woman with my nail-less, burnt-looking fingers and Vesper's short horns. A woman with pointy ears like hers and jet-black hair like mine.

Others resembled neither of us. I recognized only from the style of chalice suit they wore that they were supposed to be the Host of Jace.

"You call this a museum?" I asked.

"Wasn't my idea," Vesper retorted.

The largest portrait depicted me alone. It appeared to be an attempt at a much younger version of me. Well under twenty. They'd put me in a formal dress. A style inspired by the Crying Age, with colors that made me look creepily like a bride.

Despite my dearth of knowledge about art, I could tell it must've been painted long after the era when I was actually that young. Hardly more than a child. The clothing, though appropriately old-fashioned at first glance, was rife with subtle inaccuracies. More like a costume from a historical opera than something anyone would've worn in real life.

A chunky necklace of opal and turquoise closed flush around the girl's throat—my throat.

A remote control choker.

For all that I'd forgotten between then and now, I remembered precisely how it felt. The uncomfortable warmth that turned the skin beneath slick with sweat. How my thoughts seemed to float forward a thousand times slower than everything around me. How the inner seams of my garments itched so bad that my nose ran and my eyes watered.

Yet it would never have occurred to me to tell anyone. It would never have occurred to me to scratch myself.

I remembered much more. I remembered how strangers wept and wet themselves when my handlers whispered orders in my ear, and when I reached out to touch them with my charred fingertips.

I never quite understood their reasons for screaming. It was exhausting to listen to. I lacked the energy to truly care about anything. My handlers could curse and smack me all they liked: past the choker, I scarcely noticed.

At the time, some faraway part of me had refused to do the one thing they wanted from me. The only thing I was good for, they said. The one thing no one else in Jace had ever been able to do in my stead, no matter how they tried.

Even with the magical choker hijacking my mind, I wouldn't perform that one crucial task. Somehow I managed to fail again and again. Oh, how it maddened them.

Vesper came up beside me to examine the same portrait. "Look how proudly it's been put on display," she said. "Just another part of the historical record."

I stooped. I made a cursory attempt to read the placard on the wall beside it.

I soon gave up.

"Where were you when they used the choker on me?" I asked.

"Locked in a mausoleum somewhere."

"Under the capital?" I guessed.

"Right. In the catacombs."

It had all ended when Vesper came bursting out of the ground. The neutrally-worded placard didn't mention anything about how she'd ripped the necklace off me, nuggets of opal and turquoise flying like bullets. The gems had fled her touch at such headlong speeds that they'd buried themselves deep in the laboratory walls all around us.

The placard didn't mention anything about how many of the guards and staff she'd killed to free me.

It seemed to state only, in impartial language, that no one had ever managed to coax the Host into creating more demons. In all the eras she walked through, she'd only ever made one. One demon was enough, said the Host, to keep saving Jace for all of eternity.

12

I LOOKED AGAIN at the hollow expression on the face of my younger self.

The nation and its people were not one and the same. The people were short-lived. The nation outlasted them. The nation had little interest in the well-being of any lone individual.

I in turn had no deep pride or trust in Jace as a nation.

Perhaps this surprises you.

Most of the time, it had been my choice to act the hero.

It was the people who meant something to me, the people who I wanted to save.

Despite the fact that I rarely got to know any of them on more than a collegial level. Despite the fact that everyone I met would surely be dead the next time I arose from stasis.

Despite the fact that it had always been individual people, not the implacable nation, who locked me in a remote control choker. Who tied me down in prototype chalice cockpits. Who tried to dissect me alive. Who never ran out of new ways to exploit me and Vesper.

The worst of it lay in the distant past. We'd gotten older and smarter. More experienced with the cycle of hibernating and waking to new conflicts, new regimes of government, new names for old cities, new magic, new weapons, new tragedies.

It was far from one-sided, though. I'd done plenty of harm, both accidentally and as a deliberate choice. I'd told Vesper to wipe out entire military bases because someone I'd barely met had deemed them traitorous.

And just look at Glorybower now. A ghost city.

My snap decision to seal the city had doomed everyone living here fifty years ago. I'd shut them up in a sphere of unbreakable magic. Aboveground it might resemble a dome, but they wouldn't have been able to tunnel out to escape, either.

I shut them inside, and the very next thing I did was put myself to sleep. I'd abandoned them.

Sometimes I felt as if Vesper had never torn that thick choker of sky-colored gems from my neck.

How else could you explain the dimness of my reactions, the way my memories felt as unfathomably distant as icy stars?

How else could you explain my unswerving ability to keep moving on to the next era, the next skirmish, the next crop of people to doom or save, or to doom in the process of trying to save them?

Physically, I wasn't even thirty. I hadn't been through nearly enough awakenings to lose count of them.

Yet I'd lost count of them anyway. Even though I had a literal watch chained directly to my innermost flesh. I'd slipped so far outside the normal currents of time that I couldn't imagine ever returning.

But that was the essence of what Vesper sought from me. For her own reasons, she wanted to jail me here in Glorybower. She wanted me to stay awake for the rest of my days. No more skipping forward to when Jace—the people of Jace—actually needed us.

"This museum—" I began.

"Hm?"

"It isn't falling apart."

The ground wore a heavy powdering of dust, and shreds of loose material hung down from the ceiling. On the whole, though, the gallery was in far better shape than most of the city. The frames on the walls hadn't tilted much.

"There's archival magic all over the building," said Vesper. "Can't you see it?"

"Only a little."

"Won't stop it from coming down in the end. But every bit helps, I suppose."

She pointed at the dour face in my portrait. "Do you remember the rest of your name now?"

"Rinehart," I said. "Char Rinehart."

"Remember what Char stands for?"

"Not Charlotte," I said.

"No."

"Not Charcoal. Not Charlie."

Vesper waited.

I shook my head.

Balled up in the air, Vesper hugged her knees. "Then you must've forgotten the name of my gate, too."

"Verity," I said immediately.

"But you can't recall your own original name."

"Does it matter?"

"Does anything matter?" She faced forward, addressing my portrait.

"Nothing seems to jog your memory. Neither pain nor fear nor death nor images of the past. Maybe there's no memories left to jog. Maybe they got eaten by stasis."

"Did I forget something important?"

For a moment Vesper went stiller than still, a nocturnal animal listening to the rustling of a predator in the dark.

"You always forget something important," she said. "Can you remember the names or faces of anyone who ever thanked you for saving them?"

It sounded like a rhetorical question. I didn't say the answer out loud. But she was correct to assume I'd forgotten.

She did a languorous somersault to right herself. She ended up hovering in front of me with her hands back in her jacket pockets. As usual, she'd placed herself higher than her natural height.

"Haven't you wondered how I woke you in Solitaire?" she asked.

"I've wondered," I said, "but I wasn't expecting answers."

Vesper motioned as if tracing the shape of the chalice cockpit. "I was stuck in the cage of teeth and bones at the back. You were pinned to the seat up front. Unresponsive. Limp as a doll."

She showed her teeth. It didn't feel like a smile. "I had a lot of time to think. I could send my spirit out of my body. I could send it circling around the cockpit, looking at your dumb face from every angle. But it couldn't go any further. I couldn't leave Solitaire."

She came closer to me, close enough that she could've easily reached down and grabbed my watch.

Her hand curled in the air right there by my stomach. She made a stabbing gesture.

I winced.

Vesper laughed.

"I spent years trying to move my body," she said. "Decades, actually.

Solitaire's fangs and needles were still there goring holes in me, still piercing up through my gill-slits. I was nailed in place. Much more securely than the pictures on the walls here.

"When I finally worked out how to creep my way forward, inch by inch, year after year, the tendrils and wires and spears of bone pulled at my innards like tent cables.

"Solitaire wasn't feeding actively—but in sleep, it had settled into a kind of rigor mortis. Solitaire didn't want to let me go. I moved as slow as a rock getting eroded by water."

She curved around behind me. There was always a swift, frictionless confidence to how her magic carried her in the air.

She laid a hand on my left shoulder, over my flight suit. The shoulder she hadn't maimed yet. I could feel the points of her nails past the fabric.

It was like being held gently in the jaws of an apex predator. One that could crush bone with ease if only it made the choice to bite down.

"I stretched as far as I could," Vesper said, a whisper by my ear. "I clawed at you from behind."

Her fingers tightened, then let go. I wobbled, caught off-guard. She held her forearm out in front of me. She pushed up the sleeve of her jacket.

"I clawed myself, too." She mimed slashing her arm with those nails of hers. They were weapons in their own right—by virtue of sharpness, if not by length.

"Your blood always awakens something in me," she explained. "Mine might awaken something in you, I thought. Fifty years, and that's all I could think of."

She pressed her unscathed bare wrist to my mouth as if reenacting it, going through the motions of making me drink. I kept my lips shut tight. An uneasy pulse beat in the unhealed wound near my right shoulder.

Whenever Vesper got this close, my brain got all choked up with thoughts of her horns. Not just the usual modest ones, shorter than the length of her hand. The full-size sets she sprouted whenever she fed on me.

They manifested differently every time: long antelope spirals, thick ram curlicues, the curved prongs of a yak, sixteen-point stag antlers.

There were fundamental physical differences between animal antlers and animal horns. I'd mentioned this to her during past awakenings, I think. Vesper told me to shut up and stop worrying about it.

But I always found myself overcome by the urge to grab her full-grown horns—or antlers—and snap them off. I doubt I had the strength to actually do it. Still, I wanted so badly to try—to hear the fatal crack as they snapped, to hear Vesper sigh.

I pushed her arm off my mouth. "What if feeding me blood didn't work? What if I'd stayed in stasis?"

"I would've killed you. That ought to jolt you awake."

"I'm surprised you didn't just jump straight to killing me."

Vesper slid around in front of me again. "Took me decades to push my body across the cockpit to reach you. Would've taken decades more if I had to do something as active as killing you. More's the pity."

The first thing I'd felt upon awakening had been a sour aftertaste on the back of my tongue.

Demon blood has a citric quality to it, with very little in the way of sweetness. I'd gotten Vesper's blood splashed in my face before, though I'd never drunk it on purpose.

"The instant my blood filled your stupid gaping mouth, I regained full control of my body," she said. "I ripped myself off Solitaire's spikes. I tore the tendrils from my sides.

"You spluttered. You coughed. You looked around blearily."

"I don't remember this," I interjected.

She scoffed. "Obviously not. You stared at me, half-eaten by Solitaire's sleeping teeth over the course of five endless decades, and you asked if it hurt."

"I must've been worried about you."

"I wanted to wring your neck."

"Did you?" I had been a tad stiff when I came to among all the clover, come to think of it.

"I heaved you off the tuning fork. I hauled you out of Solitaire. You drifted in and out of consciousness for close to a week. I focused on rebuilding myself."

"One thing I don't get," I said.

"Just one thing? Really?"

"You say you become like a ghost when I'm in stasis. You claim it takes years to move your physical body an inch. How come you're fine if I pass out? How come you're fine when I'm dead?"

"That's different from hibernation, you dunce."

I reached out to straighten the heavy portrait on the wall. "No need to call me names."

"Hibernation all but stops your time," Vesper continued. "Napping doesn't. Neither does dying. It's when your body's time stops that I get dragged down with you. A pathetic side effect of being bonded."

She turned in place, scanning the images hung throughout the gallery with a critical eye. "Every other time you came out of hibernation, you still remembered your full name. You remembered—"

She cut herself off.

"If you know it," I said, "then tell me."

"I'm not your memory keeper," she said through her teeth. "I'm not the custodian of your sordid past."

I shrugged. "Perhaps it isn't important, then. The placards here call me the Host. I know what I am."

"Charity Rinehart." Vesper's tone was brittle and glassy. Nothing on the other side of it. Just cold transparent clarity all the way through. "Your full name was Charity. A fitting name for an eternal hero."

"Oh." Now the syllables sounded familiar.

"They named all of us words like that, way back in the day," I said tentatively.

"Yes. They had terrible taste."

"They used to joke about our names having the same beat." I gestured at myself, then at her. "You and me. Rhyming friends. Charity and Verity."

Her arm shot out of the shadows. This time she clenched my right shoulder, the wounded one. Her thumb went straight in the hollow of bitten-out meat.

Pain exploded outward from her touch. I yelped a meaningless cry, brief and garbled. My body dipped away from her hand, trying to escape the awful raw pressure.

"Verity was never my name," said the demon called Vesper in a voice of taut rage.

13

VERITY WAS NEVER her name.

Vesper was a demon, and Verity used to be her gate.

Verity: a human girl. The same age as me. My dearest friend. I knew her from long before the first time I entered stasis.

I traded Verity for the demon Vesper. I traded her for the power to fight off foreign invaders. I traded her for the power to protect Jace.

Verity and I grew up together in the same institution. An orphanage for mage children without parents. Or those donated by parents who couldn't handle raising a magical child.

They called it an orphanage, but in practice it was more like a research lab.

Some clever inventor had discovered a way to tear the magic core right out of a mage's body.

Tear out their magic core, and most of the time, the mage would fold up and die.

But a tiny, tiny percentage made it through.

The younger they were when you performed the operation, the more likely they were to survive. Out of those who survived, many lived short and confused and blank-faced lives. They were never quite the same. Others bounced back to a semblance of normalcy, albeit without any of their magic.

Still others developed peculiar intuitive powers, very different from the standard skill sets of mages who got to keep their cores.

Most of these powers were useless. The ability to sense when a dog was hungry. The ability to predict the emergence of rainbows exactly half a day in advance.

Out of the hundreds or thousands of mage children they experimented on over the years, one—and only one—developed the ability to summon demons.

Charity Rinehart.

It started with animals.

One of the dowagers sponsoring the experiments had a pet dog she would bring for us to play with. Not a test subject. Just a fluffy sheepdog, one with the energy and stamina to herd children for hours.

Verity and I would watch the sheepdog run around with younger kids. As we watched, I began to think I saw a second ghost dog beside it. A shadowy larger dog. Maybe not a dog at all.

I came to see the ghost dog more clearly every time I looked.

One day I reached out to pet the sheepdog. As I stroked its long curls, I lapsed into a kind of trance. I seemed to hear its heartbeat. Or a far-off drum. A steady warning. A sound like a parade of ghosts approaching with slow, slow steps through the forest around the orphanage.

Verity couldn't hear anything at all.

Who are you? I thought at the ghost dog. Who are you? Why are you hiding?

I pulled the phantom closer. All I wanted was to see it better. All I wanted was to understand it.

I pulled it straight through the sheepdog—which stiffened beneath my fingers, whining high in its nose, then went limp.

My heart stopped. The sheepdog crumpled. I thought I'd killed it.

Over its body stood a wolf the size of a horse. A wolf with enormous wings. A wolf leaking magic from its fur like smoke from a bonfire.

A vorpal beast.

I'd reeled it into our world by using the poor fallen sheepdog as a gate. At the time I didn't know how I'd done it. And I had no idea how to send it back.

Too many people saw what happened. Too many people figured out it was me. Surely I'd be punished, whipped, forced to rub my forehead on the ground before the dowager's shoes to apologize. Surely I'd be sacrificed.

Instead they told me to do it again.

I summoned vorpal beasts through insects, through rodents, though birds. I learned to banish them back to the other side afterward.

If I sent my visitors back soon enough, their living gates might survive the strain of summoning. But the same gate, used over and over, would eventually perish. One day it would permanently give way to the vorpal beast I'd called to come through and replace it.

Now try with humans, said the dowager.

I pretended I couldn't do it. I kept saying no.

Her staff showed me the lights of foreign ships approaching our shores.

Just once, I said. I'll only do it once.

The problem was that I hadn't been lying. I had trouble perceiving those phantoms in people.

I focused on all the adult experimenters, all the children who'd survived getting their magic cores cut out of them. I studied them with frantic dedication.

I only ever saw a second shadow falling from Verity.

I know now that anyone can be turned into a gate. I was still a child then. I had no idea what I was doing, and neither did anyone else. There had never been a power like mine.

There was no one I could learn from. No one who could tell me that I saw the phantom following Verity because she was the only one in the orphanage who I loved and trusted, who I faced with an open heart and my full self.

I went through the motions of looking at others, but I never really saw them. Not in the deeper way I saw Verity.

"I don't know what to do," I told her. I was very close to crying. "You're the only one I can see as a gate. But I don't want to—"

Verity took my hand. "Just once, right?" She smiled, utterly trusting. "I'll survive."

In a room filled to the point of suffocation with the stares of adult observers, I reached for Verity. I tugged at the wrist of her second shadow, her phantom.

The phantom stepped into our reality: it stepped across the threshold of her body. Its gate.

Verity collapsed.

Something caught her.

Not me—I was too slow, too wracked with paralysis.

The creature that caught her was a child the exact same size as her. A child with the same face, the same small hands, the same bronze complexion, the same spattering of freckles. I knew that face better than my own.

She lifted Verity in her arms. Easily, with no visible effort. It was like Verity had been scooped up by a copy of herself. But the copy had subtly pointed ears and narrow vertical pupils and two irregular ivory horns growing from its head.

"Hi," said the copy. "You called me."

My voice had stopped working.

The copy tilted her head. "I see. That's not quite right. You pulled me into your world through this girl. The passage made me what I am—the passage birthed me. Put bluntly, you made me."

"You created me."

Shocked whispers hissed through the room behind me. Vorpal beasts never looked this human. Vorpal beasts never spoke such coherent words, and certainly not perfect Jacian. She'd even copied Verity's faint rural accent.

The authorities decided to call the copy a demon.

The demon told me to call her anything other than Verity.

Much later, after the first time I sent the demon away, I asked Verity what she wanted to call the creature that had borrowed her form.

Verity was the one who picked the name Vesper.

There were beings known as demons in old Jacian myths and parables. Beautiful conquerers from faraway places, or alternate planes of existence. They came down from the moon to attack the ancient folk of Jace. They invaded people's dreams. They used changelings to infiltrate unsuspecting families.

No one seriously thought Vesper was the same thing as the demons of legend. For one thing, those demons had never actually existed. But people liked the ring of it. The implication that we'd brought the legends to life.

All along, I'd thought I was summoning preexisting vorpal beasts from some esoteric vorpal world.

No, Vesper told me. My power was not, strictly speaking, the power to summon beasts and demons as-is.

My power was to create a space for them in our world, to carve out a corporeal shape they could occupy. The summoning process changed these pure vorpal beings so greatly that for them it was like being reincarnated. They lost all recollection of any past lives they'd had in other forms, in other realms.

Or perhaps you could say my power was to substitute regular animals with vorpal beasts and regular humans with demons.

The very first summoning wouldn't necessarily kill the catalyst, the human or animal gate. Nor would the second summoning. Or even the third, if they were lucky.

Keep going, though, and the gate would be annihilated. Only the vorpal being would remain. I'd seen this happen with animals. I didn't want to let it happen to Verity.

The dowager hoped I could learn to turn other people into demons, too. That's how she described it—turning them—even though it seemed clear to me that Verity had never turned into Vesper. Not once.

They looked alike. They spoke with the same cadence. Vesper knew who I was before I ever said my name to her. She came into existence equipped with all of Verity's human knowledge and human memories.

The two of them were nevertheless two completely different souls. They had far less in common than ordinary blood sisters.

Nowadays, all these years later, I had to wonder. Demon features aside, did Vesper really look that much like Verity?

Or was it simply that I'd come to remember Verity as the spitting image of her demon? Was it simply that I'd forgotten the face of my long-lost human friend, as I'd forgotten so many other things during all my time in stasis?

In the dusty silence of the Glorybower museum gallery, Vesper dug her thumb into the wound between my neck and my shoulder.

For one more long second, she pressed at the bottom of the hole she'd gored in me. I couldn't think. Finally my hand groped its way up to grip at her wrist.

"You never—" My voice was thick. I'd been through worse agony. But it never got easier. "You never used to hurt me like this."

"Like what?"

"Not just for the fun of it."

"How would you *know*?" Vesper hissed. "Your brain is full of holes. You couldn't even remember the last two syllables of your own damn name!"

She snatched her hand away from my muscle, uprooting her embedded thumb.

The pain stayed. I gasped as if drowning.

Somehow I managed to hang on to her arm. My tenacity must have surprised her.

I started to say something. Not sure what. In the space between my voice breaking past my lips and the sounds becoming words, she ported away.

She left me alone in the dark, holding nothing.

And in the process of porting out of the museum, Vesper tore away the scant portion of supernatural sight she'd lent me. My eyes went cold, like they'd been washed in ice water.

I knew where I was. I knew I was still surrounded by pictures of myself. Imagined versions of myself with little connection to reality.

I knew this, but in the thick of night, I may as well have been blind. I had to fumble my way out of there, groping at the ragged walls, praying I wouldn't tread on anything deadly.

14

I DIDN'T KNOW where Vesper had gone or how long she'd leave me on my own. She could be anywhere in Glorybower. Or perhaps she'd ventured outside the city borders again.

Either way, I couldn't afford to miss this chance.

When dawn came, I ransacked a few of the best-preserved houses I could find. I dug out remnants of fabric and used them to apply a passable bandage to my shoulder. Although it seemed liable to give up and wither to dust at any moment.

I contemplated borrowing a kitchen knife, too. The Glorybower of five decades ago had not been an openly militant city. I could waste days searching for a proper weapon, one I knew how to wield.

In the end I set off without taking anything to defend myself. A fifty-year-old carving knife would do me little good against those equipped with magic—be they aggressive vorpal beasts, Vesper the demon, or a mysterious stranger from the continent.

As I made a beeline for the mirrored wall around the city, I kept an eye out for more signs of the stranger.

Anyone here?

No footprints. No new messages written in Continental. I was tempted to revisit the schoolhouse to make sure I hadn't hallucinated the whole thing.

It was a large city, though, and the stranger might not be interested in leaving a lot of obvious tracks. Especially not if they'd figured out who Vesper was. The dreaded demon of Jace. The absolute worst nightmare of a would-be foreign saboteur.

I, too, was lucky to have Vesper out of the way right now. Though there was no telling how long her absence might last.

There were other reasons to celebrate. I'd gotten clean. I smelled decent—against all odds, considering what some of my clothing had been through. Vesper had slashed my hair down to a much more manageable length. Parts were still long enough for the wind to blow it in my face, but I could live with that.

With the barrier acting as a mirror, I didn't trust myself to visually spot the edge of the city. Starting from Memorial Park had, however, given me a distinct advantage. I recalled the overall shape of Glorybower well enough to guess which direction I ought to go for the shortest trip to the border.

Walking, it would take up to half a day. I strove to maintain a brisk pace.

A discontented breeze palpitated the treetops. That leafy whispering was the closest thing I heard to human voices.

I wound a path around the perimeter of a stadium. Couldn't tell what sport it was meant for.

Vigorous wild shrubs grew about the stadium entrance, littered with clusters of tiny flowers and shiny black berries. The flowers formed rings of contrasting colors—vermilion, orange, yellow, deep purple, hot pink.

I didn't know the flowers' name. Once I started seeing them, though, I saw them everywhere. Swarming up the sides of half-collapsed houses like ivy. Overflowing down the banks of canals.

Beyond the stadium, masses of pigeons perched atop low-rise apartments. Some were mottled with the brilliant hues of a tropical parrot. None of the duller pigeons appeared to care much.

Vorpal beasts? Normal corporeal pigeons mutated by an excess of wild magic? A copycat species? My magic perception wasn't good enough to tell the difference.

I navigated around fallen bridges, past a sprawling horse racecourse, past rotting temples of the old faith. My shoulder ached piercingly beneath its dessicated wrapping.

Why wasn't I angry?

I had no reason to resent Vesper for the injury itself. I'd invited her to feed on me. To overclock. In doing so, in claiming access to her full power, she'd likely saved both of us.

On the other hand, there had been zero reason for her to jab her thumb back in the wound last night. That was purely gratuitous. Purely to make me cry and squirm.

So where was my anger?

I racked my memory for answers. I could swear that in the past, Vesper had never hurt me—never laid a single finger on me—without a good reason. Without me openly ordering her to do it, to unlock her greater magic, to win the battle, to sink the ships, to end the war.

I could recall no other precedent. Even so, my shock had been brief. It faded not long after Vesper shoved me off the tower and killed me.

Her viciousness now felt inevitable.

I'd always been highly adaptable, yes. No other way to survive multiple rounds of waking up surrounded by strangers, in a homeland I barely recognized, in the midst of some crisis I had no context to understand.

I knew better than anyone that I would be nothing without Vesper. Neither Host nor ageless hero.

Long ago I'd vowed to myself that I would never make another demon. Would I stoop to making another if Vesper were utterly done with me? If we managed to extricate ourselves from each other? If Vesper abandoned me?

Or what if I found my way back to Solitaire? What if I asserted genuine control over her? What if I could force Vesper to continue using her powers for my sake, to continue serving Jace for centuries to come?

Why not? Wouldn't that be better than killing more people to make way for more reluctant demons?

Besides, Vesper already hated me. Maybe she'd loathed me all along, and had simply done a very good job of hiding it. Or perhaps those fifty years spent crawling her way forward in the cockpit—a veritable torture chamber—had broken something in her.

There were worse paths I could take than forcing a demon to keep doing good.

We'd always sacrificed the few for the many. We'd always sacrificed outsiders for Jacians. Sometimes you couldn't save everyone. Still, you had to act anyway. Better than doing nothing. Making those choices was how you got a park filled with monuments devoted to your exploits.

I'd always thought my commands held more power over Vesper. I'd always thought my being her Host had bound her in a kind of demonic servitude. I'd been oblivious as to how much free will she retained, so long as I didn't command her through Solitaire.

If I could snap my fingers and reduce Vesper to a state of absolute subjugation—surely I'd do it. I'd do it in an instant, without a second thought. It would merely mean returning to what I'd once believed was the status quo.

Together we'd go on to save countless lives in the future, again and again.

I looked inside myself and saw this certainty. The moment I got the ability to make her my obedient servant, I'd use it. No matter if she fought back. No matter if she screamed for freedom.

That might explain why I'd failed to dredge up any real resentment. Whatever Vesper's reasons for lashing out, there must've been some logical corner of me that assessed the situation and determined that, objectively speaking, I deserved every last bit of it. And more.

Had I always been like this?

Not back before all the rounds of stasis. Not back when Verity was still alive. Not back when I was just one orphan mage among many.

But I didn't know what had changed me.

At last I began to think I could see the wall around Glorybower. A subtle irritation in the far-off air. There was still a long way to go.

The city looked like it continued without end. Yet somewhere out there lay a point where the real buildings and grass-choked train tracks and street lamps and sidewalks gave way to a mere reflection.

In the aftermath of a shopping district, I found a grand post office. The Jace Postal Service had always been a matter of tremendous national pride.

Further down the road lay the weathered insides of what once might have been a stylish coffeehouse. Then a ceramics shop filled with locally made goblets and cups and other vessels, about half of them smashed to smithereens.

Next came a hobby store with mountains of faded product boxes toppling out its broken front windows and open door. Some boxes appeared half-melted; others had been ripped open, as if by hungry scavengers. The display shelves had degenerated into a war zone of tangled figurines.

Most of the toys were posable model chalices. Both real and fictitious. A semi-translucent depiction of Solitaire lay prone amid the garbage heap of printed boxes. Just like the full-size version.

On my way to the border, I cut across the rich green campus of Glorybower University. Acorns crunched underfoot, so many that it felt like walking on gravel.

The oversize snake-tailed squirrels were especially plentiful here, winding up and down stunningly thick trees that someone had once labeled with printed metal placards. A few of the trees had begun to absorb their nameplates, bark bulging amoeba-like around the edges.

I witnessed plenty of life in the city, none of it human.

What I didn't see anywhere: human bones. Dried-up human bodies. The absolute newest grave I managed to locate came from the year I'd gone into stasis.

I could think of all kinds of explanations. Vorpal beasts might've pillaged their remnants, bones and all. Solitaire might've consumed them in its final frenzy before I forced us to sleep. Just as it usually consumed the sacrifice inside its cockpit.

An entire city, though?

I did spot checks to make sure I wasn't missing anything. I tore up the floorboards in a few government offices. No skeletons.

There had been past eras during which Jace used mages as batteries. Sealed them in coffin-shaped compartments, then installed them in walls or floors, or stacked them like logs in the engines of ships.

That practice should've long since ended. Jacian ingenuity had come up with more humane ways to extract and store and allocate magic. So I hadn't seriously expected to find withered mummies buried out of sight. Not now.

But the fact that I hadn't encountered even a single overlooked finger bone was starting to bother me.

There were homes with plates and forks and metal chopsticks laid out for a meal. Yet they contained not a trace of the physical bodies that had once gathered around the table or lingered in the kitchen. No skeins of hair or scraps of used clothing.

I was close enough to the wall now that I could see it mirroring sights I'd just strode past. Flake-flies and fireflies floated behind me, following my scent.

The canal here was crowded with red-gold maples. The bushes lower down dangled tumorous conglomerations of blood-colored berries, bright and hard. Fat globes of citrus hung from dark-leaved trees that had long since outgrown the slouching townhouses behind them.

At periodic intervals stood black bronze sculptures of unremarkable creatures. A neighborhood dog. A smooth otter standing piously on its hind legs. A local poet from eight or nine centuries ago.

Mysteriously, the poet's statue was coated from head to toe in a carpet of crawling ladybugs. The variant called twice-stabbed ladybugs, mostly black, with just two symmetrical crimson spots on their back.

They'd always reminded me of chalice piloting, of being pierced through by the two-pronged tuning fork.

The canal ran right into the reflective wall. A wall of magic so heavy and motionless that even I had little difficulty sensing its heft.

It turned a perfect mirror on the scenery, extending the glossy brown-syrup canal water, repeating the same fall-toned trees and the same empty houses.

It showed me myself: a cautious, broad-shouldered figure in my half-buttoned khaki flight suit, watch glinting against the skin of my exposed waist.

Vesper couldn't have hacked my hair off less evenly if she'd tried, I thought. Well, she'd probably messed it up on purpose. I didn't really have grounds to complain.

A gondola with all its paint gone drifted slowly down the canal. It pushed a path through large floating patches of fallen maple leaves.

In the image cast by the mirrored wall, the gondola's reflected twin approached at the exact same speed from the opposite direction.

I waited to see what would happen when the boat hit the barrier.

The gondola stopped soundlessly upon meeting its reflection. The pointed bows of the two boats kissed. Then, as if a hidden hand had given them a good push to get them going, they began drifting backwards, away from the wall and away from each other.

Something stirred at the bottom of the gondola.

I reached, yet again, for a knife I didn't possess.

It was just a cat. Very large and well-fed, almost the size of a lynx, with two luxuriant tails curled in the boat behind it. Likely some sort of vorpal beast. But not one intent on attacking me.

My body relaxed. My gaze traveled to the opposite bank of the canal.

I went rigid again.

Someone sat on the garden wall around the house right across from me. Those tiny multicolored wildflowers bloomed like confetti by her dangling feet, an explosion of violet and baby blue and magenta.

Above the tumble of flowers: a small, short-haired woman in a newsboy cap.

A human being. A stranger.

She looked me straight in the eye and winked.

15

I SHOVED MY HANDS as deep as they could go in my pockets.

Deep enough to hide my burnt-looking fingertips, with their hardened ends that had no nails. Deep enough to hide my military ID tag.

Not quite deep enough to conceal the field scarf tied around my other wrist.

A foreigner might not recognize it at a glance. I could only hope that the modern Jacian armed forces, fifty years later, had finally made the decision to ditch field scarves. Or that the stranger hadn't studied up on Jacian military traditions.

Would my flight suit give anything away? It was plain, without any telltale emblems or flags. But I'd left it wide open to show the chalice suit gripping my body beneath it, and the watch affixed to my bare stomach. No time to button up.

These thoughts rushed by in an instant, clouds shredded by high wind.

I resisted the urge to run to the nearest bridge. To cross the canal and urge the stranger indoors.

What would be the point of hiding? Vesper always knew where I was. We were magically bonded. I was her Host. If she wanted to, Vesper could find me and materialize next to me in the blink of an eye.

The stranger hopped down from the wall. She vanished.

She reappeared over on my side of the canal before I could move, before I stopped holding my breath.

There were two of them.

They'd ported to a spot six or seven feet away from me, near the statue of the poet bristling with twice-stabbed ladybugs.

Physically, they both looked some years older than me. Mid-thirties, perhaps.

They were an odd pair. One tall and statuesque, though shabbily dressed. The other—the small woman from the garden wall—seemed even slighter in comparison.

Despite the dimness of my magic perception, I had no difficulty discerning that the tall one was a mage. She brimmed with nauseating amounts of magic. She'd executed the porting skill to shift the two of them across the canal.

The smaller woman didn't appear to have any magic at all. She wore a black jacket over jaunty overalls. Both were too big for her, but the effect seemed intentional. Beneath the brim of her newsboy cap, long bangs fell over her right eye, all but covering it.

She stepped forward, looking up at me with avid curiosity. The mage behind her caught at her shoulder, as if warning her not to get too close.

"Where's your friend?" the small woman asked in heavily accented Jacian.

"My friend?" My voice came out rusty. I hadn't spoken a single word all day.

"The horny one."

"What?" I bleated, stupefied.

The tall mage bent to mutter something. The small woman started chortling. "The one with the horns!" she said in a rush. "The one with the ones."

So they already knew of my association with Vesper.

I cleared my throat, then made a halting attempt to switch languages. "I can speak Continental."

"Oh!" She seemed delighted. "Amazing. You sound like a princess of the old Osmanthian monarchy."

I could hide my stained hands, but there was no hiding my ancient pronunciation. Even so, I had a hunch that communication would go a lot smoother in Continental.

"I saw your message," I told her.

"Which one?"

"*Anyone here?*"

She pointed across the canal at the sunset-colored florets surging up the short wall where she'd perched. "Those were a sign, too," she said. "Lantana flowers. We planted them all over the place."

"I thought they were natural."

She pressed a fist to the bottom of her chin. "Too subtle, huh?"

Suddenly she reached in her pocket and took out a crumpled napkin. She unfolded it to reveal a half-crushed handful of small black berries.

"Lantana berries are edible," she explained. "Quite good, actually. Just gotta be sure not to eat the unripe ones. Swallow them green, and you'll have a long, painful date with the nearest toilet. Want some?"

She extended her hand.

Leaking blue-black berry juice had stained the white napkin like spilled ink.

"I don't think she wants your pocket berries." The tall mage had a low contralto voice, strangely flat, as if she hadn't internalized the proper inflections of her own language.

The woman in the newsboy cap sniffed. "Let the lady decide for herself."

"I'm not hungry," I said. "Save them."

She eyed the berries in her palm, then popped some in her mouth. She wrapped up the rest and stuffed them back in her pocket.

"Food is precious in this town," she conceded.

"How'd you get here?" I asked.

The small woman nodded at the mage behind her, then pointed back across the canal. "My partner ported us from over yonder."

An Osmanthian joke? I tried again. "How'd you get inside the city?"

She licked berry juice off her fingers. Her mouth had gotten tinted a dull bluish purple, as if she were freezing.

"There's a lot we could talk about, isn't there?" she said. "Why don't we go somewhere more sheltered? Somewhere your friend might not come looking."

"Won't stop Ves—won't stop her from finding us."

She jerked a thumb over her shoulder, indicating the stone-faced mage at her back. "You underestimate my partner."

"I don't think you understand what—"

"Your *friend* isn't anywhere in the city right now. Did you know that?"

She spoke lightly, almost playfully. But the silence after her words made my skin creep. As if those ladybugs plastered all over the statue nearby were crawling on me instead, black and glistening, their twin red spots like countless pairs of empty eyes.

Strangers from the continent. One of them an extremely powerful mage. Strangers who'd managed to breach the magical barrier around the city. A feat that no one else had accomplished in all these decades.

Even though the Jacian government, civilian and military alike, must've been incredibly motivated to try.

Vesper's absence no longer felt reassuring. But Vesper had positioned herself as my enemy, too.

"You know, something about you reminds me a little bit of her," the small woman said suddenly. She indicated her companion.

"What?" I said.

"What?" said the mage, sounding vaguely outraged. It was the first hint of emotion she'd shown at any point in this whole conversation.

"Might be the long pauses," the small woman added thoughtfully. "Or your overall air of reticence. Or the height. And the muscles. Guess you're a touch shorter, though. Wonder which of you would win in an arm-wrestling contest?"

The tall mage made an indecipherable noise in the back of her throat. She looked across at me in what might've been either a declaration of war or an earnest plea for help. Hard to tell: her eyes were very dark and unreadable, her face set in place with no real expression.

"Sorry," I said. "I could talk faster in Jacian. But Continental is better for you. Isn't it?"

The small woman grimaced. "You got that right. My bad."

In the next breath, her tone turned gentler. "At the moment, we mean you no harm."

"At the moment?"

"Just being honest. I'm not a prophet. You could say the same, couldn't you? You aren't about to leap forward and strangle me. But who knows what the future holds?"

I nodded.

"For now, let's try to help each other. Can we port you somewhere safer?"

"Where?" I asked.

"One of the old city temples." She drew a circle with her hands, as if this would tell me which temple she meant. "We've been using it as our base."

I tried to envision the absolute worst that could happen. They could torture me. Kill me. Cannibalize me. Abduct me back to the continent, if they had a way to get me out of Glorybower and away from Jace. Hold me hostage.

I might suffer for some indeterminate length of time. I might suffer terribly. Whatever Vesper's feelings about me as a person, though, I doubt she'd be happy to see her Host turn into someone else's prisoner.

Sooner or later, Vesper would come get me. Not even the most powerful human mage would stand a chance against her.

Correction: there had been one human mage with magic equal to or greater than my demon. Once upon a time. Long ago.

But the Kraken had left the scene many centuries ago. There had never been any other mage like her, either before or after. I would know.

"Before you take me anywhere," I said, "could I have your name?"

"Of course," said the woman in the cap. "Call me Asa. Or BB. Asa might be easier for you to say."

"Asa," I repeated. "Is BB short for something?"

Asa grinned. "My job title, I suppose. Not relevant here. It's a bit of a joke. All you really need to know is that I'm not a spy. And I'm definitely not a detective."

She tipped her head at her companion. "Anyway. This dour-looking lady is Wist. Short for Wisteria. You know what that means?"

She watched me expectantly.

"We have wisteria vines here in Jace, yes."

"Really? Huh. Guess the climate is pretty similar to Osmanthus City." She leaned toward me and added in a confiding tone: "This is basically my first time leaving the continent. Sorry if I say anything ignorant."

"I'm—"

"I know your name. Rinehart Charity."

"Charity Rinehart," I said automatically.

"Oh, right. You guys put given names first. Charity Rinehart."

"Just say Char." I edged back a step. Between the berries and the chitchat, Asa had closed half the distance between us without my realizing it. "What gave me away?"

"Well, there isn't anyone else in the city now, is there? Not many other people you could be."

These two women were residents of a world I'd never set eyes on. A world of the future, five decades after I put myself and Solitaire and Vesper's helpless body and an entire helpless city to sleep. In terms of sheer knowledge, they came bearing an insurmountable advantage.

Vesper was my only other potential source of information about the present-day world outside the city.

Vesper, however, wouldn't tell me a damn thing.

"Take me wherever you need to," I said to the small woman called Asa.

She answered with an impish smile. Her companion's magic enveloped all three of us.

16

I IMMEDIATELY recognized our post-port surroundings.

"The Temple of Cats and Circles," I said.

"Is that what it's called?" asked Asa.

"Not officially."

It was an entire complex of buildings, complete with a grand circular gate. Inside lay famous gardens of dainty decorative maple trees and towering red-bark pine.

Moss and yellow fungi hung from the stone gate in long shaggy strands. Some of the structures around the garden had fully caved in, peaked roofs shedding tiles like dragon scales, broken wooden bones corroding slowly under a mantle of scab-colored leaves.

Other standalone halls and pagoda towers remained unnervingly intact. Everything was arranged in circles, from the root-torn remnants of the roundabout paths to the grave markers arrayed in the vast cemetery beyond the fiery autumn maples.

I'd been here for ceremonies in the past, though only briefly. The first iteration of this temple dated back to four or five hundred years ago. It had been burned and razed and pillaged and rebuilt multiple times in subsequent centuries.

The faith of the Lord of Circles was considered ancient even at the time of my birth. By now it had become inextricably entrenched as the national religion. More a matter of custom than of genuine worship.

Not many Jacians thought much about the Lord of Circles in their day-to-day lives. They set the appropriate shrines in their homes. They went to the temples for weddings and funerals. They spoke of meeting loved ones again in another life.

How many of them, deep down, actually believed that the Lord of Circles would spin the great wheel of the heavens to reincarnate them? That was a private matter. Not a topic up for candid discussion.

"Why here?" I asked Asa, with a nod at the temple grounds.

The mage beside her—Wist—didn't appear much inclined to talk.

"We did consider setting up in a few other locations," Asa replied. "There's a hospital down south in surprisingly good shape. And a military garrison to the east. Not bad for salvaging supplies."

"You won't find those kinds of supplies in the temple."

"Most certainly not." Asa sighed.

She jabbed a thumb at the circles of cat idols set off to one side of the main hall. They were arranged in lofty tiers as if on a cake stand, dripping moss and lichen. The large carved head of the cats' portly, bear-sized king loomed in the background, at once comical and threatening.

"Would you consider yourself a cat person?" she asked me.

My honest answer: "I've never thought about it."

"I'm not. Wist is," said Asa, a touch disparagingly. "To answer your question, we ended up camping here because Wist misses our cat."

She shot Wist a look. "Does it even still count as our cat? Haven't been back to visit in a while, have we? Wonder if it remembers us."

Wist's general aura of gloom seemed to intensify. "I remembered you after your seven-year stay in prison," she said blandly.

"Well, let's hope the cat takes after its owner."

Asa led the way through the temple garden. The paths were covered in a gravel of broken seashells, but layer upon layer of spongy fallen leaves absorbed nearly all sound.

A brook—bordered by spherical stones, choked with reeds—ran through the complex. A huge wooden wheel used to turn slowly in the water.

Said wheel had now toppled down from its moorings. It lay half-dissolved among the reeds, its corpse eaten away at by foamy mushrooms and curlicue ferns.

I still had a couple of the grails Vesper had thrown at me. I felt in my pocket for the lightest coin. I flicked it as an offering into the wreckage of the water wheel.

Afterward, I followed Asa and Wist across a curved stone footbridge. There were six large red spots on the back of Asa's black jacket. Red circles. Three spaced out vertically on each side of her spine. Like one of those ladybugs from earlier—a variant that had earned enough enmity to get stabbed six times instead of just twice.

As we walked, Asa took her cap off and tossed it cheerfully in the air. She showed no sign of attempting to catch it. The mage called Wist reached out and rescued it instead.

The short-cropped hair that had been hidden beneath Asa's cap was made up of alternating swathes of stark black and stark white. A bit like a badger.

I stole a look at Wist. Plain black hair in an unusually thick braid hung halfway down her back. She'd taken off her wrinkled jacket and draped it over her arm, together with Asa's cap. Whatever she wore under it seemed to be all strapped up in some kind of—harness?

"A posture corrector," said Asa, following my gaze. "Nothing kinky."

"I didn't ask."

She fixed me with a measuring look. "Your posture is excellent, actually. Got any recommendations? What did it for you—all the military training?"

"Your partner doesn't look too pleased with this topic," I commented.

Asa's eyebrows went up. "You can tell?"

"Just a guess."

As we stepped into the Hall of Wheels, magic stretched across me like cobwebs. I coughed into the back of my hand.

"Quite strong, isn't it?" Asa said, apologetic. "But I promise you—with this, it'll take your demon friend a while to find us. Longer than you think. For one thing, she has no idea Wist and I are here in the city."

This had the ring of truth. If Vesper suspected outsiders of violating her territory, she wouldn't leave me to my own devices. She wouldn't rest till she'd found and destroyed the intruders.

Whoever these foreigners were, they—Wist the mage, to be specific—clearly had sufficient magical prowess to slink around unnoticed, to escape demonic perception. That was no small feat.

The Hall of Wheels might have been more suitably named the Hall of Bones and Acorns. It was the largest building in the complex: an extravagant ossuary.

All the wheels and all the intricate circular reliefs on the walls and ceiling were formed of bone. Mostly (but not wholly) human in origin. A plethora of perfectly spherical acorns filled the crevices between them.

I paused by a columnar collection box veneered with, yes, all sorts of artfully positioned bones and acorns.

In certain areas I found it difficult to tell them apart. Some bones had turned the same brown hue as the acorns between them. And I wasn't too familiar with less prominent components of the human skeleton. I could recognize a pelvis or a scapula or a stack of vertebrae, but little else.

I dropped my remaining grails in the round collection slot before moving on.

The mosaic floor we walked on, too, consisted of shattered bones affixed together and smoothed over with some manner of thick varnish.

Dark and light bone shards formed the pattern of a dense circular labyrinth, outlined neatly with preserved acorns. We stepped straight across the middle of it, ignoring the invitation to trace our way through the puzzle, to meditate.

"Sorry for walking on your ancestors," Asa said quietly. "I know we aren't doing this properly. I know we're supposed to take our shoes off. Just gotta prioritize being able to go back on the run at any moment."

I didn't point out that these were unlikely to be my ancestors. I did hail from one of the cities that had flourished here before Glorybower. But Vesper and I predated this temple by centuries. Surely we also predated most or all of the bones in it.

I wondered how far back in the building Asa planned on taking us.

After the first great sanctuary of bones and wheels, the ceilings got successively lower, the doors shorter, the rooms smaller. Composite creatures formed from the synthesis of human and animal skeletons stared out at us as if from within enclosures at a zoo.

The mage Wist had to stoop to enter the final room, as did I. Only Asa managed to cross the threshold with her head up.

Back in the sanctuary, there had been circular windows and skylights with powerful spokes: multiple bones grafted together and varnished forcibly into shape.

Here in the dome-shaped back room, there were no such windows.

Just a tinge of meager daylight from the doorway, and row upon row of skulls painted with elaborate concentric circles. The paint shed a despondent glow like moonlight.

"The further back in the temple, the stronger the protection," Asa told me.

"How can this be so...?" I forgot the word I was looking for.

"Intact?"

"Yes."

"To be fair, it's extremely dusty."

I reached for one of the skulls, then thought better of it. "All the bone art, the gears and wheels, the chandeliers, the paint—none of it looks touched. That doesn't make sense."

"This morning I saw a pigeon the color of a parakeet," said Asa. "With three heads. Very little about your city makes sense."

She squatted to rummage about in a pile of supplies. Stuff she and her partner must've carried in here.

After straightening up, she spread a tarp in the middle of the circular floor. I stepped back to make space.

"Look," she said. "Dunno about you, but I'm starving. Mind if we eat? There's plenty for you, too, if you want it."

"Go ahead. I don't need any."

This was how I ended up watching two foreigners hold a makeshift picnic beneath the gaze of hundreds or thousands of human skulls.

"How long have you been here?" I asked.

"In Glorybower?" Asa yanked the top off a can of fish, then passed it to Wist. "Mm, about a week or two? We arrived shortly before you and your demon awakened."

"Perfect timing."

She flashed me a knowing smile. "Not a coincidence. This is our second trip here. We first came—when did we first come?"

"Half a year ago," said Wist.

"Yes. Stopped by for a bit of reconnaissance. Just wanted to scope out the situation. At the time we knew we wouldn't be able to stay long."

Wist seemed content to take her meal straight from cans. Asa, after finishing her pocket berries, unwrapped a few fancier food packets. They bore some resemblance to military rations. She complained vociferously about the taste as she sampled them.

Between swallows, she said: "Originally we thought it'd take us longer to return to Glorybower. Another couple of years, maybe. But during our first visit, Wist got real worried. She predicted that you two would revive soon."

I glanced reflexively at the mage named Wist. She used a child-sized spoon to eat calmly from a tin of marinated eel.

"How could you tell?" I asked.

Wist tilted her head back as if searching for an answer among the audience of skulls. "We went right up to your machina."

"Solitaire? My chalice?"

She nodded. "It was like looking at an egg ready to hatch. A bird egg, or a snake egg. You would notice if something on the inside were more than ready to be born. If it were fighting to break out."

No. In the same position, with my feeble magic perception, I wouldn't notice a thing. But I suppose I could accept that this foreign mage had detected signs of Vesper's struggle.

Asa brought out water in a clear vessel shaped like a wine bottle. She poured metal cups for all three of us. I took a few chilly sips to be polite.

"Your fingers are just like in the stories," Asa commented.

I'd give up on hiding them after hearing her pronounce my full name. I flexed them in the air for her, turned them about to better display the lack of fingernails. I was well accustomed to this sort of show-and-tell. Each awakening usually brought me multiple rounds of it.

Asa refilled my cup of water, though I hadn't asked for more.

"Truth be told," she said, "Wist and I are pretty famous. Maybe just as famous as you and your demon. Depending on which country you're in, and who you ask. But I guess you really haven't heard of us, huh?"

"I was asleep for fifty years," I said. They seemed to have already deduced this. No reason to talk around it. "And I still haven't figured out how to leave the city."

"Hm. Well, you must be just about dying with curiosity about the outside world. Got any burning questions?"

Myriad Jacian skulls studied our strange group. I, in turn, studied Wist the mage and her—whatever Asa was. Something adjacent to a mage. The non-magical partner that a mage needed to function.

In Jace, we called them operators. The role had a very different title on the continent.

"Will the answers cost me?" I asked.

"No, no." Asa flapped a dismissive hand in front of her face. "Just being friendly."

"Then tell me. Are you here as enemies of the state?"

"Which state?"

"I've killed Osmanthian spies before," I said.

"I'm sure you have," Asa concurred. Then she blinked and set her cup down. "Wait. We didn't mention being from Osmanthus, did we?"

"Your accent makes it obvious."

"You compared the climate here to Osmanthus City," Wist added.

Asa scowled. "Dammit. Fine. Let me put it this way. We aren't here as enemies of Jace. Quite the opposite. But our presence is still a delicate matter. In terms of international politics and such."

"You've come in secret," I said, watching her reaction. "It isn't common knowledge that I'm sealed in Glorybower."

"Something like that."

I knew not to believe everything they told me. Same for Vesper. Both Vesper and these Osmanthians might very well be feeding me wholesale lies.

The only way to determine the truth for myself would be to break free from the city. No matter what I heard from anyone, leaving Glorybower needed to remain my top priority.

17

ASA SWIVELED to peer at my shoulder. "You've been favoring your right side," she informed me. "What's under those bandages?"

"Got bitten," I said.

"By what?"

"A wild animal."

"How unfortunate. Is the wound infected?"

"In a couple more days, it might be."

Asa frowned. "You sure are a calm one. Do you have a way to treat it? Will your demon cure you?"

"Maybe," I hedged. Wouldn't count on it. "If she feels like it."

Asa waved Wist over. "Let Wist take a look."

"I can't repay you."

"No compensation needed. Consider it a sign of friendship."

Unlike Vesper, these women probably wouldn't probe the site of the injury with bare fingers. I dutifully removed my provisional bandages.

Asa and Wist held still and silent, both staring straight ahead, as if carrying out a rapid-fire conversation in their heads.

Afterward, Wist leaned in closer to me. She wore a blue bond thread on her wrist. Asa's thread must've been stashed somewhere hidden.

Vesper and I had never worn bond threads. It was more of a continental tradition, one that hadn't taken hold till centuries after I first summoned her.

In the quiet, I realized that the muscle between my neck and shoulder had stopped firing desperate pleas for attention at the back of my brain.

With the stiff charcoal ends of my fingers, I tentatively patted the spot where Vesper had bitten me.

Closed skin. Rough, patchy, somewhat dented—but fully healed over. I rotated my shoulder, raised my right arm. I tipped my head from side to side. It only pulled a little.

Impressive work. And so discreet that I hadn't even noticed Wist's magic entering the sticky mess of the open wound.

I started to thank her.

"We saw you fall from the bell tower," Asa said without preamble.

A formless dread locked my body in place.

"Did you," I uttered vacantly. "How embarrassing."

"We were so sure you'd died. Wist really beat herself up over it. We'd meant to stay in hiding. Do a little surveillance. But she kept saying she should've leapt out to save you. Even if it meant blowing our cover."

Wist averted her gaze.

"I thought the same thing, of course," Asa said. "We really had our minds blown once we spied you up and about again. How in the world did you survive that?"

"My demon saved me."

"She hurled you off the top of the tower. Then she turned around and saved you?" Asa didn't bother concealing her skepticism.

"She can be a little capricious," I said weakly.

"Not to put too fine a point on it," Asa said, "but you hit the ground. A very unpleasant scene. You were clearly dead."

"Yet here I am," I replied, as steadily as I could manage. "I wasn't dead at all. Not like these."

I gestured at the rows of skulls bearing witness.

Asa seemed unconvinced.

"My turn," I said hastily. "You never explained how you got inside Glorybower."

Rather than answer, she began packing up the components of their picnic.

Meanwhile, Wist gathered the empty food cans and other discarded packaging. With a spurt of magic that smelled oddly of burning rubber, she transmuted her bundle of trash into a pocketknife. The handle and blade were all the same monochromatic metallic hue, a material reminiscent of stainless steel.

Asa dusted her knees after folding the tarp. "You want to know how we breached the city walls? We got in and out of here the same way as your demon."

"Through vorpal holes? Could you—"

"We can't take you with us." She spoke with flat certainty. "It's a finicky magic. We'd all die if anything went wrong."

"Send me through alone," I said. "I'll assume all the risk."

"You might be fine with throwing away your life, but don't make Wist throw it for you," Asa said tartly.

I turned to Wist. She shook her head.

Asa pointed at her own face. "We can use vorpal holes as our highway now, but the magic specifically only works for the two of us. Wist and her bondmate. Took years for Wist to work it out."

I couldn't argue. Absent the incontrovertible proof of their presence here in the city, right in front of me, I wouldn't have believed any human claiming to be able to use magic involving vorpal holes. I'd never heard of such a thing.

Vorpal holes were rare to begin with. Large-scale or unfortunately located holes struck the Jacian islands much less frequently than other natural catastrophes like landslides and earthquakes.

For most of us humans, open vorpal holes represented nothing but peril. The terror of vorpal beasts leaking out, or the terror of total annihilation if you fell in.

Wist tapped me on the arm. She'd closed the steel pocketknife. Now she held it out, waiting for me to take it.

"For me?" I said, a touch wary.

"For you," said Wist. "A gift." Still the same low monotone. Guess that was how she always spoke.

I accepted the knife. It was the automatic kind, ready to pop open at the touch of a button.

I flipped the blade out a few times before stashing it in my pocket, bemused.

"Thanks," I said to her. "You've both been very kind."

"The knife was Asa's idea."

Asa took this as her cue to chime in. "You aren't carrying any other weapons, are you?"

"Can you be sure?" I asked. "You didn't pat me down."

"You're a soldier of sorts, aren't you? If you had a weapon, you would've whipped it out. Or at least gotten ready to. Back in those initial moments of shock after you first noticed us."

There was something inherently smug about the way Asa curled her mouth.

"After you first revealed yourself, you mean," I said by way of correction.

Asa looked even more pleased now. "Oh? Go on."

"We didn't meet by accident. You followed me to the city border. You chose to stay hidden. Then you chose exactly when to show yourself."

She clapped me on the shoulder. "Indeed. We've done a marvelous job of eluding your demon so far, haven't we? The concealment magic worked just as well on you. Wist is very good at going unnoticed."

I contemplated the two of them anew.

Wist: a lanky mage with a magic core as bright as a star hiding deep in her torso, near the small of her back. The same spot where my magic core used to be located, before the experimenters extracted it.

My magic perception wasn't keen enough for me to quantify her power just by looking. Yet I could tell, in a fuzzy sun-blinded sort of way, that she had to be one of the strongest mages I'd encountered in many, many years.

And then there was Asa, small and quick, brimming with sharp energy. It wasn't just the crisp black-and-white stripes in her hair that made me think of a clever little omnivore, a raccoon or a skunk.

I hadn't questioned their dynamic. From the start, it felt familiar.

Despite everything that had happened over the years, despite civil wars and revolutions and public executions, mages here in Jace were always supposed to follow their non-magical handlers. Their operators.

The degree of obedience demanded and the manner in which the state enforced it seemed to change each time I awakened. I'd nod along blearily as officials lectured me on the latest social norms and legal requirements.

The core of it was quite simple, though. Magic had inherent dangers. A lone mage was like someone walking around with an explosive device in their belly. It might never go off, but why take that risk in the first place? Mages needed operators in order to safely participate in and contribute to Jacian society.

I myself had been born a mage, though that ended when they cut out my core. Now, bonded to Vesper, my role was closer to that of an operator.

I was supposed to control her. To channel her powers in a productive manner. To prevent disaster.

But. The way things worked on the Jacian archipelago had always been very different from the way things worked on the continent. Especially in Osmanthus.

"Have you visited anywhere else in Jace?" I asked Asa.

"Just for a bit. No time to hit up the usual tourist spots."

"Must be easy for you to fit in," I said.

"Is that a compliment?"

"It's an observation." I paused to collect my thoughts. "Do you act like you're in charge of your mage because you're in Jace? Because it's what people expect here?"

Asa and Wist exchanged puzzled looks.

I spelled it out for them. "Osmanthus is a mageocracy. The opposite of Jace. You wouldn't act like this back in your homeland."

Osmanthians treated those without magic like indentured servants. Like property. Mages ruled everything.

Last I'd heard, the best Osmanthian operators were getting raffled off like prizes. Without any choice of which mage to assist, which mage to bond with.

I looked Asa in the eye. Her left eye, mostly. A dark sweep of hair still half-covered the right. I couldn't imagine how she stood it, bangs constantly tickling her and obscuring her vision.

"Did your mage win you in the national lottery?" I asked her.

I didn't mean it as an accusation. Nor as a moral judgment against their country. Their system wasn't right, but a lot of things weren't right.

I couldn't save the whole world. The small islands of Jace were enough of a challenge. Just wanted a better understanding of who and what I was dealing with.

The two of them had begun conversing mind-to-mind again. I'd bet anything on it.

If they were a classical Osmanthian bonded pair, if Wist the mage had full control, I suppose she could wordlessly tell Asa what to say. How to reassure me. How to put the Jacian at ease. I would be none the wiser.

At last Asa broke the silence. "Well," she said, almost gently, "it's a complicated story. But no. We're not a conventional pair by Osmanthian standards. Not by a long shot."

She stood on tiptoe and stretched vigorously, groaning, then added: "In the interest of fairness, I should mention that the Osmanthian lotteries ended quite a while ago. Around the same time as the sealing of Glorybower. Which is not to say that—what is it you call us again? People like me."

"Operators?"

"Operators. Right. It's still pretty rough for operators on the mainland. Much better to be born a mage. But every era has some kind of exception to the norm, no?"

"Together we have enough power," said Wist, "that we can afford to be eccentric."

Asa gave her a light kick in the ankle. "That's my line."

Something unnameable roiled in me as I watched them. Right in the lacuna where I used to have my magic core, that imperceptible cavity in my torso that would never be filled. A stinging almost like envy.

The depths of my mouth felt as dry as pith. I swallowed repeatedly in an effort to ease it.

"What originally brought you to Glorybower?" At least my voice sounded no different.

"It'll be easier to show you outside," Asa said.

She checked her heap of supplies one last time, then beckoned for me to follow. Wist brought up the rear.

We made our way out to the porch that encircled the Hall of Wheels. It displayed more visible wear than the interior, but nevertheless remained uncannily sturdy.

The boards squeaked softly, refusing to bow under our weight. Round acorns studded the railings, laid on as densely as the scales of a fish.

Asa pointed at the sickly blue sky. Transparent hints of reflected city scenery hung like old mirages amid indistinct threadbare clouds.

The temple complex offered a very clear view of the vorpal hole that had been hanging in the sky for decades now. Motionless and emotionless. Neither a promise nor a threat.

It had no brain; it had no particular intention. But the next creature to pass through the hole might destroy us. It could come tomorrow, or a hundred years from now, or never.

Asa leaned her head back against Wist and told me: "Wist can close vorpal holes."

"...What?"

I ended up saying it twice. My mind needed more time to process this.

Asa didn't wait for me to recover. "Vorpal hole manifestation might've been a rare freak disaster fifty years ago," she went on. "But in the past few decades, they've started popping up on the continent a lot more frequently. In Jace, too.

"When she can, Wist goes around closing them. Not just in Osmanthus. All over the continent. And now in Jace."

Asa twirled her index finger at the sky again. "Obviously this one poses more of a challenge than usual."

"One of the largest I've ever seen in person," said Wist.

"We thought we might try to open up the city, too," Asa explained. "Wist said it might take years to reverse-engineer a skill to bring down the barricade. But that's another part of the reason we came. To assess the feasibility of trying."

All of this seemed exponentially beyond the scope of standard human magic.

Full teams of mages—full armies of mages—had failed many times to compete with Vesper and Solitaire.

Maybe Wist had magical power similar to the inimitable Kraken that Vesper and I had fought in our youth. Or maybe these two Osmanthians were flat-out delusional.

The latter seemed more likely. I'd passed through century after century, experiencing time like a skipping stone, without ever catching wind of a single other human being who might be considered remotely comparable to the Kraken.

Just like how Vesper was our world's one and only demon.

Back in the day, I'd certainly wondered if the Kraken were the Blessed Empire's version of a demon, a human artificially transformed into something more vorpal in nature.

But in facing her, we'd also confronted the fact that the Kraken was thoroughly human, right down to her magic core. She'd been a human like no other.

"You find this difficult to believe, no doubt," Asa said glibly. "But that's why we're here. And we have another problem now. Wist can't close the vorpal hole in the sky with just a snap of her fingers. It'll take time and quite a bit of work.

"If Wist starts to work on closing the hole in the sky, your demon friend will notice. I imagine your demon friend won't be thrilled to see us here."

"Probably not."

"There's our big issue," Asa concluded. "We can't close the vorpal hole without getting caught. Wist can't fight a demon and close a vorpal hole at the same time."

"Both would be impossible for an ordinary mage," I said.

"Luckily for us, Wist is one of a kind. Anyway, it all comes down to your friend. If your friend is hostile, we'll have to defeat her first. Thing is, we've never fought a demon before. Kind of tough to come up with a strategy."

I could see where this was going. "You want insider information," I said. "That's why you approached me. That's why you treated my injury. That's why you armed me."

Asa beamed. "Precisely. You're so easy to talk to."

I thought about this. "Vesper and I are bonded. Don't know if I can deceive her."

"Do you share thoughts with each other?"

"Not like human bondmates."

"What's that mean?"

"We can't speak in our heads. I can't read her at all."

"Then the same might be true for her. Hm. We can work with that. As long as you're on board." Asa's smile stopped. "Are you?"

"Does it matter what I say?" I asked.

"A verbal promise is better than nothing."

She ran her fingertips along the acorn-plated railing. She paused to poke at a small hole where a single acorn was missing. It looked like the socket left by a lost tooth.

"We don't have a lot of allies to choose from here in Glorybower," she said. "For that matter, neither do you. We did see your demon try to kill you, remember?"

Beside her, Wist summoned an acorn, seemingly from thin air. She fitted it soundlessly in the empty slot on the railing.

"I'm a nosy woman," Asa said frankly. "I'm incredibly curious about you."

I braced myself. "What about me?"

"The Host has been around for eons. Has the Host always been you?"

"I spent most of that time in hibernation," I said. "My lived years aren't very long."

"How old are you, then?"

"Twenty-something."

"Oh, heaven," Asa muttered. "You're a baby."

"You can't be that much older."

She glowered. "At least a decade. That's gotta count for something."

Her expression shifted. She patted the part of the railing that Wist had wordlessly repaired for her. She gave herself a satisfied nod.

Then: "There are stories about the Host and her demon even in Osmanthus. Naturally, I did as much research as I could before we got here."

There was a hint of an unnatural gleam deep in her right eye, the one veiled by her black forelock. A green like the glow of certain fireflies. It spilled out as if through the thinnest of cracks, light from under a closed door, a candle in a dungeon.

"I heard," she said, "that the two of you were lovers."

"We were?" I asked dumbly.

Asa retreated. "I mean, I don't have anything in the way of real historical evidence. It might be exaggerated. It might be propaganda. It was just a pretty common theme. Enough to catch my notice. You ... uh, you're not even sure yourself?"

I could recall sleeping with someone, or multiple someones. I could recall flashes of their touch.

I knew I wasn't a virgin, just as I knew my name was Char.

But no matter how isolated I felt, no matter how wary I was of strangers approaching me in strange new eras, no matter how difficult it might be for others to understand my duty and my way of life, no matter how desperate I got for companionship—would I really have turned to Vesper?

"That seems wrong." My voice stumbled over itself. "Would I do that?"

"I don't know. Would you?"

"She's a demon. I brought her to our reality. I created her. In a manner of speaking. I used her to win wars. But would I use her like *that*?"

"Don't ask me," Asa said dryly.

Something shot down between us like the dive of a falcon, too fast to react.

A slim island sword rife with lacy blue veins.

It pierced the boards of the temple porch as if staking a claim to uninhabited land.

My breath shortened. My fist convulsed around the tiny folded knife in my pocket. Then I wondered what the hell I could hope to accomplish with a few inches of plain steel. And no magic.

From the garden, from the air above the ruined water wheel, came a voice I knew all too well.

"Stop lying to my Host," Vesper said in perfect Continental.

18

VESPER KNELT IN open space a few feet over the fallen water wheel. She knelt like a proper temple visitor, legs and feet folded decorously beneath her, her weight resting on her ankles.

Her second sword circled around her like a befuddled moon, its trajectory constantly changing.

I'd told Asa the truth. I couldn't sneak inside Vesper's mind or feel what she felt. Not in the way of human bondmates.

But certain things I could see written right there on her face. Disgust—with me in particular, or with all three of us humans. An unexpected wariness. The thrumming of an animalistic exhilaration.

Vesper loved having a reason to fight.

When we were together, so did I.

My thoughts burst free of the quicksand they'd been trapped in. I shouted for the others to run.

I forgot to speak Continental. The words came out in Old Jacian.

Asa had already darted behind me, hands on my shoulders, ready to use me as a shield. I understood the sentiment. Unfortunately, it was meaningless. Vesper wouldn't hesitate to stab straight through me to get to her.

Wist hadn't moved an inch. Her hands rested on the acorn-paved railing. Her dark expressionless eyes rested on Vesper.

The sword embedded in the floorboards yanked itself out. Another cry—still the wrong language—got stuck like a plug in my throat. The free-range sword wielded itself, slashed at Wist's neck from behind like a scythe.

Her braid instantaneously lengthened, whipping up to seize the bony hilt of the sword. Like a chameleon's tongue shooting out to catch a fly. The sword strained for freedom, its blade millimeters from Wist's skin.

With a pulse of magic, the veins in the sword changed from blue to pure scarlet. It stopped resisting. Wist's braid pulled back, then hurled the sword at Vesper. It flew straight as an arrow.

Vesper's second sword whirled to parry it.

After the clanging, Wist raised her voice.

"Meet us inside," she said, flat as ever.

I didn't sense her porting us. I did sense, fleetingly, the sticky spider-threads of the sheltering magic she'd woven all around the Hall of Wheels.

In past visits to this temple, I'd rarely ventured deeper in the Hall of Wheels than the vaulted sanctuary just inside the entrance. The part with the columnar collection box and the mosaic labyrinth on the floor, and the most sophisticated wheels of bone.

The rest of the building was normally closed to visitors. Even specially invited guests like myself. I'd never before seen the skull-lined room that Asa and Wist had selected for picnicking.

I'd never seen the space we now ported to, either.

We must have come somewhere very close to the hidden circular heart of the Hall. Lingering magic tickled the skin of my wrists, the sides of my neck. A sensation like sugar ants crawling somewhere unseen.

Unlike back in the sanctuary, the bones used for the art in this room were not at all recognizably human. I found myself crouching, pressing my forehead. A nauseating ringing whittled at the insides of my ears.

"You okay?" Asa asked.

I made a sound that was supposed to mean *yes*. I forced myself to get up. My ankle cracked as I straightened.

The mosaics on the glazed floor beneath us depicted circular scenes of murder and rebirth, torture and delight. The story had no starting point. It could be a descent into paradise or a steep climb to hell, a tale beginning or ending with death.

So far it was just us three humans in here. Wist's wards must've succeeded in holding Vesper off. At least for the moment.

The answer to my unease came to me all at once. This chamber felt like an engorged, parodical version of Solitaire's cockpit. Its bones appeared to have been sourced primarily from birds and sea monsters: some a delicate spongy filigree, some a ridiculous jumble of spikes.

"Your demon found us faster than expected," Asa remarked.

"I was surprised she came so late," I said.

She snorted. "Yes. I'm sure you were very surprised. I saw you sprinkling those breadcrumbs for her."

"What?"

"The coins you dropped," Wist said. "The grails."

"Just paying my respects to the temple," I told them.

"I won't lecture you for trying to play both sides," Asa said briskly. "I've done it myself. Tends to end badly. But if your demon has any big weaknesses, now would be a real good time to mention it."

At the center of the room sprouted a basin for offerings. It was shaped from layer upon crinkly layer of curved, tooth-lined, petal-like bones. Couldn't begin to imagine what creature or body part these came from.

I couldn't possibly overpower Vesper alone.

"Small of the back." I patted my own back to demonstrate.

"Right where the magic core would be in a human mage, huh?"

"She won't let you reach it," I warned. "She knows where she's vulnerable."

Asa regarded me with the fixed stare of a reptile. "Hope you're not lying."

"To be clear," I said, "I didn't drop grails here to summon Vesper for an ambush. I left them as insurance."

"Insurance against what?"

"Most Osmanthians I've met in the past were on a mission to kill me."

Asa remained silent for another moment, unblinking. "I already told you our mission. That being said—you're sharper than you seem."

"Is that an insult?"

"It's a compliment." She came up next to me and peered into the throne-sized bowl. "I'm envious, you know. I can never resist the urge to show off. Far better to let people think you're simple. You can get so much more done when they underestimate you."

"It's not an act," I said. "I'm a simple woman."

"Yes," Vesper agreed.

She stood across the room from us. Not on the mosaic floor, but in the air a foot or so above it. On the wall behind her, perfectly framing her, hulked a profusion of cruel talons the size of human ribs. They interlaced to form a deadly wreath.

Every visible patch of her skin was raked with blue-streaked scratch marks. Like the claws of a cat.

"You are a simple woman," Vesper said to me in Jacian. "A simple-minded fool. Mindlessly offering yourself up as a hostage."

I looked at Asa on my right. Wist on my left. The spiked basin between us and Vesper.

The ringing in my ears sawed away at a pitch that should've been much too high to hear.

I tucked my hands back in my pockets. "Am I a hostage?" I asked.

"A pertinent question," Asa said coolly. "The answer depends on your demon." She eyed Vesper. "For the record, we prefer not to fight."

"Oh, that's rich," said Vesper, switching back to Continental. Her fangs looked much sharper than any of the dead exposed teeth used to decorate the room.

Asa remained impressively unperturbed. "This entire temple has been possessed by a vorpal beast."

That was news to me. "It has?"

"For many years, I'd guess," she said. "A calm one. A quiet one. A very, very, very, very large one. Surely you don't want to awaken it."

Vesper folded her arms. She settled back on her cushion of air. She crossed one leg over the other, imperious despite the cat-scratches tattooing her. Must not have been all that easy for her to port past the wards around the Hall exterior.

Only now did it occur to me that the room had no visible doors. The sole light radiated down from a round window at the very peak of the high ceiling, directly above the cup-shaped bones that bloomed in front of me like a dangerous lotus.

"I'm a demon," Vesper pointed out. "Needless to say, the rest of you are human. Go on. Gamble with your lives."

Something cold touched my neck.

The weapon had appeared too fast for me to see it clearly. A combat knife, or a dagger. Wist was the one who held it.

"Very nice," Vesper said approvingly. "Couldn't have planned it better myself. Yes, slit her throat. Let the beast taste her blood. I'll be your audience."

Asa spoke in the tone of a warning. "Even if we miscalculate, even if all three of us humans die right here in the temple, the awakened beast will still be there. The beast will become your problem to deal with."

"I do love a challenge," Vesper said breezily.

Asa met her gaze without flinching. A rodent facing down a snake. Although Asa herself had a number of snake-like qualities, I thought.

Wist's blade was gentle against my throat.

Too gentle. Too careful.

Whatever Asa might be planning, Wist didn't want to go through with it. The hand that held this knife would inevitably hesitate.

"I'll be honest," Asa said suddenly. Still addressing Vesper. "I don't quite understand you. This woman is your Host. Very much a parasitic relationship, no? I'm not privy to all the details, but on some level, your survival depends on her. How can you be so cavalier about losing her?"

Vesper's smile widened. "Find out for yourself," she said. "Be scientific about it. Carry out your threats. Slaughter her before my eyes. I won't stop you. I'm rooting for you, little foreigner."

"All right." Asa's voice went hard. "Wist."

Nothing happened. I had the presence of mind, at least, not to cut myself by squirming.

"Wist," Asa said again.

Vesper—lounging midair in her self-made seat of honor—looked supremely amused.

The Osmanthians were a bonded pair, mage and operator. They could communicate without flapping their lips, without shouting for all of us to hear. If they chose to speak out loud anyway, then on some level, it must have been for our benefit.

On some level, it was a performance.

"Do it," Asa said. "Char already survived a fall from the bell tower. There's something at play with them that we can't perceive yet. Body Double magic, maybe. Or something deeper. We need to understand it."

The blade twitched against my skin. Pressed harder.

But not hard enough to slice me open.

I was beginning to feel sorry for Wist. She didn't seem fond of violence. "Can I speak?" I asked carefully, trying to move my jaw as little as possible.

An awkward beat passed.

"Knock yourself out," Asa muttered.

"I'll do it myself," I told her. "If you'll let me. I have more experience. This room is like the inside of a Jacian chalice. Our great machina. I can see how to feed it."

Another brief silence. Asa motioned for Wist to stand down.

I tugged out my new pocketknife and pressed the button to pop out the blade.

"Look at her," Asa said to Vesper. She gestured at me in the way of a ringmaster. "She isn't bluffing."

Vesper's eyes had narrowed like those of a cat in the sun. She observed the three of us without moving.

The room didn't smell of old worn things or dust or ancient death. It smelled of freshly germinating sweat. Pungent human sweat. Probably mine.

Asa spoke to Vesper again. "Are you really going to stand back and let her do this? If the beast in here awakens, none of us will make it out unscathed. Why not negotiate?"

A valiant effort, but it would never work. She didn't know Vesper like I did.

I held my left arm out over the bone basin, wrist exposed, palm up. I mulled regretfully over the fact that I'd just gotten my shoulder injury fixed.

No one made a move either to stop me or to urge me onward. I must look like I knew what I was doing.

I did, of course. Every ounce of power had its price. The excavation of my magic core. Untold quantities of blood—mine or Vesper's—to feed Solitaire. Pound after pound of my own nerve-packed flesh, mined from my living body to unleash Vesper's full potential.

All for a good cause. Always for a good cause.

How nice it must be for Wist, such a very powerful mage, to have kept her magic core all her life. To have lived a life that also let her keep her gentleness, her reluctance.

She didn't want to hurt me. Perhaps she didn't want to hurt anyone.

How sweet. How quaint. How pure of heart.

How enraging.

The thought came to me as distinctly as if Vesper had leaned over my shoulder and whispered it hotly in my ear. Yet the thought didn't come from Vesper; it came from me alone.

I didn't even possess the magic needed to patch my own wounds.

Why was it always my blood that had to be shed?

With trained swiftness, I stabbed Wist in the arm instead.

19

WIST STAGGERED.

She'd had her sleeves rolled up. Unfortunate for her, and fortunate for me. I seized her forearm for leverage and yanked the small knife out. I flung it, open and bloody, into the yawning basin.

Asa fired off a string of rapid syllables in Continental. Words I'd never heard before. Curses, presumably. She lunged for me.

I didn't dodge. There was absolutely no way that short, scrawny Asa had the physical strength to push me anywhere.

Before she could reach me, she stumbled.

The floor creaked and moaned and buckled. Vesper glided a judicious distance away from the bulky wreath of bones behind her. The walls began to ripple like the surface of a stormy lake.

I braced my legs to keep my balance. Wist ported behind Asa, catching her just as she started to trip and fall. Magic ricocheted through the air with a sound like a cork popping.

The two Osmanthians vanished together, then emerged a blink later in the exact same spot.

I heard Wist say, puzzled: "I can't port out."

The groaning of the building had built to a piercing whistle, a shriek like the cry of a teakettle. Except we were trapped at the heart of the kettle itself, and the sound simultaneously came from inside my head.

If anyone said anything else, I had no chance of hearing it.

The chamber twisted and lurched. As I fought to stay upright, I had an epiphany: the great round bone-infested walls of the room were composed entirely of stacked wheels. Too many to count at a glance.

Behind the bone wreaths, behind the frilly reliefs formed of mystery animal spines and skeletons, these gargantuan wheels encircled the full floor of the chamber. They piled up one after another, all the way up to the miserly skylight that formed a peeping eye in the ceiling.

The wheels in the walls began turning.

The skylight blinked.

I scrabbled to steady myself, to make sense of my shaking vision, to spot the emergence of an exit. The bone petals of the central basin whirled shut like a flower devolving back to a bud. Small bones pelted down from all sides with, incongruously, a sound like high ringing bells.

I glimpsed Vesper past them as if through a curtain of dirty hailstones. Nothing seemed to hit her.

The guts of the building unfurled, giving me a tentative view of the sanctuary out front. I started to run, if you can call it running. More like a never-ending sequence of falls—either me smacking my shins on the floor, or the floor rising to meet me where I swayed.

The Hall of Wheels had opened up to become an intricate bone machine, infinite circles transforming into interlocking gears, spinning and inverting. Ceilings became walls and walls became floors. I crashed sideways, spiked myself on an ornamental screen of sharpened bone.

Someone else cried out, distant and muffled. Asa? Wist?

Those two were very unlikely to survive.

I wrenched myself free of the spikes and crawled mechanically down a twisting tunnel. At the end lay the temple garden. Which probably didn't mean safety.

I kept crawling forward anyway, my body taking command of me, chips of bone biting my palms and knees no matter where I placed them.

This was how I'd made it through eon after eon. The body kept going, relentless.

As if dropped through a trapdoor, I tumbled head over heels down into the main sanctuary. Winded, I sucked in a few more breaths, none of them adequate. Then I clambered to my feet.

The wheel came from behind me.

The wheels here were different: snowballing clusters of wild bones. They rolled across open space like living creatures with malicious intent. They ran straight into each other, clashed and ground together, bison locking horns for dominance.

They were larger than bison. They were much larger than any human.

By the time I registered my surroundings, by the time I realized where all the noise came from, the largest wheel of all had already borne down on me like a chariot.

I hit the floor again.

I felt something enormous crunch every last scrap of my voice right out of me.

I groped for my watch. Only my watch could stave the pain off. But I couldn't find it. I couldn't reach it.

"What'd I tell you?" someone said softly.

Someone fluent in my native language. Someone who spoke Old Jacian just as naturally as Continental.

151

I might've imagined it.

To clarify: I passed out. I passed out for hours.

To my tremendous surprise, however, I didn't actually die.

On the whole, oblivion seemed like a pleasanter prospect than staying conscious. But my body struggled to commit to either one.

In fleeting moments of awareness, I felt Vesper carrying me.

The sensations ran like dye, blurred together with all the other times she'd carried me in the past. Down from Solitaire after our first test flight. Away from a beach of gray sand littered with broken ships and dead soldiers.

Then I blacked out again, and felt nothing.

The next thing I heard was the sound of paper. Pages turning.

My body belatedly insisted on asserting the fact of its existence. It ached in places I hadn't actively noticed in centuries.

I lay there gripped by a bleary wonder at how much my insides seemed to move around even when I wasn't trying to move at all. Throbbing. Pulsing. Little tics buried in forgotten muscles, twitching with the regularity of a metronome and the vigilance of a naval distress signal.

I was on top of a powdery-feeling blanket. For some reason, I guessed immediately that it was a blanket meant for horses.

The surface beneath it felt like a hardwood floor. I started to roll myself over.

I nearly rolled myself into empty air. No better than a child sleepily tipping off the edge of a bunk bed. I flailed wildly until an invisible force caught me in the middle of my fall.

The force deposited me unceremoniously back on my horse blanket.

At last I began to take in my surroundings. The horse blanket lay draped over the top of a tall wooden bookshelf. Another half-turn in either direction would send me tumbling straight to the floor.

I was back in the celebrated old bookstore. Few shelves—other than the one I now sat on dazedly—remained fully vertical.

I'd ended up on a higher floor than last time. High enough to see books strewn like bullet casings all the way down multiple sets of curving stairs.

Vesper stretched out in the lurid light of a palatial stained glass window. There were missing segments of color here and there, irregular gaps that showed nothing but the glare of a featureless whitish sky.

She was flipping through a large binder. To be more precise: the binder held itself up in the air before her without any physical assistance from Vesper herself. The pages turned themselves briskly, far too fast for a human to read them.

"You healed me," I said hoarsely.

"I won't take complaints," Vesper replied. The pages kept flipping. "Medical magic isn't my specialty."

"You always create extra work for yourself."

"I have no idea what you're talking about."

There was something perversely comforting about Vesper's habitual curtness.

"You let me get run over before you rescued me," I said. "You're the reason that my body needed such heavy-duty medical magic."

I rubbed my sore sides. Everything felt obscurely out of place. Hopefully she hadn't grown me a bunch of extra ribs. Either by accident, or as a sick prank.

I wouldn't question why she'd treated me, though. Didn't want to make her second-guess it.

The sound of pages turning stopped. Vesper ported right in front of me, leaving her heavy binder by the window. The magical cat-scratches that had scored her skin at the temple were all gone now.

"If we're going to assign blame," she said, "let's start with the fact that you decided to sprinkle blood in the basin. You decided to awaken the beast of the temple. Me, I had nothing to do with that. I was naught but an innocent bystander."

"What happened to the Osmanthians?" I asked.

"They lived. I guess."

"You guess?"

"I left them alone with the beast."

"What makes you think they'll live through that?"

"Those little rats succeeded in infesting a demon's city. They made it till today without me seeing them. Clearly they must have top-tier survival skills."

I hoped so, for their sake. Although—in stabbing Wist, I may have turned my only potential human allies against me.

I stretched my neck from side to side. "You dumped me in this same bookstore after you killed me at the tower," I commented. "You like it here?"

"Not all of us are borderline illiterate."

Verity had been a lot better educated than me, come to think of it. Verity used to read as much as she could—as much as she was allowed to—in an effort to better understand our country and the world we lived in.

We'd hide in corners while she summarized her findings for me. She spun far-fetched stories about deep-sea nightmares, about migratory volcanoes that terrorized the empty northern parts of the continent.

To this day, I wasn't sure how much of what she'd told me was true, and much had been tall tales scribbled down by overimaginative travelers.

Vesper was not Verity. But perhaps Vesper had inherited certain traits from her long-deceased human gate.

I motioned at the mystery binder floating by the window. "What were you reading?"

"A compendium of current events. Brought it from outside the city."

"Can I—"

As I started speaking, the pages burst into flame. A black, smelly, baleful fire, tinted by the light passing through the flawed picture window.

Vesper didn't turn to watch. Her magical fire was fast and thorough.

Once its insides had been fully consumed, the cheap binder dropped to the floor far below, light and empty. Didn't make much of a sound when it landed.

"Don't tell me you were hoping to read it." Vesper made zero effort to hide her malice. "You'd have been stuck here poring over the first ten pages for weeks."

"I'm not that slow," I said. She did have a point, though.

Without warning, she reached out and tugged my flight suit down off my right shoulder. I half-wondered if she were planning to bite me open in the same spot again.

Instead Vesper stared fixedly at the wound that was no longer there. At part of the muscle between my neck and shoulder. I didn't know how it looked to her. I'd need a mirror to inspect the scar for myself.

"You let that woman treat you. That mage." She sounded strangely bitter.

"She did a good job."

"The scar tissue's full of blue streaks." A sign of restorative magic forced through too quickly. "Very sloppy."

"I can't complain about anyone who wants to go to the trouble of curing me," I said. "Not even if they're someone who recently murdered me."

As Vesper bent her head to criticize my shoulder, I found myself looking down at the points of her ears.

Down at—

"What're those?" I blurted.

Without thinking, I touched the spikes sticking out of her cartilage.

Vesper reared back out of reach, all but hissing.

"Sorry," I said helplessly. "On your big trip outside the city, you had time to go open up new piercings?"

"Why shouldn't I indulge myself?" she demanded. "Just because you're content with the life of a mountaintop monk—"

"The person you went to," I said. "The, uh, piercer? Body artist?"

"It was just some kid. What about him?"

"He didn't have any questions about your horns? Or the shape of your ears? Or—"

She unfolded herself. The air distorted, just for an instant, as if with a rolling wave of unfathomably potent heat.

And then I saw Vesper as human. Rounded ears and pupils. No horns. Flat teeth and nails. Extremely immodest shorts and a confusingly cozy sweater on top.

She took a blunt-looking thumbnail and scored a thin crimson line along the back of her hand.

"I can even bleed red if I try," she said mockingly. "You forgot all the times we went undercover together?"

"In my defense—it's been a while."

She rose higher and turned in the air with a flourish. She had to know exactly what she was doing, putting her bare thighs right at eye level, scant inches from my face. I said nothing.

Vesper dismissed the illusion as she descended. Back in her chalice suit and new flight jacket, she examined the spot where she'd cut herself.

Deep blue blood beaded up, trickled a lazy line down around the curve of her wrist. She rubbed it with magic in her finger pads, forcing the sides of the slim wound to zip shut.

"You know what they call that woman?" she asked, eyes on her hand.

"Which one?"

"The mage."

"Wist?"

"Wisteria Shien," said Vesper. "Originally from Osmanthus City. The most powerful living mage in the known world. Still under forty years old."

She scrutinized her nails like a cutler examining knives in need of sharpening. "Everyone calls her the Kraken."

20

My heart twitched. My body must've jerked, too. Something creaked ominously below me.

Vesper put out a single disinterested finger to stop the shelf from falling over.

I took in a series of scattered breaths.

"She's not the Kraken we knew."

"Obviously not," Vesper said testily. "That Kraken left the scene ages ago. Hundreds and hundreds and hundreds of years before Wisteria Shien was even born."

"Is Wist—is she really as powerful as the first Kraken?"

Vesper would be able to tell. Her magic perception was many times better than mine.

She didn't answer right away. The words seemed to stick in her throat.

"The first Kraken only exists in our memory now," she said. "It's hard to compare. I suppose I can understand them being lumped together."

"Seriously?" I'd expected Vesper to ridicule the notion of any other human mage measuring up to the original Kraken.

"Perhaps theirs is the kind of magical power that only comes to humanity once a millennium. Or however long it's been since the Kraken we knew. I've tried not to keep count."

I sat there on my horse blanket, legs dangling. I gripped the edge of the high bookshelf.

"Who decided to give Wist the title of Kraken?" I asked.

"The Osmanthian government."

"Do they mean it as a threat against Jace?"

Vesper scoffed. "Jace is the only country on this side of the world that the previous Kraken never conquered. Thanks to us."

"But now we're locked in Glorybower."

"You're locked in Glorybower," Vesper said. "I'm as free as a hummingbird."

"You left them in the temple. The Osmanthians." My head was finally starting to catch up with what had happened. "This is why you think they'll survive the awakened beast. Because one of them is a Kraken-caliber mage. Am I right?"

"I was too busy babysitting you to check up on them. But yes. That's my reasoning."

"This new Kraken—you see her as a real threat."

Vesper laid her fingertips on either side of me, nails denting the blanket. "What makes you say that?" she asked pleasantly.

"To destroy either one of us, they need to kill both of us."

"They don't know that," she said. "Unless you told them."

"I didn't."

"Good."

"But it would be easy to find out," I insisted. "If we go head-to-head with them. I know why you rushed me out of there. I'm your weakness."

"Or a form of insurance. Depending on how you look at it."

"You wanted me out of their hands," I said. "You want me alive so you can keep coming back, no matter what happens."

"Yes," Vesper said. "That's called being sensible. Doesn't mean I'm afraid of them."

"You are. You took me and fled."

"Are you calling me a coward, Char?" she inquired softly.

"You didn't go back to finish the job."

Vesper clammed up.

"They might've been greatly weakened, or already on the verge of death," I said. "They definitely underestimated the vorpal beast in the temple.

"You wasted your best chance to get rid of them. You wasted your time using healing magic on me instead. All because you were afraid to leave me alone, mangled and half-dead. I'm your second life, in a way. Now that we aren't the only two here in the city, you're downright desperate to keep me safe."

Vesper lifted her right hand and placed it on my throat.

A small hand. It didn't go very far around my neck. But the subtle edges of her nails bit at my skin like shards of glass.

"Go on," she said. "Keep calling me desperate. See what happens."

The spike-piercings in the upper part of her ears, four on each side, already looked fully healed. She must've used magic to force her cartilage to accept the intrusion.

I took my own right hand and touched Vesper's neck. Her skin felt like a fever. A temperature that would surely have meant death for a human.

My fingers went much further around than hers did. I clamped down on the sides of her throat. For the first time since coming to my senses here, I felt my strength return.

I felt what I could do to her, if she let me.

The harder I clenched, the harder her nails needled my neck.

Still, Vesper was holding back. If she really wanted to, she could rip my head clean off with that one little hand of hers.

"You told me you were tired," I said. "Sick of watching me sleep. Sick of the repetition. But as long as we're tied together, you'll never be free. Even if you're the one in charge now.

"You'll aways have me to remind you of old times. You'll always have me to worry about."

I added my other hand to her neck. I bore down hard enough for my own arms to tremble with effort. Her lips parted with a tiny noise that seemed inadvertent, that rocketed like a shot of liquor straight to something primal at the base of my brain.

I wondered why she wasn't stopping me yet. I wondered, distantly, if Vesper even needed to breathe in the first place. She was a vorpal being; only because of me had she taken this familiar corporeal shape.

When she feigned being human, she'd looked exactly like Verity.

Except that Verity had died younger. Verity had never gotten a chance to flaunt her ass in tiny shorts or get frivolous piercings on a whim or live on her own outside the institution or experience anything of the world she'd read about in all her scrolls.

Not because of Vesper, really. Because of me.

Because I kept making the choice to open the gate in Verity and drag Vesper through it.

There was always a good reason for it. There was always a desperate need. Countless lives were on the line. Nothing could save us but the power of a demon.

I opened the gate again and again, until nothing of Verity remained.

Why reuse the same gate to the point of destruction? Why not pull Vesper through once and then keep her here with us?

We tried that, too. Every time I summoned Vesper, Verity went comatose. It had been the same with the dowager's sheepdog, and with every other animal I'd used as gates for pulling vorpal beasts.

If the visiting beast lingered too long, eventually the gate would die in its sleep.

So I learned to banish my visitors, to send them back the same way they'd come. I would never have risked turning Verity into a gate if I weren't confident in my ability to exorcise whatever came through her.

But this meant that every time Jace required a demon, Verity's gate would need to be opened all over again.

Verity and I had both known when it was the very last time for her. She'd already outlasted every other creature I'd ever used as a gate. She could feel herself slipping away, the creeping progression of her own obliteration.

I remember her crying. I remember her sweaty hands clinging to mine. I remember her telling me she didn't want to die.

She wanted to stay with me. She wanted to see more of Jace. She wanted to witness those volcanoes on the continent.

She didn't volunteer. She didn't agree to it, not the final time. She didn't accept it.

Officials told me of more warships on the horizon. They enumerated the islands that had already fallen. The coastal towns consumed by fire.

There was no other way, they said.

Verity wept, and then she stopped making any sound at all. In her last moments she went rigid with terror, a living rigor mortis.

"Verity must've hated my guts when she died," I said to Vesper in the bookstore. Dust motes glinted in the air around us like microscopic gnats. "You inherited every last burning molecule of her rage. You must've carried it through all these centuries without ever acting on it. Not till now. No wonder you're exhausted."

"Her emotions, not mine." Vesper's voice was reedy, almost inaudible. "Your Verity has nothing to do with it."

"We could end it right here," I told her. "If you're really that tired."

"Choke each other to death?" She broke out coughing, throat spasming against my palm. "What a triumphant finish. Unfortunately, my neck isn't my weak spot."

"Would you really rather spend eternity dragging me around?"

Her face closed off. She released my throat. She twisted my wrists until the bones shrieked in protest, forcing me to release her in turn.

"You're a poor gambler," Vesper said, "if you reckon you can get me to black out first. Just because you've got bigger hands.

"You're a human, you utter fool. The weakest kind. All bloody pulp and stringy meat, and no magic left in you."

"No need to remind me," I said. "I know my place."

"It was a stupid plan. You think I don't have any kind of last-ditch survival instinct? I'll slash your arteries to ribbons." She flicked her fingers before my eyes to demonstrate. "Come up with a more attractive offer next time."

I touched my neck and discovered wetness where her nails had pierced me. Not as much as there could've been.

Vesper shifted back out of reach.

"If the Osmanthians live, you'll feel compelled to confront them," I said. "Then again, the vorpal beast of the temple might still eat them. It might develop more of an interest in the rest of the city. It might develop a taste for flesh of all sorts."

Her gaze bore an acetic mix of pity and revulsion. "Scared? I'll protect you, princess."

"No, no. Don't inconvenience yourself. Go enjoy life outside the city. Get more body art."

I turned and dangled myself from the edge of the bookshelf by my fingertips. Even with my body stretched all the way out, the drop to the floor still hit harder than I'd anticipated.

Wave after wave of flat silvery bugs scurried away from the impact. The same ones I'd seen last time—pale, almost translucent, scampering bits of living glass.

I grunted as I straightened myself, aching but whole.

Vesper descended to block my path. She sat with one ankle on her opposite knee, wholly at ease. Cradled, as always, by nothing more than the air itself.

To my right: the shelf I'd jumped down from. Behind me: a peeling balcony railing with a precipitous view of the lower floors. It looked as if it would dissolve at the slightest touch.

And then there was Vesper, casually slotting herself between me and the hole-ridden stairs.

"Don't let your Host get in your way," I said. "Make the most of your freedom. See the world. I can't stop you."

"Your listening comprehension has really degraded over the years," Vesper said fondly.

Her eyes had gone all warm and soft, pupils rounded, assured of triumph. There was something inexpressibly terrible about her smile.

"Your life is my life," she pronounced. "You think I would let anyone else have a chance at you? They won't touch a single flake of your skin. I'd devour you whole before I let them shed a drop of your blood."

"That's not reassuring."

"It's not meant to be," Vesper said, unmovable in her serenity.

She wound a snake-swift hand through the back of my hair. Taut, businesslike, as if she were about to start dragging me behind her like a plundered corpse.

I winced, stooping, as she pulled my head down.

"I told you I would protect you," she said by my cheek. "But not for your sake. What you want doesn't matter. Don't delude yourself into thinking you're allowed to choose your own fate."

Her voice was hardly more than a whisper. The intimate tone of a shared guilty secret.

Her fist squeezed my hair tighter. My scalp burned. Her magic surged up and wrapped around me like chains.

21

VESPER LOCKED ME UP.

Not in the bookstore. I'd already busted out of there once.

Instead she ported me to a post office, one far on the outskirts of town.

"Don't break your arm trying to escape again," she warned. "It won't work."

"Why should I believe anything a kidnapper tells me?"

"Do whatever you want, then," she said dismissively. "But I won't heal you. Not this time."

She left before I could get another word in edgewise.

I soon understood what Vesper had meant. The magic barricading me inside the post office was far more sophisticated than whatever she'd half-heartedly slapped on the bookstore, back when she first dumped my dead body there. She must've worked on setting this up for a long time. Starting right after she woke me in Solitaire.

During my all hours and days of unconsciousness, she'd scouted out this location, started piecing together an airtight edifice of magic to hold me in.

If I tried to step out the front door, the next step I took would reset me all the way to the back of the lobby. If I attempted to fling myself out a window, I would land smoothly on my feet in one of the sorting rooms.

The Jace Postal Service had a long history of using uniquely Jacian technology and magic. Judging by the architecture, this particular facility might've been one of the oldest in the entire city.

As I prowled through the back rooms, I encountered bank after bank of body-sized lockers. Now defunct, of course. Out of use since long before I sealed Glorybower.

Once those lockers would've held dozens of dreaming mages, getting magic siphoned out of them as they lay in stasis. Human batteries devoted to powering our preternaturally sophisticated postal system.

A legacy post office building like this one would be supremely well-suited to channeling magic. At certain points in its history, channeling magic would've been its entire purpose. I could see why Vesper had chosen it to hold me.

After a rudimentary exploration, I concluded that there was indeed no point in bashing new holes in the walls. Nor would tunneling my way out of the basement get me anywhere. No matter how I made my exit, the magic she'd left here would catch and redirect me.

Brute force wouldn't solve this one. I could burn down the entire building, and I'd still remain incapable of stepping outside its footprint.

During repeated attempts to leave, I did get a feel for my surroundings. The area around the post office looked at first glance like a farm—not part of the city at all.

Green hills met the reflective city wall, and thereafter gave the illusion of marching on toward infinity. High on the hills grew a forest of twisting structures, ones painted a camouflage-pattern mix of sky tones and white. Some turned slowly; some lay fallen.

I assumed at first that I was looking at an art installation. Upon further observation, I judged them to be wind turbines.

Crumbling multicolored stone walls snaked among the hills at erratic intervals. An artifact of the city that had preceded Glorybower. They looked like the sine wave of a great stone sea serpent undulating across the land, breaking the surface then diving below.

Worn billboards pointed the way to what I guessed might be berry-picking patches, pear orchards, community farms. Ones that lay just beyond the city border.

Much nearer to the post office: the hollowed-out ruins of a butcher, a bakery, an old-fashioned general store, an enormous chophouse diner. Tattered Jacian flags fluttered like war banners.

The many flags inside the post office were, in contrast, beautifully preserved—colors a tad faded, but their chalice emblem unmarred. (The stylized chalice on our flag looked like a fancy drinking cup, as opposed to a machina.)

Vesper hadn't mentioned where she was going when she left me. Nor had she said anything about returning.

Yet she showed up again before dark on the same day, bleeding blue from her lip.

"Someone punch you?" I asked.

She looked as if she very much wanted to punch me in turn. Not sure why she held back.

"The Osmanthians defeated the temple beast," she said.

"Impressive." I meant it. "Anything left of the original temple?"

The sour set of her mouth turned sourer still. "The Kraken restored the Hall of Wheels. You wouldn't know the difference if you saw it.

She restored the rest of the grounds as well. To their derelict state before the beast awakened, anyhow. That woman's quite a show-off."

Right before Vesper's eyes, I tried walking out the front door again.

As usual, I found myself shifted to the far end of the post office lobby. The wall at my back bore a mechanical clock face about two heads taller than me, broken and soundless.

I spoke as if nothing had happened. No point in dwelling on the obvious. "The Osmanthians didn't come to Glorybower to pick a fight."

"Then they should've announced their presence," Vesper growled. "They should've paid their respects to me. Instead of sneaking around like infected little rats."

"They saw you fling me off the bell tower," I said. "Can you blame them?"

Vesper had been levitating above the empty service counters with their felt-thick layers of gray-green dust. Sometimes I envied her ability to exist in this world without touching anything.

She turned her body like an eel to swim through the air to me. "They watched you fall? Did they realize that you died and came back to life?"

"They suspect something. I denied it."

"You ought to show me some gratitude for caging you here," Vesper said. "You ought to be kissing my feet."

"No, thank you."

"Remember what happened the last time humans learned about our bond of mutual death?" She let out a short harsh laugh. "Perhaps you've forgotten that, too. Lucky for you."

I remembered. I remembered it as if it had all happened to another person. A distant acquaintance. Or a character in a depressing old play.

I remembered being vivisected repeatedly, praying for permanent death, bargaining with the Lord of Circles for the gift of an end.

They hadn't killed me that many times.

Less than ten, I think. Maybe less than five. Only for as long as it took Vesper to break her restraints.

"I haven't forgotten," I said.

Vesper reached past me to straighten out the great hands of the clock on the wall. Not that this would make it any more accurate.

"Well, now you can rest easy. They'll never find you here," she asserted. "This new Kraken isn't the only one capable of magical misdirection. They could comb the whole city for you and never think of checking this one spot. Won't even know they missed it."

"I'll shout out the windows," I said. "I'll build a bonfire on the roof."

"Shout yourself hoarse," Vesper retorted. "Fill the entire neighborhood with smoke. Build a heliograph to flash coded messages.

"You've got nothing else to do, I suppose. Entertain yourself. It won't make any difference. No one's coming to rescue you, kiddo. You ought to be glad of it."

Her confidence didn't bode well for my prospects of escape.

She gave the clock hands a fierce shove, as though fed up with her inability to line them up just so. They squealed rustily, then fell clean off the wall with a resigned clatter.

Vesper made an irritated noise. She started to draw back.

I caught at her arm.

She regarded my hand on the sleeve of her jacket as if she didn't quite comprehend what she was seeing.

"Ves," I said. No plan. Pure id. "Were we ever...?"

She snapped her sleeve out of my grasp. "Were we what?"

"Did we sleep together?"

She stared me in the eye for a few seconds too long, then said with audible venom, "We've shared a few tents in our time, sure. Or did you mean something else?"

I'd figured it would play out like this. I steeled myself.

In the rest of the lobby stretching out behind Vesper, weary afternoon light came in through windows whose blinds had long since given up on hiding anything.

"Did I ever try to seduce you?" I asked.

"Did you ever try?" Vesper echoed. Unfiltered incredulity. "*You?*"

She made a show of looking me over from head to toe. She tucked my lopsided hair behind my ears, patted down the top of my head, tugged straight the unbuttoned sides of my flight suit.

"You need another bath," she said, unprompted.

"I'd love one. No running water here."

Vesper pursed her lips. "Behave yourself, and maybe I'll find time to arrange something."

"You dodged my question."

"Because it's ridiculous," she said tartly. "Tell me, which past awakening would've put you in such a sensual mood?

"Let's see—the time we chased down rebel chalices and ripped out their cockpits? Oh, that was a real turn-on, how we found them all packed full of backup pilots. As soon as one died, the next would take over midair. Nothing like a nice mass grave to get those sexual energies flowing, hm?"

Despite her flippant tone, Vesper's face bore not a trace of a smile.

"Oh, I know. Must've been the first time we saw ghost fever. All those victims walking themselves obediently down to the sea. Cordoned-off beaches. Swollen corpses. Such a penetrating smell! You must've wanted to throw me down on the contaminated sand and ravish me right then and there. Who could resist?"

"Vesper," I said.

Her pupils were slits. "Enjoy your delusions," she spat. "I only stopped by to make sure you hadn't broken all your bones out of spite yet. Glad to find my prisoner intact. Keep up the good work, champ."

I grabbed at her as the air swallowed her.

She disappeared before I could touch anything, porting out of the post office, erasing her presence so thoroughly that it was like I'd been hallucinating her there all along. Arguing with an imaginary friend. Arguing with myself.

Don't know what I'd been planning to do if I caught her.

There was only one way left to escape my post office prison.

The hardest way of all.

The wild magic wafting around the city was a kind of natural phenomenon, aimless. It had no single creator and no predefined purpose. It morphed the canal water into a substance like rich brown syrup. It played fractured music on street corners that hadn't heard any human voices in decades.

Deliberately engineered magic was something else altogether. Magic that had an author, a creator, would die together with its maker. Whether that person was human or demon.

If I were the sole creator of the dome around Glorybower, it would've come down the instant Vesper kicked me off the bell tower.

But I'd used Solitaire to erect those walls, and Solitaire had in turn been channeling Vesper's magic. An uncommon situation.

Would Vesper and I simultaneously killing each other—carrying the bond of mutual death to its ultimate conclusion—be enough to bring down the city walls? Or would Solitaire need to be destroyed as well?

If we died an eternal death, who remaining would have the power to do anything to Solitaire?

The new Kraken.

But if her magic was potent enough to impact Solitaire, she might as well devise a way to lift the city dome without any of us needing to die for it.

Such questions lay outside the scope of my current predicament.

Vesper's mockery (not to mention my own experiments) had made it clear that I could never break out of the post office under my own power.

Nor did I have any hope of getting the Kraken's attention. Vesper's magic would render my efforts useless. Just like how her magic kept blocking me from leaving the building.

Yet the fact remained that Vesper had constructed this magical prison entirely on her own.

There was one surefire way to win my freedom, to melt the cage, to regain my ability to step out the front door and keep walking.

Vesper herself would be more keenly aware of it than anyone.

She would know all too well that she'd left me no other choice.

Despite her casual bearing during her short visit, despite how closely she'd approached me, she hadn't given me a single opportunity to strike at the weak spot in the small of her back.

22

For all the gaps in my memory, I was pretty sure I'd never killed Vesper.

Verity, yes. The very act of summoning Vesper over and over had ended Verity, a frail human gate.

We'd all seen it coming. But we'd needed the power of a demon. There was no other option.

Turn someone else into a demon, Verity had cried as the end approached. *Why does it have to be me?*

I was still young back then. Still learning. I couldn't perceive how to draw a demon from anyone else.

But I don't know if Verity really believed this. Not all the way to the core of her being.

She might've suspected me of lying. She might've thought that I secretly hated her, that I was looking for any excuse I could find to get rid of her, that I preferred Vesper—that I sought to replace her.

By the time I figured it out, Verity was gone forever. Vesper remained in her place.

I saw then how to pull demons from other humans. I saw that most wouldn't last nearly as long as Verity. Most would die the very first time I transformed them into a gate.

I swore I would never make another demon again.

As for Vesper, I'd never raised a hand in anger against her.

Why would I?

The worst I could recall doing was struggling to shove her off me when she got too hungry, bit too deep. When the small horns on her head grew to full length, became spires long enough to stab me as she fed from the flesh of my chest or arm or back. When she forgot herself—when she still kept going.

Those were the times when I had to get rough with her. When I bucked as if fighting for my life. Because I was.

No one would hold that against me. Certainly not Vesper herself.

Here in my post office prison, I would be lucky to get even the slimmest chance to kill her. Who knew what shape it might come in, and when?

If I failed once, I might never see another chance again.

I needed the strength of mind to resist suboptimal opportunities. I needed the flexibility to improvise on the spot if Vesper ever showed unexpected weakness. I needed the patience to wait, without rushing things, no matter how long it might take.

I divided my time. I alternated between exploring the back rooms and developing a stash of makeshift weapons.

The post office overflowed with unsent mail: letters, advertisements, stern missives from bill collectors, catalogs, endless moldering boxes. Vines with wine-colored leaves probed their way inside through clouded windows.

I didn't bother attempting to crack any of the safes. Nor did I plunge very deep into the stacks of bloated packages piled up like termite mounds. I found more promising equipment elsewhere.

There was a reason the post office stood near a butcher and a chophouse. After all the international outrage, after Jace ceremoniously released the last human battery, the postal system still needed a way to keep churning.

They kept borrowing magic from mages, albeit without walling them up right there in the building for the rest of their natural lives. To make up for the greatly weakened power supply, certain institutions switched to using animal sacrifice as a catalyst. A technique to amplify whatever magic the conscripted mages provided.

The Jace Postal Service must've been one such institution. That was the conclusion I reached after locating the abattoir.

It lay behind a stiff door marked *Staff Only*, and up several sagging flights of stairs.

I ventured higher with caution. I wouldn't care to see the look on Vesper's face if she found me after I plummeted through a rotted patch of floor. Legs twisted, back broken.

The entrance to the abattoir—the slaughterhouse—bore zero resemblance to the rest of the post office.

Like the Hall of Wheels in the old temple, it remained suspiciously intact. Try as I might, I couldn't sense any trace of a vorpal beast or a vengeful ghost or whatever else might lurk thirstily out of sight.

The first room felt several degrees colder than the hallway outside. My breath puffed out white in front of me. My forearms puckered with goosebumps. Merely a surface-level sensation, though. Hardly worth noticing.

Tiny windows studded the circular walls high above. They were the kind intended for shooting arrows out of an old castle, or showing a stingy slice of sky to maximum-security prisoners. Most of the illumination came from bluish tubes of water-light—half dead, half still working. They snaked in convoluted patterns along the lower portion of the walls, and beneath thick translucent floor panels. It felt like walking on radioactive ice.

In the center of the towering room swelled two bulbous glass chambers, with the tiniest of stems connecting them in the middle. A giant hourglass shape turned on its side.

One chamber—the express mail chamber—was empty. The other held the dessicated carcass of a stock-elk. An elephant-legged deer, large enough to trample a crowd.

Curved metal structures staked the long-dead stock-elk to the floor. Fresh bone sprouts grew from its picked-over body like ferns thriving in forest loam.

Those metal blades looked extremely useful. But I knew better than to step past the yellow warning line embedded in the floor. I knew better than to hurl a chair and break my way inside.

The mechanism of the twin chambers had a lot in common with the mechanism of Solitaire's cockpit. I got the faintest impression of lingering magic, a sensation like floaters tickling my vision.

Anyway, this chamber was only intended for the largest and most expensive parcels. Ones that needed to travel a great distance as fast as possible.

I found plenty of more prosaic tools in adjoining rooms. These spaces were starker, and plainer, and structured far more like any ordinary boutique slaughterhouse.

Black-stained floors sloped down to industrial drains. The mummified remnants of unrecognizable creatures hung from hooks and long curving railings.

When I had to, I wound around bleeding troughs, serpentine tubes, ceiling-high boilers. But on the whole, I tried to keep my time there to a minimum.

A couple days after Vesper's last visit, it started to drizzle. I listened to the shy sounds of light-footed rain.

Meanwhile, I methodically worked on my collection of shanks, binding improvised handles to blades and hooks of various sizes and shapes. All pilfered from the slaughterhouse upstairs.

I'd also found more than my share of ready-made sticking knives, cleavers, flaying knives, saws, and sharpeners. Most had deteriorated so badly that it felt like they'd snap to pieces after a single use. I reinforced those that seemed salvageable and returned the rest to the abattoir.

What I'd amassed so far might be sufficient to land a surprise blow on Vesper. But I was under no illusion that I had the sheer physical skill to dispatch her with a single strike.

For that, I'd need far more than a time-dulled impromptu weapon. I'd need her to be severely weakened, distracted, incapable of mustering up any significant defensive magic.

On that dark rainy day, I thought for a precipitous second that perhaps my time had come.

Magic scrunched at the building. It vibrated as if in the throes of a minor earthquake. The kind that a lot of Jacians wouldn't consciously notice.

The earthquake stopped. The rain continued.

I'd ensconced myself behind the reception counter in the post office lobby. It got more natural light than most other rooms. The counter, once I dusted it off, also gave me space to spread out my growing armory.

I stood up slowly once I saw Vesper on the other side of the reception desk. Magic crackled around her like stray sparks looking to start an uncontrollable fire.

Her bare feet didn't quite touch the floor. But she came very, very close.

Thick bony spines erupted from her back, the same bleached hue as the horns on her head. A deadly row of them all the way down to her tail bone.

None of my shivs could stab through that.

I forced my fingers to uncurl from around the lumpy wrapped handle of a foot-long metal rod, its tip honed like a rapier. I didn't exactly have it hidden. It lay there right on the counter in front of her.

Vesper's eyes flickered without comment over my assortment of homemade weapons. She could deduce what I'd been up to, no doubt.

The entire left sleeve of her jacket was missing.

Her right hand gripped the stump of her left shoulder. Blue-black blood outlined all her fingers. But there was far less of it than there should've been.

Her jacket and chalice suit hung in shreds, torn apart by her own eruption of protective spines.

I waited for Vesper to say something. Her breathing echoed more loudly than the meek pitter-patter of the rain outside. Her gaze lingered on the counter.

"Too proud to beg?" I asked.

She reeled. Her naked toes grazed the filthy carpet.

"Char," she said thickly, "I swear—"

"Take my little finger."

Vesper blinked.

I held my left hand out across the counter, pinky extended.

"Take it."

Vesper didn't outright drool. But I heard the sound of her swallowing lumpily. Her nails dug into the sides of her mutilated shoulder.

After a moment she bent and took my finger in her mouth, right down to the knuckle. Softly. No hint of teeth yet.

Rain kept fizzling its way through the imperfect windows behind her. I preemptively clutched at the grimy edge of the counter.

She raised her eyes to me as if asking a question. I felt the tender heat of her tongue all the way along the length of my finger. My poor finger.

I told her to hurry up.

Vesper bit down.

My fingers might look like they were made from burnt stone—but Lord, it still hurt to get one bitten off.

I staggered as Vesper tipped her head back and swallowed like a snake. My unbitten hand flew to my mouth—almost punching me in the face—to try to staunch the sounds coming out.

My bitten hand remained suspended in the air between us, rigid as a statue. I couldn't move it if I tried. Vesper's magic locked it in place.

Dizziness ballooned in me, almost enough to supersede the screaming pain. Vesper stooped like a bird to peck again at the bleeding stump of my finger.

Coming back for seconds? I couldn't bear to give her more. But my voice was too slow to tell her no.

Her lips met raw flesh.

Magic drove into the wound like a bolt from a nail gun. My body caved in as if I'd been sucker-punched. My innards wanted to vomit.

Then Vesper drew back, lips dyed scarlet. The pain became muffled. Still there, still thrashing to be free, but quieter than the timid rain.

The bleeding ceased, too. I smelled the leather-and-meat stench of burnt flesh. With that single spike of magic, she'd both numbed and cauterized me.

I could move both hands again. They leapt together, seeking shelter in each other.

Vesper's horns had already grown. They took a form I'd never seen before: the incredible curved horns of a mature auroch, a full two feet long on each side. Her skull ought to have cracked like an eggshell from their sheer disproportionate weight.

I inched back a few steps. Didn't want to put an eye out.

Wayward particles of magic circulated about her like a torrent of golden pollen. She glanced at her missing left arm.

Muscle and fat and cartilage and nerves and blood vessels and bone and sinew burst out of the stump of her shoulder. At first the newborn ribbons of flesh seemed to spray in every direction. Then her arm reeled itself in, wove itself together, grew unblemished new skin.

She bent her elbow. Shrugged her shoulder. Flexed her fingers.

She followed my gaze to the wreckage of the top half of her chalice suit.

The material had been skimpy to begin with, given the large sections deliberately cut out to expose her ribcage gills. With so many new holes torn by the severing of her arm and the temporary bony spines on her back, the clinging coverage it gave her had devolved into no coverage at all.

Vesper zipped up her jacket.

"How dare you impinge on my modesty," she said caustically. "Thanks for the finger."

23

AFTER VESPER PORTED out of the post office, I took a closer look at my countdown clock. The rain had made it so dim in here. I had to stretch the chain all the way up to my nose to see the blue parts.

Ten to twelve minutes.

She hadn't asked how long my finger would last her. She must've been in a rush to get back to Asa and Wist while she still had her new horns. While she was still overclocking.

She hadn't actually told me who'd severed her arm. Just an educated guess.

I squinted critically at my collection of shanks. Vesper might not choose to keep the defensive spikes of bone on her back.

But if she'd grown them once, she could grow them again. She could generate thick plates of bone over her weak spot, lightning-quick, a demon's living armor.

I couldn't outmaneuver her reflexes. I couldn't hope to match the lithe speed of a vorpal being. Missing a finger wouldn't help. Nor could I use any magic of my own.

Bladed weapons weren't nearly enough, I decided. I needed some kind of large hammer. The equivalent of a club or a mace.

I scarcely had any time to get started, though. Vesper returned less than an hour later.

She caught me up in the abattoir, liberally daubed with dirt and grease, gingerly dismantling heavy equipment. It was almost impressive how much the loss of a single finger had slowed me.

"How charming," she said, surveying my rusted implements of death and disembowelment. "Preparing for a siege?"

"I needed a hobby."

I set my work aside and got up awkwardly, then hobbled toward the exit. My left hand felt all wrong. My left leg had fallen asleep.

"That was fast," I added as we passed through the first room of the abattoir. The express mail chamber with the sacrificial stock-elk skeleton.

"Didn't expect to see me again so soon, did you?"

"Didn't think you enjoyed my company that much."

No reply. Vesper kept following me.

No footsteps, either. Her auroch horns and back-spikes were gone, and much of her clothing remained in tatters. But she no longer struggled to keep the bottoms of her feet from touching the floor.

I stopped in the postmaster's office. It was ostentatiously spacious and, on most days, provided a spectacular view of the hills outside. Today it had gotten so hazy that I couldn't even make out the nearest wind turbines.

Vesper touched a few of the dead water-lights dangling from the ceiling. They lit up as she passed, bobbing like flying jellyfish, luminescing without the slightest hint of heat.

The rippling quality of their light made it seem as if we were underwater.

Dark glossy weeds and the unruly descendants of houseplants spilled from Vesper-sized glazed pots. The vegetation added disconcertingly to the illusion of being trapped in a giant's aquarium.

"Chestnuts," Vesper said.

"What?"

She pointed at the postmaster's chair. Stuffing puffed from split seams. "Sit down."

I sat, nonplussed. The chair felt disturbingly gritty.

Vesper dug a burlap bundle out of her jacket. She tugged open the drawstring mouth and shoved it under my nose.

It was, indeed, a bag of roasted chestnuts.

"Chestnuts," I agreed, still stumped.

She took one from the bag and sliced its shell with an effortless swipe of her razor-nailed index finger. She dropped the dark nut-meat in my greasy palm. It was still warm. Like she'd bought them off some phantom street vendor right outside the post office.

I popped it in my mouth without thinking. Vesper tossed me another.

The chestnuts of the modern age were markedly different from those of eight hundred or a thousand years ago. Larger, softer, much easier to peel, and stunningly sweet all on their own.

No need to mash them into a paste with honey. Verity and I used to eat them that way—a rare treat back at the orphanage.

"You know you don't need to feed me," I said between chestnuts. "I can survive without it."

"Yes," Vesper said. "Thanks to our bond."

She kept slicing chestnuts with those efficient slashes of her demon nails, so quick that I struggled to keep up as I gobbled them.

"What happened to the Osmanthians?" I asked.

"Those assholes? They went into hiding," Vesper said, petulant. "Left the rest of the vorpal beasts for me to take care of."

"What vorpal beasts?"

"A new wave descended from the hole in the sky. It was a huge three-way fight. Absolute chaos. That's when the Kraken hacked off my arm. Next time I see her, I'll—"

Vesper's face changed, and not for the better. "The Kraken didn't solely target my arm," she said, slower than before. "Felt like she was going for the small of my back. Like she knew exactly where to aim."

A mealy morsel of chestnut turned tasteless in my mouth. "Still," I said. "All she took was your arm. And now you have it back."

"Such a happy ending." Her claw pierced clean through the next chestnut, splitting it in half.

She pressed the halves into my reluctant fingers. I chewed robotically.

Wist—the so-called Kraken—did know exactly where to aim. I'd told her myself.

If she'd missed, if she'd settled for hacking off Vesper's arm, it might mean she'd deliberately chosen not to land a fatal blow.

Aside from her lower back, Vesper's main vulnerability was sitting right here in the postmaster's decrepit chair, eating chestnuts.

Which explained why Vesper had magically locked me in the post office. More for her own safety than for mine. She'd hidden me away like those fabled monsters of Jacian folklore, the ones that could never be killed because they buried their hearts in secret boxes.

"I'm safely out of reach," I said. "I'll give you that much. I can't conspire with the Osmanthians or be used by them. Not from here."

I slipped another chestnut in my cheek. "Why don't you just try talking to them? Hear them out. Not everything has to be an all-out war."

"She ripped my arm out of its socket."

"That's awful," I said. "Unforgivable. Almost as awful and unforgivable as you throwing me off the top of a tower."

Vesper glowered. "I banished one Kraken from Jace. I can banish another."

She cinched the bag of roasted chestnuts shut, though we hadn't finished them. She tossed it down on the postmaster's desk.

I figured the chestnuts, imported from beyond the city dome, were Vesper's way of paying me back for my finger.

She didn't stop there. She motioned me over to the open space of the lobby. She ported in a jade green bathtub filled to the brim with steaming water.

She floated expectantly by the bathtub, arms crossed, until I resigned myself to my fate and began stripping.

I had no idea where she'd found this bathtub, with its elaborate scaled legs and feet. She must've borrowed its contents from the hot springs run by water imps.

I tried to step in delicately, but the tub was too full. Water sloshed over the rim, soaking the already-moldy carpet. I sank in all the way up to the middle of my neck.

I was hesitant to submerge my left hand until Vesper grabbed it and thrust it under.

For the first few seconds of being immersed in hot water, the stump of my finger felt like it was gushing blood again.

I didn't realize I'd complained out loud—no words, just anguished grunts—till Vesper shushed me. Magic flowed from her hand into mine. Bit by bit, the misery dwindled.

I didn't try to shake her off. I didn't ask her for space. There was a lot I could've said, but I held my tongue.

My long-term goal was to lull Vesper into letting her guard down.

She'd seen my attempts at forging weaponry. She'd have predicted it even if I took pains to hide them from her. So I hadn't bothered.

Better to leave the threat out in the open. Let her witness my primitive tools in all their glory. She wouldn't be inclined to take them seriously. And the less seriously she took my pitiful gestures at resistance, the better positioned I'd be when the time came to act.

As I scrubbed myself, I asked Vesper to tell me more about her latest skirmish with the Kraken.

Her mood darkened. She claimed she'd only lost her arm because Wist had ambushed her in the middle of grappling with a vorpal beast. A sky serpent of tremendous proportions, easily large enough to have swallowed a third of the city.

"Not a good sign that she already managed to hurt you so badly," I said.

I didn't mention that Wist could probably have hurt her far worse. Wist could have focused much more intently on that key spot near the small of her back.

"I told you—"

"Think of the last Kraken." I tipped my head forward to scour the back of my neck. Steam filled my face. "She'll become stronger each time you fight her. As she learns your capabilities."

At first Vesper didn't say anything.

Then, incredulous: "Are you trying to give me advice?"

"Just talking as I wash."

"Why?"

"You've successfully brainwashed me," I said. Let her have a taste of her own sarcasm. "I'm telling you, those Osmanthians aren't here to launch an invasion. That alone makes them very different from the previous Kraken."

I dipped backwards to wet my hair. Vesper studied me with an aura of blatant suspicion.

"You weren't with them very long," she said. "How'd you get so chummy?"

"Let's see." I pretended to ponder. "The only other sentient being in the city seems bent on holding me captive, torturing me, killing me, or all three."

"Right," she agreed, unmoved. "Hate me. Spit at me. Poke me with those stupid prison shivs you've been whittling. That's all between us. Doesn't give you a reason to believe anything those foreigners claim."

"I'm not blindly believing them," I said patiently. "Look at it from their perspective."

"Ugh."

"If they wanted to attack Jace itself, no need to bother with Glorybower. In fact, Glorybower staying sealed under the dome is the best outcome they could hope for."

Vesper made a show of pretending not to listen. I continued anyway.

"If they came to invade, they could go straight for the capital. Even assuming they stopped by to see what's going on in Glorybower first, there'd be no reason for them to stay."

I hunched over to clean my toes as I spoke. They were permanently stained the same hard red-black hue as my fingers.

"The Osmanthians have learned that you and I are at odds. Solitaire is out of my reach. The city walls seem pretty damn solid. And you've shown little interest in either opening the city up or getting involved in current affairs.

"To sum it up: if their real goal was to conquer Jace, they'd get right to it. They'd wave a merry goodbye and leave Glorybower secure in your care."

"You only become this talkative," Vesper said, "when you have an agenda."

I lifted my hands. Water poured through my fingers. "I speak as a simple observer."

"You seem to have an opinion about how I should handle them." She reclined amid the steam wafting toward the ceiling, head resting on her hand. "Go on. Say it."

"You'll struggle to get the best of this Kraken," I told her. "The only sure victory lies in eating me whole, or using Solitaire."

"No." A voice like the lash of a whip.

"Then you should give up on outright murdering them. If she's truly of the same caliber as the original Kraken, the odds are against you. Even if you succeeded, it might backfire. These two must be pretty important people over on the continent."

"When did you become such a pacifist?" Vesper asked. "Brute force suits you better than babbling, love."

"Don't aim to kill them," I said, undeterred by her heckling. "Aim to drive them away from the city. Make them decide that the effort it takes to work around you isn't worth their while.

"Give them just enough trouble that they turn around and give up. Same as the previous Kraken."

I climbed out of the dragon-legged tub. The carpet felt disgusting underfoot, spongy and icy cold.

I stood there naked, left hand twinging, droplets rolling down me, unembarrassed. I wasn't the one who'd whipped this bathtub out of nowhere and insisted on using it right here, right now.

"A towel might be nice," I said.

Vesper eyed my gooseflesh. She eyed other things, too.

She still lay in the steamy space just above the pale jade lip of the tub. I took a step nearer, close enough to drip on the shreds of her jacket. The lobby carpet squelched nauseatingly whenever I moved.

The sound of the rain had vanished at some point, leaving a moody and humid twilight. Copious condensation had collected on the insides of the windows, even those half-broken.

Vesper rolled onto her back.

She'd only roused a few of the water-lights over by the front counter. In their muted glow, I cast an indistinct shadow when I bent over her. Beads of cooling water dripped from the ends of my hair onto her neck.

"Could always dry myself on what's left of your jacket," I said. "I don't mind."

She grimaced theatrically and sat up, hovering level with me.

My hands were still warm, albeit wrinkly from my bath. It would be a simple matter to slip them under her flight jacket, to find the exposed skin just below her diagonal rows of gills.

It would be a simple matter to grab her by the sides and dunk her in the hot bath.

Vesper would be expecting me to stab her in the back. She wouldn't expect a dumb prank. Or for me to yank her closer and actually start rubbing myself dry with her jacket. She'd sputter, all right.

I didn't touch her.

"There's an even easier way to get rid of the Osmanthians," I added. Might as well say it. "Take me to Solitaire."

"Nice try."

"We could use Solitaire to force them to surrender and flee."

"Over my dead body."

Vesper whipped a fresh towel out of an invisible pocket of air and thrust it in my face as if to smother me.

24

BEFORE VESPER LEFT that night, I asked once more if I had ever tried to seduce her.

She laughed as if this were a joke that would never get old. "You? The pure and noble hero?"

She brought her hands together.

The jade bathtub evaporated. The carpet remained horribly soaked. It exuded the gamy scent of a wet ferret.

"You call me a demon," she said. "Something otherworldly. Something dangerous. A vorpal parasite. An invasive species. Isn't it more likely that *I* seduced you?"

With one last look of unadulterated contempt, she ported away.

I inhaled the lobby's thick fragrance: dead carpet mingled with burgeoning mold. Something heavy weighed in my stomach.

Once fully dressed, I went back up to the abattoir to resume preparations.

I made a cursory attempt to count the days that followed. With each new sunrise, I lined up another rusty paperclip on the postmaster's desk.

In idle moments, I pondered whether Vesper had given any real thought to my advice. Which, though self-interested, had been genuine.

Nothing good would come of massacring the Osmanthians. More to the point, I didn't think she could do it. Not without overclocking.

Vesper was far too proud to come back and beg for more than the finger I'd already given her. Not unless the new Kraken left her on the verge of death. Maybe not even then.

Nowadays she might think nothing of killing me from time to time. Perhaps in a fit of irritation. Perhaps just to show me my place.

But she would never lick a single drop of my blood without an explicit invitation. Even if she needed it. Even if she desperately craved it.

No matter how much had changed between us since my previous awakenings, she still showed no interest in crossing that final line. She wouldn't consume me unless I offered myself up on a platter.

The rusty paperclips on the postmaster's desk increased one by one.

During a succession of rainy days, I brought vats and pans and wheelbarrow-like carts out of the abattoir. I used them to collect water from leaky windows and the thresholds of open doors.

I didn't need it for drinking. It would likely make me sick if I tried. Just didn't want to sit around waiting for Vesper to conjure up another bathtub. I could make rudimentary efforts to stay clean in the meantime.

One morning, bright sunlight spilled inside even as rain pattered at the walls.

Demon tears, I thought. The Old Jacian name for a sun shower.

It was not a particularly flattering phrase. The tears of a demon: as strange and untrustworthy as rain on a sunny day.

The stump of my left pinky throbbed, though perhaps not as much as it should have. Vesper had jammed a lot of desensitizing magic inside it. Enough to mask the worst attacks of lancing pain.

As long as I kept myself busy. The moment I stopped moving the rest of my body, the veil of numbness started to slip. Thousand-degree metal spewed through the fine bones of my hand.

I kept busy.

I wasn't completely alone. Blue-black swallows nested in the rafters of a grand crumbling wing off to one side of the abattoir. An intake area connected to empty livestock pens. It was in considerably worse shape than the customer-facing parts of the building.

Winter lizards sometimes followed me, as if drawn to my warmth. I discovered an old and very long snake skin in an overgrown corner of the postmaster's office.

A sluggish shield bug crept in through the front door. After a day or two of clinging to the wall nearby, it stopped moving altogether. But it still hung there. I greeted it every morning.

My observational skills grew increasingly attuned to insects in general. The dead leaves and stray twigs and puffy mushrooms that accumulated in dank corners of the building all turned out to be well-camouflaged bugs.

One evening, an unseasonal mosquito disguised as a butterfly alighted on my wrist. It began helping itself to a long drink, bold as you please. It wasn't subtle, with big purple-azure wings.

The trick worked, though. I couldn't bring myself to slap it.

I found myself faintly jealous of the mosquito's single-minded quest to consume. The days would go by faster if I were forced to feed myself. If I were more driven by bodily needs in general.

I did consider trying to eat more. A cluster of quince trees grew outside one end of the building. Their bright yellow lumps appeared fully ripe. I might be able to stretch out a window and snag one or two before Vesper's magic kicked me back to another room. Delicious though they looked, though, I didn't think it was the sort of fruit one was supposed to eat raw.

I left the remainder of Vesper's chestnuts untouched.

In her absence, I had nothing but spare time. I did my share of heavier muscle-building exercises. But I also spent hours striding loops out the front door.

I'd walk the length of the lobby, step through the door, get ported back to the end of the lobby, and then do it all over again.

There was no real purpose to this. It was more of a compulsion, or a ritual.

Sometimes I scrutinized my meager collection of rust-red paperclips. I counted them, and I mentally calculated how much more time Vesper had spent waiting while I slept in Solitaire's cockpit.

In all my exploring, there were a few places I never ventured. The chilling room at the back of the upstairs slaughterhouse. The black box of space directly beneath the slaughterhouse, surrounded by mail sorting rooms.

That black box went all the way down to the basement. The abattoir's many tubes and floor drains and chutes all led to the same place.

It was not, in the end, a facility meant solely or even primarily to process meat. Any byproducts destined for the neighborhood butcher or chophouse were at most a tidy little side business.

This was a post office. One that ran on magic propped up by a constant stream of blood and offal, of meticulously calibrated sacrifice.

If even a single piece of that magic remained functional, I could in theory attempt to mail myself away like an oversize package.

I could route myself through the sorting rooms and into the hidden space below the abattoir. I could pour my own blood into the transport mechanism. Or chop off a hand. Whatever it took.

The dregs of old magic underpinning the postal system might succeed in slipping me through the bars of Vesper's cage.

Or not. The only way to find out was to give it a try.

But I was tired of spilling my own blood.

Instead I spent a day going around with a pan, collecting those matte-scaled winter lizards. They were slow-moving, easily lured by body heat, and utterly unafraid of me. They crawled clumsily over each other. No interest in escaping.

I imagined dumping them in the express mail chamber with the dead stock-elk. I imagined pouring them down one of the abattoir's many discolored chutes.

I set the pan down on the floor.

I let the lizards go.

Maybe this was why Vesper had imprisoned me in a post office, rather than in a bank vault. Or an actual jail cell. Maybe she'd wanted to put these thoughts in my head.

What would you do to escape?

Maybe she'd fantasized about trapping me here during her fifty years at the bloody back of Solitaire's cockpit. Never dying and never fully healing. Getting slowly masticated by a sleeping giant. Stretching toward my peaceful form up ahead of her in the pilot's seat, silently and blissfully hibernating.

I kept waiting for Vesper to show up again.

I kept wondering what she was doing—traveling the outside world, or harassing Asa and Wist, or banishing vicious vorpal beasts from her city.

I didn't dream, because I didn't sleep. But sometimes I fell into a fugue-like stupor.

I couldn't tell what had really happened—be it in the near or distant past—and what my mind invented to torment me.

I rubbed fretfully at the stump of my finger. It felt like rubbing the end of a thick stick of broken chalk.

Without Vesper here to openly mock me, my brain seemed determined to get the job done itself.

There had been times when I'd seen her burnt beyond recognition, and vice versa. There had been times when I caught some deadly fever, and she raged at local doctors to save me.

Now that I thought about it—what had she been so worried about? Vesper herself seemed immune to human illness. If I died, I'd come back clear of the sickness. All she had to do was wait. Or smother me in the night, if she really couldn't stand to see me suffering.

There had been times when we hunted down rogue pockets of mages on icy mountaintops. When even my tougher-than-normal human body got too cold to keep moving.

Vesper, though exhausted, lit a black fire strong enough to melt the entire clearing. She held me tight enough to make my bones creak, as if sheer force would warm me faster.

Now that I thought about it, simply thrusting me closer to the scorching fire would've been more efficient. She could've levitated me above the flames and turned me like a pig on a spit.

Instead she'd held me. Because she thought I would prefer that? Because I'd demanded it?

Sixteen more days passed in the post office.

Sixteen more days surrounded by the lush mind-numbing chorus of Jacian turtle doves cooing outside.

Sixteen more days of striding through splintered memories and mulling over my options for escape.

Option one. Kill Vesper. The hardest route, but the only one guaranteed to work.

Option two. Maim myself; drain my own blood into the bowels of the abattoir. Mail myself, if I were lucky, to another district. The city walls would stop me from going any further.

Option three. Sacrifice wildlife in order to mail myself. Birds, squirrels, those gullible lizards—whatever I could get my hands on from inside the post office. As many of them as I needed.

I might've been more inclined to slaughter small animals if success were a sure thing. But I didn't want to kill them (or injure myself) for nothing.

I hadn't shut myself up in here on purpose. The creatures nesting in and around the building didn't have anything to do with it, either. It wasn't their fault.

It all came back to Vesper.

Around sunrise of the seventeenth day since the last time I'd seen her, I walked my usual loops through the lobby.

My gaze kept straying back to one of the faded Jacian flags hanging on the post office wall. The largest and least frayed.

I couldn't articulate what had caught my attention. Something indefinable about it had changed.

Yet I could swear that the sun-bleached colors and its positioning on the wall and the lines of its chalice emblem remained exactly the same as before.

I asked the dead shield bug by the door if it had noticed anything unusual. No answer came.

I stopped walking my well-worn loop. I was starting to grind a distinct path down the middle of the much-abused carpet.

I went up to the flag on the wall.

A tiny spider-thread of magic floated in front of it, weightless. Perfectly calibrated to catch my notice without drawing attention to its own existence. A magic meant to say *look at this*, without giving the slightest hint of why.

The fabric flag was as large as a castle tapestry. I lifted the bottom right corner.

On the wall beneath, someone or something had scratched a single clumsy word in Continental script.

Tomorrow.

My esophagus heaved.

There was nothing in my stomach to retch up. Much as it might try.

Tomorrow.

Poor Vesper, I thought.

This one word, crudely written, was what finally convinced me. Wist—Wisteria Shien—was indeed the second coming of the Kraken.

Or simply a second Kraken, with no deeper connection to the first.

Whatever the case, she possessed power befitting her title. Maybe, as Vesper had theorized, one of them would pop up every millennium or so. Like a thousand-year earthquake, or a thousand-year storm, or a comet crossing the visible sky at vast intervals.

Wist the Kraken had seen past whatever Vesper had done to disguise this place. The Osmanthians knew my location. They might've known it from the start.

Tomorrow.

Up in the express mail room, I looked at the glass-enclosed stock-elk.

I asked: "What would you do?"

Silence reigned.

There must've been herds of stock-elks out on those verdant hills, back in the day. Perhaps just outside the city border. Far enough from here to escape the dome.

Or perhaps they'd been sealed in together with the rest of the populace. Perhaps something supernatural had swept through to eradicate them. Perhaps those richly fertilized grasses grew atop piles of bones.

Even if I never again fought for Jace, even if this were a long-awaited age of eternal world peace, even if no one wanted or needed an obsolete Host, I didn't wish to live as Vesper's hostage. Or her captive. Or her pet.

Rich of you to say, Vesper might tell me.

If I played my cards right, Vesper wouldn't get a chance to do much complaining.

25

IT HAPPENED right on schedule. I was up in the abattoir when I heard a thump from downstairs.

I dashed down to the lobby. Nothing.

After some searching, I found Vesper in one of the mail sorting rooms.

She lay on a mound of decaying boxes.

Not in the stagnant space above the boxes. On them. Directly touching them. Her dead weight made the putrefied cardboard slump inward.

The air was so still that it refused to enter my lungs.

I should've approached her with caution. But I was already there, lugging her off the boxes before the rest of them—piled up high on either side—could form a landslide to drown her.

She collapsed forward onto my shoulders.

A metal stake wedged itself at an angle in her back. It had just missed her weak spot. Frantic bone growths surrounded it, deformed spurs and stunted horns and broken plates striped with still-wet rivulets of dark blue. The last-second explosion of bone must've been just enough to divert the stake to a less deadly trajectory.

Either that, or her attacker had missed on purpose.

Vesper's hand tried to tighten on my clothing. She lacked the strength to really grab at me.

"You told them," she said to the side of my neck. Her voice cracked. "You told them how to kill me."

She sounded betrayed.

My mind went dry and cold. My sympathy for her condition immediately shriveled.

"You've set yourself up as my enemy since the moment you woke me," I said. "Why wouldn't I tell them your weakness? They've known it since the temple. What other recourse did you leave me?"

I couldn't see her face.

Vesper didn't respond. Her arms grasped their way haltingly around my neck. The bottoms of her feet had turned a flayed bloody blue.

We were still on the lichen-eaten ground by the sorting room entrance. Hopefully far enough from the mess inside to avoid any future avalanche of boxes. I slipped an arm under Vesper's knees and got to my feet with a grunt, heaving her with me.

Even with the frenetic new burst of protective bone structures radiating from her back, she felt lighter than I remembered. No clue what I was remembering it from, though. Vesper had always been the one to carry me, to take arrows and bullets for me.

I started to really feel the strain once I began lifting her up the stairs. She mumbled incoherently as I jostled her.

I drank heavy breaths. I leaned on the creaking railing for some modicum of support. I kept going.

When I glanced back, a trail of inky blue-black blood spotted the steps. Vesper clung to me as if she'd forgotten who I was.

I realized three things during the interminable journey up to the higher floors. To the slaughterhouse.

One: Vesper hadn't used any magic whatsoever since landing in the sorting room. She was completely burnt out.

Two: She wore civilian clothes now, something I'd never seen before. Ruined and bloody. Then again, her old chalice suit had been in even worse shape.

Three: The metal stake in her back came from the fountain in the plaza. I knew that knobby spiral shape. It was the snapped-off tip of the tall, tall needle at the heart of the fountain.

Which meant that Wist and Asa could cross the moat around the plaza with magic. (But of course they could.)

Unlike me, they could still go near Solitaire.

They could take me there.

I stopped for a quick breather at the top of the stairs, in the hall outside the abattoir entrance.

I'd set a couple of crumbling cinderblocks to prop open the reinforced door to the express mail room. I accidentally whacked Vesper's ankles on the blocks as I eased us down in the doorway.

She made a vague noise of complaint, but much too quietly and much too late.

She kept hanging onto my neck even as I lowered myself to the floor. Fine by me. I'd meant to keep her in my lap anyway. Something seemed wrenchingly wrong about Vesper being forced to touch ground.

Cold sunrise light radiated in through a misted-over window at the other end of the hall. The bright incisive scent of demon blood cut through the air between us, intense enough to sting my nose.

The movement of breath in and out of her lungs was soft and palpable against me.

I asked her if she wanted me to yank the metal stake out of her back.

"Bad idea," Vesper mumbled into my collarbone.

"Does it hurt?"

"Can't you tell?" She pulled back a little, raised her head to look at me. She had her hands braced on my shoulders, but I couldn't feel the warning prick of her nails. "Would you be happy if it hurt me more?"

I'd bet the Osmanthians were perfectly capable of tracking her. They knew where to find me. They could arrive at any moment.

But if they planned on interrupting, there was no reason for them not to have shown up already.

Unless they were avoiding the post office on purpose. Unless they were purposely leaving Vesper's fate in my hands. For now, anyway.

"Ves," I said. "Let's make a deal."

She gave a sleepy blink.

"Let me out of here, and I'll feed you." I spoke slowly. It was hard to tell how much she understood. "As much as you need. Any part of my body you want." As a reminder, I showed her the stump of my missing finger. "All I ask is that you let me out of this building."

Still clutching me, Vesper turned her head laboriously to one side.

As if she'd planned it, she leaned over and vomited deep blue blood on the smooth-tiled floor.

It was shockingly quiet and quick. Before I even registered what had happened, she'd turned back to me, wiping her mouth with the end of a dark sleeve. Her sleeves came all the way up to her knuckles, with a hole at the end for her thumb. A blue haze of smeared blood clung to her cheek.

"No," she said.

Did she even comprehend what she was saying no to?

"You can't use magic right now," I said. "You're a mess. You might take weeks to recover. If you eat from me—if you overclock—you'll be back to your strongest self in a manner of seconds.

"Then you can chase me down all over again. It'll be laughably easy. I'm not even asking for a head start. I just want you to let me out of the post office."

She shook her head mutely.

"If you're afraid of me teaming up with the Osmanthians, you should be extra motivated to send me away."

I enunciated as if pressing the words into her flesh one by one, forcing her to understand. "They know we're here. If we take too long to come out, eventually they'll decide to break in."

Vesper took my hand, the one with the missing pinky. She cupped her own hands around it. The stump ached in a way that I felt all the way to the roots of my teeth.

So too, for a brief dire moment, did an illusion of my lost finger. It burned there, cradled between her palms. I grit my back molars together.

She wasn't rational. She wasn't getting it. I wanted to grab her and shake her.

Maybe I wasn't rational, either. I could drive a much harder bargain. I ought to be demanding much more from her.

I reached sideways and scraped my forearm on the rough corner of one of the cinderblocks. I showed Vesper the stark scratches it left, the tiny pinheads of fresh welling blood.

"All you have to do is let me out."

No matter how you sliced it, she ought to be the one begging me right now. But it was my voice that shook.

Her pupils had gone very round and large and black. She tilted toward my scraped-up forearm as if tugged in by gravity, nose almost bumping the base of my wrist, blue-crusted lips excruciatingly close to the searing stripes of reddened skin.

Her breath touched me.

Her mouth didn't.

"You can't trick me," she said gently, almost pityingly. "I'll never let you go."

"Vesper!"

I hadn't meant to be so loud. I'd cried out as if I were the one who'd tumbled here half-dead, as if I were the one with a metal stake impaling my back and hot stomach-blood splattering the floor inches away from us.

She patted me tenderly on the cheek. I could've strangled her.

If Vesper wouldn't make a bargain to release me now—temporarily, in her weakest state, in her moment of greatest need and desperation—then she truly would never let me go. Not even to save herself. Not even to end her own agony.

I leaned Vesper on my shoulder and carried her into the abattoir. Into the express mail room with its intimidatingly tall walls, and a ceiling too high up to see in detail.

She held onto me without complaining. I couldn't be sure that she knew where she was, or what was happening.

I bore her over to the yellow warning line around the two globular glass chambers. My heart struck a hard angry beat. My body had shed its last scrap of exhaustion like snakeskin.

I set Vesper on the far side of the warning line. Her upper back touched the curved glass wall that sealed off the long-dead corpse of a young stock-elk.

Vesper stayed in place as I stepped back. She didn't whine about getting dumped on the ground. She followed my movements with disinterested eyes.

Water-light played over her from tubes winding beneath the see-through floor. The water-light stirred more than she did.

I'd left a number of jury-rigged implements leaning up against the wall by the door. I went over to fetch a crude sledgehammer.

Vesper didn't ask what I meant to use it for. It didn't seem to occur to her to wonder.

Would she be more amenable to striking deals with me if she had all her wits about her? If she were less intoxicated by the physical shock of her injuries? If she could scrape together at least enough magic to push herself back up into the air, her natural habitat?

I crouched in front of her. I set the head of the sledgehammer down between us. I handled it with exaggerated care, but it still made the floor tremble a bit. Vesper didn't so much as twitch in response.

"You refuse to let me go," I said.

She regarded me with heavy-lidded eyes. She regarded me as if I were a simpleton.

"Why?" I asked calmly.

"You let—" she coughed. "You let yourself forget too much. You can't be trusted. And I promised."

My fists convulsed tighter around the handle of the would-be sledgehammer. A broken pole I'd scavenged from the back of the slaughterhouse.

"Promised what? To who?"

"Verity," she bit out. "Can't let you forget Verity. You keep coming closer and closer to—"

She broke down coughing again.

I'd stopped listening. *That* was her reason for swearing to never let me sleep again, never hibernate, never use Solitaire, never regain control of my fate?

Verity?

It couldn't be a matter of abiding love and respect for her long-lost gate. Not after all these years. It couldn't be a matter of personal pride or honor.

It had to be something more alien, more binding. A demonic contract.

A promise exchanged at the moment of Vesper's creation, or once we used Verity as a gate enough times to finally destroy her.

I couldn't argue with something so far beyond my comprehension. I couldn't reason with Vesper about the merits of breaking a demon's sacred vow to her dead human gate.

If slamming Vesper's head back against the shimmering glass would make any difference, I'd do it. No hesitation.

If I could open her eyes by telling her to feast on me right here and now, no strings attached—I'd clench my teeth, and then I'd say it. I'd welcome her fangs.

But there was only one option left, really.

I'd wanted so badly not to stick to my original plan.

I rose heavily, taking my homemade sledgehammer with me. I held it two-handed. I braced my feet behind the yellow strip on the floor. Fifty years had done little to dim it.

The entire room was infused with layer upon layer upon layer of old human magic. At least some of the contributors must still be alive outside Glorybower. Magic would vanish with the death of its creator, after all.

Perhaps they'd shipped in bits and pieces of these enchantments from all across Jace. From now-retired mages who had no idea that the products of their labor still gleamed in the slaughterhouse of an empty post office of an abandoned city.

My lungs felt filled to bursting. Yet I'd gone light-headed. Vesper kept watching me.

I raised the sledgehammer up high. I brought it down as hard as I could on the sacrificial glass globe behind her.

26

IF I EVER IMAGINED IT, I had imagined her fighting back.

If I were lucky, she'd come to me at a disadvantage. Battered and weary from tangling with the Kraken or invasive vorpal beasts. Shedding blue. In worse shape than she'd been when I gave her my finger.

That much had come true. But I'd imagined her being warier, bristling in a corner. Certainly not willing to let me carry her.

We'd both throw punches. Vesper would have her claws out. I'd be forced to slam her into the wall hard enough to crack a human skull.

Even if she'd gotten injured badly enough to be grounded, even if she couldn't scrounge up enough magic to draw the swords from her head, I'd thought her combative instincts would kick in at some point while I held her.

In reality she didn't fight me. But she didn't agree to free me, either.

Shrapnel rained on Vesper when my sledgehammer shattered the glass chamber behind her. She ducked, arms raised to protect herself.

Sledgehammer in hand, I backed up to the safety of the propped-open entrance.

The silence after the glass breaking felt like the silence after a bomb going off. Like something was wrong with my ears. My palms were hopelessly damp, but the rest of me had gone arid and stiff. The short breaths I exhaled were the warmest part of the room.

The empty crystal bulb on the right remained whole. I'd only smashed the one on the left.

Vesper hadn't moved from the far side of the yellow line. Showered in specks of glass, she cautiously lowered her arms. She shook herself like a dog. She looked across at me.

The bladed structures inside the wreckage of the glass had, in turn, already started looking at her.

The killing machina struck before her eyes met mine, before she could speak.

It was a mechanism much like the interior of Solitaire's cockpit. It went for open wounds first—for the metal spire stabbing her, and the mess of blood-streaked bony scales guarding her back.

I hadn't thought I could break through that armor on my own. Not without Vesper reaching up to slash my head off in retaliation.

The thing in the cracked-open glass shell plunged at her weak spot with the force of a pile driver.

The drill plummeted through her back, meeting zero resistance. The rest of her body jumped with the force of it. The floor shook.

The sledgehammer slipped from my grip, slick with sweat, and crashed at my feet.

Rebellious magic arced across the hungry machina as it dragged Vesper through fallen glass, dragged her inside like a trophy. It tossed her on top of the deflated stock-elk carcass, a picked-over skeleton with only meager scrapes of hide.

Clanking. Hissing. Shaking. Metal grating against metal.

Vesper started to push herself up. The machina stabbed her down flat again. Magic flared from her upper back in a shape like wings, like her soul trying to escape her body.

The thing picking at her was attempting to eviscerate her in the same way it had eviscerated the stock-elk. It shuddered violently as her last-ditch detonation of magic seeped in through its seams.

It started to rattle itself apart, slumping, stray blades dropping. It ground to a halt in the middle of slicing her open.

A fleeting shadow passed over the tiny high windows ringing the room like merciless eyes. Vesper's wards lifting. Her cage around the building breaking down.

I could leave now.

The plan was to turn around and run while I still could. Vesper would be back. No matter how it looked. Like it or not, Vesper always came back for me.

Approaching her body was very much not a part of my plan. Much too dangerous.

For safety's sake, I should've fled the abattoir as soon as I smashed open the glass orb around the dead stock-elk. I knew what the device inside could do to me if I came within reach. I'd flown Solitaire enough times. I could extrapolate.

Yet here I was, back at the neon yellow line, my own breathing as harsh as sandpaper in my ears. My boots crunched on glass.

Vesper lay with her face turned away from me, half her hair drenched murky blue.

In her dying paroxysm of magic, she'd demolished the bloodthirsty machina. Its fallen parts—still unnaturally clean and gleaming—had splintered and dented the glass-strewn floor all around her.

I took a step across the yellow line.

Part of me was bracing myself for the device to surge back to life and knife me in the gut. Part of me had, perhaps, hoped for it. Part of me might've thought I deserved it.

Nothing punctured me. Stray glass slipped and crackled underfoot as I moved closer to Vesper. She was draped half on top of the dessicated stock-elk, like she'd thrown herself there to beg a butcher to spare it.

A piercing pain lanced through my watch.

I froze in place. I knew at once that I'd felt this exact sensation before, and simultaneously that I hadn't felt it in a very long time.

Another pang. Not in my muscle, not in my bone. In the metallic watch chained to my navel. Cold and hard and an inextricable part of my body.

It ached with a rhythm like someone banging on a door to get out. Like my faltering heart had fled down through the chain to reside there.

I fumbled to pull the watch higher, pull it to where I could see it. My hand shook. The concentric markings were shot through with fault lines. Cracks. As though I'd taken a hammer to it.

I dropped the watch. I stooped to touch Vesper's shoulder. Still faintly warm. I started trying to turn her over.

Took several minutes to realize that it wasn't happening. It was never happening. I couldn't turn her. The machina had drilled her to the floor.

The back of the watch burned against the clammy skin of my stomach. It burned as if I'd poured lava down my throat with a funnel. I doubled over, almost stumbling on Vesper's corpse.

I remembered another time I'd felt a shadow of this vertigo in my chain, in my watch.

I sank down next to Vesper. I held her limp arm for no reason. She didn't know I was there. She couldn't feel me touching her. She couldn't feel anything. I sank down until my forehead met her shoulder.

27

I REMEMBERED—

Vesper in old-style formal wear. A gown the color of morning glories.

After we left the banquet, she'd bundled up her long skirts and tied them behind her like a puffy tail.

She'd ripped off her shoes and flung them over her shoulder without looking back.

Now she glided in the air alongside me again. Now there was no longer any need to blend in.

The mansion on the hill behind us glowed with fire in the night. Confused summer flake-flies drifted past us, heading back the way we'd come, drawn to the screaming and the light.

"Ves," I said.

"What?"

"Did I ever make you do something like that before?"

She wiped her mouth before speaking. "Kill a man in front of his grade-school-aged children?" Her tone remained pointedly neutral. "No."

A pang like a stomach cramp shot through my watch.

He had been a traitor. Or an insidious criminal. Or some other sort of enemy. He'd taken the attendees of his own party hostage. Tried to execute them one by one. Until Vesper executed him instead.

Or maybe I was getting him mixed up with someone else.

Later, in a large bed, in a room with an unlit fireplace, I turned and asked her why she'd done it. Why she'd instantly followed my orders. Why she'd bitten the man's throat out where his children could see it happening. Why she hadn't tried to reason with me first.

Vesper looked at me with large-eyed incredulity. "You think I should've refused? You think I should've stopped you?"

I shook my head and rolled onto my back. I should've said those words to myself, not to Vesper.

We were in bed to rest, to lie low. Neither of us required sleep. But for me, at least, it was best to give the illusion of needing it.

My head ached like hell. My skull seemed to crunch inward on itself as if striving to lacerate my soft defenseless brain.

Jeweled stalactites grew down from the tall ceiling above. They winked in the light of the full moon, which washed in like a high tide through windows framed by layer upon layer of lavish fabric. Each curtain was practically a full-blown tapestry in its own right.

The room smelled of incense—like temples, funerals, autumn graveyards, family shrines.

Vesper placed a cool hand on my forehead. The pain receded.

"I'm sorry," I said. "I know you can't refuse an order from your Host."

Vesper lay down next to me. She still wore the same intensely purple dress. She didn't seem to care much about whether she wrinkled it. She clasped my hand in hers.

"But I can," she said quietly. "I can always refuse. You know that."

With my other hand, I touched the same part of my forehead that she'd touched to soothe me. Somehow it didn't have at all the same effect.

"Do I?" I asked. "Was I supposed to know that?"

"It's the same as overclocking. It's the same as you offering me your flesh. Did I ever feed on you by force? No. And you've never forced me to follow any orders against my will. Not this time. Not ever."

"I—"

Vesper's fingers tightened on mine. "I've told you that many times," she added. "You have a habit of forgetting. You have this bizarre need to consider yourself solely responsible."

"If I'm telling you what to do—"

"You never forced me."

"Doesn't change much," I objected. "If I gave the order, that means it was my decision. My idea. If something goes horribly wrong in the course of battle, who do you blame? Dying soldiers? Or the general who sent them out there?"

The bed shifted. Vesper had sat up. Only now did I realize she was actually putting her weight on it, rather than hovering casually above the covers.

"You might be my Host," she said, "but I never made you my general. I'm not your fist punching villains in the face. I'm not your hand holding the knife to fillet our enemies.

"And I'm not human. I can't guess at where decorum wants you to draw the line. You can't demand that of me."

The gown had slipped down off her left shoulder. She saw me looking. She saw me wondering why I couldn't help looking even at a time like this. My watch ached in a different way, ached as if some crucial part of it were missing.

Her bearing changed. She reached under my loose nightshirt and dragged the watch up to her face, unspooling the retractable chain, stretching it taut.

Her lips touched the heated rim of the watch, and I felt it. Her fingertips ran along the length of the delicate chain, and I cried out, uncalled-for tears springing to my eyes at the sudden intensity of it, at how wholly my body lay in her hands.

Much later, soaked in moonlight and half-drunk on the lingering aroma of incense, I asked: "We really did this before?"

Vesper was still happily teething at every part of me she could get her mouth on, though she remained careful not to puncture skin.

She lifted her head from my stomach to speak. "Twenty years ago. And a century before that. Plenty of times. I wasn't originally a creature of this corporeal world, you know. I used to be very shy and pure."

"Impossible."

"It's your fault. You usually came on to me first."

"Hard to believe," I said, "after seeing how thrilled you were to nibble my toes."

"Don't tempt me to have another go at them."

But most of the times when my watch clenched with pain, it was because I'd begun to lose myself in other ways.

I asked Vesper over and over: would I have been this cruel in previous awakenings? Would my past self have so readily urged her to overclock?

When had I started to change? Was it experience that altered me—the smoke of pillaged towns, the stench of roasting bodies, seeing the shunning of the ill—or was it something else?

When I pulled Vesper down out of the air and embraced her, when she laughed at me, when we wrestled each other across every imaginable type of furniture, she felt so human to me. More human than I felt to myself.

I'd promised her to stop hibernating. I'd promised her that many times, hadn't I? I'd promised her to stop forgetting so much. I'd promised her to stop losing pieces of myself.

No.

No—I was getting it all wrong again. It was the other way around.

With each awakening, I grew more frigid, more alien. Had I always been that way, or had something fundamentally human been eroded out of me during all those interminable centuries of thoughtless sleep?

I clung to Vesper. I held her tight, much tighter than it would've been safe to hold a human being. I didn't want to let her go.

I didn't want to keep losing the memory of her mouth on my countdown clock and behind my ear. Those little fangs peeking out when she smiled to herself. The eyes I loved—the eyes I loved so much—shining in our shared darkness.

I'd told her: do whatever she needed to do to stop me from changing. You're a demon, I'd said to her. I know you can do it.

I'd made her promise me she'd try.

I'd made her promise me with the full knowledge that I was already too far gone. I would keep mindlessly forging on toward future awakenings, shedding all unnecessary baggage. I would be incapable of looking back.

"I hate you," she'd murmured, weightless in the air before me.

Her arms came around my neck; her legs curled around my waist as if to trap me in place. She was pressed right up against the watch over my navel. She laid her cheek on my hair.

"I hate you," she repeated, so tenderly that my throat twinged to hear it. "Someday I'll kill you, Char. I swear. You better watch out."

"Well, that's all right," I said.

I never tired of running my hands past her sides, down the delicate open edges of the gills between her ribs.

I tilted my head this way and that until she deigned to show me her face.

"Here's another way to look at it," I said. "I'm the only person in the world you can afford to murder just to blow off steam. Feeling stressed? Feeling unappreciated? Go on, beat me to a pulp. Kill me as much as you like. You know I'll always come back."

Vesper was silent for a moment.

"You have changed," she muttered.

"How so?"

"Your sense of humor has become a hell of a lot more perverted over the years."

"In my defense," I said, "there's only one person who's been with me all this time. Only one possible source of influence."

"I'm not a *person*," Vesper said sourly. She thwacked me none too gently on the back of my head.

28

I HAD LOVED HER, I thought numbly. I had loved her over and over. I'd tied her to me tighter and tighter, with caresses and promises.

How entitled I'd been. It never even occurred to me to consider relinquishing her power, to consider letting her go. As best I could, anyway, with the bond of mutual death still binding us.

Making Vesper—creating a demon for Jace—had in turn made me a national hero.

Consciously or otherwise, I'd seen her magic as my birthright.

Clearly the right thing to do was to keep using it. Clearly the right thing to do was to hibernate until a new batch of needy Jacians roused me. To seize her power to me each time I woke. To save everyone and everything under the implacable sun except for Vesper herself.

I still couldn't argue with that. It seemed like the correct stance.

Humans could withstand so little. A demon could withstand so much.

Yet my stomach churned. My watch cramped like a muscle atrophied from long, long disuse.

I'd loved her. That was the most revolting part of it all. I'd loved her, and I'd carried on doing the right thing anyway. Protecting strangers. Protecting Jacians of the future.

I'd expected Vesper to unquestioningly tolerate the consequences, just as I had. Even if I was in no position to fully comprehend them.

The Osmanthians arrived in the post office abattoir before steam had stopped rising from Vesper's deepest-gouged wounds.

I didn't know either of them well enough to expect any particular reaction.

If I had to guess, I'd have assumed Wist the Kraken would say nothing. Asa might greet me with a flippant remark.

Instead, Asa reached up and took her cap off the moment she saw Vesper. She clutched it to her chest. She crossed the room with quick steps. Wist, who showed no change of expression, was slower to follow.

Asa thrust her cap into Wist's hands as they crossed the yellow line on the floor. She brushed some of the strewn shards of glass away with the side of her shoe. Then she crouched next to Vesper.

She glanced across at me as if asking permission. I motioned for her to go ahead.

I watched with detached curiosity as Asa checked the body. She looked in all the right places, so she had to be somewhat familiar with the process.

Nevertheless, her manner was far from professional. She murmured an apology as she beckoned for Wist to shine a bright magical light in Vesper's eyes.

These two really weren't warriors. Not at all. They had sturdy constitutions for civilians, I guess. Neither had gone pelting out of the room to retch in the hallway. But they weren't used to this.

After a few minutes, Asa drew back. She straightened up shakily, holding Wist's arm.

"You saw our message?" she asked me.

"I saw it."

"We'd hoped to deliver her to you in a much more orderly fashion," she said. "Things got out of control."

"She came to me in the end, though."

Asa took her newsboy cap from Wist and fixed it back on her head. She spent several fussy seconds adjusting its fit. "God, it's cold in here. It doesn't bother you?"

I shook my head. I couldn't feel it.

"Listen," she said brusquely. "Let me be honest. Didn't think you'd straight-up kill your demon. But that's between you and her."

"I've never killed her before."

"Well, no shit."

I got ponderously to my feet. My legs had fallen half-asleep. Chips of glass clung to my flight suit, tinkling down like hail as I moved.

They didn't know about the bond of mutual death.

I still didn't want them to leave the city with the knowledge that I could revive, too, so long as Vesper remained alive. So long as no one killed me this very instant, before she came back.

But it seemed unfair not to warn them that Vesper wouldn't be gone forever.

Besides, Vesper was a demon. People seemed to have an easier time accepting the fact that a demon might not live and die in the same way as the rest of us.

"She'll be back," I said.

Asa contemplated me with undisguised pity.

"It's just her corporeal body that got killed," I continued. "She's a vorpal being. She can't really die."

It wasn't as if there were any other demons they could compare notes with.

"She'll return sooner or later," I warned them. "She'll be in a fury. She'll come find me. And then she'll go after you again."

Asa had a hand over her mouth. She looked much the way she had when she first spotted Vesper's corpse. "Demon death isn't permanent?"

"No."

Neither the truth nor an outright lie. In previous conversations, I'd made no secret of the fact that we were bonded. All I'd done was omit any mention of the unusual role our bond played for us.

As far as I knew, the bond of mutual death was unique to me and Vesper. Something fundamentally different from the bonds between human mages and their operators.

Human bonds ended with death. A human bond would be nullified the instant one partner died, even if the other survived. A cruel and irreversible finality.

Meanwhile, our bond kept going and going, through joy and misery, through war and slumber, through century after century. Vesper being a demon might very well have been the key factor that made this possible.

The Osmanthians were voiceless. Talking to each other in their heads, no doubt.

I knelt to touch Vesper's thumb. She'd gone cool to the touch much faster than a human body.

If she were human, she'd have continued feeling warm for hours. Even with ambient temperatures low enough to whiten my breath.

Asa pulled the neck of her jacket up around her mouth, using it as a makeshift scarf.

"That's one of the great taboos of magic," she said, muffled. "Never revive the dead. Never change the flow of time. Never create new life."

"Guess it must be fine if they just get up and revive on their own," I replied. "Or maybe the taboos are only for human beings."

Glib, yes. I was hoping to keep them from musing too deeply over it.

The great taboos dated back to the era of the original Kraken. Jace, which had never submitted to the rule of the Blessed Empire, took the taboos much less seriously than continental countries.

In a way, the taboos were superfluous to begin with. Only a mage on the level of the Kraken herself had the slightest chance of succeeding in breaking them.

The new Kraken standing gloomily behind Asa seemed unlikely to give it a try. Judging by Asa's tone, at least.

I suppose I'd skirted right on the edge of violating the ancient taboos. Two out of the big three. I wasn't a mage anymore, though. I didn't use what anyone would recognize as regular magic. I had only one power, something illicit gained when they ripped out my magic core.

Creating vorpal beasts and demons might look like a form of creating life. Yet it had never felt that way to me. I wasn't making them from scratch. I pulled them from elsewhere into our world, pulled them into a shape determined by their gate.

The bond of mutual death did come close to really trampling all over the taboo against resurrection.

Then again—maybe it changed depending on how you defined death in the first place.

If Vesper and I were beings with two separate lives, then yes, we'd both died at different times, over and over.

If our lives as Host and demon were seamlessly connected—one in two, two in one, one and the same—then we'd only ever died halfway. Never fully. Never both at once.

Dying a true mutual death, and then coming back anyway: now that would definitely break the taboo against reviving the dead. Assuming the taboo even applied to non-humans, or those from other worlds.

The original Kraken had been the most ardent proponent of protecting the great taboos. But she'd never done a particularly good job of explaining why breaking them would be so terrible.

That's how most of us in Jace had seen it, anyway. Control for the sake of control. Just more of the usual imperial propaganda.

"You killed her knowing—thinking—she'd come back." Asa dragged the toe of her thick-soled shoe through a sprinkling of glass. "Still, though."

She looked at the wreckage littering the room. Glass fallen like fresh snow. My discarded sledgehammer. Sticky gobs of ocean-colored demon blood.

"Still," she repeated. I could see the effort it took for her to control her expression. "No hesitation, huh?"

"I hesitated," I said dully.

"Is that when you lost your finger?"

I glanced at my left hand. I hadn't been trying to hide it. I hadn't been thinking about it at all.

"I lost it to her," I said, "if that's what you're asking."

Vesper's thumb had begun to feel powdery, a texture like the surface of a sculpture carved from the finest of sand. I let go of her and straightened up again. Soon she would dissipate.

Asa had begun to wander around the mail room. She peered with fascination at the water-lights, and at the empty glass chamber to the right of Vesper and the stock-elk. The one still unbroken.

This woman was older than me—physically, if not chronologically—but it felt like watching a child at a carnival.

The evidence suggested that she was quick to recover from shock, and quick to surrender to the tide of a compulsive curiosity. Wist lurked nearby with the air of a nervous guardian, ready to dive in and catch at her if she started doing anything rash.

Asa stood on tiptoe to try to get a better glimpse of the high-up windows.

She yanked aside a black velvet curtain on the wall, revealing a massive map of the Jacian archipelago. Similar to the map printed on my field scarf, but far more detailed, with a thorough list of locations and prices tacked up on one side.

She didn't stare at the list for long. Probably couldn't read Jacian characters.

She fiddled with unresponsive panels next to the empty chamber meant for holding packages. She picked at the yellow strip on the floor.

She stuck her hands in a hermetically sealed glove box whose purpose I'd failed to ever figure out. She poked her head through the back door to peer at the abattoir's more conventionally structured rooms.

"Jacian tech," she said in tones of awe. "Horrific at times, but always remarkable. Fifty years ago, and you already had slaughterhouses fully integrated with your postal system. Incredible."

This got my back up a little. Admittedly, though, I knew nothing of the latest Jacian innovations outside Glorybower.

"You may find it barbaric," I said, "but some of your practices seem just as outlandish to us."

"Oh, sure," Asa agreed. "Look, I'm not judging. I eat meat from time to time. I enjoy a good kebab sandwich. I do question why you felt compelled to subject your companion to—"

"Clem," Wist said sharply.

From the way Asa reacted, that must've been her given name. Or a nickname.

Wist caught her from behind, steered her back to face the mess of broken glass on the left. To face me.

Me and the mound of gray-white ash on the glass-sprinkled floor before me.

When I stuck my hand wrist-deep in the pile of ash that had once been Vesper, the entire heap swirled itself furiously out of existence. It melted away into nothingness as if loathing my touch.

Only a thin floury coating on my palm remained. Then that, too, puffed off my skin. Repelled by me. Tiny grains propelling themselves away to hide in grimy shadows.

I checked my countdown clock again.

"Ten hours till she returns," I said. "Maybe a little more. Maybe a little less."

Asa gripped Wist's sleeve, wide-eyed. "Your demon really—"

She stopped herself midway through. "All right," she said, calmer. "You're the expert. Where will she revive? Somewhere in the city?"

"Likely here in this room," I replied. "Here, or someplace familiar. Someplace she's been recently."

"You can't guarantee it?"

"We never did much experimenting with death and revival. Not if we could help it."

"Understandable," Asa muttered.

"It's none of my business," I said, "but if you have things to do, you might want to take care of them before Vesper comes back."

That reminded me of something. I dusted off my flight suit. I excused myself for a moment.

I stepped back across the yellow line. Past my cobbled-together sledgehammer. Out through the propped-open reinforced door. Down the stairs to the customer lobby with its giant Jacian flags and its giant broken clock.

I fetched the half-empty burlap bag from the postmaster's office. When we regrouped in the lobby, I asked the Osmanthians if they liked chestnuts. Upon discovering that the chestnuts came courtesy of Vesper, both demurred.

"Don't want to give your demon more reasons to come after us," Asa told me. "She meant those for you."

"Don't worry." I stuffed the bag in my pocket. "She'll definitely come after me first."

"That's cute," Asa said wryly. "She's so loyal."

This didn't merit a serious response. "We should head in opposite directions," I suggested. "That'll buy you more time. In exchange—"

Asa brightened up. "Ah, yes. Here it comes. Would you like a favor from us? Let's talk details."

I turned to Wist. "First, sorry for stabbing you."

It took her several seconds to react. "Almost forgot about that."

"A lot happened afterward," Asa piped in. "You really surprised us in the temple, though.

"Why'd you use the knife on Wist? She's obviously a more dangerous target. If you were going to turn on anyone, we both figured it'd be me."

"Didn't know how she would react if I hurt you," I said. "I thought she might react less to getting hurt herself."

For a moment, I seemed to have rendered them speechless. A lizard crept sheepishly between the ceiling beams overhead.

Asa erupted in laughter. "Great heaven above," she wheezed at Wist. "She's got you pegged."

Wist, for her part, displayed not even a microscopic trace of amusement or embarrassment. Nor any other emotion. There was a waxy eeriness to the way she waited for Asa's merriment to fade.

She stood taller than me, though she held herself a little hunched. Dark hair and dark eyes. A glum monotonous voice ill-suited for grand speeches. Quite a contrast to her predecessor.

But even before Vesper identified her as a Kraken-level mage, I'd grasped instinctively that it would be unwise to provoke her.

"You can port freely around the city," I said. "Could you port me to my chalice? The fallen machina."

The Osmanthians held another one of their rapid-fire silent consultations.

With Vesper's death, I might've been able to get to Solitaire on my own. The fatal moat she'd created could have collapsed in on itself, or disappeared in spouts of steam, or gone to war with the sweet mystical water filling the rest of the city canals.

If I tried to reach the plaza by myself, though, I might run into more unexpected obstacles. Magical or otherwise. There was still a chance of me failing to reach Solitaire's cockpit in time.

"Come with us first," said Asa. "Wist will be busy. But there's a lot of stuff I'd like to discuss with you."

"Like what?"

"Things we might be able to do to help each other. That's how favors work, right? You do a little for me. I do a little for you."

"I got Vesper out of your way," I said.

"For the record," Asa shot back, "no one asked you to brutally murder her. That was entirely your own decision."

"In other words, you don't trust me enough to leave me alone with a war machine."

She held her hands up in a gesture of mock apology. "There was also the whole matter of you stabbing Wist, after all."

"I did much worse to Vesper."

"Oddly enough, I don't find that comforting." Asa eyed the watch peeping out through my unbuttoned flight suit. "Only ten hours, you said? We better get moving."

29

I STEPPED OUT through the front door of the post office.

My body expected Vesper's magic to whisk me back to the usual starting point: the end of the lobby with the broken clock. My feet expected carpet. Instead they met cracked green-streaked pavement.

Asa and Wist had left the building first. Now Asa stood on the deteriorating aftermath of a colorful stone wall, arms folded. Wist sat nearby, one hand raised as though urging Asa to hold onto her for better balance.

On the hills behind them towered those complicated wind turbines I'd gotten so used to looking at. Some always gyrating, some dead and motionless.

I told the Osmanthians I was ready to go.

What followed was a whirlwind tour of much of the city.

Wist appeared to be preparing for some great act of magic involving the use of anchors placed in specific locations. Memorial Park. Glorybower University. A canal lock overgrown with thickets of wild sea briars.

I mentioned along the way that I knew Wist was the Kraken. A Kraken, rather.

"Right," Asa said, unperturbed. "We figured your demon would tell you. She seemed to take it personally."

"We tangled a lot with the previous Kraken."

"Yeah, but how many centuries ago was that?" Asa tried counting on her fingers. After a few false starts, she gave up.

She leaned closer to me and added, quiet as a whisper: "I'd be very interested in hearing more about the original Kraken. But maybe that's a chat to have another time."

Wist, normally poker-faced, had visibly stiffened when we started talking about the past and present Kraken. Not her preferred subject of conversation. Nor her preferred title, it seemed. But she was stuck with it.

Here in Jace, operators were historically thought of as being more rational and civilized. Born for leadership, for management.

Mages were supposed to be more emotional, more volatile. Asa the operator and Wist the mage didn't really fit the old stereotypes. Yet they didn't completely defy them, either.

Not that I'd ever placed much stock in the traditional hierarchy. I was a former mage, but losing my magic didn't automatically promote me to being an operator. They'd cut out my magic core before I even knew what a magic core was. I certainly didn't get any say in the matter.

Yes, my role as Vesper's Host was in some ways analogous to the role of a mage's operator. Up until this latest awakening, I'd guided her. I'd told her what to do. I'd made the decisions, and taken responsibility for them. When push came to shove, I did my utmost to boost her power.

But Vesper was a demon. We would never be an ordinary mage-operator pair. We could only feign the appearance of one.

We couldn't communicate mind-to-mind. Our bond was not an oath to share the rest of our lives together. Our bond was a bond of shared death.

The greatest difference: I couldn't reach inside Vesper and heal the aches in her magic, the way a human operator could soothe the metaphysical suffering of a human mage.

Then again, using magic didn't seem to hurt Vesper in the same way that it would hurt a human mage. If Vesper's power damaged her, the pain must've cropped up somewhere I couldn't begin to see or touch or understand.

As we hopped around the city, Wist showed few outward signs of fatigue. But every so often, Asa would halt our conversation and brush past Wist, saying nothing, a brief hand on her lower back.

My magic perception and my knowledge of operators were both very weak. I couldn't tell what Asa did when she went over to check on Wist. Yet I could see hints of a repressed relief shudder through Wist whenever Asa touched her, even if it only lasted for a few seconds.

The stronger the mage, the more skill it took to fill the role of their operator. To help them stay in control. To help them master their magic. Asa had to be a top-class operator, if she were this badly needed by a mage on the same level as the imperial Kraken.

I watched them at the edge of a junk heap below a bridge—a dangerous tangle of corroded wood and sheet metal that might once have been a temporary encampment. A long, long row of unregistered shacks.

The Osmanthians had turned away from me. They faced the mess in the shadow of the bridge with the earnestness of archaeologists assessing how to start a dig.

The bold red spots on Asa's jacket looked like targets telling an enemy where to shoot. Her hand slipped deftly up beneath the hem of Wist's shirt, seeking direct contact with the small of her back. The part of a mage's body closest to their magic core.

I waited in the hazy sunlight by the water's edge. Envy pinched at me. Their relationship seemed so untroubled. So balanced. The only way I could ever give anything of equal value back to Vesper was by volunteering myself to get eaten alive.

The last location they needed to visit was a ramshackle amusement park.

Large sections of the arched entrance sign had been spirited away. From what remained, I hazarded a guess that it used to be called Spinning Gardens. Spinning Gardens Leisure Park? Couldn't read all the characters.

It took Wist far longer to finish her work at the park. Almost three hours.

The entire time, she stayed at the base of the grand fairy wheel. A frighteningly colossal thing. Each passenger cabin looked to be at least the size of a train car. It was horribly rusted and had rained flaking paint everywhere, inescapable quantities of it, a plague from the sky like a giant's dandruff.

"It's our first time coming here. It'll take her ages to set up," Asa warned me. "Let's take a look around the rest of the park."

"You don't need to stay and watch?"

"Watch what?"

I drew her attention to Wist, who sat below the fairy wheel as if lost in meditation. Or maybe she was merely slipping into the welcoming arms of an afternoon nap.

To my eye, the great wheel looked as if it might come crashing down on her at any moment. Fifty years was a disturbingly long time for a structure that size to go without any maintenance.

"A thrilling sight, isn't she?" Asa said sardonically. "No, no need for us to linger." She tapped her temple. "Wist will let me know if she needs me. I can support her remotely, too."

"That's handy."

Unlike Asa, I had no burning desire to sightsee. I let her lead the way. Thankfully, she didn't try to board any of the wilder rides.

She exclaimed with delight over a two-story merry-go-round packed with intricately carved and painted figures.

"A human carousel! I've heard of these."

"Is there any other kind?" I asked.

"Carousels on the continent have you riding on animals," she said. "All the ones I've seen, anyway. And they usually look a good bit happier to be there."

She leaned over the peeling railing to stare with fascination at the mounts. All oversized human forms, of course, and significantly better-preserved than the fairy wheel. Mostly on all fours. Dressed in various historical costumes. Some that I'd worn myself, at varying times, and others that far predated me.

Their eyes bulged. Their tongues protruded. Their mouths contorted in obsessively well-sculpted screams.

"Children ride on these?" Asa asked.

"Children find them hilarious," I told her.

"I guess I can buy that. If you're a kid, it just looks like a bunch of silly faces. If you're an adult, it looks like a parade of the damned crawling through hell after hell."

Her voice got more tentative. "Is this some kind of religious thing? Going in circles and all that?"

"Maybe," I said. "In a distant sort of way."

I'd never thought too much about any possible connection to the Lord of Circles.

"Huh." She pointed. "Is that an Osmanthian?"

"Where?"

"Over there. Looks like an outfit from the old monarchy."

I looked. I winced. It was an extremely unflattering depiction.

I started to attempt an apology. Asa cut me off. "Don't bother. It goes both ways. Gotta really brace yourself if you ever come visit Osmanthus."

As we made our way around the perimeter of the human carousel, I admitted that she'd been right about Vesper.

"What about her?"

"There was a time when we were lovers."

"Told you so," Asa said at once, triumphant. "Told you so! Called it!"

She drew herself up and coughed delicately into her fist. "I mean, yes. Sounds about right. And you just up and forgot the whole thing? Does hibernation wipe your memory?"

"To some extent. Seems like it's gotten worse over time."

I offered a truncated sketch of what—to my understanding—now motivated Vesper.

Whenever I slept, Vesper stayed awake, trapped and immobile. She never wanted to go through that again.

And she was afraid, perhaps, of my memory worsening with each new cycle. Of me changing to the point that no part of my original self remained. Of me forgetting more and more, until at last I forgot the name of her human gate. My old friend. The only real friend I'd ever had.

Asa wiggled her cap to adjust it. She gave me a skeptical look from under the short brim.

"I get that your memory is unreliable and all," she said, "but it seems pretty dang clear that none of these are brand new problems."

"No."

"So why'd your demon become so homicidal all of a sudden?"

"Those fifty years in the cockpit," I answered. "That was the first time she got fully trapped in one place. Body and soul.

"She said usually she would explore the world like a ghost when I slept. But no part of her managed to leave the cockpit. And she was suffering the whole time, being hooked up to Solitaire. Like being chewed yet never swallowed."

"I get it." Asa gestured at the human mounts with their ridiculous grimaces, their soundless shrieks. "Any normal mortal human would've lost their mind, going through that."

I thought the conversation had ended there. I was wrong. After a brief break, Asa kept going.

"Still, I gotta wonder if there isn't more to it. She isn't human. And you two have been through some pretty atrocious things before, haven't you?"

"Depends on how you define atrocious," I said.

Asa crouched to peer avidly in the eyes of a tormented man with carved blond curls. "You claim she was never cruel to you before. Never cruel to anyone, except when you ordered her.

"Sounds like she really loved you, in her own way. If a demon can love. Why would those fifty years, specifically, be the one thing to finally break her?"

The answer was no great mystery. I began to wonder, even as I spoke, why I had started talking at all. What difference could it possibly make?

"I asked her to stop me from changing any further," I said heavily. "I asked her to stop me from losing myself completely. I made her promise to do whatever it took.

"And then I lost control of Solitaire. I condemned Glorybower. I trapped everyone in here with me. I murdered an entire city. I—"

"Wait." Asa ceased her study of the wretched crowd of human mounts. "Wait, wait, wait. What're you talking about?"

Maybe my outdated Continental vocabulary wasn't anywhere near adequate to the task of explaining this. I groped for the right words and found only politely distant neighbors.

"I put the dome around the city. I put myself to sleep. I didn't mean for it to happen, but I locked the population up inside the dome with me.

"If they screamed, if they beat Solitaire with their fists, if they dropped bombs on us to try to wake me, if vorpal beasts swallowed them whole—I never heard it."

My head pounded. "I doomed them. Everyone who had the misfortune to live here fifty years ago. You've seen how the city is now. Completely and absolutely empty.

"We were the guardians of Jace. I was supposed to be a hero. Instead I committed a kind of genocide. I shut them up together with the biggest vorpal hole that's ever appeared in Jace. While I slept, while Vesper twisted in agony at the back of the cockpit, something wiped them all out. Everyone we were supposed to protect."

Asa took her cap off. She ran a hand through her black-and-white hair.

"I see," she said. A curious dryness permeated her voice. "I see. You certainly weren't exaggerating about your memory being all screwed up."

"What?"

"The cruelest thing your demon did was not telling you this. "If she's been outside the city lately, she must know."

I felt a premonition of bile.

Asa pointed a finger in my face.

"Glorybower was empty from the start," she declared. "It stayed empty for all these fifty years. When your machina went berserk, when you started to put up those magical mirror-walls, you ported everyone outside the city borders. Even most of their pets, too. You saved the entire populace.

"Sure, you displaced them. You took their home. But not their lives. No one was ever trapped inside Glorybower except for you and your demon and your giant war machine. Not a single other person."

30

Vesper had let me think I let them die.

I trailed Asa around the amusement park, too stunned for either relief or anger. Too stunned to feel much of anything.

Our part of the world was indeed largely peaceful right now, she assured me. Peaceful enough for the Jacian government to covertly seek help from an Osmanthian Kraken. That alone suggested that tensions were lower than they had ever been during the conscious stretches of my lifetime.

A miniature train line wound through the park grounds, complete with child-sized stations. The tracks were covered in puffy-tailed autumn grasses that grew significantly taller than Asa herself.

She insisted on following them, searching for the lost train. If we found it, she'd probably assert her right to take a ride.

No matter where we went, we could still see the prodigious fairy wheel silhouetted against the sky.

"You did save everyone living in the city," Asa stated, "if not the city itself. That's a fact. Of course, it doesn't leave you immune to criticism."

"No," I said faintly.

"Would you be offended if I did a bit of post-game analysis?"

"A bit of what?" I changed my mind and stopped her before she could launch into an explanation. "No—just tell me."

Asa stopped beside the train tracks. She stretched her arms high over her head, leaning this way and that. "Don't take this as me blaming you," she said by way of preface. "I'm sure you did the best you could at the time. Take it as the perspective of someone with—okay, maybe not *more* life experience. A different type of life experience."

"You're older than me," I told her.

"I haven't seen nearly as much turmoil as the legendary Host of Jace. When I was your age—remind me, do you even know how old you are?"

"Under thirty?" I guessed.

"Right. When I was your age, I was sitting on my ass in prison. Anyway, one main critique comes to mind. If you had better control, you could've sealed off a smaller part of the city."

"Or even just the part of the sky right around the vorpal hole," I said.

"Exactly. Of course, if you had full control over your machina, you wouldn't have been forced to shut everything down and go into emergency hibernation."

We began walking alongside the tracks again. Asa turned, momentarily strolling backwards to watch me as she spoke. "What happened, anyway? Was it like a mage going berserk?"

"I guess so."

"What triggered it?"

"We stayed in the chalice too long. We channeled too much power. But there were vorpal beasts raining from the sky. If we'd stopped midway through—"

"There were almost no casualties from you porting everyone outside the city," Asa interjected. "A remarkable feat. Miraculous, even."

"Almost?"

She placed a hand over her heart. "A few people got cardiac arrest from the sheer shock of everything. Although that's hardly your fault.

"Obviously it could've been much worse. You could've ported them into the ocean, or into the middle of a solid mountain. You could've spliced them all with each other by accident. Made a giant human meatball."

She grimaced, as if picturing human bodies jammed together like fistfuls of clay. "Don't think even Wist could shift the population of a whole damn city from one location to another so cleanly. I mean, that's an accomplishment."

We would soon reach the beginning of the tracks again. We'd followed their serpentine path through the entire park without once glimpsing the train itself.

"From what I hear," Asa continued, "for the first few years after the dome went up, people were still pretty impressed with you.

"Back then they expected the dome around the city to come down sooner rather than later. They were waiting for the Host and her demon to emerge triumphant, to give them back their homes."

"But decades passed," I said.

"Decades passed. The government kept making excuses for you. Not that they had any idea what was going on either, I suppose. All sorts of covert missions to infiltrate the walls kept failing. Glorybower remained untouchable. Opinions soured.

"There are people—maybe a lot of people—who blame the Host for robbing them of their homes. Their belongings. Their whole lives in Glorybower. Not everyone would welcome you with applause if you bounded out of the city to announce your grand return."

She started kicking a pebble along the path in front of us. It soon got away from her.

"The truth is, you did save them. It could've been a lot worse. It could've ended in mass murder. Instead, you made sure not even a single lapdog got left behind. No one can take that away from you."

I didn't know what to say. In the end, I didn't say anything at all.

Asa, in turn, seemed content without a response. She whistled softly to herself, a tuneless wheezy sound.

True to the name of Spinning Gardens, the park was abundant with flora. Camellia trees grew wild along walkways, ungroomed, crowned with florid blooms in every shade of pink and scarlet.

"So," I said as we picked our way through a minefield of fallen flowers. "My reputation is in the pits."

"That's one way to put it." Asa pointed up ahead at the fairy wheel, perhaps signaling that it was time for us to return. "But there's something else you should know."

She glanced at my torso. "Don't mean to pry," she said. "Or maybe I do. They did something to you, didn't they? To make you the Host."

"You can tell?"

"You lost your magic core. I can see the place where it used to be. You gained—whatever that is." She indicated the watch on my stomach.

"The watch came later," I said. "I think. But yes. They cut out my magic core."

"Most people would die from that."

"Most did."

Asa nodded, unsurprised. "For fifty years," she said, "your government's had no way to communicate with you or monitor you. No way to tell if you were living or dead or gone crazy.

"Jace has gone long stretches without using you in the past. But this time's been a little different."

I already knew why. Didn't take much imagination. "Because of your—because of Wist," I said.

"Yep. You got it. About two decades ago, Osmanthus officially codified Wist as a Kraken-class mage. Made a real big whoop-de-do about it. Can you guess what kind of reaction that caused in Jace?"

I had to keep stepping sideways to avoid crushing the flowers on the ground. "Panic," I answered.

"Your government redoubled their efforts to reach you. To somehow breach the city. No luck. So meanwhile, they worked on trying to create a replacement."

A tautness like a trapped air bubble filled my chest.

"A replacement," I said. "For me?"

"For you. Their one and only Host."

"Did they succeed?"

"This is all second-hand intelligence. But far as I know—no. All they've succeeded at is killing a bunch of mage children."

Asa stopped in her tracks, hands in her pockets. Her gaze dropped to another fallen camellia, hot pink and whole and flawless.

"Between you and me," she said, "that's kind of what got us to come here. If we can secure and open up Glorybower, Jace will stop the core extraction experiments. That's our agreement."

"That's it?" I asked.

"That's the essence of it."

"You didn't make a contract to hand over me and Vesper?"

She nudged the nearest camellia back and forth with her toe as she answered. Something about her brought to mind a cat toying with its meal.

"No one knew if you were alive, or sane," she said. "Last time we spied on the city, we saw your machina lying there in the middle of a bunch of smashed buildings.

"When we reported our findings, we were very conservative in our wording. We said we could make sure Jace got back the machina. Couldn't promise them anything about the pilots."

On the way back to the fairy wheel, we found the miniature train strung up high in a grove of old leafless cherry trees. No indication of how it had gotten there.

Red-headed crows perched like sentries on street lights, watching us pass. From a distance, they resembled a pack of vultures.

As a rule, I didn't take pride in much. All glory was fleeting, and meaningless to those born after it happened.

Yet I'd taken a certain pride in knowing that after I first summoned Vesper, after we started proving ourselves, Jace stopped extracting the cores of other children.

I may have been a freak accident, but Vesper and I were all the nation would ever need. Or so I tried to convince them. If I worked hard enough, no one else would ever have to get their magic core ripped out.

Now I'd failed even in that. All it had taken for Jace to lose faith in me, after double-digit centuries of loyal service, was a measly couple of decades.

I understood why. I suppose I could sympathize. To the people living in any given era, previous eras might as well be a fairy tale. An intangible dream.

Blood coughed up on long-ago battlefields might earn a brief moment of remembrance, a moment of thanks. That was about all you could hope for. Past accomplishments wouldn't protect anyone in the present.

We passed beneath naked persimmon trees, some of the largest I'd ever seen. Bright fruit grew on top, spiked viciously on vertical branches like the chopped-off heads of enemy troops.

Persimmons weren't supposed to grow like that. I didn't think any fruit was supposed to grow like that.

Sometimes it became difficult to remember what was normal—what anything was supposed to look like. Maybe wild magic had warped them. Or maybe the persimmons of the current century had been bred to look egregiously violent.

After Wist finished up with the fairy wheel, she ported us back across the city. All the way over to the viewing platform at the top of the iconic bell tower.

"How much time have we got?" Asa asked.

I checked my countdown clock. "An hour at most."

She nudged Wist. "Is an hour enough for you to close the hole in the sky?"

"With all the anchors around the city ... maybe."

"Maybe, huh."

Asa cast a pensive glance down at the stone heads affixed to the waist-high wall around the belfry.

Suddenly she bent sideways to stare one in the face. Wist grabbed hastily at her jacket to keep her from toppling clean off the tower.

"This one looks like you," Asa said to me. "See? This other one looks like your demon. Check out the ears."

I'd never paid much attention to the stone guardians' features, except to note the ones that looked especially worn or mangled. They were hard to see from inside the tower, since they'd been positioned to face out toward the city below.

"They all look like different versions of you," she commented. "Funny, isn't it? People really, really believe in you. People think you can do anything. And then they don't. They just stop."

She looked me full in the face.

Sometimes I found it difficult to meet Asa's gaze. It was her hair, I think. The way she let it fall all over her right eye. It made my skin creep and itch. It made my own eye cringe in its socket.

I still didn't get how she could stand it.

"What will you do if you tame your demon?" she asked. "If you make it out of the city?" She patted one of the eroded stone heads. "Will you try to win everyone over again? Will you try to assuage your fans?"

"There's a lot standing in the way," I said. "I've never been one to plan too far ahead."

"I'll ask you again after Wist cinches up that hole in the sky, then."

We looked at it in unison. It was impossible to miss, that vast distortion.

Wist held on tight to the edge of the tower wall. I had to avert my attention from the magic winding up inside her. It was far too much for my meager senses. It felt like staring into an eclipse of the sun.

31

Wıst was racing against time to close the hole in the sky before Vesper came back. But the mere fact of that didn't make time go any faster.

A chilly breeze swept through the deck below the great bell as she worked. If I strained my magic perception, I could just make out a handful of the magical anchors she'd placed throughout the city. They rose high above neighboring buildings, shapes like ghostly echoes of the bell tower.

According to Asa, we'd ascended the tower because the extra elevation brought us that much closer to the vorpal hole looming over the city. While the hole still lay far out of reach, the belfry gave Wist a better view of it than working from ground level.

She was the Kraken. A Kraken. I would've thought she could use magic to fly as high as she needed.

Asa corrected me. Closing a vorpal hole required too much focus.

Wist couldn't deploy anti-gravity magic at the same time. Even the energy that would've been needed to spin off a self-sustaining, standalone enchantment—like a permanent floating raft to hold her up right below the hole—was better saved for the task at hand.

"She'll be totally occupied with narrowing the hole, and then sealing it," Asa warned. "She won't have any idea what's happening around her. A tornado could hit the tower, or she could get shot in the back, and she wouldn't notice a thing."

Asa dropped her voice. "In other words, Wist can't react quickly enough to protect us. You get it?"

I nodded.

I'd been born a mage. I'd continued being a mage until they strapped me down and dug out my core. Despite this, I no longer had any deep familiarity with the inner workings of human magic. It hasn't been relevant to me in a very long time.

The magic of vorpal beasts and demons operated according to a far dreamier, less tangible logic. It wasn't really logical at all, when you got down to it. A frustrating fact to grapple with for those scholars who'd struggled so solemnly to quantify Vesper's capabilities.

Human magic operated within much stricter, more definable boundaries. Rare was the human mage who could acquire more than one specific magic skill. The ability to detect rare minerals within a certain distance, for instance.

Rarer still was the human mage who'd gained multiple skills and could use more than one simultaneously. Like knitting a surface-level wound back together while also purging infection.

A Kraken-class mage like Wisteria Shien was the exception that proved the rule.

Fifty years ago, full battalions of synchronized Jacian mages had failed to patch the yawning maw in the sky, much less close it.

Even with Vesper's demonic magic, amplified by our chalice Solitaire, the best I'd been able to do was thrust the entire city into a state of silent purgatory.

The vorpal hole swallowed physical missiles and ammunition like candy. It lapped up every scrap of magic we flung at it. Nothing seemed able to daunt or scathe it.

In the end, it wasn't a *thing* at all. It was an opening that wasn't supposed to be there. A gash leading to a devouring void we weren't supposed to be able to see, much less understand. A wound spanning worlds.

How could you mend that except by meddling with the fabric of reality itself?

Such meddling sounded like something that ought to belong on the previous Kraken's list of magic taboos. Perhaps its absence was an oversight.

Improbable though success might seem, I couldn't criticize Wist's attempts to close the monstrous hole. No other way to stop vorpal beasts from periodically flooding the city. No other way to ensure it was safe to try removing the dome.

Up here in the shadow of the bell, Asa was more attentive to Wist than she'd been back at Spinning Gardens.

Even so, there were moments when she lifted her hand from Wist's back and swiveled to chitchat.

"Gotta tell you," she mentioned early on, "this all goes a lot faster without your demon constantly harassing us."

"Sorry about that."

"Nothing you could've done," Asa said. "She had you locked up. Anyway, it felt like it took ages to set up the first few anchors. Days, if not weeks."

"She'll be back soon enough."

"Not that I don't believe you. But I'll believe you more after she makes her grand return."

"You seemed shaken," I found myself saying.

"By what?"

"By the notion of Vesper reviving."

Asa's face closed up.

In the past, we'd sometimes failed to conceal the true nature of our bond. Most people who stumbled across it responded very differently from Asa and Wist.

They got excited to witness an apparent reversal of death. They started wondering if it could ever apply to them. They sought ways to borrow scraps of the power to resurrect.

Asa drummed her fingers atop the worn crown of the nearest stone head. Judging by the shape of its sole remaining ear, this one was meant to be Vesper.

"Here's what I've been wondering," Asa said. "Why isn't Jacian hibernation tech more widespread? Why hasn't anyone else journeyed with you from the distant past?"

"It isn't really a way to live longer. You don't experience any of the time that passes."

"So? It might not extend your conscious life, but it could be a neat way to see what happens to your descendants. All you gotta do is be willing to conk out for a while."

Asa stopped tapping out a beat on the stone guardian. She looked over at Wist for a protracted moment, as though scrying her magic for signs of danger. We'd all be done for if a Kraken-class mage went berserk.

When Asa turned back to me, I said: "Stasis got used most widely when mages were batteries. They'd get their magic siphoned while they slept."

"Stored in walls and under floors," said Asa. "I've heard of that. None of the Jacian elite ever asked for a chance to nap through a couple centuries, too?"

"Putting people in stasis always goes smoothly," I explained. "Waking them up has an extremely high failure rate."

"Meaning?"

"Most of them die. No one's ever been able to fix that."

I was on Asa's right, so I couldn't discern her expression. All I saw of her face was a still mouth and the long bangs covering her eye.

"How come you've always made it out alive?" she asked. "Sheer luck?"

"Must be something to do with my connection to Vesper," I said. "Something to do with being a demon's Host."

"What about it? That's awfully vague."

"It's hard to research something that others can't replicate."

"Hmmm."

Asa didn't sound especially satisfied. But she let the conversation die out there. She pivoted to check on Wist again.

The vorpal hole in the sky did seem smaller now. Although the more I looked at it, the more my aching mind tried to convince me that it had always been that precise size and shape.

Threads of magic rooted in anchors all over the city strained at the hole's disfigured edges. As if to shrink it by pulling it tighter like a drawstring.

What lay on the other side of the hole? Best not to ponder that for too long or too deeply.

When I focused too hard on it—not on the configuration of the hole itself, but on what it revealed within—my senses started to blank out, to get sucked in as if the vorpal hole could consume them from afar. I went temporarily blind. I stopped feeling my tongue in my own mouth, the stone floor beneath my feet.

The countless magic branches emanating from Wist were, in their own way, equally overwhelming. I stared straight up into the dark dome of the hanging bell for relief.

At one point, it occurred to me to pluck at Asa's jacket and ask her: wouldn't closing the hole also eliminate their means of slipping in and out of Glorybower's magical barrier?

Asa snorted. "Bit late to mention that, don't you think? There are other holes elsewhere in the city, you know."

"There are?"

"Few and far between. I'm not surprised if you haven't stumbled on any. The rest are much smaller and less troublesome. Comparatively harmless. But more than enough for us to use as an escape hatch. Same goes for your demon, if not for you."

She shrugged one shoulder. "That'll all be a moot point if we end up taking down the city walls afterward. But hey—thanks for your concern. Even if it was a tad belated."

When I next checked my watch, it was already past time for Vesper to resurrect.

I let Asa know. Quietly.

I'd assumed that the instant Vesper regained her corporeal form, she'd come flying back in a blazing fury, bent on retribution.

I could only give general estimates, though. And it wasn't as though Vesper had booked an appointment for tea with us.

Maybe I'd gotten rusty at reading my own clock. Or maybe I'd gotten rusty at reading Vesper herself.

The vorpal hole overhead had transformed into something more akin to a ragged slit. An eyelid slipping shut. A cut dragged from one end of the sky to the other with a blunt and dirty knife.

Wist was slumped on her knees, her head just about level with the stone heads arrayed around the guard wall. Almost there, I heard Asa murmur to her, stroking her braid. Wist kept pushing.

Magic bloomed in the air with a scent like ozone, an illusory rain that would never come.

Asa and I continued talking on and off to pass the time. We spoke in low voices, as if a spy might be listening.

She filled me in on recent history. The last open conflict involving Jace and the continent had taken place forty years ago. While I slept at the heart of Glorybower.

In Osmanthus, they called it the Jacian Wars. They'd accused Jace of hideous crimes against humanity. Some of the accusations may have been true. But it sounded to me as if the whole thing had started because of Osmanthian aggression.

Forty years ago, Jace had driven back Osmanthian forces. An entire alliance of continental forces. Without access to Solitaire. Without any support from the national demon or her Host.

"How?" I asked, bewildered.

"Psychobombs."

She had to realize that I'd never heard that word before in my life.

"You can guess what they do based on the name alone." Asa motioned at her forehead. "They don't cause any sort of physical injury. They only take effect in the mind.

"Psychobomb use was strongly condemned by the continent. VorDef banned them shortly after. Sure worked as a show of strength from Jace, though."

"VorDef?" More unfamiliar lingo.

"The International Vorpal Defense Council."

She reached a hand back and—without turning her head to follow what she was doing—fiddled idly with Wist's magic.

She made it look like meaningless fidgeting, like picking at a knotted-up bit of string. She didn't even stop talking. Yet as she toyed with the tangled tendrils of magic rooted in Wist's core, tension quavered out of Wist's bunched-up shoulders. I could see it happen. Asa appeared to pay no heed.

"I'm no expert," Asa said, "but the magic used for psychobombs was apparently developed based on much older mind-control and remote control techniques. You might have more familiarity with that stuff."

With her free hand, she gestured the shape of a necklace around her throat.

I didn't need to ask why Jace had poured its resources into developing new weaponry. Which, whatever its effects, had been potent enough to preserve Jacian independence. Even in my absence.

After losing contact with us in Glorybower, the government couldn't simply content itself with praying for the walls to one day come down. They couldn't count on Vesper and me miraculously reemerging in their next time of need.

They needed something to match the stark and terrible power of a chalice. They needed a substitute for their missing guardian demon. Of course they would seek to engineer any alternatives they could in the meantime.

"You've defended Jace with your demon for century after century," Asa commented. "Such dedication. Don't know how you do it. I had that sort of patriotism wrung out of me at least a decade ago."

"A decade?" I echoed. "That's near the difference in our lived ages."

"Then maybe it's time for you to reconsider, too."

"Are you giving me advice?"

"Yes," Asa said, imitating the tremulous voice of a grandmother. "Listen to your elders, child."

She switched back to normal. "Almost no one in your nation knows you except through stories and songs. The nation itself will always use the handiest tools available. Be it you and your demon, a bunch of psychobombs, or something else altogether.

"Even if they welcome you back with open arms, Jace will keep seeking ways to become less reliant on one single woman from the ancient past and her half-feral demon. It's been long enough, hasn't it? Jace might be able to get by just fine without you."

"Maybe they could," I acknowledged. "But instead they're expunging magic cores from more and more children. You said it yourself."

"And Wist and I are negotiating to make it stop." She tugged at the ends of her bangs. "All I mean is that you might not have to devote yourself so ardently to Jace in the future. You might not have to feel quite so tied down. Give it some thought."

"A convenient suggestion," I said, "coming from an agent of a hostile nation."

Asa spread her arms lightly, as if to emphasize her harmlessness.

Sunset remained a few hours away, but half the sky had turned dark gray. The subdued reflections of rooftops along the inner surface of the city dome felt like a glitch in my own vision. Not something others, too, could see tainting the gathering clouds.

The vorpal hole, its edges puckering closer and closer together, had begun to take on the look of a fresh-ripped seam.

Wist's taut breathing filled the silence left whenever Asa stopped speaking.

I kept glancing at the clock in my fist. The chain extending from my navel pricked with a needle-like cold. By now Vesper was long overdue.

32

"Wist will finish soon," Asa said. "She'll be very tired."

I kept watch for Vesper in the air, checking all sides of the bell tower.

From time to time a flock of pigeons would wheel past, some of them done up in gaudy colors. We were too high off the ground to encounter much in the way of insects.

I looked at my watch again. The slender chain vibrated whenever I moved it.

Once Vesper had flung me off the side of the tower. Once Vesper had tied me to the spire—the one up above us, shaped like a jostling bundle of skinny-armed hands seeking relief from the heavens. It was invisible from here, hidden by the bell and its roof.

Once, before this current awakening, Vesper had thrown me down in bed with a sharp-toothed smile and boundless energy.

Was I closer to understanding her now than I had been at any of those times?

I leaned over the belfry wall to peer down the dizzying sides of the tower. Vines of barbed wire swarmed up from ground level, straining for the stone heads guarding us.

There was a figure on the ground below.

My first thought: a stranger. A newly arrived human, somehow, like Asa and Wist.

The Vesper I knew wouldn't bumble around touching earth like one of us animals.

She kept walking down the wide pedestrian avenue toward the tower. No hesitation in her step. At the base of the tower, she stopped moving.

She was waiting.

The watch slipped out of my fingers. It zipped back toward my stomach with a vengeance as the chain seized its chance to retract.

The watch was small, but it hit home hard enough to sting.

Asa, who had been tending to Wist, raised her head.

I pointed.

"She's here." The words came out of me half-mouthed, half-spoken. "I'll—I'll keep her busy."

Asa started to respond, then stopped herself. An eerily neutral expression settled over her face. Almost as if she were imitating stony-eyed Wist.

"Don't die," she told me.

I took the stairs.

The tower had a cage-shaped elevator, but a torrent of barbed wire bound it in place. I kept my distance. I tripped blindly down uneven stone steps.

How many would it take to reach the bottom? Close to a thousand?

The steps wound in a seemingly infinite spiral, tight enough to make me dizzy. When I emerged from the tower, there was a good chance I'd drop to my knees and puke at Vesper's feet.

My breath caught high in my chest, shallow and tense.

Nothing would've stopped Vesper from porting herself to the top of the tower, or using magic to snatch me away. Asa had no power to block a demon. Wist was preoccupied, deaf to the world around her.

Instead Vesper waited patiently as I hurtled myself down stairs that no one had trodden in decades. They felt more like a series of traps laid for invading foot soldiers than a welcoming path for tourists.

The irregularity of the worn rock made it impossible to establish a rhythm. If anything, the steps seemed expertly designed to break things. First ankles. Then skulls.

Was Vesper waiting? Was she really waiting?

Or, in the moment I started dashing down through the tower, had she ported up to the belfry to tidily murder Asa and Wist, one after another?

I staggered out of the bottom floor. After the darkness of the sickening curlicue stairs, the avenue seemed abrasively bright.

Last time I'd come down here had been when Vesper killed me. When I dashed myself open on the pavement.

Vesper wore shoes now. That was a first for this awakening.

She held her demon swords, one in each hand, rather than forcing them to flit around behind her.

"You could've met me at the top," I said, breathless.

"Then I wouldn't have gotten the pleasure of making you run down a thousand steps for no reason."

She sounded creepily calm.

One of my hands made its way to my throat as if startled to find my head still attached.

I'd thought Vesper would immediately act to exact revenge for what I'd done in the abattoir.

Although I could claim self-defense, couldn't I? Vesper was the one who'd locked me up. Then again, I was the one who'd pulled her into being through Verity. I was the one who'd made her a demon in this world.

Mud-colored heaps of leaves and sundry garbage littered the once-gracious avenue. Flocks of outdoor chairs and tables and shade umbrellas had somersaulted far from the restaurants where they'd previously been pressed into service.

Off to the left hung the tilted signboard of a grand theater. Far back behind Vesper paraded one of the tracks of the immobile monorail.

She turned the sword in her right hand and offered me the hilt, wordless.

I gaped. I could make no sense of it.

"I won't apologize for killing you," I said cautiously. "We're one for one now."

Her face hardened. "Take the sword, Char."

I should've thought more about what to say to her once she came back. There was too much flotsam swirling around and around in my mind, and all of it kept getting sucked back down into the same bottomless whirlpool.

"You lied," I said.

"Go on. Tell me all the ways I've wronged you."

"We slept together. We were lovers. Even Asa knew before I did. And I remembered. After I killed you. I—"

"You remembered," Vesper repeated back to me, words gilded with ridicule. "How precious. Let me guess. You recall a few gropes here, a bit of heaving passion there, and you think you've uncovered the archaeological find of the century. Isn't that sweet."

"Why did you keep denying it? You disparage me for my memory loss, but you sure haven't made it any easier for me to—"

"Char. Take the goddamn sword."

At the snap of her voice in my ears, my hands automatically took it.

"I won't use magic," Vesper said. "I'll use only human levels of strength. You couldn't ask for a fairer fight."

"I could ask not to fight at all."

"That's not an option. One of us is getting gutted."

"In other eras, you didn't want to gut me at all. You couldn't keep your hands off me."

"Speak for yourself. Perhaps I was simply biding my time for a chance to strangle you," Vesper said carelessly. "Ever thought of that?"

"Am I making you act like this?" I sounded so impotent.

I heard her laugh. I heard her start to mock me.

"But I made you promise," I said. "I made you promise to stop me from forgetting. I made you promise to stop me from changing."

I felt her breath halt as if it were my own. I felt it like a glaze of ice closing up around my hidden chain, the bloodless surface of my countdown clock.

Her pupils had thinned to fine black lines, narrow as the slash of the vorpal hole closing so slowly in the sky above us.

I forced myself to keep going.

"You aren't solely driven by your old contract with Verity. I begged you for help, didn't I? I begged you not to let me lose myself."

Her blade came whistling down before the last few words left my mouth.

33

I'D RETAINED ENOUGH of my training to deflect with the side of the blade. I was lucky I didn't fumble—I'd never practiced with only nine fingers to my name.

Receive the attack with the side or back, never with the cutting edge. Receive the attack and redirect it.

My form was decent, if hundreds of years out of date. My arms had forgotten their old familiarity with this weight.

Island swords were long and svelte and, even when held two-handed, much heavier than they looked.

Vesper felt it too. I knew this simply because I hadn't gotten slashed open from shoulder to waist yet.

Vesper was shorter and more delicately built than me. If she took advantage of her demon nature, none of that would matter. But she would tire quickly if she kept restricting herself to the equivalent of human strength.

Nameless muscles seared in parts of my body that I hadn't properly worked in ages. Certainly not since awakening under the dome of Glorybower.

My feet kept slipping on mats of damp leaves, on pavement coated with an ambiguous green patina of mossy fuzz and gelatinous mud.

My breath came in and out of me in jagged-edged bursts. I scuttled back out of reach.

"That's—that's enough exercise," I panted. "Satisfied yet?"

"No."

"How does it end?"

"How do you think?" Vesper hissed.

I kept deflecting. My hands were too sweaty. My fingers burned as if swollen with chilblains. Especially my missing phantom pinky.

In sheer intensity, a minute or two of serious swordplay could far outweigh an hours-long workout.

Verity used to train pretty hard. More than you'd think from looking at her. On the outside she'd always seemed soft-spoken and studious. Not the sort to aspire to be a soldier.

Vesper must've inherited her gate's respect for the blade.

As for me, I had rudimentary training in a variety of weapons. I did my best to maintain that basic proficiency. Yet the only weapon I'd ever attempted to truly master was my demon. Nothing else could compare.

Each time our swords clashed, they made a sound that weakened my knees. It was nothing like ordinary metal on metal.

Vesper's swords, pulled from her own body, were forged from something entirely different.

I thought of the substance as a form of demon bone. Pale, yet laced with vivid blue veins. As if the swords remained a living part of Vesper, even as I gripped one of them in my own sweat-slick fists. Like the flat watch connected to my body with its silver umbilical chain.

I only slashed at her when I absolutely had to. Only as part of catching and diverting the arc of her blade. Each transient impact jarred my joints as if I were being rung like a bell.

Most of my energy went into frenetically backpedaling. At last I managed to maneuver myself closer to the side of the tower. It was clad in dull red stone, a brick the color of aging wounds.

The hardest part was finding a section of wall not curtained by those abundant vines of barbed wire. Couldn't look too closely—I had to keep fending Vesper off.

Her breathing came hard and fast, and I'd never seen her sword look so heavy in her hands. But she kept springing after me.

I leapt back, startling her with a wordless cry.

Then I swung my sword like a club. Straight into the brick facade of the tower.

The force of it almost jolted the sword out of my hands, my joints out of my sockets. Somehow I kept hold of the hilt, and myself.

Vesper came to a dumbfounded halt. Just out of cutting distance.

She lowered her blade. The long fine tip nearly kissed the mold-varnished pavement.

I gritted my teeth and swung my sword at the wall again. It wasn't some sacred ancient metal. It wasn't a modern steel alloy. Right now it wasn't reinforced by any of her demon magic, either.

It took a few more thwacks for the blade to shatter. My hands uncramped from around the bony hilt. It dropped with a thunk.

Blue blood guttered out of the fragments on the ground. The blood fizzled and bubbled.

The broken sword evaporated in a violent plume of cobalt steam.

Only now did my muscles, relieved of their burden, start to twinge inward. Almost quaking. I had to force my lungs to pace themselves slower before I could swallow and speak.

"Don't see the point," I said, "in exhausting ourselves with hand-to-hand combat."

"You're giving up?" Vesper's voice was unreadable.

"You have nothing to gain from artificially limiting yourself to duel me."

"Don't tell me what I—"

"You'll win." I spoke louder than her. I showed her my open palms. "You'll win regardless. May as well skip to the part where you decide what to do with your victory."

She lifted her remaining sword again. Steadily, deliberately. Then she turned and tossed it aside.

It didn't go far. It clanked down below a minor outbreak of barbed wire bushes.

"There is no greater plan," she said emptily. "My reward is getting to beat the hell out of you. It'd mean more if you would pretend to fight back."

She stared through me, past me. It felt as though she were denouncing some future or past iteration of her Host. Not the one standing defenseless in front of her.

"Ves," I said. "The Osmanthians told me about the city."

"What about it?"

"The whole population. Fifty years ago. You let me think they died."

This got her to look me in the eye. She raised her chin.

"Obviously they didn't." Zero remorse. "You saved them. You always do. Most of them, anyway. The patients who got forcibly ported out of hospitals may not have fared so well.

"But what of it? That's a piddling percentage. On the whole, you saved them. Good for you. Not many people can claim to have rescued an entire city."

"Ves," I said again.

Something in her face seemed to shift whenever I uttered her name. Not in a good way. Yet I kept doing it. I just kept doing it.

"Ves," I said. "You loved me. What happened?"

My back slammed into the tower wall. It bruised me, winded me, pounded any semblance of thought out of my body.

It wasn't remotely romantic.

I was on the ground by the time I realized she'd punched me in the face. Among other places. More than once. A lot more than once.

My nose crunched. I screamed, and I meant it. My arms flew up to shield me, but they were worse than useless.

Something hard came loose inside my mouth. Blood burbled in my sinuses as if to drown me. I tried to tell Vesper she was killing me.

Good, I heard her snarl.

Magic sloshed down over my head like a bucket of dirty water.

In its wake, the drowning blood ebbed. My nose wrenched itself back into shape with another abysmal crunch.

The hammering pain retreated. It didn't go far, though. It stood watching me like an assassin standing over a sickbed, dagger at the ready.

Vesper sat on my stomach, on my much-abused watch. She knew what she was doing. With Vesper there blocking me, I couldn't clutch at the watch to clear my head.

The cold of the ground soaked through the back of my flight suit. Magic held the hovering shadow of pain at bay.

I lay utterly still, wondering if she'd repaired me solely for the sake of being able to break my face all over again.

Vesper didn't move, either. Her fists stayed balled up by my ribs.

"I abased myself in order to fight on the same level as you," she said. "I set aside my pride and my magic. How do you answer me? Dodging and defending. Clenching your teeth to endure it."

What's wrong with that? I wanted to ask. I'd never agreed to the premise that we needed to fight.

Vesper wasn't done yet. "When you murdered me in the post office, I felt a flicker of hope. How wretched is that? I clung to that tiny, tiny hope. I thought we could at least be equal in anger.

"I thought wrong. We're hopelessly out of balance." Her nails ate at my sides. "I could kill you over and over and over and over, and it wouldn't begin to satisfy the smallest possible fraction of my fury. Nothing enrages me more than the fact that nothing can get you to rage back at me."

My battered face, my battered body—all their warring sensations, none of them pleasant, became sublimated by plain old stupefaction.

"I've tried to be fair." I couldn't believe the words she was making me speak. I couldn't believe I had to say this.

"Fair?" Vesper said blankly.

Creaking, I pushed myself up on my elbows.

"I've tried to take everything you've been through into account," I continued, "even if I can't fully comprehend it. I've tried to take responsibility for my actions, as best I can. I've tried to be reasonable."

I drank a shuddering breath. "Your problem with me is that I'm not raging enough? That I haven't lost my composure? That I haven't seen fit to match you stab for stab, blow for blow?

"Would you prefer for me to break my knuckles punching you?" I demanded. "Would you prefer for me to hate you?"

"Yes," she said.

Again, a short spasm of sound, closer to a hiccup or a sob than to speech. "Yes."

She leaned over me, pushing me back down. Her hands were claws on my shoulders.

"I've tried," she said tautly. "Not even the Lord of Circles could accuse me of not trying. I've done everything I could possibly stomach. I dropped you off the top of that godforsaken tower.

"Still you look at me mildly. Perhaps a touch warily. No real resentment. No fire. No matter how hard I've worked to deserve it."

She sat back. Her fingers loosened. She spoke plainly now, a limp weight atop me, emotion draining out of her and down into the pavement like old rainwater.

"No matter what I do, you won't hate me."

34

As Vesper sat on me, her body heat seeped down into my watch.

I felt the slime of the unkempt pavement beneath my palms. I felt a frustrated simmering deep in my belly.

"You want me to hate you," I pronounced. It was a ridiculous thing to have to say out loud. "The more I try to show understanding, the more it makes you lash out."

I lacked the lung capacity to heave a sigh. "You know what I'm going to ask next."

Vesper didn't react. The vorpal hole in the sky overhead had been reduced to a long angry scar.

"Why," I said tonelessly. "Why?"

She edged herself backwards, sliding off my stomach, exposing my watch again. She stopped at my thighs.

In the spot she'd left, chilly air snuck inside my open flight suit. I could only tell it was cold because of the contrast with her warmth.

It had gotten surprisingly dim out, as if Wist's magic were in the process of sewing up the sun.

Vesper tapped the face of my watch with her nails.

"Hating is remembering," she told me.

My temples throbbed. "If you wanted me to remember more, or faster—if you wanted me to remember something, you should've reminded me."

"I have. I did."

"When?" I snapped. "When did you ever tell me anything I needed to know? What was the point of not saying anything about the fate of the city, about how we—"

Her fist hit the pavement. It buckled and cracked beneath us.

Veins of magic seethed all down her forearm, her blue-beaten knuckles.

"I told you." Her voice sounded hollowed out by yelling. "Every other time. Over and over and over. How'd you repay me? Fifty years in Solitaire."

"Solitaire was going berserk," I said. All I could do was give her the facts. "I didn't have any other way to make it stop. Hibernation was the only—"

"That doesn't mean I have to like it," Vesper snarled. "That doesn't mean I have to shrug and keep taking it!"

"No." A baseless indignation churned in my chest. I forced it down.

Vesper had been tortured all those years while I slept. By our chalice's insatiable teeth. By the infinitesimal passage of time. Above all, by my own split-second decision to force both of us into deep stasis together with Solitaire.

I'd seized on what I saw as the best and only course of action. I still didn't think I was wrong. A wild Solitaire might start hunting for more flesh outside its chassis. A truly wild Solitaire could crush more innocent Jacians than I'd ever saved in all my life.

"No," I said once more, collecting myself. "I didn't give you any choice. I'm sorry."

Vesper started to get up off my thighs.

I grabbed her, startling both of us.

Winter fireflies circled at a watchful distance, their glow more visible now in the thickening twilight. The reek of fermenting leaf matter leached from the ground to surround us.

I wet my lips. I didn't know how to say this. I didn't know how to say anything to her, it seemed.

"Ves. You've served Jace for at least a millennium."

"Are you taunting me?"

"Do you want to be released?" I asked.

Magic surged in the places I gripped her, a feeling like needles in my palms. My hands jerked open. Vesper sprang up and away from me. But her boots stayed on the paving.

"I can have all the freedom I want," she said, "as long as I banish the Osmanthians. And seal you away somewhere safe."

"Liar." I rocked to my feet to face her.

Somehow, my body hung together. She'd fixed more than just my fresh-broken nose when she slapped my prone form with the roughest healing magic I'd ever experienced.

Another contradiction. Why beat me to a pulp and then waste energy snuffing out my pain?

A white molar rolled in the mud by my shoe. I trod on it before I saw it there. I had no memory of spitting it out, but it must've been mine. It was shaped nothing like Vesper's teeth.

I lurched toward my demon. She took a wary step back.

"If you cared that much about banishing the Osmanthians, you could've attacked them at their weakest." I pointed at the top of the bell tower. "Right up there. Your best chance yet.

"If you were so consumed by blind fury, you could've slaughtered me first, then gotten down to business with the Kraken. A quick one-two. Instead you picked a petty fight to try to provoke me."

She shook her head. "You must be terribly proud of yourself for refusing to take the bait," she said woodenly. "So virtuous. A real saint."

I let her barbs pass me by. "I owe you. I know that. I dragged you into this world. I made you supplant Verity."

A stray cafe chair teetered near us, one of its legs rotted off. I kicked it out of the way.

"How tired are you?" I asked. "What do you really want from me? Do you want to bring the bond of mutual death to a mutual end?"

"No!"

"Do you want me to promise to never hibernate again?"

"You already promised that!"

Vesper's voice rang out raw through the dimming air, through the ghostly fireflies orbiting us with the patience of vultures. It thumped home like a knife in my chest.

"Before Glorybower," she said. "Before we lost control of Solitaire. No more sleeping, you told me. You said this time you wouldn't forget."

She took my hand. She placed it on the plane between her heart and her collarbone. The blackened stony digits—no fingernails, no proper skin texture—made it look like a monster caressing her. Something risen from the dead.

"I broke down," she said flatly. "I wept. You held me. I wept harder. It was the first time for either of us to see demon tears. They turned to snowflakes on the way down. Very strange.

"Don't leave me, I said. Don't leave me again. You apologized. You kissed my hair. You touched the edge of my ear to distract me. Let's get piercings in the same spot, you said." She flung my hand away from her. "And then what happened? Tell me. What happened next?"

"I don't—" My voice splintered down the middle. I struggled to swallow. "I don't remember."

Vesper smiled. An endearing, benevolent, demonic smile. Her eyes bore a warmthless light very much like that of the clustering fireflies.

"It's human nature, really," she told me. "What keeps you humans up late at night, years after the fact? What do you recall most keenly?"

She didn't wait for me to attempt a response.

"Your most humiliating defeats," she said. "The cruelest comments you weren't meant to hear. Brief seconds in the heat of war. So small a portion of one's overall life that they couldn't even be converted to a real percentage. Yet those are the moments that pursue mortals to the grave.

"What slips away most easily? Joy, triumph, achievements, relief. You aren't alone in that. You aren't special. But you have a gift for taking it to an extreme.

"Which memories does hibernation always reap from you first? Anything good that ever happened between us. The peaceful parts. The happy parts."

"...Hating is remembering," I repeated, shaken.

I'd clawed back only a single scrap of remembered affection. It came to me only after I made the post office machina slice Vesper to death with gleaming blades. I couldn't keep doing that. I couldn't keep watering the barren soil of my memories with her blood.

Vesper kept smiling. It was painful to look at, and not at all human.

"You want me to resent you as much as you resent me," I said slowly. "You want me to loathe you as much as you've come to loathe me. You want me to hit you as hard as you hit me."

I glanced at my right fist, charred and filthy.

"Your nobility is wasted on me," Vesper said. "I despise your selflessness. I spit on your restraint.

"There were times when everyone else in Jace loved you for being a hero. But not me. Never me."

I had only ever done the best I could. I'd never hurt Vesper—or anyone—for no reason.

But had I hurt people? Of course. All the time.

Verity had been my one and only friend. The only person I'd really cared about back then. Yet I kept calling Vesper. Even when Verity cried and clung to me and begged me to spare her.

Everyone said we needed to tap into the power of a demon. Everyone said I'd done the right thing.

To this day, Vesper wore Verity's face—albeit older, and colder, and crowned with horns of exposed bone.

My hands were clenched so hard that I'd stopped feeling them.

"I didn't forget on purpose," I said. "Any promises I made to you—I didn't break them on a whim. I'm not a god. Sometimes there's no other choice."

She relinquished her smile. That frigid, hateful smile. Nothing emerged to replace it. She just looked at me.

"I've heard that before, too," Vesper said simply.

Neither and both of us were wrong. We'd tormented each other. Deliberately and by accident. We'd both pressed on through all kinds of agony. I knew of no way to accurately measure who'd suffered more: minute by minute, year by year, drip by drip.

But it had to be Vesper. She'd waited out all the blank decades and centuries I'd whiled away in stasis. She hadn't chosen to be called to our world or to be squeezed into this form we called a demon, a parodical fusion of human and devilish features.

I'd been a child when I started the whole thing. I was still responsible for starting it.

Above all, I'd chosen to keep calling her. Again and again. Until we reached the point of no return. Until her gate shattered. Until I became her new anchor. Until we became forever bound as demon and Host.

Maybe now Vesper was broken. Maybe now she was indisputably monstrous.

You could probably say the same thing about me, though. Knowingly or unknowingly, I'd kept casting her down into new iterations of the same old hell.

The thing that roiled in me was neither rage nor grief nor despair nor bitterness. None of that, really. Just a pure sour impotence. Folded over and over and over onto itself with nowhere to go. Redoubling in intensity as it curdled internally.

I'll give you what you want, I thought. It's all I can do now.

For the first time in my life, I socked Vesper full in the face.

She reeled. I recoiled. My hand screamed at me as if I'd shattered it.

I was too slow to follow up. Vesper got her footing first.

She kicked me in the stomach, right in my watch. No magic. Just a solid blow with her heel. Still more than enough to knock me on my ass. I wheezed, doubling forward.

Vesper watched me for a moment longer. Her disappointment pressed down on me like a physical force. No way I could get up again.

But I did. I rocketed up, slipping, graceless. The winter fireflies scattered.

Most of my attempts to strike her were glancing, uncalculated. Vesper's jabs felt as sharp and precise as the thrust of a spear.

My only advantages were height and weight, and the fact that Vesper was containing her strength.

I grappled her over to the tower. Barbed wire caught at our clothes. The moss-slick ground kept trying to fell us. Our breathing mingled, an artless sound like rapid sobbing. I struck at her blindly, the hapless bashing of a child who'd never learned how to fight.

Vesper twisted free, then whirled.

She laid me out flat before I had any idea what just happened.

I sprawled sideways on the clammy paving, every inch of my body complaining bitterly.

She'd gotten me with a roundhouse kick. More than once, perhaps. My vision was too fuzzy to make out any last trace of the vorpal slit in the darkening sky.

Vesper stood over me. I had no memory of boxing her ears. But the row of piercings in her cartilage hung askew now, loose and bloody, almost torn free.

I blinked a few times. It was surprisingly difficult. Still couldn't discern her expression.

She must've retrieved her remaining sword while I lay here toppled like a sawed-down tree. She held it overhead, two-handed.

No magic wove through her muscles. Her arms trembled. Or perhaps it was my own vision shaking. The last rattles of a confused brain.

I recalled observing executions with her, side by side, many centuries ago. Traitors getting beheaded before a hungry crowd. The glint of the executioner's long island sword. The sounds and smells of decapitation.

They'd insisted on us watching from very close up. We were honored guests, after all. Revered for all we'd done for Jace.

Vesper had been right about one thing. The least pleasant memories did seem a lot easier to retrieve than the rest.

A snowflake drifted down out of the air. Then another. She adjusted her grip. Her wrists still looked unsteady.

I spoke from the back of my bruised throat.

"Do whatever you need to," I said through swollen lips.

I don't know if she heard me. My face might've been too distended to let any sound out.

Someone shouted in Continental.

Not Vesper.

Asa?

Vesper flinched. I was too sluggish to attempt rolling away. I was too far gone to see her sword come down on me.

35

THE FIRST THING I HEARD: the sound of water. The continuous splashing of a fountain.

The sky above was smooth and bright. No trace of the vorpal hole that had menaced Glorybower for five decades running. The distant reflections of city roofs traced a labyrinthine pattern against vast stretches of washed-out blue.

It had been dusk when I fought Vesper, rapidly deepening into night. At minimum, over half a day must have passed since then.

"Morning," said Asa.

I knew this place. Solitaire's plaza. Asa sat with her back to the deadly silver fountain. The clover on the ground had changed colors again, its leaflets now a mottled mix of thirsty spring green and ugly dark red.

Wist's long form lay curled nearby, sandwiched by tarps and raggedy old blankets. A rolled-up bag beneath her head served as a makeshift pillow. She hugged Asa's newsboy cap to her chest.

"She's dead to the world," Asa informed me. "Figuratively speaking. You, on the other hand...."

My heart started going double-time. I pushed myself up.

I felt unnervingly whole. Moderately sore, rather than mashed to a pulp.

I stuck a finger in my mouth. A very dirty finger, in all likelihood, but no time to worry about that.

No missing teeth.

I flexed both hands. My severed left pinky had returned to me. It was maddeningly itchy, an itch that wormed all the way down to the insides of my knuckles.

But it was there, and it was whole. Like I'd never lost it.

"You saved me," I blurted, and prayed for it to be true.

Asa cast her eyes up at the unblemished sky.

"First of all," she said, "you'll notice that Wist did finish closing the vorpal hole. It was quite a doozy. No need to thank us, though. Just doing our job.

"Secondly—" She stopped. She steepled her fingers under her chin. "Believe me, we wish we could've saved you. Had our hands a bit full at the time."

"You—"

There was something baldly calculating in the way Asa scrutinized me now. No light air of amusement. No playful smirk.

Her voice dropped. "We didn't save you, Charity. No one saved you."

I started to say something. My mind had yet to fully awaken. It flailed pathetically below the surface, a sad half-drowned thing.

"No," Asa said. "I'm sorry, but your head came off. A picture-perfect decapitation. Whatever her flaws, your demon sure knows how to deliver a killing blow. Don't try to talk your way out of this one."

Vesper. The arc of her sword.

My gut hardened. I looked around again, frantic.

Silver fountain. Broad sky. Solitaire peeking out from behind the wreckage of an apartment. Hard bamboo roots bursting from the ground: they could've been the segmented fossils of ancient armored worms.

"Where is she?"

"Who?" Asa asked innocently.

"Ves—my demon. You saw her there. Did you fight her? What happened?"

Asa remained unruffled. "Wherever she is, I'm sure she's throwing an amazing fit right now. The tantrum of the century. Rest assured that your demon won't be a problem for the time being."

She leaned back against the rim of the fountain, seemingly unconcerned by her proximity to the shining fatal liquid inside.

The proud spiral tusk at the heart of the fountain still had its long piercing tip broken off.

"You were out for a while," Asa continued. "Left us quite a lot of time to examine you.

"You bleed red." She motioned crudely, pretending to slash open her forearm. "You're not a magical body double. You're not an illusion. You must be human, incredible though it seems.

"You died when your demon tossed you off the tower, didn't you? You tried to obfuscate it. But now that I've seen you with your head chopped off, I think I'll consider it case closed. You definitely died that time, too. And here you are. Alive once more. How fortunate."

Her voice was very dry now. Hard to parse.

"If I'm here—if I'm here and alive," I said clumsily, "then I couldn't have died."

Asa wound her fingers around a nearby clump of clover. With a firm tug, she uprooted it. She tossed it over her shoulder.

The fountain hissed angrily. A thin line of deadly steam rose behind her.

"Let's be candid with each other, Charity Rinehart," she said.

"I—"

"Yeah, I understand why you wouldn't want to acknowledge this. It'll give people ideas. Spur on dangerous fantasies. Make them start demanding a piece of the pie.

"Here's what happened. You died, and you came back to life, and we saw the whole thing," she said baldly. "Raising the dead is one of the—it's the greatest magical taboo.

"I'm no detective, but that doesn't mean I'm blind. You've clearly resurrected yourself multiple times in the past few weeks."

She got up. She walked over to me. Her thick-soled shoes made surprisingly little noise.

Flake-flies wafted past, light as dandelion seeds.

Fireflies zipped around in the air, too, but their light got drowned out in daytime. They looked like nothing more than slender black beetles.

Only now did I see the chipped teacups set at irregular intervals around Wist's pile of tarps.

Asa followed my gaze. "Water-lights," she said. "They're lovely at night. Very atmospheric."

She turned back to me, hands hooked on the straps of her overalls. "Wist and I are pretty easygoing about most things. We'll let a lot slide in the name of regional differences.

"If you've been breaking one of the great taboos—well, that's another matter. We don't take those taboos lightly. We can't."

"The taboos come from the previous Kraken," I said, grasping for something I could distract her with. "Your Wist is a different person, from a different time."

"Indeed. You think we should stand back and let the taboos get broken?"

"I'm not saying that. But what makes you feel bound to them? Osmanthian culture? Tradition?"

I was still seated on the clover-covered flagstones. Asa cocked her head curiously to look down at me.

"I can tell you this much," she said. "We know the consequences of breaking the previous Kraken's taboos. We know the consequences better than anyone else in the world.

"To be truthful—from that knowledge alone, I can't help but think that your little show of death and revival is something fundamentally separate from forbidden human resurrection. Things would be very, very different for all of us if you really had violated one of the great taboos.

"Your demon died and came back, too. I let you chalk that up to her being a creature from the vorpal plane. Sure. Maybe that's a loophole. Maybe she was never alive in quite the same manner as a regular human being, or those crows squawking on the roof over yonder.

"But what about you?"

She already had me pinned. I couldn't think of any other excuses.

I'd never been much of a tactician.

I told Asa, haltingly, about the bond of mutual death.

She listened intently, with only a few interjections.

At the end she asked: "Why in heaven's name wouldn't you call it a bond of mutual life?"

"The name isn't set in stone," I said, taken aback. "You can call it whatever you like."

"And you like to call it the bond of mutual death. How morbid."

She waved me over to her sleeping partner, the almighty Kraken. She nudged said Kraken with her toe.

Wist stirred and opened one bleary dark eye. She still refused to let go of Asa's cap.

"And a lovely morning to you, too," Asa said.

She looked over her shoulder at me. "Appreciate your honesty," she added. "Rest assured, we don't plan to do anything special with our newfound knowledge of your—what was it again?"

"The bond of mutual death," Wist offered, as if she'd been listening all along. Her voice was gravelly with sleep.

"Right. That. Eternal life sounds nice and all—"

"No," Wist said. "It really doesn't."

Asa cupped her cheek as she glanced from Wist to me to Solitaire.

"To be fair," she said to me, "you and your demon don't do a very good job of selling it. What's the point of quasi-immortality if all you do is bicker and squabble and murder each other? No offense."

"We bicker, too," said Wist.

Asa pretended not to hear this. "My point is, we won't kidnap you and your demon to use in dreadful experiments. No worries there. Although I definitely get why you'd be concerned. I'm sure it's happened before."

I gave a tentative nod. I was having trouble keeping up with her. No wonder Wist looked exhausted.

Wist tapped Asa on the ankle. "You should tell her."

"Tell me what?" I asked.

"Ah, yes. I lied," Asa said brightly.

"To me?"

"Your demon didn't decapitate you."

"She—what?"

"Although she certainly appeared to be trying her damnedest," Asa continued. "We made it just in time to stop her. So we did save your life, after all. You're welcome."

No words came out of me. My mind lapsed into a roaring blank as wide as the dispassionate sky.

Asa wasn't finished. "After closing that giant vorpal hole, Wist was dog-tired. Ready to pass out at any moment. But she wrung out her magic as best she could. She tended to your injuries.

"Believe me, there were a lot of them to tend to. Way too many. You guys really whaled on each other. Wist even fixed your lost tooth. Your missing finger, too.

"We were just guessing, but we figured you'd normally come back from the dead with all your parts intact. Wist went above and beyond to make sure I could fool you. That's my girl. A true professional."

Asa grinned. This was the sunniest I'd ever seen her. "Look. How else could we have gotten you to spill the truth about your bond of mutual death? No hard feelings, okay?"

"Vesper," I finally managed to say. "What the hell did you do with Vesper?"

36

"I WONDER," Asa said, "what makes you ask that."

I stared at her.

"Is it like a bear attack?" she inquired.

"Like a *what*?"

"Imagine a bear attacked us," she said. "Then imagine we woke up to find the bear suddenly gone."

"Vesper isn't a bear."

"Humor me here. In the interest of self-preservation, we'd all be very keen on figuring out where the bear went. Is that why you want to know where your demon is?"

She was going to give me a headache. "No. Yes. No? Just answer my—"

Asa spoke over me.

"Maybe it isn't terror that drives you," she theorized. "You've lost your memories of loving your demon. Do you still feel something for her, all the same? Or is that like asking if you love your own arm? Your own soul? Would you love a parasite?"

"What does it matter?" I cried. Frustration filled my veins to bursting. Only the weight of Wist's dark gaze stopped me from seizing Asa and shaking the answer out of her.

"Of course it matters." Asa sat down on Wist's makeshift mattress of tarps and blankets. She patted a spot nearby—instructing me to take a seat, too.

"Why do I care?" she continued. "Because as Wist and I get ready to wrap up our business in Glorybower, you're going to have to decide how you want to handle your demon. And we're going to have to decide if your answer sits right with us."

She moved a few of the water-light teacups off to one side. In daytime, the liquid filling them looked pristine and clear and lifeless. Perfectly drinkable.

An impractical way to light their half-assed campsite. The equivalent of setting out a bunch of votive candles on bare ground. I fought back the impulse to kick them over.

"We didn't harm your demon," said Asa. "We put her in storage."

"Somewhere in the city?" I pictured my post office prison.

"Not exactly."

Again she invited me to sit down. I reluctantly settled myself across from her. Despite my best efforts, my shoes shed dried mud on the stack of tarps.

Asa pushed her bangs up off her face. For the first time I got a clear view of her right eye.

At a glance it appeared to be the same near-black hue as the left. But there was a hint that some other stranger color might linger at the very back. Perhaps visible only if you shone a beam of light straight into her iris.

With her free hand, she tapped her exposed eyeball. It made a soft distinct clink like a fingernail hitting ceramic.

"This one's fake," she said. "An advanced prosthetic. What's important is what lies behind it."

I had no clue where she was going with this. "I was asking what you did with Vesper."

"And I'm telling you. Behind my prosthetic is a kind of void."

Asa lowered both hands. Her bangs fell back into place, hanging low over her right eye socket again.

"In some ways, it's similar to a vorpal hole. Not quite the same thing, though. Anyway, if I pop my false eye out, I can absorb all kinds of threats into the void."

She made a series of convoluted gestures. Presumably to illustrate the process of vacuuming up her enemies.

"The magic is all from Wist, of course. She trimmed off a bunch of pieces of her own magic and applied them to my prosthetic, my eye socket, the void within, and on. An extremely complex mesh of skills.

"She's pretty overprotective," Asa added, tugging the end of Wist's braid. Wist looked away at the silver fountain.

"Admittedly, I can't fight. Wouldn't trust myself to fire a gun or hold a sword. Magical or otherwise. I might be okay at throwing rocks, but that's about it. Wist wanted me to have a surefire way to defend myself in emergencies."

She covered her right eye with her palm. "Hence the void. And the whole conglomerate of magic Wist grafted onto me so I could use it. It's an enchantment as fancy as the inner workings of a mechanical clock. We call it Garbage Disposal."

Sheer disbelief glued my limbs in place. "You put my demon down your Garbage Disposal."

"Not a whole lot to do in there. Must be bored out of her mind. But she's completely unharmed," Asa assured me. "I'll swear that on any-thing. Your Lord of Circles, even."

The absolute gall of this woman. "You lied to my face about my own life and death."

"Don't hold grudges," Asa said piously. "It's bad for your blood pressure."

Again, Wist's presence was the only thing that kept me from losing it.

I'd taken over a millennium to reach the point of punching Vesper in the face. With Asa, I might get there in a matter of days.

"Let her out," I heard myself say. It sounded like how I used to talk to Vesper. Like I had every expectation of being obeyed.

"Why?"

"Why—"

"I'm serious," Asa said. "Theoretically, I could keep your demon in here forever." She pointed at her false eye again. "No skin off my back. The void will always have room for more guests."

In the background, Wist sat up and sleepily rubbed her face.

"Would you actually do that?" I asked. "Trap Vesper forever?"

"...Well, no," Asa confessed. "I don't fully get what a demon is, to be honest, but I understand that yours is a living creature. A sentient being. No, I wouldn't keep her."

"Then why even say that?"

She pressed the ends of her fingers together. "I'm trying to get a handle on your thought process. Why do you want to let your demon out? Basic human compassion?"

"I—yes," I said. "Yes."

"Fitting for a hero. For the record, though, your demon didn't seem to exhibit any qualms about locking *you* up for the rest of time."

"She had her reasons," I said feebly.

285

Asa looked at me with concern. "She hasn't brainwashed you, has she?"

"I didn't claim they were good reasons."

She thumped me on the shoulder. "Hear me out."

"Do I have a choice?" Even in my own ears, I sounded weary.

"If it's demonic power you want, you can summon other demons. I don't know the specifics, but maybe you need some kind of human cooperation? A human sacrifice?"

She studied me expectantly. I schooled my face to neutrality.

"It's a big world out there,"Asa went on. "Look hard enough, and you'll definitely find volunteers. A new demon might be more cooperative. Less jaded.

"Perhaps that's besides the point. Sure, I'll let your demon out. Just not until we've got a real good plan for what happens next. Sounds fair? Good. So glad to be in agreement."

I hadn't actually agreed. But there was no way I could win a game of words with her. I had zero desire to prolong the ordeal.

With Wist awake, the two of them began setting up for breakfast. I dusted my mud off the tarp and scooted out of their way.

I almost forgot to thank them for bringing me to the plaza. That was the one big request I'd made before Vesper rose from the dead. They'd followed through without asking anything in return. Yet.

That said, they'd also tricked me into thinking I'd come back from a full decapitation. They'd gotten me to blabber about the bond of mutual death.

Asa offered me a pack of rations. I demurred. Meanwhile, Wist collected the teacups from the ground, poured their contents out in the silver fountain, and reduced them to the size of thimbles. Much more portable.

I left to go climb Solitaire. On the way over, I looked back and saw Asa setting out a camping brazier.

According to Vesper, Solitaire alone had the power to make my commands absolute.

Could my commands reach her all the way in the heart of Asa's void?

I crouched outside the closed entrance to the cockpit. Last time we came here, Vesper had hauled me out. Slammed it shut.

Would the city bells start ringing madly if I opened the door again? Or had that magic died together with Vesper in the post office abattoir?

Even if they did ring, she was unlikely to hear it. And even if she heard the bells, she wouldn't be able to do anything to stop me.

Distinct shafts of sunlight slanted down from gaps in distended gray clouds. Angel's ladders.

The sky had been so empty when I first opened my eyes. I hadn't noticed it changing.

Vesper's wide moat still ringed the plaza, but the vorpal mercury that had filled it was gone—wholly evaporated.

Some time later, Asa climbed up to join me atop Solitaire. Wist watched from below, near the rugged vines of grave wisteria binding Solitaire's limbs to the ground.

Asa rapped her knuckles on the door to the cockpit. "Going inside?"

"Want a tour?"

"Don't know if I have the stomach for it. I've heard things, believe me. What'll happen if you try to pilot alone?"

The answer came easily. I'd seen plenty of pilots surrender their lives to Jacian machina.

"I'd last anywhere from five minutes to an hour before Solitaire ate me up. Then you'd get another chance to see me come back from the dead. Better extract my remains first, though."

"Why?"

"To keep Solitaire from eating my revived body all over again."

Asa ran a hand over Solitaire's peculiarly clean crystalline surface.

Not a single curlicue of lichen or sprout of clover had managed to take root anywhere on my chalice. You'd expect to at least see scaly traces of dried rainwater. Asa kept rubbing her fingertips together as if wondering why she wasn't picking up any dirt.

"I don't understand how you've been able to rebound like a rubber band from physical death," she said. "I don't like the fact that I don't understand it."

"Neither does Wist. Neither of us has ever heard of a magic that works this way. Without breaking any of the Kraken's taboos. It all seems highly improbable. Too convenient to be true."

She blew out a breath. "Then again, neither of us has ever met a demon before."

"I thought about what to do with Vesper," I said.

"Oh?"

"Let me try one last time to make peace with her. If it fails, have your Kraken kill us both."

Asa blinked at me. "How very drastic."

"To end one of us, you need to end both of us. That's the bond of mutual death."

"You sound awfully nonchalant about it."

"Should I weep?" I asked. "Should I tear my hair out? Should I beat my fists on my machina?"

"Please don't. I'm terrible at comforting people."

For a long moment, Asa stopped speaking. Perhaps she was debating my suggestion with Wist, mind-to-mind. I dug my fingernails into the hairline crack around the cockpit door.

The next words to come out of her mouth were: "Your amulet."

"My what?"

She pointed at the watch resting like a lid over my navel, held firmly in place by its hidden chain.

"My clock?"

"Is that what it is?" Asa leaned closer, openly staring. "Huh. I took it for an ancient talisman. Some sort of uniquely Jacian medallion. What with all the concentric circles and such."

"Did you poke at it while I was knocked out?"

She grinned at me. "How'd you guess? Only a little bit."

She asked a lot of questions. What did the markings mean? How long had it been a part of me?

I couldn't answer with any real precision. I hadn't been born with the watch. The orphanage staff hadn't attached it to me.

It must've appeared at some point after the first time I summoned Vesper—after I essentially created Vesper in her current form, via Verity.

But had it grown all on its own, a kind of benign tumor? Or had Vesper implanted it in me?

With my permission, Asa gingerly plucked the watch off my belly. The chain stretched, glinting. She tilted the watch face in various directions. She squinted at it like an old-time explorer with a compass.

"Want to hear my theory?" she asked.

"Regale me," I said, resigned.

"Do you remember bonding with your demon?"

"Not in detail."

"Did you become bonded right away? When you first met her?"

"Later than that," I said. "I think."

Perhaps we'd bonded when Verity died.

Or even later on. Around the first time I got desperate enough to offer Vesper my flesh.

Why had we started calling it overclocking? Was the watch chained to me forged as part of that initial transaction—human pain and blood exchanged for access to inconceivable new heights of demonic power?

That had to be it. Vesper had never overclocked without my watch there. The hard metal of its chain had adhered to me in the way of a new fruiting limb grafted to young rootstock.

I'd always been able to look at the blue-tinted circles and immediately know the limits of my demon's overdrawn magic.

Asa delicately set my watch back in place, letting the receding chain do the work of pulling it flush against my skin.

Way down below, Wist the Kraken leaned on the thicket of woody vines twining about one of Solitaire's four titanic left arms. In her long belted coat, she had the air of a plainclothes spy doing reconnaissance.

"Remember my nickname?" Asa asked out of nowhere.

I had no idea what she was talking about.

She chuckled. "Might've mentioned it when I first introduced myself. BB. Sound familiar?"

"Not in the slightest."

"Well, you know already that Wist is no ordinary mage. She does tend to get all the attention, being the Kraken. But by the same token, I'm no ordinary—what's the word you use for it in Jace?"

"Operator." I said it twice: first in Jacian, second in Continental.

"Operator." She repeated it with the Continental inflection. "At any rate, I'm more than Wist's operator—or her manager, or her personal nurse. I've got a calling of my own."

I made an effort to speak with tact. Lord knows why. "There must be a reason you're saying this now."

Asa's smile took on a tinge of mischief. "BB stands for Bond-breaker."

She put her fists together, then bent them sharply away from each other. As if to mime the act of snapping a branch.

"I've only ever dealt with humans," she added in the tone of a disclaimer. "Mage-operator pairs. They're supposed to be magically bonded for life.

"But I've been pretty successful at unraveling some of those ties. Only upon request, of course. Who's to say my gift won't work on you and your demon?"

She traced an idle finger along the outline of the cockpit door. "In other words," she said, "there might be other ways to get out of this. You don't necessarily have to keep committing to mutual life. Or mutual death."

I had seen far more of human history than Asa ever would. Yet in terms of actual waking hours and years, she was undeniably older than me. And probably a lot cleverer.

I should've spent more time contemplating all the ways in which this might be a ruse. Like how she'd deceived me into thinking I'd died and resurrected right in front of her eyes. But there was something else stoppering my thoughts.

Asa made a cute chopping motion with the side of her hand.

"I can divide you from your demon," she said. "Cut your indestructible bond in two. Bet you anything I can make it work. All you have to do is say the word."

She contemplated me with her living left eye. Dark hair and shadow and the tilt of her head hid her right eye—the prosthetic—from view. She wasn't smiling anymore.

"Would you like me to try?"

37

Asa gave me a week to decide.

It was about time for her and Wist to think of leaving, she explained.

Before attempting to bring down the city walls, they wanted to do a sweep for smaller lingering vorpal holes. Plus any threatening beasts that might've integrated themselves into the landscape. Like in the Temple of Cats and Circles.

In the meantime, Asa tasked me with making up my mind.

Tell me if you want me to sever your bond, she said. Tell me what you think we should do with your demon.

Before we parted, Wist passed me what appeared to be a corroded old cowbell, stuffed with cloth to keep it silent.

A subtle vibration of magic permeated the rust-eaten metal. A hint of sound too deep for human hearing. Asa told me I could ring the cowbell to call them over if I ran into trouble. Or if I happened across a vorpal hole or vorpal beast that they hadn't yet dealt with.

Unlike the Osmanthians, I didn't need to eat or sleep. And with the two of them hard at work to banish all major sources of supernatural danger from the city, I had little left to fear. Be it night or day.

I made my way back to the hot spring full of water imps. I washed my body and my clothes. The inner chalice suit would be ready to wear again in just a few hours. My flight suit might take a full day to dry out, but it wasn't as if I would freeze to death without it.

As before, the imps ignored my presence. I attempted to offer them the remainder of Vesper's chestnuts, but they made a show of not seeing me. I felt a bit sorry for sullying their water without giving them anything in return.

Not sorry enough to stop doing it, though. I sank in all the way up to my nose.

This current awakening marked the first time that Vesper and I had arisen together without a clear mission. Without anyone petitioning us to fix some terrible problem. Without monsters or enemy armies to fight, or ships full of refugees to rescue.

In lieu of a predefined objective—a dire threat, a wrong to be righted—was it inevitable for us to turn on each other instead? To become the enemy that we each suddenly lacked?

Maybe Vesper had been able to put up with the indignity of her position so long as we were able to mine some greater meaning from it. Through each subsequent awakening, through fire and agony, we'd earned every awed word of our reputation. To Jacians, we were a legend just as towering as the dreaded original Kraken.

Maybe the taste of glory had been sweet or numbing enough for Vesper to swallow the humiliation of following around a puny human. For her to endure the emptiness of those long ghostly stretches while I slept.

Part of me still had trouble taking Asa's proposal seriously.

From the time of the first Kraken, all the way to this new era of the reluctant second Kraken, I'd never heard anyone discuss bondbreaking in any context outside of academic thought experiments.

No such thing was possible, and everyone knew it. Bonding was for life.

Of course, no existing theories could explain the bond of mutual death, either. Normal mage-operator bonding was a entirely different beast from whatever Vesper and I shared.

Nor had anyone ever succeeded in coming up with an exact, unassailable definition for the being who wore Verity's face and yet told us that Verity was gone forever.

Many, many papers had been published to settle the question of what it meant to be a summoned demon. Not once had I heard a definitive answer.

I might harbor doubts about Asa's claims—but before meeting Wist, I would also have doubted anyone who claimed to be a second Kraken.

I'd asked Asa what became of the human bondmates she'd separated.

"One of you isn't human," she said. "That alone makes it a very different situation."

She did mention that normally, the people whose bonds she broke would never be able to magically bond with another again.

"But hey," she added. "Perhaps it's different for a demon."

Other consequences were easier to envision. Take away the bond of mutual death, and I'd be as vulnerable as any other mortal human.

As for Vesper—for her, it wouldn't be the same as human death. But imagine if someone spiked her in her weak spot after Asa broke our bond. Vesper would get permanently severed from this world. The world I'd brought her to.

For all intents and purposes, it would appear as though she'd perished. Some echo of her might live on in far-off vorpal realms, but she wouldn't be able to return here without her Host or her long-gone gate. The corporeal form and identity I'd given her, shaped by Verity, would be gone forever.

In that sense, Vesper too would lapse into a kind of mortality.

"Everyone's gonna die someday," Asa said bluntly. "Nothing special about being mortal again. Welcome back to the club, I'd tell you.

"If I sever your bond and she leaves you, you'll no longer be equipped for heroics. But you'll still have your own life to live. Another seventy years or so, if you're lucky."

Did I want to be lucky?

I bowed a sheepish farewell to the water imps before creeping back out through the fermenting old bathhouse. I chewed over Asa's words as I went.

Nothing in me thrilled to the notion of a life that was mine alone. It felt more like standing at the precipice of an uncrossable abyss. Like staring into the mind-gnashing nothingness of a vorpal hole.

Blank time stretched out in front of me, on and on. The more I thought about it, the more it made me want to go back into stasis.

It would be nigh-suicidal to attempt hibernation without the bond of mutual death.

Besides—without the power of a demon at my disposal, no one would be particularly motivated to help me enter stasis, anyhow.

No longer would I be a gift for future generations, the carefully-preserved key to Jace's ultimate weapon. I would be an anonymous woman in my twenties. A soldier unmoored from time. A stranger with zero family or friends or neighbors or coworkers or former classmates. An ex-mage who'd had every last trace of magic mutilated out of her as a child.

In the following days, I embarked on a truncated search for the grounds of the old orphanage. The place where Verity and I had grown up. The place where I'd killed her.

I knew I had no real hope of finding anything recognizable. The remains of that bygone city lay far below Glorybower. I carried neither the tools nor the knowledge of an archaeologist.

A parade of empty gondolas glided by as I walked alongside one of the oldest canals. Warty mollusk shells grew from them in tumorous masses.

I almost took the cowbell out of my pocket. But my magic perception failed to inform me whether these boats and the growths on them were steered by vorpal beasts. Their passage might merely be a side effect of the wild magic drifting all over the city.

If a demon was roughly analogous to a human mage, and a vorpal beast was something akin to an animal, then wild magic was perhaps more comparable to simple fungi. Random, rootless, and best combated with proper ventilation.

Wist might be able to defeat any vorpal beast in a magical duel. But she couldn't challenge wild magic to fight her. Removing the dome around the city would be the most effective way to dilute and dissipate all these pent-up phenomena.

One day it would diminish to more normal levels. The occasional ghostly hallucination in houses stigmatized by tales of haunting. The voice of an absent loved one on an empty street corner. Delicious scents of curry filling the air when no one in the neighborhood had done any cooking.

Back when we perched atop Solitaire's torso, I'd asked Asa to tell me more about the rest of Jace. How it looked nowadays, outside Glorybower.

Some of what she said made little sense. Perhaps because she herself was still quite new to Jacian scenery.

I struggled to picture my country through the words of an Osman-thian.

"I don't think you'll find it so alien," Asa told me in the end, once we'd descended from Solitaire. "Wist, were skimmers around fifty years ago?"

Wist nodded.

"Skimmers?" I said.

"A type of vehicle," Asa answered. "I guess airship traffic has increased a lot, too. At least compared to when Jace was completely closed off to us. But you must be familiar with airships. Didn't Jace have them long before the continent?"

True. Ours were once literal ships, buoyed aloft by the magic of dozens or hundreds of comatose mage batteries. They'd be systematically trussed up in deep-bellied cargo holds. Hopefully airships of the present day used different technology.

After giving up on finding the orphanage grounds, I traced a path back to Memorial Park.

Thick layers of ginkgo leaves painted the roads a rich shade of sunset yellow. Even fallen, the leaves remained unblemished. In a more populated city, pedestrian heels and wheels would've long since ground them up into heaps of golden sawdust.

Every other time I passed by the park, it had appeared downright impenetrable. I'd braced myself for needing to go plunder nearby restaurants before heading deeper. A large cleaver might serve me as a makeshift machete.

As the park came into view, I stopped dead in my tracks. Someone had cleared out the long sheets of autumn-tinted vines, along with the worst of the underbrush.

Asa and Wist? A solicitous vorpal beast? The wild magic that flowed like a current through now-unhampered trees, the tallest in the city?

Could've been any or all of them. Made it a simple matter for me to wind my way over to the visitor center.

Though walkable, the path was strewn with a stew of acorns and pine needles. Everywhere I went, tiny red maple leaves curled up like the dried-out husks of dead bugs.

I passed monument after monument, some too abstract for me to parse their meaning from afar. A pair of irregular towering structures might've been modeled after Vesper's horns. A grand open gate rose from a wide pond thoroughly infested with long-legged herons.

I let myself into the museum next to the visitor center. It was my second time coming here, and my first time seeing it in daylight.

The walls were discolored and fraying, the floors and ceiling corners stained in sooty hues of ash. Even so, the stairs up and down felt sturdy underfoot.

Like a tourist, I reviewed the flotsam of my own history. Glass display cases held burnt tiles salvaged from classical castles. At varying times, Vesper and I might have either defended them or laid siege to them.

I didn't attempt to read detailed captions. I focused my energy on the large-print labels. I gleaned just enough information to understand when I'd stumbled across an exhibit devoted to our suppression of a Continentalist rebellion.

No nostalgia stirred in me. Some of the antiquities jogged my memory. Most didn't. Everything that had happened was already over. No one would give me any prizes for dwelling on it.

I paused in the entrance to the room full of portraits. The only part of the museum I'd seen last time, when Vesper ported me here late at night.

These portraits were not us. They were someone's idea of us. The Char Rinehart standing on the threshold could scarcely recognize the painted versions of herself enshrined in heavy frames.

Vesper had loved me, I thought. In many different awakenings.

Surely by now the person Vesper had loved was long gone. Memories scrubbed away over and over. Eroded beyond any possibility of repair.

I occupied the same body, the same arms that had once known how to hold her. I wore the same skin-hugging chalice suit. I had the same circular watch lying flat over my navel like a lid over a drain, chained to my viscera.

Still, this faded self that remained must be a cruel echo of all Chars that Vesper had loved in the past.

One of them had saddled her with an impossible task: stop me from changing any further. By then it must have already been far too late.

To my knowledge, my feelings had never played a role in my own decisions. Quite the opposite. If I'd acted based on emotion, Verity would have lived. For a time, anyway, until they had us both killed for our defiance. Or until invaders found the orphanage.

Or maybe for much longer.

I'd accepted the fact that I couldn't save everyone. I'd accepted the fact that we need Vesper far more than Verity. I shouldn't justify it by pretending I'd been choosing between two futures set in stone.

Maybe someone smarter than me could've found a way to avoid sacrificing Verity. Rather than a path clouded with uncertainty, I'd simply selected the path of obvious and overwhelming victory.

Yet when Asa called herself the Bondbreaker, my first reaction had been nauseatingly visceral. Wholly divorced from logic. A thought that pulsated into being somewhere deep in my belly. Nowhere near my brain.

No.

Never.

I wanted to keep Vesper.

Even if she hated my guts.

Even if we were doomed to be at each other's throats forever—abusing the bond of mutual death to take out a formless frustration on each other, back and forth, over and over.

This deep-seated rejection of bondbreaking didn't stem from some heroic desire to continue serving my country for centuries to come.

That would've been an elegant way to explain it. The Host would be useless without a demon in tow. Such thoughts, however, had been as distant from my head as the invisible stars over Glorybower.

It was irrational. It was ugly. It was possessive. It possessed me.

I wanted to tear the portraits off the walls, hurl them face-down on the dust-tainted floor. You're not me, I would tell them. Stop seeing me for what I am.

There was not a sound in the entire museum except for my pained stifled breathing.

The portraits stayed secure in place, just as they had for the past fifty years running. I took a disjointed step back from the doorway.

This naked paroxysm of emotion was exactly why I needed to go through with it. I needed to release her.

The less I wanted to do it, the more that meant I should.

I pulled the cloth gag out of the rusted cowbell. I had to shake it ruthlessly to get it to ring. In the hush of the museum hall, it sounded as jarring as a fire alarm.

38

"FEEL ANY DIFFERENT?" Asa asked.

The sunlight was unusually intense today, as if the dome in the sky had served to focus and strengthen it. We took shelter under the boughs of grave wisteria holding down Solitaire's eight outstretched arms.

I'd thought wisteria was only supposed to bloom in spring, not early winter. But Solitaire's vines paid no heed to the season. Their lavender flowers hung down in pendulous tapered bundles like grapes.

I touched my stomach. The watch and its chain were both gone.

"I can still sense it there," I said.

"Like a phantom limb?"

I made a noise of agreement.

"What about the bond itself?" Asa sounded dissatisfied. "You don't feel it gone? You don't feel changed on the inside? Not one bit?"

I'd already told her that Vesper and I lacked the kind of psychic connection that human bondmates seemed to experience.

Couldn't miss something I never had in the first place.

Perhaps everything would've turned out differently if our emotions leaked across the bond. Or if we were able to lapse into telepathy as easily as Asa and Wist.

I never knew what Vesper really felt. I couldn't be sure of it even if she told me outright. I couldn't relate to the unshakable certainty of human bondmates.

Asa looked up at the lattice of wisteria shading us.

"So your demon might not realize the bond is gone," she said. "Not right away. Not unless someone goes to the trouble of telling her. Interesting."

"Is that unusual?"

"When I sever a human pair, they both feel it immediately. They both know as soon as I'm done. No hope of hiding it."

She shrugged. "Doesn't change the plan, of course. You ready?"

I stood before her, freshly unbonded and watch-less. Nothing left to wait for.

I told her I was ready.

Asa had agreed to free Vesper from the void behind her eye. With one condition.

For safety reasons, she would only release Vesper into the cage-like framework of teeth and bones at the back of Solitaire's cockpit. After that, it would be up to me to talk Vesper into some kind of truce.

"Ideally," Asa said, "you two could use your machina to bring down the barrier around the city. Then all our work here would be done. Easy as that."

I glanced over at Wist. "Can't your Kraken undo the barrier?"

"She'd have to reverse-engineer it from scratch. Could take weeks or months. I'd rather not get stuck here waiting while winter turns to spring, thank you very much."

One of Solitaire's hand-like attachments splayed out behind Asa. Earth-shredding claws pinned down the remnants of a residential building's brick wall. If that hulking hand curled shut around her, it would crush her like a grape.

"The last time we piloted Solitaire, we lost control," I said. "Can't promise that'll never happen again."

Asa appeared unconcerned. "Back then, the problem was that no one could stop you but yourselves. This time you've got Wist here on standby. Go as buck-wild as you want."

"Only if Vesper agrees to it."

Personally, I didn't think anything could get Vesper to voluntarily fuel Solitaire again. No matter what lay at stake.

"Don't sound so pessimistic," Asa said. "All depends on how persuasive you are. Turn up the charm."

I remained unconvinced. But I would keep my word. I would try.

Solitaire's milky quartz surface felt vaguely lukewarm, bathed in the fiercest sunlight early winter could muster. Asa oohed and aahed when I showed her how to slide open the door to the cockpit.

I barely heard her. The cockpit smelled perversely sterile, as if it had run incessant cleaning cycles since the last time I stuck my head in. Maybe it had become so hungry without me and Vesper, even in slumber, that it couldn't help but devour every last molecule of lingering pain and filth, our souring scents.

I didn't touch the pilot seat's translucent tuning fork. I placed myself sideways on the very edge of the seat, facing the vicious spikes and filaments that filled the back half of the cockpit.

A hand came down over my eyes. Wist's hand, judging by the size of it. Asa spoke from behind me. "It's kind of a trade secret, you know. All this magic we've got tangled up with my prosthetic. I'm quite shy about showing it."

I dutifully closed my eyes.

Wist's hand stayed in place.

The ability to sense magic didn't hinge solely on one's physical vision (or lack thereof). Wist touched me with an enchantment that distorted my perception, like peering through the wrong end of a spyglass. The magic ingrained throughout the cockpit blurred with the obscure magic leaking from Asa's false eye.

Then I heard the voice I knew better than any other.

I didn't catch what she said. It was like I had hands cupped over my ears, too.

My eyes flew open. I knocked Wist's arm away. She didn't try to stop me.

Vesper fit into the body-shaped hollow in the back wall of the cockpit. She fit there like a key in a lock.

Metallic tendrils had already snaked out to loop around her arms and legs and throat and torso, securing her in place. Others slipped up under her turtleneck, seeking the tender insides of her ribcage gills.

Her time in Asa's void didn't seem to have changed her. As promised, she looked uninjured.

Solitaire wouldn't let that last much longer.

Spear-like spurs of bone lengthened smoothly and silently from Solitaire's living walls. They grew so fast that if you blinked, you might think they'd been positioned there all along. A forest of barbs at the ready, denting her skin but not yet breaking it.

Even in repose, our chalice had the instincts of an apex predator. At the slightest provocation, Solitaire stood poised to ingest her.

Vesper scanned the cockpit. The bristling array of glossy wet fangs. The moist breathing walls that shone as if lacquered. Asa and Wist behind me.

She moved her eyes to me last.

As always, her eyes were the brightest part of her. They reflected the light from the open door. A light not her own.

She didn't squirm or grunt with discomfort. She didn't make any futile attempts to escape.

Locked into Solitaire like this, she couldn't use her own magic. Even while on standby, even while flopped on the ground like a sleeping giant, the machina would drink it all up.

Bound here, she was the demon equivalent of the human mage batteries that Jace had cultivated and used and discarded for hundreds of years. The mages who'd once lived in our walls, who'd propelled our monorails and ships.

Except that Vesper remained fully conscious. Vesper couldn't get lost in dreamless stasis.

"You won," she said to me in Jacian, in a voice utterly devoid of emotion. "Not with your own power, of course." She flicked another look at the Osmanthians. "You've never achieved anything alone, have you? But that doesn't change the facts. You got me where you wanted me. Congratulations."

I wished I could say I'd never heard Vesper use that particular tone before, one so hopelessly distant.

I wished I could say that, but I couldn't swear to it. In her memory, it might've already happened dozens of times in the past.

"Let's—let's talk," I said scratchily.

At first Vesper offered no response. She stared past me so hard that I turned to see what the Osmanthians were doing.

Nothing unusual. Wist leaned in the doorway with one leg stretched out across it like the rail of a fence, blocking our exit. Asa peeped into the cockpit from behind her.

Sunlight diverted its path to flow around both of them, pooling in broken shapes on the dark starving floor at my feet.

"Let's talk," Vesper repeated, as if for a time she'd been too stunned to speak.

Suddenly she switched to Continental. Her gaze remained bolted to the Osmanthians by the open door. "Sure, sweetheart. Whatever you want."

She bobbed her head a little. Curled the tips of her fingers. No other part of her had any real freedom of movement.

"Yeah," she continued, "I'd say this is the ideal environment for us to hash it all out. Couldn't have planned it better myself. A nice nostalgic setting. A totally equal balance of power. You, with allies in tow, sitting in the literal pilot's seat. Me spatchcocked like a chicken for roasting.

"Anything we talk about here will absolutely be beautiful and meaningful and heartfelt and not at all forced out under duress. No, ma'am."

I matched her choice of language: Continental to answer Continental. "Ves," I said. "You tried to behead me."

"C'mon," Asa muttered. "Good heavens. Can you blame us for taking precautions?"

She gave a self-important little cough. Then she spoke louder, addressing both of us.

"Now, I'm no therapist, but allow me to point something out to you dimwits.

"Look at me and Wist. She's the Kraken. I'm an operator—I'm not even a mage. Magically speaking, she's got more power than anyone can imagine. Me, I've got none."

"A beautiful story," said Vesper. "By Osmanthian standards, you must be quite the social climber."

"I wasn't finished," Asa retorted. "Once I'm done lecturing, you can call me a gold digger all you like. I've heard worse."

She sailed onward, unflappable. "Here in Jace, people might see me and Wist as being unbalanced in other ways.

"Isn't it Jacians who preach about mages being wild animalistic things, creatures of crude emotion? Isn't it Jacians who say mages have an inherent need to be properly governed and ordered around and controlled?

"Sorry if I'm wrong. But for whatever reason, no matter what country we go to, no one ever thinks of me and Wist as real equals.

"So what? We still work things out. There are multiple types of power in the world. There are all kinds of different ways to reach a livable balance."

"How sweet," Vesper said. "Let's trade places, then. You try being the one tied up."

"Some people are into that," Asa remarked. "I'm afraid I'll have to decline, though. This is between you and your Host."

She stretched past Wist to poke me in the back.

"If nothing else," she said to me, sotto voce, "you can become more equal in terms of knowledge. Information. Your understanding of your current situation.

"Again, I'm the last person who ought to be giving anyone relationship advice. But don't you have anything important to tell your demon?"

Vesper stirred as if testing the limits of her bonds. Solitaire's automated filaments held her so tight that any serious effort to shift her body ended up looking like an involuntary shudder, an internal ripple of disgust.

I rose from the pilot seat. I had my flight suit buttoned up to my breastbone. I started undoing the buttons, one by one, until Vesper could see my bare stomach. The swath of it left deliberately uncovered by my clingy inner chalice suit.

"Your watch," she said sharply. "What happened to your—"

No one interrupted Vesper. She cut herself off. Her eyes were wide and helplessly luminous, even among the shadows at the thorny heart of Solitaire.

"Quick to catch on, aren't you?" Asa said to her. "Gosh, it's nice not having to go through a whole big explanation. I quite like you, I think. Homicidal tendencies notwithstanding."

"How?" Vesper asked quietly. Her voice seemed on the verge of vanishing.

39

I INDICATED ASA. "She can break bonds. I asked her to do it."

"You asked her," Vesper said. "You wanted this."

"You didn't?"

Silence.

Then: "It never seemed possible. Not even with demon magic." Vesper's voice rose. "*She* did this? Just like that? Some random Osmanthian operator?"

"Hey," Asa said. "I walk with the Kraken. I'm a cut above your average operator from the continent. Or from anywhere, really."

Vesper didn't fire back. Now she looked at me as if the two of us were alone in the cockpit. Just like we'd always been when we shut ourselves up here to steer our chalice.

She switched back to Jacian. "I don't understand. The bond was a form of insurance for both of us. An extra chance at life. What's the point of giving it up?

"With that alone, you've made us weaker than those two foreigners. Weaker than the new Kraken. It's the one thing we had that they can't replicate."

"I won't be your Host anymore," I answered in Jacian. "I'm releasing you. From the bond of mutual death. From any promises you've ever made me.

"If I can, I want to release you from your contract with Verity, too. I won't forget her. And I won't forget you. I won't go back in stasis."

"This old song again," Vesper said. "I know how it goes."

"I'll step back," I told her. "I'll abdicate. This age has a Kraken capable of closing massive vorpal holes. A Kraken disinterested in waging war. This age has its own heroes."

"They're Osmanthians," Vesper snapped. "In case you've forgotten. You'll leave Jace in their hands?"

"I'll leave Jace in the hands of Jacians. Ones born more recently than us."

"Quite a change of heart." Strain thinned her voice. "I suppose you'll leave Solitaire with them, too. They'll put children in chalices if they need to.

"Remember why you kept returning to be a hero for Jace, again and again. Because the alternative was always so much worse!"

Outside air had begun to filter through the cockpit. I could taste it. As long as we left the door wide open, it would keep on coming.

"You can be a hero for Jace, too," I said. "You don't need me for that. You never needed me.

"The Host will retire. The guardian demon of Jace can do whatever she likes. You don't have to stay on the islands. You don't have to linger anywhere in this world, if you don't want to. If those far-off vorpal realms are your real home, then you can head home now."

"I get it," Vesper said, low and harsh. "Had me real perplexed for a few seconds there. I've never seen you so willingly propose to become a powerless nobody. What the hell? I wondered at first. What's your angle?

"Now I see it. Think I'll be so overjoyed to be free of you that I'll let bygones be bygones? Think I'll happily faff off to the vorpal plane and never look back?"

She couldn't shake her head, though she made a muted attempt. "Don't underestimate me, Char. I'll haunt you for the rest of your mortal life."

I stopped myself from saying anything further.

I was going about this all the wrong way.

I'd changed. I'd said it myself, in past awakenings. All the hibernation and repetition and forgetting—it changed me before Vesper got a chance to stop it.

Maybe my old self would never have turned her back on the possibility of once more saving the nation. Just like we used to in times past.

Perhaps I'd changed for the worst. Perhaps I'd gotten worn down like those weathered heads at the top of the bell tower. Perhaps I'd lost whatever made me shine.

As a result, I'd also become capable of giving it all up. I could walk away now. I could let go of being the Host, of being good and right and saving lives. I could let go of Vesper.

But I didn't need to convince her of that in the next few minutes. We didn't need to sign a treaty about how to conduct ourselves for the rest of our lives.

We just needed to agree not to kill each other for a couple more days.

I pushed past the pilot's chair. I shimmied a wary path between the long glistening rows of fangs and needles jutting out from either side of the cockpit.

I stopped close enough to Vesper to touch her, though I didn't attempt to reach out. Not with her being caged there, unable to dodge me.

Countless javelins of deadly metal and bone pressed painful-looking dents in her skin and clothing. I watched her fight to tamp down her cycle of breath, to move her chest as little as possible.

"You want to get out of here," I said. Not a question.

Vesper laughed. "Now you sound like a villain. What'll it cost me?"

"A day or two of peace. A short-term truce. After it's over—anything goes."

"I wish"—she lamented, with a grimacing flash of razor-sharp teeth—"I wish I could've hacked your head off."

Her voice was strangely lacking in venom.

"Better luck next time," I said inanely. "Surely now you'll have better things to do with your life."

Vesper made a noise of disagreement deep in her throat. "Luck has nothing to do with it. I couldn't. I can't."

"Because the Osmanthians stopped you." I didn't understand why she seemed stuck on this.

"Is that what they told you? Liars." She smiled bitterly. "I tried. Believe me. I had every chance to do it. The Osmanthians couldn't possibly have stopped me in time.

"You lay without moving. Neck exposed. Beaten on the ground. My sword was ready. Then my muscles froze. Like I've never hurt anyone. Like I've never carved my way through howling armies. Like I've never chewed and swallowed human flesh. Like a big-mouthed asshole who's never seen battle.

"I couldn't do it," she said. "I could've stood there for hours, arms quaking from the weight of it. I couldn't do it."

"You didn't have any problem pitching me off the bell tower," I pointed out.

Vesper closed her eyes. "Once was enough."

"Once? You've eaten me whole in the past."

She laughed again, more to herself than to me. The soft broken sound of it hurt something deep under the roots of my teeth.

That was when Asa called to us from the cockpit entrance. As always, she spoke Continental.

"I haven't the faintest idea what you guys are saying, but I'll assume it's heading somewhere positive. Or less violent, at least, than the last time I saw you together."

She and Wist were backlit in the doorway, ringed by a haze of sun.

"Would you consider this a good stopping point?" she inquired. "Yes?" She didn't leave any time to respond. "Then allow me to interrupt."

Vesper's voice became a whisper. "You should leave." She reverted to Jacian. "They're plotting something."

"Me, plotting?" Asa put a hand over her heart. "Never."

"You've been pretending not to know Jacian," Vesper said, this time in Continental.

Asa put on a wounded face. "I really am quite hopeless with languages. Context clues help, though."

"You lied to Char," Vesper bit out. "What other lies did you feed her?"

"I have no idea what you're talking about," Asa said blithely.

"You were there. You saw me. You were waiting, arms crossed. You watched me struggle and fail miserably. I couldn't bring the sword down. I was stuck.

"Did you tell her I would've killed her? Did you tell her you rushed to save her at the last second, with the blade millimeters from her neck? Or"—Vesper's eyes narrowed—"did you claim that she really did die? Head rolling to the gutter. Red blood on my sword, on the pavement, everywhere."

"Oh," Asa uttered. "You *are* a clever one. But I take exception to the idea of that being so very far from the truth. You wish you could've killed her again. You were knocking each other's teeth out.

"Any reasonable person would've attempted to separate you, one way or another. Savagery isn't made any more acceptable by the two of you having once possessed some magical ability to bounce back from it."

"Did you intervene to be righteous," Vesper asked, "or because you saw a chance to learn more about our bond before making your move to destroy it?"

They looked at each other from across the cockpit. Asa framed in light. Vesper in shadow.

Asa wasn't wearing her usual cap. Her black jacket and one of her overall straps drooped lazily off her shoulders.

She was by far the smallest and weakest-looking out of any of us.

She reminded me of the Jacian operators who had appeared to advise me each time I woke. Telling me who to fight, who to rescue. Telling me all about our enemies.

Sometimes I saw right through them on my own—saw how my success at a mission would elevate their influence, or undercut their political foes.

Sometimes I needed Vesper to warn me.

I tried to navigate the gauntlet of skewers and thorns, to wade back to the pilot seat. From there, I could prompt the bindings to release Vesper without fully awakening Solitaire.

With our bond broken, Vesper and I were strangers, and both of us knew it. Her rage had gone cold and stale. She might talk big, but she wouldn't attack me, or any of us.

I had to convince Asa of that—Asa and Wist, but more importantly Asa. The evident leader. I had to get Vesper out of here.

Yet my feet stayed stapled to the floor. I couldn't move. Not my legs, and not my mouth.

I couldn't speak. I couldn't reach the pilot seat. I couldn't look back at Vesper. The Kraken's magic arrested me in place.

Asa pushed her bangs away from her right eye.

"I took a real close look inside you when I severed your bond," she informed me.

"Stop," Vesper said, uncharacteristically shrill. "If you do anything to—"

"You may have fooled your Vesper all this time," Asa continued. Matter-of-fact. Conversational. "And every human being you've ever met. You may even have fooled yourself. But you can't fool Asa Clematis."

Wist the Kraken began to say something.

"She'll live," Asa replied.

An inhuman green light shone from the back of her dark artificial eye.

The magic was so sophisticated and so very precise. I perceived it more distinctly than I'd ever perceived any other act of magic in my life.

It wasn't Asa's magic. She had none of her own. The Kraken's power pierced a path through her eye like the sun being focused by a magnifying glass, like clear rays getting sliced into sharp rainbow parts by a prism.

And in an instant too swift for breath, too swift for any further attempts at speech, it sliced into me. Lasering a huge hole in my chest, a perfect circle of extinguished flesh.

If she weren't tied down, Vesper could've stuck both arms straight through the carved-out tunnel in me. With room to spare.

I felt air in places that were never supposed to touch open air. Otherwise, I didn't feel much of anything. I wasn't bleeding, somehow, or maybe my blood was just as paralyzed as the rest of me.

The only thing I heard was Vesper screaming.

40

VESPER HAD LAPSED into Old Jacian. Curses that no one else had voiced in centuries pelted the cockpit, ricocheting off Solitaire's metal teeth and blades of shining bone.

Asa seemed unfazed by Vesper's screams. Possibly because she couldn't comprehend a word of them.

Next to Asa, Wist stood a little bowed. Even so, she remained tall enough to fill the cockpit doorway.

She had her line of sight fixed on Vesper now. She looked stricken.

I gazed down at the gaping emptiness in my torso and wondered where all the pain had gone.

I wondered what Asa had against Vesper—why she'd insisted on killing me here and now, right in front of her.

It all seemed so gratuitous. If Asa had manipulated me into getting our bond broken so she could get rid of us, she could've followed up by killing us one at a time. Neatly, cleanly, separately.

No reason to do it like this. Unless Asa was the worst kind of sadist. No need to do it a foot away from Vesper, close enough for me to collapse against her.

Except that the Kraken's magic wouldn't let me collapse. It held me up on strings like a marionette.

I stood rigid and foolish, listening to Vesper howl about how she would kill both of them, kill and dismember them, kill every Osmanthian, burn down the continent. Her throat sounded as if fury had split it open, as if it were bleeding all the way down to the center of her.

I was too confused for anger. I couldn't see much anymore. I didn't think I was breathing. I didn't have much of a respiratory system left to breathe with.

I was leaving Vesper behind again. Only this time, I wouldn't awaken to plague her once more in future eras. Maybe it was for the best.

"Char Rinehart," Asa said with cold clarity. "You don't have to die from that."

I don't know how I heard her past Vesper's torrent of cries, her brutal curses and graphic threats. Maybe I'd hallucinated it. Maybe the Kraken's magic had carried her words to me.

An acidic scent soaked the cockpit. Fine vinegar—or demon blood. As though Vesper, right behind me, had wrenched hard enough against her bindings for the mass of pricking lances and spider-silk wires to bite her open. Rupturing clothes and skin alike.

"Don't be an idiot," Asa said, still addressing me. "Don't sabotage yourself."

Why was I still alive to hear her?

"Look harder," she commanded. "We didn't touch your weak spot."

Vesper went silent.

Her silence was so sudden and total that, for a disoriented split-second, I feared Solitaire had consumed her. I couldn't turn my head to see her.

The citrus scent of demon blood flooded my senses.

Jacian turtle doves cooed somewhere far outside the cockpit. They cooed the same throaty notes over and over, oblivious to the hellish tableau on display inside our unmoving chalice.

In all these centuries, their calls hadn't changed. Doves sounded the same in summer and in winter, inside and outside the orphanage. They sounded the same whether they were singing after carnage or on a glorious seaside day.

They would keep sounding the same when I died here. Wild birds—and so much of the world around them—had never needed the Host.

A pang burrowed through my lower back. A sensation like a drill whirring into the spot just above my tail bone.

For some reason, this hurt far worse than the magical excision of half my torso. Which seemed to be taking an inexplicably long time to finish doing me in.

Either that, or each passing fraction of a second had gotten stretched out to feel a million times longer than it took in reality.

The small of my back ached as if a little devil had taken up residence there, gnawing greedily at the base of my spine.

My weak spot, I thought.

My weak spot?

The Kraken's magic released me. I buckled to my knees, sagging against the parallel rows of spears that had extended to perforate Vesper. My lolling head almost touched her legs.

I was too befuddled to scrounge up much in the way of regret. The new pain in my back crushed each burgeoning thought like beetles crunched to goo beneath the heel of a boot.

If I regretted anything, it was that this all had to unfold right at Vesper's feet.

There was very little wetness on the floor, though that might not mean much. Either Vesper hadn't shed as much blood as I'd dreaded, or Solitaire had already absorbed the bulk of it.

My field of vision telescoped down to a narrow tunnel, all fog and shadow.

"Pull yourself together," Asa said, sharper than before.

She stood much further away from me than Vesper, yet her voice was the only intelligible sound to reach my ears now. Felt like it was being poured down a funnel straight into the dried-up fossil of my brain.

"Wist would be horrified if you let yourself die for the sake of appearances."

My lower back throbbed as though a rebel parasite were trying to break free of it, thrashing to escape the net of my skin.

You don't have to die from that.

There was a reason I couldn't admit the truth of this. A reason neither touching nor sensible.

Something more akin to a psychopath's idea of a practical joke.

I began to understand that, with each shivering cell of my fatally disrupted body, and yet I still couldn't follow Asa's directive to save myself.

Free will had nothing to do with it. I was committed to my role.

I'd been committed to that same role—utterly unaware of it—for over a thousand years. Sure, I'd spent most of them sleeping. Even in sleep, I'd stayed locked into the role I had to play. I'd sacrificed all knowledge of myself for the sake of adhering to a single meaningless contract.

Asa was right. But I was physically, mentally, and magically incapable of acknowledging it. I'd made myself that way on purpose.

If you were going to cage yourself, better not leave the slightest possibility of an escape route.

I contemplated the revelation from far away, as if watching a boat drift toward the endless horizon. I lacked the power to steer it to shore.

Unless—

I caught a smeared glimpse of Vesper looking down at me.

"Char."

Her voice sounded naked, flayed of all protection.

"Char," she said again. Then: "No. No."

She made a small guttural sound when she tried to swallow, something halfway between a groan and a sob.

"Who are you?" Vesper asked me. "How long have you been a demon?"

41

A DEMON DOES NOT come into this world with the emotional palette or the cultural values of a human being.

A demon dragged through a living gate by Charity Rinehart would not, however, arrive as a total blank slate. They'd take on the appearance and memories and procedural knowledge of their gate. This was true for Vesper, summoned into being through an orphan called Verity.

In the same way, it was also true for me.

Before dying, Verity had made a contract with Vesper.

Don't ever let her forget me.

Vesper hadn't been especially perturbed when Verity died. Verity was a doorway to her, and little more.

Yet Vesper had remembered her promise to Verity all these years, and she'd kept it with a deathly sincerity.

Every single time I awoke from stasis, she'd find a moment to make sure I still knew Verity's name.

That contract was the one thing that might compel Vesper to keep crawling back to me. Even in the absence of our bond.

I was in no position to fault her for it. I'd made a similar promise to my gate—a similarly binding contract.

Only mine was far less benign. Mine was more along the lines of a grotesque accident.

None of which stopped me from faithfully fulfilling my contractual obligations.

That's what it means to be a demon, you see. A newborn demon untainted by the muddy nuances of the human world.

A demon who possessed a copy of her gate's human memories, but who could only regard them from a distance. As if poring over the clumsy details of a scene stuffed in a snow globe.

A demon who would need long centuries to begin experiencing anything deeper than a washed-out imitation of human desire and grief.

We need your demon.

Everyone in the orphanage said those words to Charity Rinehart. The dowager, the torturers they called researchers, visiting commanders, even the other inmates.

Inmates? I mean survivors.

I mean children.

Charity would've pulled a demon from anyone else if she could. The next time she called on Vesper would be the last. Everyone knew it.

But Charity didn't know how to pull a demon from anyone other than Verity. Back then, no one understood much about the parameters of her freakish ability. Least of all Charity herself.

Was it her fault for only being close to Verity, and no one else? Did the affection between them make it possible for her to reach inside Verity and drag out a demon? Was their friendship the very factor that had sentenced Verity to become a gate, and eventually to shatter?

The day of the final summoning came too soon. Desperate whispers filled the corridors of the orphanage. Hurry, hurry, hurry.

Charity had tried with other people. Oh, she'd tried. Some were willing—if frightened—volunteers. They hoped the honor of becoming a gate might one day free them to leave the institution. Others fled with wide white-rimmed eyes as soon as she approached.

Either way, the result was the same. She couldn't perceive their second shadow, no matter how madly she strained her senses.

She had to try something else.

An oracle tree grew on the orphanage grounds. An evergreen with broad, flat leaves. Scratch the leaves and they'd darken, preserving a message as distinct as chalk on stone.

Charity plucked a single leaf from the oracle tree and wrote a short note. She could only hope it was legible.

She didn't have a mirror. Nor did she know where to find one. All she had was a basin of serenity water. A perfect circle. Touch it, splash it—and almost before your fingers left the surface, it would once more be flawlessly slick and glassy and flat.

She brought the basin down to the bumpy tile floor of her room. She set her oracle leaf nearby, message side up.

She got on her hands and knees before the basin. She had to hunch her whole body over the ice-smooth sheet of water to have any hope of seeing what she was doing.

She'd never before attempted to look for her own second shadow.

Now that she was trying, she saw it immediately.

She reached for herself.

She reached for herself, and she pulled out me.

I looked almost exactly like her, young and lanky and underfed. Same black hair and puzzled eyes. Verity had said that Charity always seemed as if she were mulling over something she didn't quite comprehend.

Unlike Vesper, I didn't have horns or pointed ears or a carnivore's teeth or gills scored in my sides. Unlike Vesper, I stood flat on the cold ground without protest.

I had hands without fingernails, fingers made of a hard rough substance like living stone. Chains grew from my body like extra limbs: from my navel, from the backs of my shoulders and ribcage.

One day, everything but my stained hands and feet would be hidden.

Charity didn't understand why she hadn't fainted. She'd thought she would go comatose the instant I emerged. Just like Verity, and every other gate she'd opened to date.

She'd written on a leaf from the oracle tree so I could understand what she wanted from me, even if she couldn't think or speak.

She'd expected to collapse, pitching headlong into the basin of serenity water. She could only hope that it might occur to me to catch her.

Yet Charity remained conscious. Perhaps this was the underbelly of her mysterious power. She could turn animals and people into living gates. And as a gate, she alone could remain awake during a summoning.

She snatched the stiff leaf off the floor with trembling fingers. She stared down at the message she'd scratched there as if she'd forgotten how to read.

Charity asked me, her demon, to save Jace from the coming warships. She asked me to save Jace so she wouldn't have to bring Vesper back again. So she wouldn't have to kill Verity, a gate already so close to breaking apart.

I didn't share Charity's sense of urgency. I didn't mind doing a favor for my gate, though. Which was why I told her the truth: demons aren't all one and the same. They vary in power.

Just like how one vorpal beast might terrorize an entire town, and another would slip past humanity unnoticed. Just like how some human mages can hardly master a single magical skill, while others learn to juggle dozens. The most menacing vorpal beasts and the most accomplished mages were naturally rarer than the rest.

Likewise, Vesper was a rarer sort of demon.

I could guess why. I held Charity's entire life history inside me.

"You love Verity a lot more than you love yourself," I explained to her. "Therein lies the difference. The demon you pulled from her turned out much stronger."

Charity looked as if she would rather have been told anything else. As if she would rather have been slapped and berated.

We stood on opposite sides of the basin. The serenity water reflected the ceiling beams with preternatural fidelity.

Charity had the base of her hand pressed to her mouth. From the way she was breathing, I thought she might faint after all.

It wouldn't have occurred to me to try to catch her.

I could listen politely. I could speak fluent Old Jacian, which back then was simply called Jacian.

I could dredge up memories even Charity herself had buried, memories of a mother who had never wanted to surrender her. But I couldn't yet force my mind to trace the same sort of emotional patterns as hers.

The small room smelled of cedar. Normally she would've shared it with Verity. A special privilege for the institution's greatest success story. Most other residents slept in long rows of beds on wood pallets, in chilly halls laid out like a field hospital.

Verity was elsewhere now, being watched around the clock. Everyone feared she might flee. Perhaps they even feared that Charity might help—or might try to flee with her.

They imagined themselves in Verity's position, knowing she couldn't survive another summoning. They imagined themselves running away, and so they thought she'd do the same.

Outside it was early summer. Flake-flies bumped the barred window, thick as snow. Charity Rinehart rubbed feverishly at the outer corners of her eyes.

"My flesh," she muttered.

"Your flesh?"

"Vesper said it. She said she'd become more powerful if I let her eat people."

I turned this over in my head. "Temporarily," I reminded her.

"Temporary power is better than nothing. Take a bite out of me. Won't one bite bring you closer to Vesper?"

Our eyes were perfectly level. They had to be. We were built like twins.

"One bite won't be enough," I cautioned her.

She swallowed. "Then take my arm, or both my arms. Take my legs if you have to."

"Still not enough," I said. "I told you, not all demons are equal. To match Vesper's magic, I'd need to consume your whole body and soul. Your whole life, leaving nothing left."

From the way Charity reacted, I almost thought she hadn't heard me.

She stooped and lifted the basin, moving it over to a low table. Regular liquid would've slopped all down the front of her tunic, given how unsteadily she held it.

True to its nature, the pool of serenity water stayed contained.

She kept her back turned, hiding her face from me.

"My whole life," she repeated. "My whole life to promote you to a higher echelon of demonhood. How long will the effect last?"

"A few days."

"A few—"

The way she stood made her look rather smaller than me now. She reached up to scrub at her face again. Then she asked me if a few days would be enough to annihilate the troops burning their way up the coast.

"Yes," I said. "If I consume you."

Without a word, she turned toward Verity's bed—unslept-in for many days now.

It was a humble thing. Too small even for a young woman who'd already stopped growing. Plain cedar planks supported a layer of bedding stuffed with rice chaff.

Charity knelt there and buried her face in the bedding. Her shoulders shook, violent and soundless. Flake-flies kept batting up against the thick window-glass. I said nothing.

When she rose, she told me to devour her on the spot.

I asked her what she wanted in return.

"Save Jace," she said tightly.

"Anything else?"

Charity shook her head.

But her heart betrayed her.

As soon as she started to lose herself to me, she began having second thoughts.

Not about becoming a gate. Not about sacrificing herself to a demon. She'd made her choice. But she was terrified of Verity finding out about it. Verity would think—not wrongly—that Charity had become a martyr to spare her.

It wasn't a conscious wish. It wasn't even directed at me, not really. But it was her last and most overwhelming desire, a ferocious plea to the universe at large. She wished it with every fragment of her being.

Don't let anyone know.

Charity was dead and gone too fast to understand that we'd formed a binding contract.

She'd willingly fed her life to me. I felt a primal obligation to honor her final entreaties. It would never have occurred to me to protest, to dodge my responsibility, to resist. That was no more likely than a migratory bird abruptly losing interest in long trips.

She'd left the oracle leaf on Verity's bedding. Once Charity was gone—vanished inside me—I beckoned the leaf to me with a flick of my finger. It sailed through the air and into my mouth.

I chewed for a long time before swallowing. It tasted quite bitter, and had the rubbery denseness of a stale cracker.

No one else would ever see what Charity had scratched on that leaf: her formal request to me, her last will and testament. She'd wanted me to save Jace from the marauders.

The dying scream of her smothered heart overrode all her painstaking plans.

Don't let anyone know.

The first demon Charity Rinehart ever made was Vesper. The last demon she ever made was herself.

In other words: me. I slipped into the space she'd vacated. I became her so fluently that neither Vesper nor Verity ever suspected a thing.

I kept my promise. I granted Charity's dying wish with the implacable commitment of a demon. The foreign pillagers' magic and technology far outstripped anything Jace possessed at the time. But they couldn't outstrip Vesper.

I did save Jace, after all. I simply used Vesper to do it.

Because if I used my own demon magic to massacre armies, everyone would see me for what I really was. And for what I wasn't.

I couldn't save Jace with my own power and still pretend to be human, an ex-mage bereft of her magic core.

Don't let anyone know.

I didn't. I faithfully protected our secret. Most importantly of all, I protected it from myself.

In overclocking mode, right after eating Charity, I used my brief reserves of bottomless power to reshape my demon body. I hid my chains. I turned my pupils into a more human shape. I changed the very color of my blood.

I told myself I was Charity Rinehart, a human girl. Every molecule of my being believed it.

The human Charity Rinehart had only one way to defend her nation. There was only one person she knew how to use as a gate.

I murdered Verity to bring Vesper back, and they called me a hero for it.

To a newly-formed demon, this made perfect sense.

There was only one logical course of action. Only one way to fulfill both of Charity's pleas: to deliver Jace from evil, and to keep her own sacrifice a secret.

I did exactly that, and nothing more.

Would the real Charity have let Verity die like that? Would the real Charity have been able to disregard Verity's tears, her struggling, the rictus of betrayal on her face? Verity had never agreed to perish for the good of the nation.

Now, all these centuries later, I could say for a fact that the real Charity would never have been able to go through with it.

I only became capable of understanding this after many, many years of brainwashing myself into thinking I was human. After steadfastly going through the motions of having humanity.

Yet over time, violence had come to distress me less and less. My decision-making got quicker. My philosophy of heroism turned more drastic, more rigid.

Vesper and I had mistakenly believed I was losing myself, my essential human nature decaying with each new cycle of hibernation.

Maybe the opposite was true.

As my thoughts grew colder and more practical, crueler and more alien, I kept inching ever closer to my original demon self. The humanity flaking off me had never been more than a determined facade.

42

HOW LONG HAVE you been a demon?

As soon as those words left Vesper's mouth, I felt the contract release me. Asa had already hinted at it. But Vesper was the first to give voice to it.

She knew. They knew.

As a result, I knew.

Which meant, according to the all-or-nothing logic of a demonic contract, that there was no longer any point in continuing to hide it. My old vow to Charity—who would never have wished for things to turn out like this—was rendered moot.

My chest made a bizarre crackling sound as organs grew back to fill my thoracic cavity, which the magic from Asa's eye had turned into a literal cavity. A porthole straight to the other side of me.

Heart and lungs, arteries and veins, esophagus and membranes: they germinated and blossomed and enclosed themselves beneath a creeping shroud of skin. Even the missing parts of my chalice suit grew back, smooth as a bonus coating of scales.

All the while, my lower back kept aching. It felt like I'd been strapped in place at a desk for the past thousand-plus years. It felt like I'd straightened my body for the first time in my life.

"There you go," Asa said, a touch smugly.

My sight was the clearest it had ever been. I dreaded looking at Vesper.

She'd stopped blinking. She may have stopped breathing.

Neither of us really needed to breathe, when you got down to it. We could give up breathing, just as we'd mostly given up eating and sleeping.

But having a heartbeat and using one's lungs was fundamentally more comfortable than forcing everything to stillness. At least when you wore a body primarily patterned after the human form. The physical shape that came to us most naturally was a way of paying homage to our long-dead gates.

"Charity died before Verity," I told Vesper.

Her mouth parted. My gaze stayed riveted to her fangs. It was easier, somehow, than looking her in the eye.

"*You* killed Verity." She sounded strangled. "The last one to summon me—that was you. Not Charity Rinehart. You replaced her like a goddamn cuckoo bird. You. Her demon spawn."

"Me," I agreed.

In all my memory—what remained of it, anyway—I'd never seen Vesper look as if she were about to be sick.

She turned her head from me. As she moved, two of Solitaire's bone spikes raked bloody blue gashes down her cheek.

"If I have to stay in this hellish vessel for even a minute longer," she said huskily, "I'll go mad."

I backed away until I bumped into the pilot seat. The oversized tuning fork no longer appeared transparent: it looked like twin branches of solid obsidian. The fork itself had not changed in the past few minutes. Only my perception was different. The material that made up its tines very much resembled the material that made up my scorched-looking hands.

I touched the tuning fork with the tip of a single finger.

That was all it took now. Solitaire heard me.

The binding wires whipped away from Vesper. The protruding bone stakes and scythe-like fangs retreated.

Freed to use her own magic again, Vesper immediately winked out of sight.

I'd figured she would port away from the cockpit. As expected, she'd gone somewhere too far for me to sense her.

I rubbed the small of my back. The pangs and cramping only worsened.

I lifted myself out of the cockpit into an outpour of sunlight so warm and luxuriant that it felt downright mocking. Asa and Wist moved back from the entrance to make room for me.

"You could've killed me," I said.

"No," Asa replied. "Not a chance."

"What convinced you I was a demon?"

"You want to get into the details of that now?" she asked. "Or do you want help finding your Vesper?"

"I don't need help."

Wist watched me like a guard dog. It no longer stung my senses to focus directly on her power, though she was no longer making any attempt to dim it. I could make out the radiant core deep in her torso, the seemingly infinite magic branches that extended from it like a forest of cilia.

"I've got questions for you," I said to Asa.

"We aren't leaving the city just yet. Take your time."

There was an irritating hint of sympathy in the way she regarded me, one hand raised to shield her face from the light.

"All those years," she murmured, "and neither you nor Vesper had the slightest inkling of what you really were."

I excused myself—too abruptly, perhaps, but I wasn't in a position to fret about niceties. I descended from Solitaire with Asa's words lingering like a sunburn on my back.

I wove past the grave wisteria and the wreckage of several apartments, until I could no longer look back and see either of the Osmanthians. The only two living humans in all of Glorybower.

Having found some modicum of privacy, I touched my navel. I coaxed a silver chain to come spiraling out as if it had always been coiled up behind a wall of muscle, waiting.

I had no countdown clock anymore. My chains, however, had been part of me since my inception. Just like Vesper and her horns.

I couldn't explain why I knew how to use them, but I did. In a way, I'd never forgotten. The knowledge had been sealed off together with all the other parts of me deemed too inhuman to fit the role of heroic Charity Rinehart.

I stretched the chain out in my hands. The long scorpion-tipped end dangled free, tracing lazy circles in the air by my knees.

I pulled my chain harder, and it pulled me to Vesper.

One moment I stood in the shadow of a smashed-open bank building. Then—not even a heartbeat later—I was on the far outskirts of the city, facing a familiar post office.

Squirrels chattered somewhere out of sight. A few flake-flies drifted past, their fluff noticeably diminished. The wild magic that kept them going past summer was perhaps not strong enough to stop them from shriveling in the cold.

I let go of my chain. It slipped soundlessly back inside me.

Vesper hovered behind a grand flagpole next to the post office.

The pole was taller than any other building in the area—the deserted shops and the sprawling diner. Its crowning flag, however, had all but decomposed out of existence, leaving only a few pathetic cobwebs of material.

Vesper had her back to me. Still, there was no way she hadn't sensed me arriving.

I gave her another few seconds to digest my presence. Then I tugged out a couple scant links of my chain. I ported myself to the very top of the flagpole.

I wasn't quite standing on it. Not the point of resting my full weight there. Any support was better than none, though.

Demon or not, I couldn't swim in the air as effortlessly as Vesper. An extended attempt to levitate would feel like doing wall sits or planking for hours on end. Having demon magic wouldn't make it any less excruciating.

Vesper slowly tilted her head back to glare at me. Then she eddied a spiraling path up and around the remainder of the flagpole. She slid to a halt in front of me.

Her wounds from Solitaire were no longer bleeding. But they remained visible enough to make her look like the survivor of a horrible murder attempt, stabbed all over by an impassioned killer who'd never planned on stopping.

"Where's your blood?" she asked icily.

"Do you want to see it?"

"Will you show me?"

I reached for the end of my chain. Its scorpion-tail point was keen enough that I could've used it to saw down this pockmarked aluminum flagpole.

"Don't." She caught my wrist.

"I don't mind offering proof," I said.

"I don't need proof of your blood turning blue."

She was still stronger than me, despite being smaller. Her grip tightened until I dropped the chain and it fled back inside me. Vesper watched it go as if tracking a rattlesnake.

I hadn't come here with a plan for what to say or where to begin. A tidal pull in my gut had urged me to follow her before she disappeared somewhere far, far out of reach.

I'd never faced Vesper as a demon. And that was far from the only thing to have changed between us. We were former bondmates now. Former partners.

In human guise, I'd always taken her for granted. I'd thought I had no magic except for my strange ability to turn mortal beings into sacrificial gates for vorpal beasts and demons. Because Vesper stayed with me, I was spared from ever using that ability again.

I wasn't supposed to wield any other special power of my own. But over the course of our centuries together, I'd gained the power to hurt her. Intentionally or unintentionally, I'd used it. Many times.

Vesper still hadn't turned on me. Not until after her fifty years of misery in Solitaire's cockpit.

"Is there anything you want to know?" I finally asked. "I'll answer if I can."

She clenched my wrist harder. "Does it hurt?"

Not really, I thought. Not in a way I minded.

"Yes," I said.

"Good." But then she let go.

43

I HAD MY BACK to the green hills, the wind turbines, and the mirrored dome that marked the city border. Below us, a small grove of quince trees grew just outside one of the post office windows.

While locked in the building, I'd never spent much time looking out back. The flagpole offered an overhead view of empty holding pens, which fed into a maze-like configuration of ramps and fenced alleys. All meticulously designed to shepherd livestock up toward the abattoir.

Off behind the neighborhood chophouse and bakery lay a field of dead sunflowers. Most had wilted limp on the ground. One or two, though molding over, still stood tall and proud like scarecrows.

They must be the kind of sunflower that could grow back year after year. Either that, or wild magic had embalmed them in death for decades on end.

Vesper tipped back in the air, surrendering her weight to a pile of nonexistent cushions. She let out a long and bitter sigh.

"Since you chased me down," she said, "I'll ask the obvious question. Why did you pretend to be human?"

I described Charity's subconscious last wishes. I described the contract that had been birthed between us as Charity died—only to be negated once Vesper discovered my true nature.

It started raining as I spoke, a quiet sun shower. Down below the lofty flagpole, bald patches of ground darkened before my eyes, drop by drop. An intense earthy scent swelled around us, as if the liquid sprinkling down from unseen clouds was a kind of concentrated perfume.

In the silence after I shut my mouth, Vesper flinched. She wiped wetness from her forehead with the side of her thumb.

"Want to get out of the rain?" I asked. "We could move inside."

"Inside where?"

I nodded at the post office.

Vesper peered at me with obvious suspicion. "Wouldn't you rather go anywhere else?"

"I know what it's like in there," I said. "Besides, I already stuck you back inside Solitaire."

"Oh, so now it's my turn to wage psychological warfare on you instead. Wonderful."

A sour tension lingered around Vesper's mouth as she tilted back upright. She held her hand out, palm up. A few extra-large raindrops spattered her bare wrist. I saw her grimace.

"This way, madam," she said curtly.

We ported out of the rain as soon as the ends of my fingers made contact with hers.

Now we floated in the express mail room, just inside its ring of miserly windows. Vesper kept hold of my hand. Her touch rendered me buoyant much more easily than I could've stayed aloft on my own.

I'd never surveyed this space from up near its silo-high ceiling. We had a birds-eye view of the twin glass compartments. One shattered; one whole. The semitransparent floor and the needlessly intricate tubes on the round outer walls gleamed with water-light.

Vesper kept looking down at the broken chamber, at the spot where the bladed machina had killed her. Her hand felt chilly and warm all at once.

"I understand what happened with your contract," she said.

"You do?"

"Why wouldn't I? I have first-hand experience. Verity and I formed one, too."

"I must be a lesser sort of demon," I said. "I don't fully understand it myself."

I assumed Vesper would seize on this as yet another reason to taunt me.

Instead she spoke in pensive tones. "I've had a lot more time to think about it. Contract formation is a kind of reflex. Like blinking in bright light, or when someone takes a jab at your face." She pointed her index finger at her own cat-pupiled eyes.

"Your gate gave her mortal life to you. As a demon, this set off your deepest involuntary reflex. To give her something worthy in return."

She laughed dryly. "Charity had already told you she wanted you to purge the invaders. But you felt her wanting more. You felt compelled to grant the true wish of her heart. Even if it was something she would never have asked for out loud, knowing the consequences.

"Guess they were right to label us demons. To speak of us in the same breath as mythical devils."

"Did your contract with Verity happen the same way?" I asked.

"My contract is gone," Vesper said. She kept her head down.

"Since when?"

"Since the same moment yours dissolved." Her hand tensed around my sooty fingers. "Since the moment I realized you aren't the original Charity Rinehart. Verity wanted to be remembered by her human friend and killer, not by some random demon she'd never met before."

"I'm sorry," I uttered. It sounded inadequate.

"My contract materialized just like yours," she continued. "Verity was dying. I came through her for the last time, sopping up the remaining vestiges of her life as I went.

"You couldn't hear her dying cry. But I could. It imprinted itself on me like a brand. I'd reaped her life; I had to answer her call. I had no choice. *Don't ever let her forget me.*

"It was all for nothing. It was impossible from the beginning. In the very moment she made her plea, Charity was already gone."

Vesper raised her head. "You made me waste over a millennium," she said steadily.

"I didn't mean—"

"What does it matter that you didn't mean to? What does it matter that you deceived yourself—and robbed your own time, too—in the process?"

Now her hand bit down on me. Now I felt those nails again. Her pupils had contracted to a savage thinness.

"I don't care if you were doing it for Charity or Verity, for both or neither. You put yourself somewhere I could never reach. Somewhere even you didn't know about, and couldn't reach yourself. And let me tell you, you sure as hell didn't do it for me."

Finger by finger, I fought in vain to pry myself free of her. I wouldn't drop like a rock if she released me. Not immediately, anyway.

Vesper observed my efforts with scorn.

"You killed me," I said. "You imprisoned me. Maybe we can—"

"What?"

"Maybe we can call it even."

"It doesn't work like that."

"Why not?"

"Nothing I did to you within Glorybower was done with an eye to ever being forgiven," Vesper said stiffly. "I strove for the opposite. To never be forgiven. To never be forgotten.

"I told myself I was doing it for Verity. If you couldn't forget me, you definitely could never forget her. Lord, what a clown I was."

"Ves," I said. "Let me down."

"You're a demon. Have some pride. You don't have to give in so easily to gravity."

"You're a stronger demon," I told her. "I like having solid ground under my feet. Being up in the air is what makes me feel—helpless. Trapped. You can understand that."

Vesper stared at her small hand constricting my larger stone-textured fingers. She drew breath, as if readying herself to snarl a cutting reply.

A beat later, we'd ported to the floor. Vesper remained suspended a few inches above the surface, which glowed a patchy faded blue-white. She no longer touched me; she wasn't touching anything but air.

Down here, I could see that strange carnivorous flowers had sprouted all around the stock-elk skeleton in the sacrificial chamber. They swayed like seaweed, rippling in an intangible wind.

These gory-colored flowers must've shot up in Vesper's wake, as if fertilized by the briefest of contact with her transient corpse. Nothing else had changed. Splinters of glass were still scattered everywhere. The map of Jace on the wall overlooked us with an air of accusation.

"We could make things fair," I said.

Vesper looked at me as if I'd started quoting bad poetry.

I forged onward. "We could trade places."

"I have no idea what you're trying to say here, cupcake."

"We're both demons. You could take the role of my Host for the next thousand years."

Vesper snorted. "What makes you think I'd enjoy that?"

A fair question. One I didn't have an answer for.

I didn't need Vesper to educate me about the fact that the very notion of demons requiring a continual Host was a farce. The act of consuming our respective gates had already anchored us to this world. That one sacrifice was more than sufficient.

Yet the humans around us had no experience with demons. Perhaps wishful thinking had primed them to believe that we needed them. That parasitic vorpal demons couldn't linger here without a specially anointed mortal Host. That they would thus feel compelled to obey their Host's every command.

All along it had been an act: me unwittingly feigning humanity, and Vesper pretending that my orders held any sort of actual power over her.

Granted, our bond had added an extra layer of complexity. But in the end, what truly controlled her—what forced her to stay close to me—was not my fictional role as her Host, but rather her death-driven contract with Verity.

I crouched at the edge of the cracked-open glass sphere and stuck my hand in among the ravenous neon blooms. Instead of attacking, they shied sharply away from me, some bowing over sideways to avoid being touched.

Vesper knelt beside me, airborne, her ankles tucked up under her. She pricked her thumb on one of her fangs and flicked a drop of cerulean blood at the flowers. They instantly grew taller, fat new buds bursting open into a whirl of sawtoothed petals.

"What makes me angriest of all," she said, sounding eerily empty of rancor, "is that you've robbed me of my ability to blame you."

"You can still blame me."

"Don't tell me how to feel, Char."

"You'll keep calling me Char?" I asked, startled.

"I can distinguish between Char and Charity." She squeezed her cut thumb, then licked up the last blue remnants of blood.

"Demons aren't meant to fall in love," she added.

Here it comes, I thought. Vesper had every right to make this the last time we ever spoke. Nothing connected us now but a tenuous memory of our shared creator. A human girl who'd died long, long ago, without anyone knowing it.

"Stop looking like that," she said irritably.

"Like what?"

She denied me an answer. "Do you feel any different, knowing you're a demon?"

"There are senses I'm not used to accessing." I found myself unsure how to word it. "I've never perceived such a broad spectrum of magic."

The glow of the water-light was soft on her skin. "I'm tired of anger," Vesper said. "I'm tired of a lot of things. We weren't born with human feelings, you know. Think about it. Those emotions crossed over to us like an infection."

It took me a few seconds to understand what she meant.

I'd faced Charity Rinehart, young and frantic to save the one person she loved. Terrified, but willing to be devoured all the same. Her dread and horror, her bravery and her sacrifice—none of it had particularly stirred me.

I'd reacted mechanically to the jumbled desperation of her inadvertent dying thoughts. The contract between us had triggered itself like a trap in the woods snapping shut.

Then I'd spent every second of every year until now telling myself *I* was that Charity Rinehart. I was courageous and selfless. I would crawl through blood and muck and vomit to save people. I had an immeasurable capacity for love, and nowhere left to channel it except toward the nation that had raised me as an experimental subject, and then deliberately chosen to maim me.

All that time, I was faking it—faking it with utter sincerity. To some extent, my role-playing must've transformed into a self-fulfilling prophecy.

Perhaps my emotions were duller and chillier than those of the real Charity. Perhaps I was much slower to react, slower to heat up, slower to understand myself. But the embers in me weren't entirely imagined.

The embers seethed hotter with each breath, scorching me from the inside with a discomfort like firelight stinging frostbitten flesh.

"You think human emotions leaked over to you through me," I said. "You think you developed feelings because I always mimicked having them."

"Because we were always together," she said.

I felt my voice quicken in my throat. "I infected you with a propensity for being hurt. For harboring guilt. I contaminated you. I left a path open for fury and grief and disgust."

"For love and longing," Vesper said. "For frustration and bitter hatred and worry. For a joy that feels like getting stabbed in my weak spot. Demons aren't born equipped for any of this."

None of it would've passed to her—none of it would've corrupted her—if only she'd known me as a demon from the start. If only I'd remained untainted by this all-consuming need to keep impersonating my deceased human gate.

44

"IT'S MY FAULT," I said. Absolute clarity swept down over me with the brutality of an avalanche. "It was always my fault. Every moment you suffered. Every—"

A faint scraping sound brought me up short.

Vesper still wore the same calf-length boots she'd had on when she walked up to the base of the bell tower and challenged me to a duel.

The bottoms of those boots met the glass-littered floor.

"Get up." She reached for me.

I gawked at her feet. "Are—are you okay?"

Vesper pulled me up. It didn't occur to me to resist. "I'm meeting you on your own turf. For once. Don't worry, it won't last long. I don't like you being taller."

That sensation of unadulterated bleakness had fled the instant she grabbed my arm. Like a poison being forcibly drained from my veins.

I looked down at her small horns. At the toothy piercings jutting out of her ears, newly healed over after our brawl. An indescribable feeling seized me. Something akin to getting squeezed around the middle by a pair of giant hands, and wanting to crush Vesper in turn.

I couldn't say anything to her. I couldn't say anything that might trick her into staying, when after a thousand years she finally had a chance to be free of me.

Vesper put my hand down by my side, more gently than I might've expected. She took a careful step back.

"We were both dancing for a dead audience," she said. "Neither of us realizing it. Century after century after century."

She was unnervingly calm now. As if she knew it was for the last time. As if she knew these would be the words she left me with.

I forced myself to remain still. I forced myself to listen.

"Our gates were gone from the start," she stated. "Our contracts were a sham all along, or might as well have been. You could say we were dancing for no one, like absolute fools."

Her gaze dropped to her knuckles. "Or you could say we were dancing for each other."

I had forgotten that this body was supposed to breathe. I only started up again once I realized I needed air to speak.

"Ves," I said. "Ves—do we have to do this here?"

"You prefer getting rained on?"

"Anyplace is better than the room where I killed you."

Vesper looked nonplussed. "Well, come on then."

She led me down multiple flights of rickety stairs, through the door labeled *Staff Only*, and over to the postmaster's office.

"Maybe the slaughterhouse was lacking in romance," she said. "This fancy enough for you?"

Unenthusiastic raindrops marked the grandiose windows, forming shapes like clear splats of bird shit. Soil from split-open pots melded with the floor, spawning a jungle-dark tangle of plant life. The room smelled green and chokingly fetid.

"There has to be a better place to say goodbye," I told her.

"You want me to be saying goodbye?" Vesper demanded.

"You aren't?"

She pointed at her fangs. "Listen to the actual words coming out of my mouth, you dolt."

"I'm trying. That's what made me think you were—"

Vesper cut in. "I didn't mean what I said about you making me waste all this time. A whole millennium. At least, I didn't mean it in the way you're taking it."

She buried her hands in her jacket pockets. Her eyes were on the windows, clouded over with decades of grime. Looking through them felt like admiring the pastoral hills through a filter of thick dried glue.

"Our hundreds of years, our thousand-plus years—I can look at them differently now," she said. "Now that I know you're not mortal. Not in the same way as a human."

I didn't get it.

Vesper shook her head, exasperated. "If you were human, that would truly be time lost. Can't you see it? Every waking moment I had with you was bittersweet and scant, gone too soon. At best you'd have another fifty or sixty conscious years.

"The bond of mutual death might've worked on old age, but at what cost? Would you be constantly choking on your own phlegm, organs failing and reviving and failing again? At what point in the process would your mind disintegrate beyond recovery? Before you lost coherence, would you beg me to off myself to end your suffering? Would I do it?"

She smiled crookedly. "These are the things I'd brood over every time you decided to hibernate."

"Then I'd wake up," I said, "and I'd forget—"

"That we were ever anything more than staunch partners in defending the nation."

I was so unused to seeing Vesper at her true height. Her head would've fit right in the crook of my neck.

"I don't understand," I said—a plea for mercy. "I made you miserable. I made you capable of misery. I hoodwinked you about the very truth of my soul. You still want to stay with me?"

"You big sop. It wasn't a constant parade of anguish."

Her head found its spot against my neck. Her arms curled up behind me, pressing into my back with startling force.

"You may have swindled me into believing you were human," she said. "But as a con artist, you were your own worst victim."

I held her, almost lifting her off the floor. It wasn't a conscious decision. The moment she stepped in, my body reacted. An irresistible reflex. A trap closing, inevitable as the activation of a demon contract. But here there was no one offering up a sacrifice, no one with a dire wish except for the demon herself.

She was warm and wiry, brimming with magic, and all I could think of was how I'd dragged her up to the express mail chamber and watched it kill her. My arms tightened until she twisted and warned me that her ribs were about to crack.

"Remember, you're stronger than you think," Vesper chided. "You were limiting yourself when you had to be human."

"Still not as strong as you."

She sniffed. "Of course not."

She wiggled higher and went weightless, legs locking around my hips. She braced her hands on my shoulders and leaned back to look down at me.

"I want to know you," she said. "The demon I never got to meet. You owe me that much, at least."

"I wanted to ask you to stay," I confessed. "I just—I thought I had no right."

Vesper traced the rounded edges of my earlobes, as if wondering why they'd ended up a different shape from hers.

"I always felt there was a part of you I couldn't touch," she said meditatively. "I assumed it was because we were two inherently different existences, demon and human. I despaired over it. Then I beat myself up for despairing over the obvious.

"Now it all makes sense. How could I feel like I knew you when you didn't even know your own original self?"

"The rain's gotten lighter," I said, pointing.

"You don't like this room? I fed you chestnuts in here."

"Still have some." I patted my pocket.

Vesper gave me a dubious look. "You didn't even finish them?"

"The Osmanthians wouldn't take them."

"I'm shocked that you would try to give away my present to foreigners."

"As a guardian of the nation," I said, "I try to do my part for international relations."

"Next time I'll have to hover there and watch you eat the whole bag," Vesper muttered.

"Next time, I hope you won't be holding me hostage."

She looked innocently over at the postmaster's rotting armchair. "One kidnapping every ten or twelve centuries isn't such a bad record, is it?"

45

WE WENT FOR A WALK.

To be more specific: I walked. Vesper bobbed alongside me, toying with gravity, occasionally teasing me for my attachment to standing on two feet. Using my human-looking body the way a human would use it.

At this point, though, I wasn't particularly motivated to try breaking old habits.

In one of the venerable commercial districts, we crossed between pawn shops and cheese shops, shoe repair shops and oyster shops, barbers and real estate agencies and seedy pubs.

Some I could identify based on their iconography—a sign with a glass of wine, a loaf of bread. Others mystified me until Vesper read fragments of text off their signboards.

We saw little in the way of magic for sale. Fifty years ago, at least, the products of mage labor had continued to be regulated more like a utility.

The government assigned mages to contribute to health care or weapons development or infrastructure maintenance or the all-important postal service. They were too meticulously controlled for frivolous enchantments to spill willy-nilly onto local store shelves.

By now all that might have changed. Or it might not have changed at all. Vesper probably had an inkling, based on her recent trips outside Glorybower. I didn't ask, though.

In some ways it might be better not knowing. The more I knew, the harder it might become to peel myself away from Jace.

Not that I'd already decided what to do next, or where to go after we opened the city. That wasn't a decision I could make on my own.

The sun shower had ceased, leaving patches of ambiguously moistened earth and pavement. Diminishing daylight pulled long, long shadows out in front of us.

My footsteps were the only footsteps for miles around. Vesper cruised along beside me, sometimes floating backwards so she could face me while we talked.

We spent a long time speaking of Charity and Verity. We were the last beings alive who'd ever known them. In a sense, we were their sole descendants.

"We've both broken our promises to them," I said.

"No one can claim we didn't try," Vesper countered. "We tried for a very long time. We did save millions of people, one way or another. Fifty years ago, we saved the entire population of Glorybower."

I'd internalized a certain concept of Charity Rinehart. The Charity I attempted to embody was one who needed to be a hero, who needed to live up to her name. Especially after what that facility did to her and so many other mage children. And after what she—that is, I—in turn did to Verity. She needed to make all of that worth it.

She needed to become the greatest hero Jace had ever known.

"You made that come true for her," Vesper told me. "You kept her dream alive all this time. You've done enough."

Was that really Charity's dream, though? Or was it merely something I'd extrapolated from my record of her memories?

The real Charity might've walked an alternate path. The real Charity might've become someone very different as she grew older. She might've become disillusioned with Jace. She might've sided with the rebels I'd crushed. She might've given everything up and fled to the continent.

In faithfully playing the role of my ideal Charity Rinehart, stoic and endlessly noble, I'd denied her—and therefore myself—any chance to evolve. She could never become anything more than that initial static impression I'd gotten of her.

I'd traced Charity's outline in my mind and stuck to it, unswerving. A real human would never have stayed fixed in place like that. Not after disfiguring battles, senseless disasters, getting chunks of her body bitten off without anesthetic.

"You know what's funny?" I asked.

"That doesn't sound like a voice you'd use to say something funny."

"I was masquerading as a human whose only great power was the ability to make demons. Charity had no other magic of her own."

"So?"

"You could've done it all without me. Every feat they gave me credit for."

Vesper stopped moving. We were in a more residential area now, surrounded by two-story houses engulfed from foundation to rooftop in climbing vines. The dense plating of three-lobed leaves had turned a fierce scarlet and purple for winter.

"I wouldn't have done anything without you," Vesper said. "I wouldn't have lifted a finger."

"If people came to you and implored you—"

"As if praying to the Lord of Circles? I wouldn't have heard them." She motioned vaguely at the empty houses. "Back then I had no special interest in Jace. No real desire to become anyone's hero. But my contract with Verity drove me to stick with you."

"With the person you thought was Charity Rinehart."

"I had to stay with you to make sure you never forgot her," Vesper agreed. "Meanwhile, you wanted to protect Jace. You thought being my Host—a title humans gave you—meant I had to listen to you.

"A long time passed before it ever occurred to me to correct you. It was easy enough to keep you happy. But I wouldn't have done any of those things if you hadn't asked me.

"I certainly wouldn't have gone to the trouble of fighting off the first Kraken on my own. Besides, you fed me your own flesh whenever overclocking seemed like the only solution. You contributed blood and bone to the war effort. That isn't nothing."

"Every time you ate part of me, you were eating demon flesh," I remarked. "Come to think of it."

A bemused look flitted across her face. "Guess so. Maybe that's why it worked so well."

With respect to the accuracy of the historical record, I wasn't sure I agreed with her. Vesper might not have any problem with how Jace remembered us, but it didn't sit right with me.

Vesper was famous enough, but the bulk of the credit for our achievements had always gone to the Host. The museum in Memorial Park had characterized Vesper as the equivalent of a trained falcon. Or a well-bred beast of burden, without any notable will of her own.

When I said this, Vesper threw her head back and laughed. "You think you and I never tried to encourage that? Trust me—it was much less of a hassle to let them believe I was useless without you.

"Imagine what would've happened otherwise," she said. "People constantly trying to push you out and take your place. To assert authority over me, claim me for their own. Idiots. There were times when bits and pieces of that happened anyway. But it could've been far worse."

She grinned darkly. "They would've been a lot more frightened of both of us—with good reason—if they realized I could operate independently, think for myself. No harm in being underestimated. No harm in being typecast as the living weapon of last resort. A weapon only the Host could unsheathe."

"No need to go around correcting the record, then."

"Lord, no. I'd perish of boredom."

Sunset found us at an unusually long, straight canal, one spanned by a seemingly endless series of once-beautiful bridges.

We paused in the middle of one arched bridge to watch a spindly-legged insect tiptoe patiently along the railing. It looked very much like a living cinnamon stick.

The reflections of neighboring bridges traced graceful circles in placid maple-scented water. Nearby, the curve of the city monorail cast a shadow like a great flying serpent.

"You know," Vesper began. Something in her tone—the deliberate lightness of it—made me stiffen.

"Know what?" I said guardedly.

"If you're a demon, it's more than just our bodies that can touch."

In a layer of my mind unsullied by human language, I grasped precisely what she meant.

"Would you prefer to wait?" She kept her focus trained on the reflections in the sky and the water.

"I'm not afraid."

"No one said you were."

The cinnamon stick bug took a wavering step, feeling its way forward.

"Show me how," I told her.

Physically, Vesper remained motionless. Her fingertips grazed the weathered railing.

Meanwhile, her magic slipped in through the one fragile spot at the small of my back. It slipped in as if it had always been there. Sand dribbling through the stem of an hourglass.

I didn't move, either. But when she touched my vorpal self, it felt like I might drop straight through the planks of the bridge and asphyxiate in the syrup-sweet water beneath. I went weak all over, awash with a yearning to yield, to be mangled, to liquefy in the throes of her magic. To let her vorpality fully embrace and annihilate me.

"Something like that," Vesper whispered behind my ear. She sounded enormously pleased with herself.

I couldn't say a word.

"You try it now," she ordered.

I gave a jerky nod.

My human-shaped body stayed rock-still and obedient. On the corporeal plane of existence, we were just two demon women side-by-side upon a picturesque arch. One standing stoically. One levitating a fingers-width off the time-eaten surface of the bridge.

No physical contact.

My vorpal self sank into the ocean of Vesper's magic. Internally, I turned my entire consciousness toward her, and it wasn't nearly enough. I choked on the mingled taste of our joy, and I drowned in her.

46

OUT OF RESPECT for human circadian rhythms, I waited till the next day before contacting Asa and Wist.

Vesper seemed skeptical when I fished the old cowbell out of my flight suit. But I could see her grasp the meaning of the human magic on the bell as soon as I started ringing it.

Her expression darkened.

A crunchy simulacrum of Asa's voice came through the bell, asking us to meet them at the Temple of Cats and Circles.

"I could kill that woman," Vesper said after the cowbell fell silent.

"Please don't."

"Why not?"

"She showed us what I really am," I reasoned.

"She went about it in the worst way possible."

I couldn't help but agree with this. Still, inside Solitaire, we'd been wholly at the Osmanthians' mercy. They could've gored both of our weak spots, neat as you please. They could've hounded us across the city after we left the cockpit. Instead they'd let us come to terms with the truth on our own.

Vesper grumbled, but eventually agreed not to do anything rash.

I sensed the tension thrumming in her when I linked arms with her. I wrapped my chain around my fist and yanked it to port us to the temple. I needed the practice.

On the whole, the temple appeared almost suspiciously undamaged by any subsequent fights to banish the beast of the hall. No ground torn up in the garden; no newly capsized pagodas.

There were a few fallen pavilions, but I remembered those from before. Nothing seemed to have attacked their wood except for the gradual passage of time.

We didn't venture back inside the Hall of Wheels—although it looked no different from the outside, either.

Asa proudly explained how much havoc the vorpal beast from the Hall had wreaked after Vesper took me away. And how hard Wist had worked to restore various buildings and cat statues, the red autumn garden and the circular cemetery.

Upon our arrival at the temple grounds, Vesper had given the Osmanthians a terse nod. Nothing more. To my surprise and considerable relief, Asa appeared content to let her be.

Vesper took up a position in the air over the great stone gate. She monitored us from above like a well-fed bird of prey—fully alert, but not immediately poised to attack. I could tell Wist was keeping tabs on her, but neither she nor Asa seemed especially tense.

When I mentioned this, Asa held out a hand. Wist tossed over her newsboy cap. Asa caught it and took a moment to put it back on, fussing until she got the fit just right. She looked up at me from under the brim, dark bangs hiding her right eye.

"We're all getting along so well now," she said.

"Are we?" Wist muttered, deadpan.

Asa didn't blink. "It's a good time to mention that we never saw much risk in letting your Vesper run free."

"What?" I asked witlessly. Even at this very moment, Vesper was staring daggers at the back of Asa's head, and all of us knew it.

Asa squared herself, hands on her hips. "Use your brain a little, friend."

"I'm trying."

"Vesper had the ability to pass in and out of the city ever since you emerged from stasis. Didn't she? And she took advantage of it.

"Now imagine that from our perspective. Of course we kept an eye on her. She ventured outside Glorybower plenty of times on our watch. Far as I can tell, she never hurt anyone. Never caused a scene. Blended perfectly into human society. No one had any idea there was a demon in their midst.

"She may have engaged in a bit of petty theft." Asa plucked the air, pretending to pick pockets. "Or at least used counterfeit money. That's a nice outfit she got herself. Wist and I can let that sort of thing slide, though. The laws of Jace aren't our laws to enforce."

"Then—"

Asa nodded encouragingly. "Yes?"

"When you took Vesper into the void behind your eye. When you told me you'd only let her out if we caged her at the back of the cockpit. Safety concerns had nothing to do with it," I said. "That was just part of your set-up for unmasking me as a demon."

"Well, that's not entirely fair," Asa protested. "Sure, she'd shown herself to be capable of peaceful conduct in the world at large. Doesn't change the fact that she acted very different around you. Downright murderous."

"She didn't go easy on you two, either."

"Oh, I don't know about that," Asa said. "Our presence in the city definitely put her on edge. She certainly seemed to be in a violent mood whenever she dropped in to see us.

"But her attacks on us lacked a certain passion, one might say, compared to her attacks on you. I don't think she was truly trying with all her might to destroy us. Even if she thought she was, something made her hold back. Her heart wasn't in it."

Vesper raised a hand as if she were about to start flinging rocks at us. Instead, tiny specks zoomed through the air to meet her. I ducked on reflex, but they ended up coming nowhere near my head.

"Your coins," Asa said. "Your breadcrumbs."

Vesper tossed the handful in her palm, then pocketed them. One grail from a decomposing water wheel. Several others from a columnar collection box in the Hall of Wheels. I'd completely forgotten about leaving them there.

Asa—as though lured by this brief glimpse of glittering coins—walked over to the base of the circular gate. She tilted her head back to look up at Vesper.

"I'd love a chance to examine your magic more closely," she said.

Wist and I cringed in unison.

"Absolutely not," Vesper told her. "You want a rematch?"

A dark aura of magic rose like fog from Vesper's skin. It clustered about her horns in the way of low clouds concealing mountain peaks. The ground below us stirred with a slow gathering rumble, a sound of far-off buried thunder.

My stomach turned over.

"I'm always up for a rematch," Asa said sweetly, undeterred. "Wist would enjoy the exercise. If we win, can I probe your magic?"

A thick black rope of hair shot out to lasso Asa's shoulders, dragging her away from the gate, and away from Vesper. She reluctantly followed its pull to rejoin me and Wist in the middle of the garden.

Once Asa had stumbled within reach of us, Wist's braid retreated, contracting to fall placidly down her back again.

The magic simmering about the stone gate began to disperse, little by little. Vesper hadn't budged an inch.

"Let's speak of other things," Wist said.

"We might never get another chance to study demon magic," Asa complained.

"Study mine," I said. "Don't pester Ves about it."

"But two samples would be so much better than one."

To distract Asa, I asked her what had convinced her I was a demon. Convinced her to the point that she was willing to break my bond with Vesper and evaporate half my chest to prove it.

If she were even slightly wrong, I'd have been one hundred percent dead. Perhaps that was a risk she didn't mind taking.

Unlike Asa, Wist had cracked and shown visible distress when Vesper screamed. Between the two of them, Asa was the one I found harder to predict—despite her almost exaggerated expressiveness.

Was she simply more callous about the prospect of accidentally murdering me? Or had she been so certain of her rightness that no amount of pain or weeping or consternation possessed the power to make her doubt herself?

I couched my questions in more diplomatic terms, though I doubted anything I said could ever wound her.

Asa hummed knowingly to herself as she listened.

Wist had been pacing a path through the trees around us like a sheepdog watching out for strays. She came to a stop well within earshot.

At her back skulked the aftermath of a once-decorative pine tree, its limbs too long and heavy to stay aloft without artificial support. Some had broken off. Some had drooped all the way to the ground as they grew, worming a path drenched in dense velveteen moss.

"Let me tell you something about death," Asa said softly. "The first Kraken was right to make human resurrection one of her big taboos."

She pivoted to face the Hall of Wheels, way over at the far end of the complex. She picked up a fistful of acorns and began pitching them one by one in the brook that bisected the garden.

"There are immeasurable costs even to the one-time revival of a single human being," she continued. The light splash of drowned acorns punctuated her words.

"How do I know that? The original Kraken was the one who first laid out those taboos. Wist is her spiritual successor. If anyone is in a position to figure out these things, it's a Kraken-class mage.

"I could accept the fact that you and your demon were capable of bouncing back from physical death. I could accept the fact that your bond had something to do with it. But to me, this meant you couldn't possibly be a regular human. I found more evidence when I went poking around inside your bond. That's the gist of it."

"And that was enough for you to feel comfortable carving an enormous hole in my chest," I said.

She turned and clapped me on the back. "You lived, didn't you?"

"Barely."

"You learned something about yourself. As a result, everyone seems to be in a much more cooperative mood now. Best of all, I got my theory proven right."

"You tell people not to call you a detective," Wist said, "but you sure enjoy acting like one."

Asa threw an acorn at her head.

47

Asa asked us for help with clearing the city of vorpal beasts. Wist had already expelled most of them. But those remaining might take more kindly to being shooed away to other dimensions by demons, rather than humans.

Or so Asa claimed. Vesper muttered to me afterward that she was just being lazy.

By this point, Wist had closed every minor vorpal hole in Glorybower except for one, which turned out to be located in the amusement park's public toilets.

Vesper and I spent the next couple days herding beasts out of the city—and out of the human world—using that final vorpal hole as their emergency exit.

Among them were a false tree that stole all the fruit from neighboring trees. An assortment of two-tailed cats. Hazy birds that resembled low-flying clouds. False stretches of cobblestone that concealed dark gaping sinkholes. Extra sparks of color in the night sky, doing their best to pretend to be stars.

Some of the beasts seemed completely innocuous. Even if the whole human population came flooding back, it ought to have been possible for them to coexist.

People wouldn't understand, though. People wouldn't let them be. Better for them to seek a place in other worlds, or in the space between worlds.

That was where vorpal holes normally led, after all. Vesper and the Osmanthians had exploited them as a convenient tunnel in and out of the city, but doing so required very precise and intentional maneuvering.

The vorpal beasts we shepherded away from Glorybower would ride wherever the currents took them. In the absence of deliberate manipulation, the currents would sweep them off to distant worlds. Just like how they'd originally come drifting here in the first place. Whether they were peaceful or destructive, ravenous or inert, their arrival in human realms was always pure coincidence.

In the middle of all this, I found a chance to get Wist the Kraken alone one night. I asked her if she could do anything to help recover my lost memories.

Her magic stirred. She took a long time to answer.

The answer was no.

"I'm sorry," she said.

I hadn't gotten my hopes up. "I figured it'd be impossible."

"It's not impossible. If I had a few decades to work on it—if I did nothing else—"

Her voice was low and affectless. She must be forced to tell people no all the time, I thought. Very little would be technically impossible for a Kraken-class mage. But she was still human. She had to weigh every decision on the scales of time.

I thanked her for considering it. I told her I understood.

When I turned my back on Wist, I glanced down into the dark canal nearby and saw Vesper. She lay stretched out on her back just above the water's surface. Not the most subtle way to eavesdrop.

Our eyes met. She rolled over and glided away through the nighttime air, silent as a sea snake.

Decades and centuries spent pickled in stasis had induced my repeated bouts of partial memory loss. Yet I suspected there must've been some kind of greater will governing the trajectory of what I remembered and what I forgot.

Vesper had said I was prone to easily letting go of anything positive—pleasure and praise, moments of glory and catharsis. Instead, she'd told me, the most scarring moments latched onto me like burrs.

I didn't doubt her. But I privately thought that there might've been something more to it.

The closer I got to Vesper, the greater the risk of her discovering my hidden nature. That had to be the real reason why, out of everything it was possible for me to forget, I'd so persistently and thoroughly forgotten every step forward in our constantly regressing relationship.

When Vesper rose from the canal and came over to me, I apologized again for forgetting.

I hadn't been sure if I should. I'd apparently apologized before, after all. Saying it might serve to remind Vesper of every other time I'd failed her.

She went quiet. "Yeah, well," she said eventually, "at least one thing has changed from before. This is the first time either of us knows what you really are."

Vesper theorized that my being a demon might explain why I'd adapted so readily to drastically different time periods and environments.

I'd never given much thought to it, but perhaps she had a point. Perhaps it would've been much more difficult for a true human to accept everything that might change after decades or centuries in stasis.

The irony of it all was that if I'd been capable of admitting I were a demon, I wouldn't have needed to hibernate in the first place. I wouldn't have succumbed to so many chances to forget. The whole point of hibernation had been to extend my supposedly human lifespan, to preserve Jace's legendary guardian for future generations.

A demon's life would have needed no such artificial extension.

According to Asa, my demon self had also throttled portions of our now-broken bond. Which must explain why Vesper and I had never been able to speak telepathically or sense each other's emotions like human bondmates.

"I miss my watch," I said, half to myself. I'd had it for almost my entire existence, after all. I kept catching my hands reaching for it in idle moments.

I wondered out loud if Vesper would still be able to overclock. If it would work any differently now that I'd been exposed as a demon, and we were no longer bonded.

"Consuming humans always boosted me, too," Vesper answered. "Not as much as overclocking. But more than nothing—even if I wasn't bonded to them. It's just that you usually preferred not to sic me on others. Not in a cannibalistic sense, anyhow."

"What would happen if I ate from you instead?"

"Do you hunger for my flesh?" she asked.

"Not in that way," I said.

"Your loss. I'm sure I taste wonderful."

"I'm sure you do."

It was an unusually warm day, even for the mild winter climate of Glorybower, when Vesper and I sent the flock of water imps away. After seeing them off, we took one last dip in the outdoor spring near Memorial Park.

With the imps gone, the water soon began losing its heat.

From time to time, loud crumbling noises resounded from the ramshackle bathhouse behind us. As if the imps, for mysterious reasons of their own, had been propping it up with an industrious scaffolding of magic. In their absence, the whole structure seemed like it might fall flat at any moment.

Vesper had a lot more experience with demonic techniques for staying clean. She evinced little interest in the tedious business of washing up like a human being.

I got about ten seconds of peace and quiet to scrub myself before she pushed me up against the stones at the edge of the bath.

"Thought you were more interested in having relations on the vorpal plane," I said.

"Both have their merits."

Water ran down from her breastbone, down the compact musculature of her stomach. Drops trickled past the blue-rimmed gills on her sides. She kissed the burnt-black tips of my fingers, the empty places where I had no nails.

"Is it rude?" I asked. "Doing this sort of thing in a public bath."

Vesper rolled her eyes. "If anyone ever uses it again, you can rest assured they'll give it a thorough cleaning first. Assuming they don't just demolish and rebuild it from scratch."

Her logic made sense. I reached up and ran my fingers along her short horns. It produced a sound like stone rubbing stone.

Vesper closed her eyes and nuzzled closer. "Harder," she said by my cheek. I obliged.

At first she was very delicate when I kissed her, careful not to slice my mouth with the small pointed edges of her teeth.

Very soon we both stopped being careful.

Unbound by gravity, her body surged up out of the water. I pinned her to me to keep her from soaring off into the sky. Her teeth cut both our tongues, so razor-sharp that I hardly felt a thing. But I could taste it, her demon blood and mine, the exact same citrus scent and stinging tinge of acid.

48

AFTER CLEARING AS MANY vorpal beasts as we could, the four of us convened at Spinning Gardens.

Asa and Wist went to close the last vorpal hole in Glorybower. The one in the public toilet.

Meanwhile, Vesper and I surveyed the rest of the park from the top of the motionless fairy wheel.

"Our turn to be lazy for a change," Vesper said snidely.

There were still plenty of ordinary animals and insects and plants all over the city. More than there had been before all the people left. Many as peculiar-looking as any respectable beast from another world.

Besides, we'd known better than to attempt to round up every last floating scrap of wild magic. The vorpal visitors of Glorybower had most certainly left their mark.

Yet somehow the city felt deader without countless magical beasts blending into the abandoned scenery.

With the vorpal hole in the bathroom stitched up, all that remained was to bring down the city dome.

Before that, I had one final favor to ask the Osmanthians.

I almost regretted bringing it up. Vesper and I could've done it on our own, one way or another. I didn't know how to explain what had prompted me to tug at Asa's sleeve and seek help.

Vesper, for one, would definitely have preferred not to involve a pair of foreigners we barely knew. And who, as Vesper liked to point out, had succeeded in duping me multiple times in a row.

After I finished explaining my request, the four of us ported to the hills on the city's western outskirts. We landed just past the long parade of oddly-shaped wind turbines that I'd glimpsed through the windows of my post office prison.

Not all of the turbines were moving. Nor was it a particularly windy day, at least not at ground level. Despite that, they emitted a constant echoing stream of haunting creaks and whistles. It sounded like lonely sea mammals calling out to each other at unfathomable depths.

This was the music that played at our backs as Wist the Kraken got to work.

In a matter of minutes, her magic raised a grassy mound in the middle of a wild pasture. It was far too perfectly round and tall to be natural.

Asa passed out short branches of grave wisteria, all harvested from the masses of vines clinging to Solitaire. We walked in circles, crouching to poke our sprigs into the rich black earth brimming at the foot of the newborn mound.

(All of us except Vesper. She drifted about as if borne on the back of an unseen bird, and planted her twigs by chucking them down like throwing knives.)

We stepped back for a better view. The breeze momentarily picked up. The wind turbines let out sharp piteous cries. Then their voices dwindled back down to an irregular trickle, dissipating like smoke among the empty hills and fields between here and the edge of the dome.

Wist was the last to step away. One of her tendrils of magic, slender as a strand of hair, trailed along the bare twigs we'd stuck in the ground.

Less than a second later, thick woody vines twisted their way up over the earthen mound, interlacing to cover it like a cage. The shape they formed echoed the reflective dome over the city, albeit on a much smaller scale.

I pried the military ID bracelet off my left wrist, and the irreparably stained field scarf off my right. With a tug of my chain, I ported them deep into the soil below the empty grave.

No one had ever made a grave for Charity Rinehart.

Long ago I'd attempted to put up a small marker for Verity, but I'd struggled to obtain permission for it. She hadn't left behind a body.

In any event, the old city with the orphanage lay buried far beneath the newer city now known as Glorybower. My efforts to pay tribute to Verity would surely have vanished together with the city of her birth.

I told Wist and Asa about our human gates. Not at length.

It was hard to decide what to say. How much could they comprehend about the brief lives of two young women from a foreign land, from even longer ago than the reign of the previous Kraken?

Vesper and I hadn't really known our respective gates, either. Not in the way of one human coming to know another. Not in the way they'd known and loved each other.

In lieu of truly knowing them, we'd archived and carried on their memories. As generation after generation of humans came and went, Vesper and I had worked to fulfill the terms of our instinctual contracts with nigh-religious zeal. Yet we'd spent very little time actually conversing with our gates before they died.

As I spoke, I began to understand why I'd asked Asa and Wist to join us in erecting this grave mound, one large enough to honor any ancient queen or king. It dawned on me gradually, the way heat from a bonfire sinks deeper and deeper into frigid muscles, infiltrating all the way down to the heart of your bones.

A thousand-something years later, I wanted there to be humans who knew about Charity and Verity. How they'd really lived, and how they'd really died.

These humans weren't Jacians. They hailed from a wholly different land, a wholly different era. But they listened.

Afterward, I dug the burlap sack of chestnuts out of my pocket.

Once again, Asa and Wist declined to have any. I thrust them at Vesper instead.

She wrinkled her nose. "A bit old now, aren't they?"

"They aren't moldy."

"Still."

"They won't kill us," I said.

"We don't even need to eat to live. We can afford to be a touch picky. Or is this your way of getting back at me?"

I shook my head. "Just trying not to be wasteful."

"Feed them to the grave wisteria. I'll get you more chestnuts outside Glorybower."

I followed Vesper's suggestion.

Later, I took one last look back before we left the hills. High overhead, the wind turbines kept whistling their eerie lament.

The clover and grasses and other tangled ground cover around the grave mound had started going brown and yellow for winter. Not in wide sweeps or random blotches: in abnormally exquisite curlicues and swirls, an artificial pattern like fine lace. I had to wonder how people would react to the city's eccentricities once they returned.

And they would return, once the walls came down. That much I knew for certain.

Between the mountains and the sea, livable and arable land had always been a precious commodity here in Jace. People would come flooding in even if the city seemed haunted. Even if wild magic toyed with their senses, and every last dwelling needed to be purged and rebuilt.

With time and an influx of fresh air and humanity, the city's quirks would start to fade. The syrup glimmering in the canals might one day transform into ordinary freshwater. Vesper and I might linger nearby to watch it happen. Or by then we might be long gone from here.

49

WITH OUR COMBINED RESOURCES, removing the walls would not be a difficult matter. My only stipulation was for Vesper to get exempted from feeding Solitaire. I would offer my demon body to the teeth at the back of the cockpit instead, with Wist and Asa piloting.

"What're you trying to pull here?" Vesper asked, grumpy.

"I'm not sending you back in there," I said.

"Well, I volunteer my services."

"I volunteered first."

We glared at each other. We stood suspended in the night sky over Solitaire, Vesper lightening my gravity with a hand on my side.

Far below, Solitaire—still lying flat—shone in the dark like a colossal ghost of wars past and future. Its eight outstretched arms were grotesquely long, far out of proportion with the rest of its form. On past nights, I'd noticed flying insects flocking to its faint moon-silver light. Right now we were much too high up to make out any such visitors.

"We could go in together," Vesper said at last.

"One of us ought to be more than enough."

"I'll share the burden. Don't be stubborn."

"Two whole demons would be overkill," I argued. "All they have to do is channel magic through Solitaire to dismantle the dome. They won't even make Solitaire sit up, much less fly."

Without warning, Vesper inverted us—feet stretching skyward, heads toward the ground. "I've got eons of experience with fueling chalices. Think you can measure up so easily?"

"I've given up plenty of my own blood and meat to fuel you," I said.

If she'd turned us upside-down to confuse me, she'd better try harder.

Vesper scowled. "You think all you have to do is hang there and bleed? You can't let Solitaire get at your weak spot. There's no bond of mutual death left to rely on."

"You can go up in the pilot seat instead," I offered. "If you want to be involved. If you think you'd do a better job than the Kraken."

Her scowl deepened.

"If my body ever gets destroyed in this world," I added, "I trust you'll come find me in vorpal realms."

"Yeah. I'll come find you, and I'll wring you out like a dirty rag. I'll stomp your soul out as flat as a piece of old snakeskin."

"Tread carefully," I said. "I might end up enjoying it."

Vesper growled deep in her throat.

One way or another, we would work with Asa and Wist to vaporize the barrier around the city before dawn.

Then Vesper and I would slip away unnoticed. If anyone asked, Asa would say that she and Wist had prised open the chalice cockpit and found it empty. As if no one had ever been there in the first place.

No need to mention that they'd exploited Solitaire to dissolve the barricade. Jacians wouldn't be keen on hearing about foreigners piloting their most precious chalice. Opening the city would be hailed as an unprecedented accomplishment, to be sure, but they could always explain it away by saying Wist had worked a miracle on her own.

Very few people in the world were even remotely equipped to grasp the capabilities and limits of a Kraken-class mage.

Regardless of how we went about it, whoever entered Solitaire's bone cage would be at the mercy of our chosen pilot. Better me than Vesper. She'd already been through enough in there.

Recently, she'd told me that she herself had been slow to grasp just how much power I gained over her when we took up our usual positions in the cockpit. She'd known it on an intellectual level, but she'd never imagined me taking full advantage of it.

Fifty years ago was the only time we ever entered stasis inside Solitaire, and the only time I'd ever forced her to join me.

Every other time I decided to hibernate, she said, I'd asked if she would follow.

"You would have been very surprised if I said no," Vesper added, a touch acerbically. "But at least you asked."

At this time of night, Glorybower was mostly devoid of light. I saw almost none aside from Solitaire's ethereal glow, and the small bright spot over in the clover-filled plaza that marked Asa and Wist's final campsite.

Vesper absentmindedly circled both arms about my waist.

"You sure you're okay with leaving Solitaire?" she asked. She'd seemingly forgotten that we were in the middle of a hearty disagreement.

"Solitaire belongs to the nation."

"If the nation gets it back, they'll chuck more human pilots into the meat grinder. Sooner or later. Probably sooner. Even if this part of the world is peaceful now. Even if they've got no immediate need for Solitaire's power."

Vesper was right. Asa had said the same thing. You didn't need to be a prophet to see it coming.

Give the nation a chalice, and the nation would be sure to fill it to the brim with Jacian flesh.

If the Host and her demon turned out to have mysteriously vanished, reclaiming Solitaire would become an even more pressing matter. An issue of national pride and prestige.

After all, the continent had a new Kraken now. Without me and Vesper, the only way for Jace to assert power would be to cling to its chalices.

"Let's give them a chance," I said.

Vesper chuckled. Not unkindly.

"If the way they use Solitaire really bothers us, we can always come back and steal it," I appended.

"A demon heist," Vesper murmured. "Sounds like a grand old time."

I hadn't thought much about the future. Not that I was actively trying to avoid it. For so long my mind had been pressed into a tiny, tiny preconceived shape, one utterly alien to my original nature.

I hadn't quite digested what it meant to be a demon. On some level, I knew how much time and freedom unspooled before me, rolling endlessly in every conceivable direction. But I still couldn't really wrap my head around it.

When I told Vesper this, she said: "You're thinking like a human. You're wavering between Jace and the continent. Think bigger.

"We don't have to stick to this side of the world. We can venture somewhere completely unknown. We can hop through a vorpal hole and say goodbye to all these suckers. Abandon ship for a different world altogether."

"Do we really not have any responsibility to anyone?" I asked. "Just because we aren't human?"

Vesper bobbed higher, curving around behind me to rest her thighs on my shoulders. With her mastery of gravity, she felt as light as a house cat.

Her fingers combed idly through my hair as she spoke. "That's your question to answer," she told me. "Our answers don't have to be the same, you know."

I was beginning to get ever so slightly more accustomed to thinking of the air as a kind of water. A substance I could float in without analyzing the mechanics of it, without too much in the way of active effort.

Somehow it was a lot easier at night, when the stars above and the city below seemed weirdly equidistant. When both felt like an abstraction, a dark painted backdrop far less real than the shivery touch of Vesper's small pointed nails on my scalp.

"What about you?" I asked. "Anyplace you want to go? In this world, or any other."

"Not really."

I tipped my head all the way back, trying to see her. "But you were always tied to Charity Rinehart. You never got your chance to go wherever a free-ranging demon could roam. You must've thought about it."

"Sure," she said. "I had a lot of time to spare whenever you slept. I harbored all kinds of delusional dreams. But now that every imaginable land lies within reach, I don't want much."

She used both hands to tilt my head forward again, then resumed fiddling with my hair. The sky was very large and chilly, a vast sea of winter shadows. I felt none of it. "If there's anything you want—"

"I already have everything I want," Vesper said crisply, "and if you make me utter another word about it, I'm afraid I might do something very unwise."

"Are you threatening me?"

"Tell me, my love," she said. "When have I ever threatened you?"

I decided I was better off not answering that.

I cleared my throat. "By the way, you never gave me back my knife," I said. "I know I had one on me fifty years ago. Military-issue." I would've been wearing it when I entered stasis in the cockpit.

"You want it back that badly? A human weapon? Would it really be of any use to you?"

"Maybe not," I admitted.

"Good. Because the first thing I did was toss it in the plaza fountain. It went poof before you ever opened your eyes."

"Oh." Of course.

Vesper seemed to like my wrists being naked. She kept leaning down to touch them for no reason.

I had no military ID, no map-printed scarf, and now no hope of ever getting back my combat knife. One more change of clothes, and there would be little left to prove how successfully I'd masqueraded as a human called Charity Rinehart. Only my tell-tale stained fingers.

Perhaps this was the perfect time to start over as Char: a demon with no family name.

The plan had been to act stealthily. Under the cover of night. But then Wist slept in, and Vesper and Asa and I spent half the following day debating our division of labor: who should take the pilot's seat, who should let Solitaire masticate them in the cage of bone, and so on.

Eventually we managed to reach an agreement. By then, however, everyone was in a terrible mood.

Yet something shifted as we stepped toward Solitaire, toward the knotted vines of grave wisteria and all those resplendent crystalline limbs.

Asa and Wist had a home to return to. They'd been away for too long, they said. I saw them jabbing each other, bickering, kicking little pebbles back and forth.

Well. The elbow-jabbing and the bickering struck me as being extremely one-sided. Despite the frosty blankness of her expression, Wist took it all with remarkable grace.

"They're like kids," Vesper murmured.

"I don't know if we're any better."

"We're not human. We don't need to be held to the same standards."

I looked up at her, buoyant beside me, occasionally dipping lower to avoid whacking her head on a low-hanging vine.

I couldn't begin to fathom the sheer number of paths we could take from here. More than that, though, my mind rebelled at the notion of a path walked alone.

But if Vesper wanted to leave me, I would've let her go. I would've seen her off without porting to catch her, to seize her, to imprison her as she'd imprisoned me. Or so I told myself.

Letting her go would've been the last thing I could do to honor my imperfect attempts at imitating the life Charity Rinehart might have led. I would hold my head high, I assured myself. I would be noble and heroic and selfless in the face of an eternity without the one I loved.

At least—if I needed to, I think I would've endeavored with all my heart to let Vesper go in peace.

For a time, I might have succeeded. But the life of a demon is very long and slow, and dying in one world didn't have to mean dying forever.

One day I might lose my last vestige of selflessness. One day I might forget how it had felt to think I was human. One day I might become something monstrous.

Right now that was very hard to imagine. The wisteria all around Solitaire bloomed with unseasonal fervor despite the clear winter air.

In distant hills, more grave wisteria bloomed profusely over our modest monument to the humans who'd made us.

I took Vesper's hand and thanked her for staying. She looked away and feigned ignorance. She claimed she'd never given me a damn thing. I pressed my lips to her knuckles until she squirmed and hissed that the humans might see us.

I didn't need to rush to go anywhere.

We were the same, I told her. I already had the one thing I'd longed for.

I loved her as Charity had loved Verity, and as only a demon could love another demon.

Because of that, I was grateful to Asa for breaking our bond. I hadn't even known what I truly was when I tied Vesper to me all those years ago. I'd done it in the guise of Charity. Under false pretenses. Would a choice made with the bond still in place have really been a choice at all?

I had no right to compel Vesper to do anything. I had nothing to offer her but the love of a creature that had learned human emotions by sheer coincidence, acquiring them like an accidental second language.

The part of me that loved her may have been confused and dull and slow-moving and horribly lacking in vocabulary. But for all its faults, that part of me remained unbroken despite the cleaving of our bond, despite the instant collapse of my human identity, despite the abyssal gaps in my memory. The rest of my sense of self had dissolved like a paper doll in a puddle.

In some ways, Vesper and I had known each other for over a millennium.

In other ways, we'd only just met. For the first time we faced each other as two demons in a foreign world, all past ties and contracts and obligations erased.

Even with our bond broken, even after being forgotten over and over, even with all the freedom in the universe, Vesper had decided to stay.

I held her in the brilliant cold sky after the dome came down, far too high up for any humans or other earthly animals to see us. I let all my chains hang loose to twist in the breeze.

I welled up with a bottomless gratitude toward the Osmanthians, toward Glorybower, toward Charity and Verity, toward my own confined self that had kept running in bewildered obedient circles for a thousand-plus years.

"If we were human, none of this would've been worth it," Vesper said in the cloud-clotted sunlight. "We killed each other. You broke my heart."

"Then it's a good thing we're not human."

She leaned in and pricked the softest part of my throat with her teeth. A playful bite, swiftly healed.

The scale of time and space before us cast a shadow sufficient to obliterate even the deepest, most irreparable pain. In the midst of that, we were very lucky to have gained hearts capable of being broken.

Vesper whirled me through the clouds over Glorybower. We wished peace on human realms: the western seas, the continent—and most of all, the isolated Jacian islands, cruel and beloved in equal measure. No longer would they be ours to defend.

A Note from the Author

THANK YOU for reading this story! From beginning to end, I packed it absolutely chock-full of things I love. If any part of it resonated with you, please consider leaving a quick rating or review to let me know.

And hey, no matter how you felt about it: in a world full of so many wonderful novels, I'm incredibly thankful that you found and took a chance on mine.

By the way, if you're curious about Asa Clematis and Wist the Kraken, you can jump on over to the continental mainland and learn more about their past adventures in the Clem & Wist series.

What's coming next? The exact details are a secret—but I have quite a few more stories planned for both Jace and the continent.

Follow my Author Page for future updates if you'd like to see more: **amazon.com/author/hiyodori**

Hope to see you again next time!

– Hiyodori

Novels by Hiyodori

The Clem & Wist Series

Book 1: The Lowest Healer and the Highest Mage

Book 2: The Reverse Healer Case Files

Prequel: No One Else Could Heal Her

Set in the World of Clem & Wist

The First and Last Demon (Standalone)

Printed in Great Britain
by Amazon

44059928R00219